THE
EARTH, SKY & SPIRIT
SERIES

STARS
IN THEIR
INFANCY

MARLEEN PASCH

Editing: Haley Hampton, Chris Kuell
Interior Design: Penelope Love
Cover Design: Rolf Busch
Author Photo: Christina Arza

Library of Congress Cataloging-in-Publication Data
Pasch, Marleen
Stars in Their Infancy: A Novel

p. cm.
Paperback ISBN: 978-1-947708-90-7
Ebook ISBN: 978-1-947708-91-4
Library of Congress Control Number: 2022903589
1st Edition, June 2022

 CITRINE PUBLISHING
State College, Pennsylvania, USA
(828) 585-7030 · www.CitrinePublishing.com

To Cindy, my sister, my friend

To Donna, who left us too soon

And to Ruth, who put a pen in
my hand and said, "Write."

ACKNOWLEDGMENTS

With gratitude to publisher Penelope Love for launching the *Earth, Sky, and Spirit* Series. Her light shines wherever she goes. Rolf Busch and Penelope captured this series' intent in their imaginations and in *Stars'* cover design.

Chris Kuell helped shape and reshape this story. He continues to push me to explore and discover.

And what about Haley Hampton of Polished Manuscripts? I couldn't have envisioned *Stars'* final direction and flow without her wisdom and skills.

So many other kind teachers and friends along the way, especially morning friends, for warm hugs and enthusiastic cheers. I hope you know how loved you are. Then there are lighthearted Marcella, wise women Lorrie and Karen, and Joe, stalwart and steady, no matter what comes down the pike.

And, as always, thank you librarians everywhere!

NOTES

STARS IN THEIR INFANCY addresses issues of domestic violence and sexual assault.

⁓

Madagascar's history has been rich and sometimes volatile. During its evolution, its name changed many times. During the 1950s, for example, when France considered the island an Overseas Territory, the island was called the Malagasy Republic. In the 1970s, when Didier Ratsiraka assumed control, its name changed to the Democratic Republic of Madagascar. As of the date of this novel's publication, the island's official name is the Republic of Madagascar. To eliminate confusion for the reader, this author refers to the country as Madagascar, or the Great Red Island, with the understanding that, in some time periods in which this novel is set, those names may not be historically accurate.

SPIRIT OF PLACE

When he came to Pennsylvania in 1848, Martin MacMillan was hungry—for land, more than food—and he was braced for a rocky ride. He'd heard tales from widows of men who thought life would yield sweeter fruit across the Atlantic. Word of the dead came back with men who had crossed and returned, poorer, or more worn or bitter than when they left.

Still, Martin figured, it was better to breathe life into a dream in America, where boundaries were ill-defined, and limits not yet tested. Yes, better than in Scotland, where his grandfather was from, or even Ireland, where his parents brought themselves and their discontent long before Martin and his brothers were born. Sure, the spongy bogs and the rock-ragged coasts and the everlasting rain of those little islands fed a man in a dramatic, poetic way. But there was only so much land there, only so much hope.

So, a month after his nineteenth birthday, with his mother dabbing her eyes and his father wishing he had dared to dream dreams as limitless and colorful as his son's, Martin booked passage to New York on *The Majestic*. Weeks later he set sail, heading west.

Martin landed in New York on September 9, 1848, along with two hundred other Scottish-Irish and Irish, most of them attached to little more than the threadbare clothes on their backs and the need to quell their youthful hungers. With a dozen or so of them, he made his way to Philadelphia. But Martin wasn't planning on working the anthracite mines in northeastern Pennsylvania like most of his buddies, or even the less treacherous bituminous mines south and west. He wanted to own the land, not just ravage its underbelly. And he would get some of it, by God. He was young and strong and stubborn, and good fortune would be his if only he reached for it and hung on once his hands circled 'round it.

Martin arrived in the center of Pennsylvania two hundred years after the Iroquois routed the Susquehannocks from their homes there and sent them wandering, homeless. It wasn't so much the Susquehannocks' land the Iroquois raped and killed and burned for. It was the pelts of the animals that prowled and foraged there, and the easy dollars the French fur traders in Canada and western New York were willing to pay. One hundred years later, according to the terms of the purchase agreement signed in Albany in 1754, Europeans took ownership from the Iroquois of what they called Penn's Woods. Pennsylvania. And ten years after that, following the war waged and won against the great Pontiac, settlers were first allowed west of the twenty-eight-hundred-foot escarpment called the Allegheny Front.

Years later, when Martin told a new crop of Irish immigrants about his arrival in Pennsylvania, the story was gilded here and there and whitewashed where necessary. He left out the parts about the Irish who were hanged in Scranton. The ones, including his brother, called the Molly Maguires, who avenged their mistreatment in the anthracite mines with mine owners' blood. Until the newcomers learned differently, they believed Martin when he told how he personally dug the Pennsylvania Canal—called the Main Line. And how, because of Martin's own diligence and brawn, mules and horses trudged the Main Line's towpaths, drawing barges from the Delaware River in Philadelphia to the Ohio in Pittsburgh. The truth, however, was that Martin hadn't set foot in America until two decades after the canal was completed.

Some of Martin's acolytes believed him, too, when he claimed as his brainchild the Portage Railroad, which wasn't a railroad at all, but ten giant inclines, burrowed into the Allegheny Front at Hollidaysburg. Canal boats, he told them, were hauled up and over the inclines, then deposited thirty-six miles away in Johnstown. The five-day crossing was tedious and treacherous, to be sure, yet a welcome improvement over the weeks-long trip by horse.

Similarly, none of his admirers thought to challenge the great Martin, the pride of western Ireland, when he said he got the idea for the Horseshoe Curve. That stretch of track outside Altoona allowed rail cars to climb the Front one foot for every hundred feet of track, shortening the trip from Hollidaysburg to Pittsburgh, which once took days, to a mere twelve hours. The truth, however, was that John Edgar Thomson, the Curve's true architect, conceived of that engineering marvel in 1851 while Martin was still digging dirt to earn a living.

Finally, he told his devotees—and this part needed less embellishment, for it was, by and large, true—there was the tunnel his crews dug through the Front at what became known, in his honor, as the township of MacMillan, Pennsylvania. The tunnel was blasted using explosives and techniques Martin himself devised, and when it was finally possible to travel through the mountain instead of over it, the trip from east to west took only the time necessary to walk or drive from one side to the other. The tunnel's profits bought Martin his home on MacMillan Ridge, to the east of the Front, where he could survey the town below and claim it as his own.

The truth was that Martin didn't father the idea for the Canal, or the Portage Railroad, or the Horseshoe Curve. But his imagination and his shovel bought his admission to possibility and promise. From the first time he fixed his eye on the Allegheny Front, he wanted to own that escarpment. Not only because the land around it reminded him of Connemara, *Iarchonnacht* in Irish, but also because he knew the Front would own *him* for all his ditch-digging years ahead.

Martin saved whatever wages he didn't spend on food or drink. Even before the Portage Railroad was put out of business by steam-powered locomotives, and before the first rail was laid at the Horseshoe Curve, he started buying land on both sides of the Front. At first a few acres to the east. Parcels no bigger than the patches his countrymen scraped survival from in Ireland. Then more to the west, the land which men without Martin's vision and good luck deemed less desirable, maybe useless. (They beat their fists on many a pub table when oil was discovered there in 1859, however. And later, natural gas.) By the time locomotives began to haul their loads up and over the Front, along the Curve, Martin owned his part of the Front. Or, more accurately, he owned the rights to blast the tunnel that would open the western part of the state to any man willing to stake his claim there.

The day work on the tunnel began, in 1858, the town of MacMillan was officially incorporated. It wasn't much more than a village then. A few paper-thin dormitories to the west for rail-road workers, and a house for Martin and a general store on the eastern side. But by the time he died on the cusp of a new millennium, MacMillan, Pennsylvania, was called The Mountain Jewel. It boasted shops rivaling any in Pittsburgh, New York, and Philadelphia, as well as Catholic and Presbyterian churches and one of the country's finest universities.

Martin wanted the school to be a place where young men—and later young women—studied the earth that had been so generous to him and the stars that kept his sights on the heavens and on possibility. So, MacMillan University was established with well-regarded departments in Earth science and astronomy and botany and, a century later, in astrophysics and aeronautical engineering. Even the most single-minded geologist or engineer, however, could not leave before reading the classics, and the newer writers like Hawthorne and Melville and James, and not until mastering at least one language other than English. When Martin died, MacMillan University's endowment trailed only those of Yale and Harvard.

It wasn't only in Martin's imagination that the Front and its surroundings resembled the west of Ireland. When the Front was shaken and shocked and crumpled into existence, over three hundred million years before Martin dug his first shovelful of it, North America and Europe were bound into a single continent called Laurentia. Years later, Laurentia collided with Gondwana, the earth's other continent, then made up of what later became Africa, South America, Antarctica, India, and Australia. One continent was formed then, called Pangaea, "all earth."

During the collision, Africa rammed into North America's east coast and part of Europe, wrinkling Laurentia's edge and forming the Appalachian Mountains and the Allegheny Front. A hundred million years later, Pangaea broke apart, and the earth's surface began to look much like it did in the nineteenth century. Evidence proves that the geologic makeup and age of the Appalachians are identical to those of mountains in Greenland, Scandinavia, and Ireland, testimony that they once comprised one contiguous mountain chain. Although scientists in the 1960s claimed this geological repositioning was due to plate tectonics, or the shifting of Earth's landmasses over a moving, molten mantle, the theory of continental drift was first proposed by Garrison Byrne, professor of geology at MacMillan University during the 1870s. Not until Byrne's hidden journals were discovered, after his death from an opium overdose, was this fact known.

When all the mountain-building was over those millions of years ago, the underlying rock across the Appalachian Plateau—west of the Front—and the Valley and Ridge—east of the Front—was largely the same. But the topography was dramatically different. Visitors to the Plateau, even in Martin MacMillan's time, might have suspected that it was named in error, because it was not flat as its name suggested, but deeply dissected by ravines and gorges. The series of slopes interrupted by fertile valleys of the Valley and

Ridge province were created suddenly, during the orogeny, the mountain-building process, whereas the relief on the Plateau was cut by rivers and streams over thousands of years.

From its earliest days, MacMillan Township extended both east and west of the Allegheny Front, but the halves looked, felt, sounded, and smelled different then, as they still do.

In 1859, one year after Martin blasted the tunnel through the Front, oil was drilled in Titusville, in the Plateau's northwest corner. Towns with names like Wellsville and Petroleum Rock and Gusher City sprouted up, and more men came there from Ireland and Scotland, Poland, and Lithuania. They drilled oil and mined coal and the air on the Plateau took on a thick, viscous feel. In languid summer, it smelled like swamp rot; because, when, out of the Plateau's underbelly, the corpses of decayed prehistoric ferns and crustaceans and other land and sea creatures were exhumed, in the form of oil and coal and profit, their sulfur smell released into the air. It was the stinking smell of money, the miners and drillers used to say, all the while smiling in anticipation of what that cash could buy them, how it could fuel their futures.

Once the coal was gone, the miners left. Without those men to support them, the towns died. With ten billion tons of coal scraped from its guts, the Plateau fell in on itself in places. The miners referred to the resulting pockmarks as sinkholes, although MacMillan University's scientists called this process subsidence. Where coal had been mined nearer the surface, those men of science tried to ameliorate the effects by peeling back and replacing the topsoil, then planting new trees and shrubs. The plantings struggled, scraggly and undernourished, unable to develop healthy root systems, until years after the men who planted them were dead in the ground they fought to save.

Where oil had been drilled, rusted wells and pumps ornamented the Plateau, their limbs gawking like reproachful skeletons. Even dozens of miles from the mines and wells, decomposed iron and pyrite, byproducts of mining and drilling, turned streams and creeks orangey brown. The caustic sulfuric acid residue emitted a pungent smell and killed fish and birds and plants, whose rotten remains intensified the stench.

Prevailing winds crossing the Valley and Ridge province from north and west hit the ridges and deflected currents skyward, carrying the Plateau's swamp smell east. Migrating raptors paid the smell no mind as they rode the updrafts. Every autumn the sky to the east of MacMillan Mansion filled with birds of prey—peregrine falcons, sharp-shinned hawks, rough-legged hawks, red-shouldered hawks, golden eagles, bald eagles, osprey, and northern harriers— all spiraling upward, gaining the height needed to cross the state's southern boundary in search of winter warmth.

Most of Altoona's railroad tycoons built their homes farther up, around Tyrone, but Martin preferred to stay south, where the view reminded him more of Connemara. He built his mansion atop what he named MacMillan Ridge, the first ridge to the east of the Allegheny Front, so he could fix his gaze on the Front from one side of the house and the migrating raptors from the other. He imported fieldstone from Northern Ireland for the mansion's exterior and green marble from Connemara for the floors. When the last leaded window was set in place, filled with amber- and amethyst- and rose-colored glass, filtering the sun as it crossed the ridge from east to west, he went back home to Ireland to find the lady of his house and his land.

He chose Mairead O'Shea, a sturdy girl whose ever-ready laughter won his love, though she cried fierce tears on her wedding day when she kissed her father good-bye. It would have been foolish for her to refuse Martin's proposal, what with the famine still ravaging the country. Still, she feared she would miss her father's little patch of Irish land. Yet when she first saw the view of the Allegheny Front from MacMillan Mansion, so like Connemara's Maamturks mountain pass and Inagh Valley, she crumpled to the floor. When Bridget ran to wave ammonia salts under her new mistress's nose, Mairead opened her eyes. "Tell me, girl," she said, "did I dream it all and never left the west of Ireland?"

"No, ma'am," Bridget assured her. "It's no dream. You're in America, in the town of MacMillan, Pennsylvania. And to be sure, it's all yours."

Mairead embraced the valley between MacMillan Ridge and the Allegheny Front, and her role as its mistress. She decorated it as an extension of her drawing room, with stone walkways, arbors, cupolas, and fountains. She planted lilacs and wisteria and wild roses, and their fragrances, each in turn, wafted across the ridge from April through November, insulating the mansion from the sulfur smell west of town. She declared that any structures, at least east of the Front, must keep the character of those in Connemara, and that any necessary but unattractive municipal necessities, like the landfill, be relegated through the tunnel, west of the Front.

Mairead arranged for fireworks displays each Fourth of July, when everyone—east and west of the Front—picnicked on the mansion grounds, though the blankets and hampers of families from the west were laid out farthest from the mansion's steps. She set up scholarships for the children of Irish workers in the west, and she built a chapel through the tunnel, where immigrants' children could receive the sacraments of Baptism, Holy Communion, and Confirmation. But until they were schooled and cleaned up, West MacMillan's children were not permitted near the mansion grounds, even for the Christmas Eve pageant or for the Easter Sunday egg hunt, when Mairead gave away live as well as chocolate rabbits.

She cultivated the friendship and tutelage of Mrs. Carnegie from Pittsburgh and Mrs. Vanderbilt from New York. Not to be outdone by them in support of matters cultural, she hosted salons each winter and studios each summer, which—she said, at every opportunity—even New England writers and painters who had studied in Paris were eager to attend.

After Martin died in what was called an accidental fire in Buffalo, the land closest to the mansion had already become part of the university. The more remote areas were sold off to developers who built neighborhoods for faculty and other MacMillan professionals. But even a hundred years after the MacMillans' passing, their town remained divided.

West MacMillan still boasted more than a dozen pubs and taverns, frequented mostly by men who worked on the railroad and in the mines and in local garages, but also by East MacMillan's young people who wanted to drink before they were of legal age. A mall was built west of the Front in the 1960s with a J.C. Penney, a Grand Union, and a Kmart. Though it served the needs of West MacMillan's residents, the shopping there was different from that in downtown MacMillan's boutiques.

East MacMillan's cobblestone streets were closed off in the early 1980s to all but foot and bicycle traffic. New streetlights were installed, looking much like the gas lamps Mairead ordered for the town when she first arrived. Some of Center Street's shops, like Metaphors bookstore, Green's General Store, and The Smart Shop, had been in business under different names and ownership as far back as Mairead and Martin's time. Others, like the dozen or so specialty stores with names like Pizzazz and She-she Chic, came later. Those newer shops sold overpriced tee shirts and skimpy party dresses to MacU students and a lot of cashmere and corduroy to faculty. All were designed with matching brick fronts and modest black-and-gold signage. From April through November, washtub-sized planters outside them brimmed with pink astilbe, purple salvia, and chartreuse sweet potato vines.

In the 1980s, even though West MacMillan's high school ranked scholastically well above the state's average, many graduates eschewed college. They worked, as their parents had, for the railroad, in the remnants of the mining and drilling industries, or as independent contractors. Others found jobs in local businesses or in the homes of the east side's wealthiest residents.

MacMillan High School, east of the Front, ranked number two in the state, when test scores and Ivy League admissions were the judging criteria. Even so, some East MacMillan parents preferred to send their promising progeny to Phillips Exeter, Deerfield Academy, or other boarding schools in Massachusetts or Connecticut.

The smell remained. No matter how the public works department tried to chase it away, it still blanketed the Plateau west of the Front. On especially humid summer days, when the air was sulfur-heavy and sluggish, it sometimes took on a yellowish cast. As it lumbered toward the Allegheny Front, however, its acrid smell almost always dissipated before descending on East MacMillan.

CHAPTER ONE

When he came East to visit Sherman Whiting during the summer of '79, Quinn Gallagher figured they'd drink a few beers, smoke a little weed, fish some. They'd shoot the breeze and a little pool and raise as much hell as possible in two weeks' time. He figured, too, there would be things they'd say, and things they wouldn't.

Quinn knew, for example, he'd get on Sherm's case about the ten pounds that had settled around his buddy's beltline. "It's all in your damn gut, man!" he'd say, jabbing at his pal's bloat then feinting away. He wouldn't be shy, either, about pointing out how Sherm's mussed-up hair was growing in gray around his sideburns and wearing thin on top.

But Sherm wouldn't let on how Quinn kept the same thirty-four-inch waist and hard-rippled abs he'd had in Basic. Or how, even though the war had been over four, five years, he swore he sometimes still smelled babies roasted in napalm, especially on nights he couldn't sleep. And Quinn wouldn't say how, sometimes when he was out hunting, the wind across the Plains carried the sound of old women bleating like lambs during night raids along the Song Tra Bong. Or how, when he ground his teeth at night, he woke to the sound of his buddy Jonathan calling "Lela, Lela" before the kid knew he lost his legs to a Vietcong landmine in a mission that was all Quinn's fault.

He figured if they said anything at all about their time in Nam eleven years earlier, it would be about something fuzzy, with no edge to it. A lost weekend in an opium den, maybe, or the salty taste of a girl they both remembered but whose name they never knew. Then he figured he would head back to Kansas and carry on, same as before.

But Tuesday night of that week in June, Quinn and Sherman were playing a dollar a ball at the Three Bears Tavern, one of six bars on MacMillan's west side that catered to men who worked for the railroad and women out looking for those same men. They were knocking back a few without any particular goal in mind when Lorraine Jenkins came on her shift. "Another round, fellas?" she asked, threading her way through the chairs to them.

Quinn looked at her and hesitated. "You bet." When she walked away, he watched her golden hair bounce and her narrow hips shimmy long enough for Sherman to rearrange his next shot more to his liking.

"You best keep your eyes on this game, young man," he said when Quinn finally brought his attention back to the matter at hand. "Otherwise, I'll be whuppin' you even worse'n I am now."

"In your dreams, pal." Quinn chalked his cue and stepped to the table. "Number six. Side pocket." He sunk the shot and tipped back the last of his Budweiser. Then he and Sherm sat at a nearby table.

When Lorraine returned, she set down two longnecks, one for each man. She leaned in close enough for Quinn to get a whiff of her Ashes of Roses perfume, a look down her blouse, and a painful desire to cradle those bewitching breasts, round and ripe. He blew Marlboro smoke out the side of his mouth and smiled.

"If this was coffee," he said, with a twinkle in his green eyes that had served him well in barrooms from Saigon to San Antonio, "I'd ask you to stick your finger in it and make it sweet."

"Well, mister," Lorraine said, tossing her curls over her shoulder, "it's good you didn't have to ask, 'cause I don't spread this sugar around too generous." She looked at Quinn with gray eyes that would freeze a man who lacked confidence and kindle a fire in a man who didn't. Then she gave him a sour little smile and tapped her ruby red nails on the round tray she carried. When a man across the room yelled out, "Hey, Lori darlin'," she turned, her high heels clicking along the barroom floor as she sashayed away.

Sherman laughed so hard he snorted a mouthful of Bud out his nose. "That woman put you in your place, boy."

But Quinn fixed on the way Lorraine worked those tight black pants she had on. She couldn't have been more than five-three, but she was a woman who made every inch count. That much Quinn could see. He tilted back his beer and took another drink. "Only means she wants me too bad to come right out and say." Before he straightened his shirt and jeans over his six-foot frame, he said he'd bet a day's pay he'd be having himself a sugar overdose within a week's time.

Sherm had never known a woman who, once she laid eyes on Quinn, could resist him. But what the hell, he thought. There's always a first time. He took the bet.

Five days, two Italian dinners, and a bouquet of red roses later, Quinn dangled a receipt from the motel next to the Three Bears in front of Sherm. "Time to pay up, soldier." A week after that, when Lorraine asked Quinn did he want to move in, he couldn't come up with a good reason not to. He figured he could work a sheet metal job just as easy in MacMillan, Pennsylvania, as he could back in Kansas. Granted, he'd heard that come hunting season it was harder to unload an illegal rack in these parts than it was down around the Oklahoma border. And he would miss casting for flathead cats in the Caney River next spring. But he'd caught wind that Pennsylvania's whitetail herd was on the increase. Maybe now, seeing he was going on thirty, it was time he gave up his meandering ways. For a time anyway.

~

Until Quinn, Rusty Jenkins never cared much for his mother's boyfriends. Most weren't around long enough to get to know, anyway. But the ones that stayed never seemed to appreciate Rusty being there, except if he could help them get on Lorraine's good side. Rusty didn't like how those men got in the way of the little bit of attention he could wangle from Lorraine when she wasn't selling Mary Kay or working at the Three Bears or painting her nails or highlighting her hair. And he did his best to let each one know—by running his house key along the intruder's pickup truck, maybe, or on a hot day, leaving a rabbit, with its throat slit, in the trunk of the visitor's Camaro or Firebird—he didn't appreciate his butting in. Whenever a new one came around, Rusty made sure Lorraine knew he didn't like that, too, by going after the neighbor's chickens with his BB gun. Or sneaking quarters or singles out of the cookie jar where his mother kept her tip money.

Rusty couldn't sleep at night when the men were there. With them talking loud and laughing and knocking the headboard in Lorraine's room up against the wall next to his bedroom, two, three times a night sometimes. Not bothering to close the bedroom door so that if Rusty got up to pee, he was as likely as not to find Lorraine kneeling on the floor with her head in some stranger's lap while he's saying, "Work it, baby. Oh yeah, you got me now."

There were no secrets in their flimsy four-room house that a little wine and weed ever failed to bring out into the light. Like a morning after a nameless man visited, when Lorraine might come out in a tee shirt or her tangerine-colored negligee, still smelling like her guest who got up to go home to his wife, or back to his girlfriend, or on to his early morning shift at Penelec or the railroad. Never naked but always close enough for Rusty to learn whatever made him curious about a woman's body, like where the hair grew, where the curves rounded, where the breasts hung.

Most of those mornings Lorraine fixed her coffee, extra milk and sugar, then lit a cigarette. Or maybe she poured some Scotch in a glass of milk and said, "What the hell you lookin' at?" Or "Keep your eyes where they belong." Some days, though, she held Rusty close to her before he went off to school, and stroked his red hair, then gave him a couple dollars for candy or a movie. The only problem was Rusty never knew what made one day good for Lorraine and another day bad. So, he watched and waited for her blues to come and go like the wind. Only the wind seemed to have some predictable seasonal variation to it.

⌒

Before his grandmother died, two years before Quinn came along, Nana moved in with Lorraine and Rusty. Lorraine gave Nana her room and made a bedroom for herself out of half the living room, with two sheets hanging across it on a clothesline.

Even before the cancer got bad, Nana stayed in bed most days, praying her rosary, holding onto her crucifix with all her weakening might. She got to talking funny, about days gone by and, one October afternoon, called Rusty into her room after he came home from school. "Ronny Lee was your father's name," she said. "Just like yours."

That was something Rusty never knew. All Lorraine told him about his father was that she married him when she was seventeen and pregnant.

Nana handed Rusty a picture of Ronny Lee Jenkins Sr. holding his day-old son in the hospital.

Rusty could see how he inherited his father's match-stick-straight hair and his blue eyes, pale as winter ice.

"It was those eyes that give him away." Nana shook her head. "They was so clear you felt when you was lookin' at him you was really lookin' through him. Like there was nothin' to grab onto and tell you who the man was or what he was up to."

Rusty could see he had his father's compact build, too, his bowlegs and his narrow, freckled face. Even in the picture, holding his newborn son, his father's jaw muscles were close to the surface, the same as his. He imagined that when his father got mad, or nervous, his face probably worked and pulsed the same as his, too.

"I only hope to God," Nana said, looking at Rusty straight on, "you don't take up his lyin' and his wanderin'."

Lorraine started drinking, his grandmother said, when Ronny Lee started cheating. "Or, more accurate, when she found out he was cheatin'. And when Ronny Lee left, Lorraine didn't want to give up the friendships she had developed with white wine and weed.

"Your mother was runner up in the Miss Junior Pennsylvania contest over at Altoona when she was sixteen." Nana smiled when she told how it was a good six months before people stopped talking about Lorraine, how she looked like an angel that night, and sounded like one, too. "Somewhere Over the Rainbow" was what she sang in the talent contest, Nana said. "But the girl passed up a nursing scholarship over to Millertown College for your father first and the bottle second. Ever since, they been her downfall." She shook her head. "I spent many a night beggin' the good Lord for an answer as to why she turned out how she did. He never saw fit to answer, but I always suspected it was 'cause her own daddy died when she was twelve and needin' him most."

The next weeks Nana faded in and out, like the sun passing behind summer clouds. The day before she died, when she called for Lorraine, Rusty went to her room and stood by the door. "Mom's not here, Nana," he said. He was afraid of her by then, because she looked gray, like she was covered with dust. But when she talked, and he couldn't hear, he walked closer.

"Some women just don't take to motherin', Rusty. It's got nothin' to do with the child. You hear me?" Rusty nodded, though he wasn't at all convinced what Nana said was true. "It's the liquor's fault, honey. Not yours."

~

That August, when Quinn moved in, Rusty didn't say much at first. He just watched the way the man settled into the living room recliner like it was his own. The way, after he was there only a couple weeks, he bought Rusty a baseball and glove, then a rod and reel. The way he kissed Lorraine hello every time he came in the door. Lifted her up and swung her around till she giggled and flailed. "Set me down, you dirty bird," Lorraine used to say, even though she seemed happy floating through the air. His mother laughed more with Quinn around. She didn't have to work as many hours with him helping pay the rent. And when she was holding Quinn's hand, she seemed to be hanging onto something solid and safe. She slowed down long enough to answer Rusty's questions, about whether his other pair of jeans was in the wash or if he could go to the mall. Best of all, she seemed to forget what deep down was making her feel so blue.

Rusty started looking forward to the breakfasts Quinn made on Sunday mornings, orange juice, waffles with syrup, and bacon, crisp. Or pancakes and scrapple maybe. Even Lorraine put on a little weight, once she was sitting down to meals instead of standing at the counter, grabbing chips and salsa and wine on the run. Rusty liked having meals together so much he learned to cook a little, too. Scrambled eggs or French toast for breakfast. Burgers for dinner.

Quinn gave the fake-wood paneling in the living room a couple coats of soft yellow paint and fastened the curtain rods, so the sheers hung even instead of dragging on the floor. He replaced the turquoise kitchen counters with butcher block. After he put in a dishwasher and a disposal, Lorraine bought ruffled curtains and a pink and yellow cloth for the kitchenette. It was Rusty's room that looked the best, though. At least he thought so. He and Quinn steamed off the faded cowboy wallpaper, then painted it Steelers' gold and hung posters of Bradshaw throwing, Harris receiving.

Quinn fixed the gutters so when it rained there wasn't a steady stream running off the roof over the front door. He replaced the glass in the back door and patched the foundation that cracked after a sinkhole fell in on the Plateau behind the house.

Rusty liked Saturdays best, though, when he and Quinn fished for brookies in Sinking Creek or for bluegills in the Tebolt Run

Watersheds. And toward September, when the fall migrations started, how they packed lunches and hiked the boulder fields at Hawk Mountain Sanctuary and watched the hawks and harriers and peregrines catching the updrafts and heading south for winter.

By then Rusty wanted to know more about this man. "So," he asked one Saturday on their way to Hawk Mountain, "where you from? You got brothers and sisters?" Quinn told Rusty about Chautauqua, Kansas, where he came from. About his sister Cheryl and her three kids, Janey and Bobby and Noel. About what it was like to live in a place where a man could see straight ahead and straight behind for miles, with no hills or mountains in sight. How once a man got used to that kind of vision, it was hard to feel at ease in closed-in spaces.

Rusty didn't know what Quinn left out. How, when they lived in Topeka, his mother stashed quarters and dimes into hiding places under the floorboards. Anything she could sneak out of her husband's work pants when he came home too drunk to notice. And how, one night when his father was out for a week's worth of poaching in Idaho, she bundled Cheryl and Tim and Quinn into their 1967 Fairlane and drove nonstop to Saint Francis in Chautauqua County, where her sister lived. And how Glenn Gallagher found them living in a boarding house and "roughed 'em up a little," as his father said, until they couldn't do anything but go back home.

When Rusty asked to know more, Quinn said there was no need for a man to go around flappin' his mouth like any regular bird flaps his wings. "Not when he can glide like these raptors and let the winds carry him wherever it is he's meant to go."

Still, Rusty set his gaze, not so much on the birds overhead, but on this tall, strong man who seemed to know everything that mattered. He didn't ask the question he wanted answered most. "You gonna stay around a while?"

That October Quinn brought up his Winchester from the basement. A bolt-action 270. He let Rusty carry it now and again to get the feel of it in the woods. While they hiked over the creek, closer to the county line, Rusty decided he wasn't sure what he liked best, a day off from school or just hearing Quinn talk hunting. Slow and even. Like there could be no doubt whatever the man said was absolute truth.

"Man's gotta want a deer so bad, he's willing to wait," Quinn said. "No leaves crunchin' under your feet, no teeth chatterin' 'cause it's cold. No hoppin' back and forth one foot to the other 'cause you gotta pee or eat or drink or 'cause you want your momma or any other damn thing.

"Same time, you can't let any deer know you want 'em too bad. Especially a doe. You gotta stay downwind of 'em, the breeze blowin' in your face. Otherwise, they'll smell you. And once they get a fix on you?" He shook his head. "They ain't never gonna be yours."

Whenever Quinn took him to the woods, Rusty sat still and waited and watched. It was worth it, he figured. Better to freeze your butt solid out in the fresh air than to have Miss Merkel trying to glue your backside to a desk chair while you're doing your best to read, and the letters go forwards and back and you can't get them to sit still—no matter how many times Miss Merkel says you're not trying hard enough. Certainly better than being home with a mother too drunk sometimes to know if you're there and, most times, too wrapped up in herself to care.

"There's no secret to huntin' deer," Quinn told the boy as they lowered themselves to the ground, settling their backs against the base of a two-foot-wide oak. "No magic whatsoever."

Quinn rested his 30-30 on his knees and opened and closed his hands a couple times around it, waking them to the late-October chill. He lifted his Stetson while he scanned the hedgerow in the distance. Then he combed his fingers through his meandering brown hair and nestled his hat square on his head. "Just gotta look at things real close is all."

Rusty turned his gaze from Quinn to the horizon, where Quinn still fixed his sight.

"Then," Quinn said, "you gotta wait."

It was twenty minutes, half an hour maybe, before sunup. Just the time, he told Rusty, when the whitetails were rousing themselves from their beds among the fallen leaves and branches of Central Pennsylvania's mottled autumn landscape. Hunters had to notice things, he said. Like the fact that MacMillan Creek still had an orange cast to it. "No deer's gonna drink runoff from a strip mine any more than you or I would."

It was important to watch for sinkholes, too, where mineshafts were dug, and the gutted earth fell in on itself once the coal was removed. And while it was to a hunter's advantage, he said, for a deer to lose his footing in a sinkhole, a hunter who stumbled into one could miss himself a shot. Or worse, turn an ankle and be deprived of a day or even a week of prime hunting season.

"See that brush over on the right, down around where that old gate cuts in?"

Rusty narrowed his close-set blue eyes and turned his freckled face toward the trail to his right where Quinn pointed. He could make out the rusted oil pump, the one that looked like a bent-over, bony old man, at the edge of Hank Roland's property. Beyond that, he wasn't exactly sure where Quinn was pointing his chin. The boy nodded anyway.

"I bet you can't tell me why those leaves are missin' down around the center of it there," Quinn said. "Close to the ground."

Rusty saw how Quinn looked away from him, as if it didn't matter one way or the other whether he knew the answer. But he wanted to please Quinn, so he thought hard about the answer. It had to have something to do with deer, and deer eat leaves. "Deer's gotta eat."

"Atta boy."

Rusty smiled.

"And how long ago you think some old buck came along here and had himself his breakfast?"

This question stretched beyond Rusty's knowledge or his imagination. He knew he couldn't run anything past Quinn, so the smile left his face as he settled for the truth. "Not sure," he mumbled, disappointed for coming up empty.

"No guesses?"

"No, sir."

Quinn told Rusty to walk over to the hedge and tell him the color of the broken branches, whether they were white or brown.

"They look more white."

"And that means the deer passed by when? A short or long time ago?"

When Rusty realized there hadn't been time for the branches to dry and darken, that the deer must have nibbled at them only a little earlier, he spun around quickly, hoping to see the deer.

Quinn laughed. "Just 'cause that old buck came through here five, maybe ten minutes ago," he said, "don't mean he's anywhere in sight now." A man had to stay sharp. On the lookout for opportunity at all times. Not worrying about what's already gone by. "Past is the past, and there's nothin' to be done about it."

Then he taught Rusty how to look for deer droppings, how it was easier to spot them against December snow than in October or November when they mixed in with brown and gray leaves along trails. He showed him how to hold his hand close to the droppings to see if they were still warm, so he could gauge a deer's distance, and how to look for scrapes where bucks rubbed their antlers against trees or bare spots where they pawed at the ground for God knows why.

Quinn told the boy, too, how an experienced hunter could smell whether a storm was coming on, one that would send the whitetails looking for cover. Rusty filled his lungs, good and deep, but all he took in was the same old dead-rot sulfur stink that hung over the Appalachian Plateau in all but the stormiest weather.

About four that afternoon, as the sun lowered behind them, and the sky went gunmetal gray, Rusty smiled when Quinn called their day to an end. Though he hadn't told Quinn, he had watched his breath form puffs in the chill air for about the last hour and was looking forward to getting home, to seeing his mom, and to drinking hot chocolate in front of the wood stove. He rounded up their thermos and remains of the lunch Quinn had packed and stumbled down the trail. He was slight and small, even for eleven. He had to hustle to keep up with Quinn's long-legged stride. That was okay, he told himself. He kept warm that way. But he'd need some decent gloves in order to hunt. Maybe if he raked the leaves out front and kept his room picked up, his mom would agree.

Meanwhile, Quinn talked on about how, if they'd been doing serious hunting with live ammo that afternoon, and if they'd paid close attention and had a little luck, they'd be loading a carcass into the bed of his black Silverado, carting their kill home to dress. They'd hang that big old buck from a hook under the carport. Then, while the life was still steaming out of him, they'd skin and gut him and cut him into steaks and roasts to freeze.

Rusty stayed sharp and kept his eyes on Quinn in case he asked any questions. But once they crossed onto Hank Roland's property and Rusty's house was visible beyond the creek, he rehearsed in his head what he would tell his mother when he got home. "No secret to huntin'," he would say. "You just gotta look real close is all. Then you gotta wait."

But when they reached the house set back from White Ash Road, the one where Ronny Lee Jenkins Sr. left Lorraine a month after Rusty was born, Lorraine's Mustang wasn't in the carport. When they walked around front, the door was wide open. Quinn tousled Rusty's fiery red hair. "How 'bout you run down and get the mail while I go on ahead?"

Rusty took off for the mailbox, and Quinn went inside. He leaned his Winchester in the corner behind the door, unlaced his boots, kicked them off, and picked the dried burrs off his scratchy woolen socks. When he pulled the chain on the overhead fluorescent light, it flickered, hummed, then spread a bluish cast over the room. There was no note from Lorraine on the counter. No dinner in the oven. No sign of her except a thick haze in the air, still swirling, part stale smoke and part Ashes of Roses perfume.

Quinn screwed the top onto the jug of red wine that sat on the table and stowed it under the sink. He emptied the Virginia Slims butts and the stub of a stogie from the ashtray. She'd had company. He would've smelled that fact a mile away, even without the evidence. Quinn emptied the water glasses, too, both still half-full of Cabernet. Then, when he heard the boy at the door, he took a quart of milk from the refrigerator, poured some in a pan for hot chocolate, and set it on the stove.

"Your mother told you about that Mary Kay meetin' she's got tonight, right?"

Rusty tried to remember but couldn't.

"Must've slipped her mind," Quinn said. "No tellin' when she'll get back. Those hens can get to talkin' and sippin' their Chablis and forget everything except their own names." He told Rusty to clean up. That he could tell his mother about hunting at breakfast the next morning, once Rusty had time to remember the details even better. "No harm in shinin' the truth up a little now and then," Quinn said. "Not when it comes to huntin' or fishin'."

Quinn rescued a leftover meatloaf from the refrigerator and fried it with hash browns in the cast iron skillet. Some onions, too, mostly to chase away the cigar smell. Meanwhile, Rusty stirred cocoa and sugar into the hot milk on the stove, then set out three plates, in case his mother came home.

"Your momma's gonna be proud of how you spotted that doe on the ridge even before I got a glimpse of her," Quinn said while he served up dinner. And while Rusty dug into his meal, and relived their day out loud, he almost believed he had seen the deer before Quinn.

After they ate, Rusty curled under an afghan and fell asleep on the couch. Quinn sent him to bed at nine. He woke only once during the night, when he heard the front door slam and Quinn asking Lorraine where she'd been. But he was too tired to get up, even to tell his mother about his day in the fields with Quinn.

CHAPTER TWO

On Rusty's twelfth birthday, Quinn handed him a gun of his own. When he took his first shot with it, the kick of that Remington 760 would have knocked him back and down flat if he hadn't remembered what Quinn taught him. "Bend your knees," he said. "Stay light on your feet. Shift your weight forward, now, just a hair."

Rusty didn't hit the mark that day, but Quinn followed the boy's shot with one on the money. Just behind the front shoulder, halfway up, through the lungs and out the heart. After they dragged the carcass, still warm, to the clearing, Quinn hoisted it onto his Silverado's bed. Then they drove home to dress it, the life steaming out of it into the November air.

The following morning Rusty rushed to the kitchen. "The buck's hangin' outside," he said with a puffed-up grin. "All skinned and purple."

Lorraine pointed her Virginia Slim, a little curl of smoke rising off it, at Quinn. "The boy's too young to be huntin' deer," she said.

Rusty knew—even before Quinn told her how, where he was from, any boy Rusty's age already knew how to scout, shoot, and dress a deer—Lorraine wasn't picking at Quinn because of anything to do with deer. He'd felt it coming the last few weeks.

"He's not yours anyway," she said. "So don't be messin' with him." Then she turned to Rusty. "Those dishes need washin' before you leave this house."

Rusty felt his face going red, his heart racing. He'd seen his mother like this before. When she was setting about getting rid of one man and bringing in another, one who'd give her finer negligées or perfumes, or leave bigger bills on her nightstand. But he never cared before about any man's leaving. Besides, he was Quinn's boy.

"Don't do this, Momma." Then he felt everything stop around him. He stood up while Lorraine glared. He didn't know how long, but he could hear the clock on the wall. Tick-tick-tick. One thousand one, he counted to himself. One thousand two.

"Since when you had permission to tell me what to do?"

When Lorraine turned from him, she drew on her cigarette without looking at him, but didn't let go of that wrinkle across her forehead, the one that always showed up when the wildcat in her was ready to strike. Rusty knew she wasn't through with him. She tilted her head back to blow the smoke straight up. She was winding up to a bigger finish. He knew.

"Helluva time to start playin' momma, Lorraine."

Rusty heard Quinn talking, but his mother's silence rumbled louder inside his head, like thunder, warning of a storm. He'd heard it before, sometimes for days at a time, when she stopped talking to him and he couldn't figure out why. The silence ended when she wanted it to. Not a minute before.

He watched his mother set her cigarette, still curling smoke out its end, on her saucer, then eye the skillet sitting on the table on a hot pad, with half the scrambled eggs still in it, just starting to get a shiny skin on them. Rusty kept counting to himself—one thousand ten, one thousand eleven—as if measuring the time would make it go faster or fill it with something less scary than Lorraine's silence. *She'll feel better if she eats something*, he thought, when she reached for the eggs. *She'll calm down, come back to her senses. She'll ease her hand across the table and maybe even sweet talk Quinn.* They'll be climbing all over each other like they can't let go. Like they used to.

Lorraine grabbed the skillet, held it out in her left hand. Thinking how many eggs to scoop onto her plate, Rusty thought. Or maybe she'd just stick her fork in and take a bite. Meanwhile, Rusty saw how Quinn set down his coffee. How, when he pushed back from the table, his chair screeched across the linoleum. How his body looked tight. Like he had a plan for whatever was coming next. Rusty backed against the wall.

"Damn you!" Lorraine flung the skillet. Rusty didn't know if she was yelling at him or Quinn. "Damn the both of you to hell and back." Metal on metal, the pan hit the stove, eggs rolling out in rubbery clumps. Before the skillet landed on the floor, it seemed to Rusty, Quinn was up. Pulling Lorraine out of her chair. Jerking her right arm up behind her back. Wedging her belly against the counter.

"Take your hands off me," she snarled.

"You don't hurt the boy. You hear me?"

"Let . . . me . . . GO."

"You think I don't know what you been up to?" Quinn twisted her arm higher, harder. "You think I don't have friends around this town that's seen you?"

She flung her left arm behind her and grabbed Quinn's hair and pulled. He yanked her wrist until she let go, then held her arms behind her back, still pressing her to the counter so she couldn't get free.

"I give you the benefit of the doubt till now," Quinn said, "but you can't hurt the boy."

"He's none of your business. Neither am I. Rusty, go get Hank Roland."

"You stay right there," Quinn said. "Your momma's gonna be talkin' to you nice and sweet in just another minute or two." With one more quick move, like he'd played it out in his head, he released Lorraine's right hand behind her, shoved up harder against her, trapping her against the counter. With his free hand, he grabbed the carving knife from the block, brought the knife to her waist. "Aren't you, sugar?"

The tip of the blade made a hole in Lorraine's turquoise negligee when she tried to wriggle away. He pressed her harder against the counter. With his left hand he brought her left arm up her back again. With his right he slid the knife down her side, ever so lightly. A little red stream flowed from Lorraine's waist. A drop of blood spotted the floor. Another. She stopped fighting. "Now apologize to the boy."

"I said get Hank Roland, Rusty. And you get your hands off me." She tried to kick Quinn off again.

"Your momma just needs a little lesson is all," Quinn said. "About how far she can cross over the line and get away with it." He pushed his body against her again, and before she could even wiggle, he grabbed a clump of her hair. "Your new boyfriend like your pretty curls, sugar?"

Lorraine said nothing when Quinn jerked her head back, but there was a fear in her eyes Rusty had never before seen.

"You hear me?"

When Lorraine nodded, Quinn ran the knife through his handful of her hair, making a quick, staticky sound, cutting it off and exposing her right ear, her neck. He threw the hair on the floor, then grabbed another handful.

"Sonofa-BITCH!" Lorraine wrenched away, lunged toward Quinn, slid on the scrambled eggs, and fell.

Rusty looked at his mother, then at her hair on the floor next to her, still in golden curls, then at the knife in Quinn's hand.

"See how pretty your boyfriend thinks you look now," Quinn said.

Lorraine grabbed her fallen hair, opening and closing her fist around it, then dove for Quinn's legs and tried to pull him to the floor.

Quinn heard the pounding in his head. When he tried to kick loose, he felt the pumping in his chest. He swallowed. He tasted the kill. He breathed and smelled the swampy, rotten stink of it.

The rush propelling him toward Lorraine, he dropped the knife. He bent down, circled his hands around her neck.

"Quinn," Rusty yelled. "Quinn, no!"

The boy's voice broke Quinn's spell. He released his hands from Lorraine's neck. Wiped the sweat off his upper lip. He stumbled backward, watching Lorraine as she sobbed, holding her neck where her hair should have been. He turned, looking over his shoulder, then went to the bedroom.

Rusty heard bureau drawers opening and slamming shut. He looked from Lorraine—picking herself up from the floor, reaching for her bottle of Dewar's in the cupboard—to the bedroom where Quinn was packing his bags. When he felt he couldn't favor one without losing the other, he ran outside. The screen door flapped twice behind him, lonely and wooden.

He looked back and saw Quinn tossing his duffels out the window, then climbing out after them. He heard him open the metal basement doors, go inside, then leave with his rifle, shotgun, and hunting gear. *Quinn, no!*

Lorraine came out on the front step, still in her nightgown, her water glass full of Scotch in her hand, flinging what was left of her rage at Quinn, telling him to never come back. As if he ever would.

From the woods behind the house, Rusty watched Quinn drive off and Lorraine trip on the front step on her way back inside. He watched the Silverado turn from White Ash onto Hemlock. The air was still, except for the crunch of dry leaves under Rusty's feet and his breath, deep in his chest. His tears made no sound. While he ran farther into the woods, the sun rose round and bright over MacMillan Ridge to the east.

⌒

"Same as your son of a bitchin' father," Lorraine said when Rusty went back home that afternoon, waving her half-filled glass at him. "You'll have to walk to school tomorrow. Or get a ride from Hank on his way into town."

Rusty looked at the new haircut she gave herself. Short on top and around the ears, and shaggy down the back. It showed off her face more. Made her look even prettier than before. He didn't want to tell her that. She'd sent away the only man he could talk to. The only person except Nana who taught him anything about how to get along in the world. He didn't think he owed his mother anything anymore.

After he heard Lorraine turn on the shower, Rusty went outside and around to the basement. He pulled up the metal door and walked downstairs, looking for a trace of Quinn. Next to the gun Quinn had given him for his birthday, he found a hunting knife in a leather sheath with Quinn's initials on it—QMG—and a note. *You got to want the deer bad enough you're willing to wait for it.* Rusty pulled out the knife, opened and closed his hand around it until it felt friendly there. Then he sheathed it again and fastened its rawhide strap on his belt. He loaded three cartridges into the 760's magazine, one in the chamber.

He'd go after Quinn, is what he thought. Track him same as he would a deer. All the way to Kansas, where Quinn always talked about going back to. Where a hundred-twenty-point rack could bring a man twenty, maybe thirty grand if he sold it to a lazy-ass Texan who wanted all the glory of a buck's head hanging on his wall but wasn't willing to pound the fields for it. He'd smell Quinn out. That's what he'd do.

But once Rusty settled down a little, he could have sworn he heard Quinn talking, same as if he were sitting right next to him, sipping coffee or Johnny Black from his thermos, or chewing a blade of grass. "Man's gotta know his limits," he heard him say. "Gotta know when to give up the hunt and start over." Then he knew Quinn was gone for good.

After he walked back up the basement stairs and closed and latched the doors behind him, Rusty circled the edge of Hank Roland's property, fifty feet or so from where he'd often seen white-tails feeding on fallen apples. He set himself up against a wide oak, with just a few November leaves dangling off its bony old branches. He waited and watched, swallowing hard to keep his angry tears to himself.

Going on two hours later, he heard a rustle in the brush. He lifted the 760 off his knees where it was balancing, waiting. He crouched forward and raised the barrel and fixed on the doe. Not a legal target this time of year, but Rusty heard Quinn again. "Safety off. Crosshairs on the shoulders. Get yourself a deep breath and squeeze."

Rusty pulled the trigger. Then he closed his eyes, shaking, afraid he killed the deer, and afraid he might have missed. He shot again. His heart pounded, and when he opened his eyes, the doe lay on the path in front of him, her left hindquarters bleeding where the first shot grazed her.

He steadied himself against the oak behind him, then started toward her. "Nice and slow now," Quinn's voice said. He grabbed a stick from the trail to poke at the doe to see was she dead or just wounded. But before he reached her, she hobbled to her knees, looked at him, and got up on all fours.

When she took off, with a ragged gait, Rusty ran after her a hundred yards until she fell again and didn't get up. When he reached her, he stood over her and stared into the eye facing him. He watched her sides, heaving, still pulling in air. Without taking his eyes off her, he reached for the knife Quinn left him.

He knelt. He unsheathed the knife, raised it, whoosh, above his head. He grunted when the blade hit the doe's chest. Once. Twice. The skin tougher, thicker than he expected. Nine times. Most of the blows coming up against rib bone, protecting the heart he was after. He struck again, between the ribs, through the rubber-muscle. He tore in. More muscle. More bone. Blood. Spurting, then a slow little stream. He tore the flap of chest flesh. Ran the knife across it. Cut it free. Tossed it. Still no heart.

Raging. Open-mouthed and silent. Except for breath, louder, higher in his chest. Faster. He landed the knife again, below the ribs. Ripping up. Out. His hands on her, ripping again. Then standing still above her. Clenching the knife, his jaw. His fury seemed red and hot as her insides beneath him, sticky on his hands. No heart. He could not get her heart. Kneeling again and plunging the knife one final time. Then standing. Kicking. Turning. Running. He left her heart for hungry crows.

Hustling to his Silverado, Quinn looked over his shoulder. He wouldn't put it past Lorraine to come after him with a knife or even a gun. After what he did, he couldn't blame her. He started the engine with one hand while closing the door with the other. Until he came to his senses, he even toyed with going back in and trying to regain what he could of her affection. Instead, he backed out the driveway and drove. Out Route 22 to Route 80, then east to the Delaware Water Gap outside Philadelphia. He gassed up on the turnpike, grabbed a burger and fries at the rest stop, then turned around at noon and headed back toward Pittsburgh. He had no destination in mind, no purpose but the need to keep from detonating again.

He thought about driving straight back to Kansas, but in Pittsburgh he turned around and drove east again. By evening he was back in MacMillan on Sherm Whiting's doorstep.

He pounded on the door loud enough to wake Sherm from his after-work nap, the one he took before deciding which of his favorite hangouts he would visit for a beer or a game or both.

When Sherm answered the door, he was still shaking his head to dislodge the sleep from his brain. "Shit," he said. "What you doin' here, man?"

Quinn was silent, but his eyes were glassy-red, and his shoulders were hiked around his ears.

"Come on in, soldier," Sherm said. "What the hell's up?"

"Got a beer?"

"Hell, yeah, I got a beer. Got a caseful."

"Gimme two."

Sherm opened the refrigerator, took out three cans of Rolling Rock. He handed one to Quinn, set another in front of him, then sat down and popped the top on the one he kept for himself. Before Quinn spoke, he downed the one can, then half the other.

"Bitch!"

"Oh." Sherm leaned back in his chair, tipped on its two hind legs. He clasped his hands behind his head. "Can't say's I'm surprised. That girl has some reputation. She's cheatin' on ya?"

"Cheatin' on me? Hell yeah, she's cheatin'." Quinn tilted back the second can, drank the rest of it, then crushed it in his hand. "I'm not surprised, neither. But it ain't so much she cheated on me as the fact that I fell so hard for her, knowin' all the while I was steppin' into a viper's nest." He tossed the first empty can into the trash beside the sink, then the second. "It's the boy I'm worried about. He's smart and got a good heart and it's gonna be squashed if he don't get some direction."

"He's got no family but Lorraine?" Sherm asked.

"None as far as I can tell." Quinn lit a cigarette. "What you know about the father?"

"Only that he left right after the boy was born and never come back."

Quinn took a long lazy drag on his Marlboro, as if what he was about to say was of less consequence than he felt. "Boy needs a father. Needs one bad."

"Well." Sherm brought his chair back to all four legs. "It ain't you." He reached for his beer but hesitated before he drank. "What you say you down a couple more brewskis, then bunk in here a couple days. You can worry about everybody and everything else after that."

Quinn acted like he didn't hear, like what he had to say was more important than where, or even if, he slept. "I coulda killed her, you know?"

Sherman looked at him but didn't ask the obvious question.

"With my knife," Quinn said.

"How bad?"

"Hell, she's okay. I just scratched her a little. Ruined her damned negligee." He paused. "Give her a new hairdo, too."

Sherm started into a good laugh, but when Quinn didn't crack so much as a sliver of a smile, he caught himself.

"I went for her throat," Quinn said. "Soon as I did, all I had was the jungle in me. That whole mess in Nam, with Jonathan and all. Like I was watchin' a movie inside my eyeballs." He blew out a single gray stream of cigarette smoke, then looked out to the sun setting behind the Front. "Don't it never go away, Sherm?"

"It goes when it's good 'n ready. And that time ain't come yet for you."

"I hope to God it goes sometime soon," Quinn said. "There's times I'm not sure I can live with it no more."

Sherm got up from his chair and slapped Quinn on the back. "You lived with it so far, right?" He ushered him to the couch, switched on the television, and handed him the remote. "Steelers're playin' tonight. Bradshaw's still got one helluva arm, don't he?"

Quinn set up camp at Sherm's that night and went to work in the shop the next morning, taking the long way around to avoid Lorraine's place. But the next night, when Sherm came home from work, he found a note taped to the refrigerator. *Gone back to Kansas.*

"If I didn't know you better, I'd think it was failed romance that brought you back home." Quinn's sister, Cheryl, kept her eyes on the potatoes she was slicing. "You're moping around like you lost a leg."

Since showing up on Cheryl's doorstep a week earlier, Quinn had been helping her around the house, in the yard, taking the boys to the park to play ball, and the older one, Bobby, to hunt the wheat fields along the Oklahoma border. He was fixing a wobbly leg on a kitchen chair when Cheryl spoke to him that afternoon, and he set the chair upright. He didn't look at her. "Well, you know a lot, little sister, with your college education, but you don't know everything."

"So, I'm right, am I?" She cast a knowing look toward her brother before wiping her hands on the kitchen towel, turning on the stove's burner, and sliding a slab of butter into a skillet to melt.

"Okay, you're right." He sat on the newly repaired chair, leaning forward and back to test if it was fixed. "You happy now, smartass?" He manufactured a grin.

"Yeah, I'm happy. I just wish you were." The butter sizzled as she slid a pile of onions off the cutting board into the pan. She stirred them then slipped in the potatoes and set the cover on. "It seemed like you were making a life for yourself out in Pennsylvania. You had friends. The hunting was good. I just don't want you coming back because you think we need to be taken care of. You've got your own life to live."

Since her husband died in a hunting accident the year before, Quinn had been sending Cheryl money to help her and her three kids manage. "It's not that I don't appreciate the help you're giving us," she said. "And God's truth, we need it till I can get back to work full-time. But maybe you can make a new life out there. Forget about Dad, about Tim, the war, and start fresh. I mean anyone could go a little wacky trying to find some excitement in this town. Even if you're not ready to settle down, you can at least have some fun out East."

Quinn looked at Cheryl. How she managed to raise three kids with no husband, especially after she'd nursed their mother until she died from cancer, he had no idea. Then he smiled, this time for real. "You know why I can't find the right girl?"

"Why's that?" She flipped the potatoes to brown on the other side.

"'Cause no one ever measured up to you."

With a little laugh, she shook her head. "I suggest you save the sweet talk for someone else, big brother." She threw a wet towel at him and opened the oven. "Now wash up and get the kids in here before these pork chops burn."

The next day Quinn drove Janey and her brothers to school. He promised the boys he'd come back to Kansas in time for trout season and Janey that he'd be back for her art show. Then he packed his bags and pointed his truck north and east, back to Pennsylvania.

He drove through the night. The following afternoon, Sherman didn't act at all surprised when Quinn pulled in the driveway and leaned on his horn.

"You're a week ahead of schedule," Sherm yelled as Quinn took his duffel from his truck and walked to the porch. "I figured you wouldn't last more than a month watchin' the corn grow." He put Quinn in his guest room and gave him the name and number of a contractor friend of his, Lester Craig. "Needs a foreman, he was tellin' me."

The following week over spaghetti and meatballs at Luigi's, it took Quinn about a half a second to accept Lester's offer of a job supervising construction of a new elementary school in Erie. Hell, he would have taken a job digging ditches. A man had to work, after all.

After dinner he drove back to Sherm's place and stuffed his duffel with a couple work shirts and pairs of jeans. Inside the bag he found a photo of Rusty and him, the day they rode the rapids at Ohiopyle. He looked at it a good long time, thinking it might not be a bad idea to stop by Lorraine's house the next morning on his way out of town. Just to say hello and check on the boy.

But Sherm stuck his head in the door to Quinn's bedroom as he was mulling his options. "I don't suppose you're thinkin' of stoppin' anywhere on your way up north?"

"No, damn you." Quinn accepted the beer Sherm offered, drank it down in a few good-sized gulps, then went to the living room and turned on the Thursday night game.

CHAPTER THREE

Rusty waited out the five years after Quinn left, hunting, fishing, and planning his way out of MacMillan. He'd go to Kansas, he figured. Even if he couldn't find Quinn, he could at least make a name for himself poaching, and make a good amount of cash, too. He learned how to bait deer with apples turned to brown mush from Hank Roland's property, and how to spotlight, catching deer unaware as they tried to focus in the dark at a lamp shining on them. Frozen still. While his 760 was readied to pick them off.

He started skipping school and not caring, even on the few occasions Lorraine got after him. Even though the gentle way he'd had about him when Quinn was around was gone, he could still put on that Poor Rusty Jenkins face. Eyes cast down, mouth turned down, too. Hell, he could even come up with a tear if he had to. With a little work, time after time, he had the principal or any teacher wanting to protect him more than punish him.

He pumped gas on weekends at the Mobil station on Route 22 and learned to hold in his temper when the kids from the other side of town came in. The ones with futures. The ones he figured would end up at MacMillan University or some other college and then become doctors or teachers. He knew he was different from them, but not dumber. He'd find a way to make his mark. A way to make those candy-asses sit up and take notice.

He saved what money he could from helping farmers during planting and harvest and dipping into Lorraine's purse when she was too far gone to notice. Got into the weed a little. Drinking, too. It was when he was high he was most likely to lift a six-pack from the 7-Eleven, or a shirt or pair of pants from Kmart. By then he wasn't afraid to get mean either or try to take more from girls than they necessarily wanted to give. Not that he had much luck with that.

Whatever he saved or stole, he stashed in the basement or buried under trees, away from his mother and Lloyd, or Floyd, or Franklin, or whoever was keeping her bed warm at the time.

On November 7, 1985, the day Rusty turned seventeen, he took apart his Remington 760 and wrapped it in a towel. He stuffed it and a couple shirts and two pair of jeans into his duffel. *Gone for good*, he wrote to Lorraine on a piece torn off a grocery bag. Then he set out for the Trailways Station where the bus to Pittsburgh was due at six fifteen.

Good riddance, he thought while he walked down White Ash, then on to Hemlock. It was fine with him if he never again saw that big old Allegheny Front, separating him from anything that could make him as important as he knew he could be. If this was the last he smelled of that sulfur-stink coming from the mines and wells to the west, that was okay, too. He would have liked it, though, if Hank Roland's Susie came barking after him one last time. It was only five, early even for the Rolands to be about, so he kept on toward town, thinking only once how he hoped Lorraine found the note he left.

When the woman behind the Trailways counter slid the boy's ticket toward him, she picked up her pencil, bright yellow. She held it by both ends, the rounded off point in one hand, the pink rubber eraser in the other. She took his measure, thinking. "Kansas City's a long ways down the road," she said.

Rusty folded his wallet, the ticket inside, then slid the wallet in his back pocket. He knew how far Kansas was. His only concern was it might not be far enough. "Yes, ma'am."

She stashed the pencil in her teased-up beehive hairdo. "Change in Pittsburgh."

Rusty tipped his Pirates baseball cap to the woman. Then he picked five quarters out of his pants pocket, shouldered his duffel bag, and made for the vending machine to get himself some breakfast.

On the morning he left MacMillan, as the sun rose over Pittsburgh, where the Monongahela and Allegheny rivers spilled into each other to form the Ohio, Rusty boarded a bus to Kansas City. He figured he'd maybe find work there and save up some until spring. Or he'd go straight to Chautauqua County where the best game was and where he might find Quinn. When he tossed his bag into the overhead rack and settled in, he didn't know what he'd do. But as the bus crossed the state line into West Virginia an hour later, he sat wedged into the corner of his seat, head against the window, hat over his eyes. All he knew for certain was he'd never again have to think of MacMillan, Pennsylvania, as home.

That evening, when he tumbled off the bus in Kansas City, he wandered around downtown. While he ate at MacDonald's, watching people walk by, he decided there was too much concrete in a town that size. So, he went back to the bus station, bought a ticket south to Chautauqua County, and ended up early the next morning in Saint Francis, south of Independence. At the Caney River Guest House, he handed Bev DeLand a fifty to cover his first week's lodging.

"Breakfast included. Every day but Sunday," Bev said as she led him to a faded blue room on the second floor. "But most of the boys head over to the diner to set and talk with the locals." She pointed down the hall. "Bathroom's second door on the left."

The next day Rusty took a job at Alfred Cunningham's Mobil station. Pumping gas. Changing timing belts. Rotating tires. All the while learning from the locals where the biggest bucks had been sighted and who was bringing them in. Over the next few months, Rusty proved he could hold his own in the fields with the county's best hunters when they went looking for the season's biggest catch, and he went searching for the feeling he'd had when he hunted the Appalachian Plateau with Quinn.

He got himself a reputation and started making himself at home in the stories men traded in the county's pine-paneled barrooms and storefront diners. "Boy's got a helluva nose for deer," George Sullivan told the regulars tossing back shooters at the Plainview. "Temper's hot as the color of his hair, though. 'Specially with a little Wild Turkey in him." "Kid's a mean son of a bitch on the trail of a buck," Randy Waite was heard to say over ham and eggs at Rita's Diner. "Don't know when to quit."

Rusty never grew taller after he left MacMillan. But during his next three years in Chautauqua, all five-foot-nine of him filled out tight and hard. He grew a patchy little beard, just on his chin, and a little of Lorraine's golden hair threaded in with his father's red. He walked with short, quick steps, his chin pointing to where he was going. His hands worked pretty much all the time, telegraphing that what the men were saying was true, daring anyone to say it wasn't.

Rusty got himself a reputation with the women in the county, too. "Don't know when to quit," more than one of them was heard to say, giggling, when it was her turn to house and feed and love him. He drifted from bed to bed, staying until the arms that welcomed him began to wrap too tight. He kept his little room at Bev DeLand's place, just in case. Any time a woman started wanting him to stay too bad, or too long, he packed his bags. No regrets.

Most mornings, Terry Sullivan showed up for breakfast in Saint Francis, halfway between his home in Redmond and the Oklahoma border. He liked to stop at Rita's Diner before he started patrolling all twelve hundred square miles of his territory. He never knew what he might hear that would help him rout out yet another unscrupulous cheat, one who didn't care to follow the rules. After all, Chautauqua County was still known as "Outlaw Country," same as it was during the Civil War when Charles Quantrill's raiders massacred every woman's husband in town, every child's father, and when the Dalton gang rode through in the 1890s, holding up trains and rustling horses till locals took them down for good.

It was Rita herself who told Terry about a preacher and his buddy from over the state line in Miami. The ones who came in the diner two weeks earlier, bragging about kills they made up toward Granville. "A woman gets an earful if she pays attention while she's serving up coffee and eggs," Rita said with a wink. "They got a black Ford wagon, with a taillight knocked out, and Oklahoma plates."

Ten days later, just after he came off patrol, Terry saw the preacher's wagon cruise past his driveway. Smart poachers always checked to see if his truck was in the yard before they went to the fields. After the preacher passed, Terry jumped in his truck and followed, without lights. He stayed back far enough to see how, when the preacher's brake lights flashed, he aimed a spotlight out his window and how the glare froze a good-size buck, grazing in the cornfield. The preacher's nephew, waiting in the field, fired one shot, through the heart. The buck went down.

Terry sat still until the men hauled the deer to the road and heaved it into the back of the car. When the tailgate slammed shut, he turned on all his pickup's lights and roared down on his prey. "You coulda heard that Baptist Bible-thumper cursin' all the way to Colorado," he laughed as he finished buttering his toast at Rita's the next Monday morning.

When he followed them to their camp, Terry said, he found

three more untagged deer. "Total fines come to more than five grand. And that don't count the loss of guns and hunting privileges." Terry knew five was a drop in the bucket compared to what the horns would have brought on the open market. Still, he'd done the right thing, the thing his father would have done. "Nothin' gets my goat quicker, Rita, than a man talkin' out both sides his mouth." He slammed his hand on the counter and shook his head. "Preachin' on the one hand and poachin' on the other."

"You say the man was a preacher?"

Terry turned on the counter stool to see who spoke. He didn't have to guess. All eyes were focused on Rusty, who was soaking up the last of his eggs-over-easy with his grape-jellied toast. Terry wiped his napkin across his face and eyed the man, a stranger, at George Clemson's table. He crumpled the napkin, nice and slow, and reached back to set it by his plate.

"That's what I said."

"Now, I don't know about you, George," Rusty said, slapping his buddy's shoulder. "But I'm not so sure I'd be struttin' like an old Rio Grande tom turkey in full fan, braggin' about bringin' in some pansy-assed preacher." Rusty set his coffee cup in his saucer, then laughed. "What you say, George?"

Clemson shot Rusty a sideways look. He wasn't going where Rusty was leading. "Time to hit the road, son."

Rusty waved George off. "I got plenty of time," Rusty said. "Besides, I'm curious if that's what they're teachin' in college these days. How to bring in a preacher. Maybe next they're gonna teach how to catch nurses and hairdressers." A few men in the diner chuckled. Most sat back, arms crossed, or reached for their coffee or into their pockets for tip money. No one but Rusty cared to get on Terry's bad side.

"Law's the law," Terry said, leaning back, propping his elbows against the counter. "No one's above it."

"No one?" Rusty snorted. He started to speak but Ben Miller got up from a nearby table and took Rusty by the elbow, urging him out of his chair.

"Time to go, Rita," Ben said as he set his hat on his head. He laid down a five to pay Rusty's tab, talking to him in a low voice as he escorted him to the door.

"That's right," Rusty called over his shoulder on his way out. "We got to get us to Sunday school."

$$\sim$$

"Now ya got to admit," Ben said to Rusty in the diner's parking lot, "the man's got guts."

"Nothin' you or I couldn't beat," Rusty said. Ben and Rusty had worked the county's fields together for the last two years, shipping more than twenty-five racks to Texas. They weren't above spot-lighting or baiting a field with corn or apples, or any other tricks, legal or not, that could bag them a set of eighteen-karat antlers, as they were fond of calling the best and biggest racks.

"I'm not goin' up against any man with an axe to grind." Ben ran his hand over the windshield to dust off the light snow that had collected. He hauled himself into his truck's cab and turned on the engine. He cupped his hands, then blew into them to rout out the chill before he spoke. "His father was killed on the job when Terry was a kid. Made the papers from here to Denver. He couldn't've been more'n eight or nine at the time."

The chill air didn't bother Rusty. He had something more important in mind. "What you wanna bet I can't beat that man at his game?"

"Not all the tea in China."

Rusty grinned. "That's all I need to hear."

Ben shook his head, put his truck in gear, and drove off.

Rusty walked to the station where he worked, figuring how he might knock Sullivan off the pedestal the locals had built for him. From that morning on, like Quinn taught him while hunting deer, he kept his eye on the man. He waited.

He watched his house. Saw how, when Terry came home from a day or two out on the road, his wife—Carolanne her name was—greeted him. The man could hardly even breathe, Rusty imagined, given the way the woman got her arms around him soon as he walked in the door. Then there was the girl. Ashley. How, if she was awake when he got home, he swung her up in the air and she laughed and slobbered all over her daddy. If they weren't the happy family.

It came to Rusty after he downed his fourth, maybe his fifth, Wild Turkey late Thursday at the Plainview. He watched JoAnne Peterson grinding her hips against Roger Rutherford while they moved slow and close on the dance floor, hardly leaving the spot they carved out for themselves. When Roger nibbled Joanne's ear, she cradled the back of his neck in her hands. Rusty used to think he might want some of Joanne for himself again. Trouble was she hung on too tight. How it was with a man like Sullivan, who wanted a woman as much as she wanted him, Rusty couldn't figure. Then he smiled as he reached into his pocket for his wallet. Sure, he could give Sullivan a run for his money by making a big kill right under the pussy-warden's nose. But if he wanted to hit Sullivan where it really hurt? He'd have the guy's wife.

"Don't spend this all in one place, old man." Rusty laid a twenty on the bar and tipped his hat to Gus, same as every night when he left the Plainview right before closing. "Better yet," he said, "how 'bout just one more?" He needed to quell Nana's voice in his head, or Quinn's, or anyone else's that might make him think twice about where he was headed next.

Instead of going back to Bev DeLand's place, Rusty drove east on Route 17, toward Redmond. When he turned onto Black Oak Road, he switched off his lights and slowed his rusting F-100 to a crawl.

The new moon didn't give him much to go by, so he took it nice and easy. When he got to a thicket of blackjacks down the road from Sullivan's little yellow ranch, he pulled behind the trees for cover, turned off the engine, and sat. It was almost four when he woke to the sound of Sullivan's Dodge Ram starting. He waited until the truck pulled out of the driveway and headed west, toward Coffeyville.

Rusty had never known Sullivan to turn back once he started anywhere. Just in case, he waited another ten minutes. After the light in the kitchen went out again, he watched Carolanne's shadow follow her back to her bedroom. He eased out of his truck and, nice and slow, made his way around the side of the house.

By the light of the moon, dim as it was, Rusty looked in the bedroom window and saw Carolanne curled under the covers. He crept around to the back door, opened it, wincing when it scraped against the step below. Not even Sullivan locked his doors in that sleepy town. He wiped the mud off his boots to keep from leaving a trail. Then he went in. He felt his way along the walls, past the room where Ashley slept to the master bedroom down around back. He waited at the door, still enough to hear his own breathing and the small sigh Carolanne made as she turned over. When she was quiet again, Rusty took two long strides, and he was on the bed behind her.

She tried to scream, but Rusty pushed her face into her pillow. Chest heaving, he reached down and pulled the sheet loose. He tied it around her eyes. He took the cord he had stowed in his pocket. Sitting astride her, he reached around and tied her feet at the top of the bed, her head at the bottom. He raised her night-gown behind her, groped for her panties and ripped them. Holding his knife against her side, he twisted its point deep enough in her waist until she got the blade's message. She stopped struggling. While she sobbed and shook, he reached down to unzip his jeans.

Crash. The noise came from the kitchen. Then what? A chair dragging across linoleum? Rusty stilled himself, listening. He moved the knife from Carolanne's waist to her throat. He heard nothing more, but he tossed her aside. Then he bolted from the room and out the front door.

Ashley made her way from the kitchen to the bedroom. She patted the bed and felt around Carolanne's head. "Uppy, Mommy."

But Carolanne didn't move to pick her up. All she could manage, in a throaty little plea, was "Don't cry, Ashley. Mommy's here." Ashley batted at her mother again, then cried, then slept. But Carolanne stayed awake all day, until late afternoon, when Terry found his wife and daughter on the bed, the sheets damp with tears and sweat.

⁓

When he left Terry's house, Rusty hustled back to his room and packed his two bags. What the hell had he done? The best thing, he figured, was to act normal, then get out while the gettin' was good. He took the fifty grand or so he had stuffed in the mattress, under the baseboard, behind the bureau. He went to the diner for breakfast just as the sun was coming up. When Rusty stood from his table at six fifteen, to go to work everyone figured, he tipped his hat to Rita like he did every morning. Then, instead of going to work at Cunningham's station, he got in his F-100. He drove past fields full of Eastern toms wooing their mates in the sandstone hillsides, past ponds teeming with crappies and largemouth bass, and past big bucks, bounding through woodlots along the Caney River.

"And bye-bye to you, too," he yelled, waving out the window, his hand mimicking the deer's flagging white tails as they ran for safety. He slammed the steering wheel with the palm of his right hand before he popped the first Bud from his six-pack. He guzzled it down, then turned the radio up full.

He stopped in Kansas City first, just long enough to unload his truck at a chop shop in exchange for an old Buick and a set of stolen plates. Then he phoned Donna Jefferson in Minneapolis. She'd headed there from Saint Francis to be near her family when Rusty lost interest. Donna would put him up for a while and maybe he could put up with her if she didn't come on too strong.

Three weeks after he got established in town, he hooked up with a guy looking for what he called a salesman. Someone who could expand business out Pittsburgh way. Within the week, Rusty headed toward Pennsylvania, a twenty-five-thousand-dollar stash of weed in his trunk, a bucket full of uppers and downers on the back seat, and all the time in the world.

He set himself up in Pittsburgh, but once he made connections, mostly at high schools and colleges, business took him all over the state. He even made it back to MacMillan on occasion, where he sold to MacU boys and to the pansy-ass high school kids who hung out at the Three Bears because no place else in town would serve them.

CHAPTER FOUR

Class had already started when Lucy Stephenson entered Adriana's yoga studio. On any other day, she might have taken a deep breath, inhaling the calming lavender scent, and allowed herself to melt into the dreamy music coming from the speakers. Instead, she kicked off her clogs, pulled back her fine hair with a clip, and walked to an empty spot in the back corner.

After she unrolled her mat on the floor and stretched, she assumed the asana Adriana called out. "Mountain pose." Lucy stood and planted her feet on her mat, hips width apart. She pulled her shoulders back and down. She visualized her head being held erect by an imaginary string of stars, descending from the sky. But no matter how intently she focused, no celestial energy flowed down through her ribcage, as Adriana suggested. Nor did she feel Earth energy moving up through her feet, her long, toned legs. She felt hollow, like an empty shell.

"You are as young as your spine is supple," Adriana said with her innocuous little half smile.

Until hours earlier, Lucy believed that. But she had just come from her second visit with Dr. Olsen, the oncologist. She now knew she was as old as she would ever be. As was often the case with pancreatic tumors, he told her, by the time she felt the pain in her shoulder and the discomfort in her bloated belly, the cancer was too far advanced to control. Not with surgery, chemotherapy, or any other known treatment.

"I'm sorry," he said.

Sorry? What an insufficient expression of empathy. Or sympathy. Which was it? All Lucy could say was "I'm sorry, too."

"Downward facing dog." When Adrianna called out the next pose, Lucy placed her hands and feet at opposite edges of her mat. She pushed her hips in the air and held the pose, looking at the room upside down, her topsy-turvy perspective seeming more accurate than her viewpoint when she was standing upright. She looked across the room and saw her friend Corinne Kramer on her mat. She was upside down, too. "Coffee?" Lucy mouthed the word. Corinne nodded.

When class neared its end, Lucy lay on her mat, palms up, feet splayed, to prepare to meditate.

"Dead man's pose." Adrianna tiptoed from one mat to the next, adjusting each student's head and hands. "Repeat after me," she said. "I am a child of the universe, safe and protected."

When Adrianna reached Lucy's mat, and saw her tears, she patted Lucy's hand. "With all the introspective postures we did today, release is to be expected, and welcomed."

Lucy opened her eyes. She didn't smile as she would have in past weeks. She didn't say thank you. She also didn't shake her head and say, *What rubbish. You have no idea what you're talking about.* And she didn't ask, although she wanted to, *Can you promise me a death like this? Quiet and safe and still?* She nodded and waited for the calm, the peace that didn't come.

After class, Lucy and Corinne rolled up their mats, put on their shoes and jackets and went to the coffee shop next to the studio. They ordered their overpriced drinks at the counter, then settled into a corner booth. As soon as they set their yoga gear on their seats, Corinne leaned forward, her gold bracelets tinkling. "I was so glad you came this morning."

Even from across the room in class Lucy could tell that something was disturbing Corinne. Not that her eyes weren't their usual sparkly blue, or that her skin didn't look fresh and plump. It was the lines in her forehead that gave her away. She'd most likely had another altercation with Graham.

Relieved that she could focus on Corinne's problems instead of her own, Lucy held her double espresso in both hands, appreciating its warmth. "What happened?"

"I told him last night." Corinne sipped her cappuccino, then settled back into the squishy leatherette seat. "That I got the job at the Center for Hope."

Lucy tilted her head. The fact that Corinne got a paying job at the Center after volunteering there for years should have been good news. "And?"

Before Corinne answered, she raised her right hand to her head and held it there. "He . . ." She started but couldn't finish.

"He what? He doesn't want you to?" Lucy frowned and leaned forward. "After all the work you've done to get your masters? That's so nineteen fifties."

Corinne shook her head. "He said it was good I was making a career for myself . . . he wants a divorce."

Lucy reached across the table and took her friend's hand. Restlessness was epidemic among MacU's forty-and-over male faculty. Her own husband, Richard, had moved out three months earlier because he *needed a break*. Arthur Morehouse in physics and Davis Carter in American history had done the same a while back. But none of them even hinted at divorce. What was Graham thinking? Was there someone else? A graduate student? No, that would be laughably cliché.

Lucy released Corinne's hand. She sipped her espresso to allow herself a second to think. "He actually said the D word? He didn't mean he just wants a little time off?"

Corinne shook her head while Lucy reached in her bag and handed her a tissue.

"Did he say why?"

While she waited for Corinne to answer, Lucy thought back to when they each arrived in MacMillan sixteen years earlier on the arms of their tenure-track husbands. Richard had been delighted. After being banished to Saint Francis University in the-middle-of-nowhere Kansas to earn his PhD under the tutelage of Solange Bouvier, he would return to an elite school. He, his undergraduate work at Yale, and his publishing credentials would garner the attention they merited.

Lucy, on the other hand, was ambivalent. The first time Solange, Richard's comp lit department chair, brought him to dinner at Dr. Charles Schroeder's house Lucy was enthralled. What young woman who had been confined to the hushed halls of the Sacred Heart Academy wouldn't be taken by the doctoral candidate with his rather distracted brown eyes, his brown hair swept from his face, his mara-thon runner's build, and, best of all, his stories of eclectic friends in New York and Paris and Rome, eagerly awaiting his return?

The first time Lucy discovered she was pregnant, she and Rich-ard told Charles and Emily they were going for a drive one Satur-day afternoon in April. But instead of heading north for a picnic along the sandstone banks of the Caney River, they drove south over the Kansas line to the office of a grandfatherly obstetrician in Miami, Oklahoma. When Lucy returned home that evening a little dreamier than usual, she told her parents she had had "a smidge too much wine" with her fried chicken.

She stayed in bed for two days, even though the cramps subsided the day after the *procedure*. "I'm just tired," she told Emily, but didn't mention the abortion or how she dreamt about the pictures of the doctor's grandchildren, set out in silver frames along his office credenza.

After that, when things started to go very wrong—when Emily was diagnosed only weeks later with Parkinson's, and a crop-pun-ishing rain started and didn't stop, Lucy got on her knees and begged forgiveness. Whether it was the Holy Spirit speaking, or her determination to make up for her transgression, she wasn't sure. But she decided the only way to compensate for the baby she let go of was to make another.

She skipped a pill one week. A couple the next. And when she felt nauseous in the mornings, and unendurably tired in the afternoons, she told Emily before she told Richard. Not just about the previous pregnancy but about the *procedure*. After visiting her mother's gynecologist, she invited Richard to dinner. But not before Emily led him into Charles's study for a closed-door talk.

"Solange and I can make your academic future as full or as insignificant as we like," Charles told Richard that evening, in private, before dinner. Three days later Richard proposed, Lucy accepted, and they married in a private ceremony in the university chapel.

That summer, they flew to Ireland so Richard could study Celtic manuscripts at University Galway, and so Lucy could return to the States to have her daughter without anyone—except Charles and Emily—counting days and weeks before Lucy gave birth. For the next year, Richard worked on his dissertation, Emily tried to channel some of Lucy's creative energy away from painting and sketching into homemaking and child rearing, and Charles avoided all of them. Only Emily cried when Richard finished his dissertation, defended his *viva voce* in front of his committee, and accepted a tenure-track position at MacMillan University.

From their first faculty spouse's orientation in 1972, Corrine and Lucy found comfort and camaraderie in their similar plights. They traded everything from recipes to political opinions over coffee or after their weekly meditation group. Later in the seventies, when they both got into therapy, they helped each other *own her feelings*—with limited success—and to not *give away her power*—to their husbands, the butcher, or anyone else who might try to curb their ambitions or their creativity.

For Lucy that meant working at Metaphors bookstore, chairing church committees, and helping her daughter, Allison, fire up her imagination and cultivate her independence. Corrine, meanwhile, volunteered at the Center for Hope, studied for her masters, and raised her two daughters to always look their best as they achieved and accomplished.

They took yoga and, yes, shimmied into hot-pink and periwinkle spandex to work out with Jane Fonda. They tried eating macrobiotic, but neither could give up coffee or cheesecake. They both swore off nicotine several times, though occasionally Corinne snuck Virginia Slim menthols under duress, like when her younger daughter started kindergarten or when Graham was late, again. And, despite their ventures into New Age practices, each continued to attend Sunday Mass and went to confession with Father Malone once a month.

⁓

All the work we did, all the hope we cultivated, Lucy thought, pulling herself back to the present, *and here we are, my body as broken as Corinne's spirit.* She raised her eyes to her friend's.

"I'm embarrassed to say." Corinne looked away.

"A graduate student?" Lucy asked.

Corinne dabbed her eyes again. She turned back to Lucy and nodded. "That exquisite-looking Swedish girl. You remember her?"

Yes, Lucy remembered Annika from Graham's last department gathering. Who could forget all magnificent five-foot-ten of her? Then she started to cry, too, when she thought of Richard's new secretary. A French beauty named Jacqueline. In a few months, when Lucy was gone, Richard would become officially available. If not to Jacqueline, then to someone else. What would happen to Allison? Who would help guide her, protect her?

"I didn't mean to make you cry," Corinne said. "You're getting along without Richard. I'll manage, too."

Lucy attempted a wistful smile. "It's not about Richard. Or—and I'm sorry to say this—it's not even about Graham." Her smile faded. "I have cancer. Un-fucking-treatable cancer."

Corinne thumped down her coffee. "Cancer?"

Lucy nodded.

"What kind of cancer? What do you mean it's not treatable?"

"It's in my pancreas. Or it was. Now it's spread. All over. I don't even feel that bad. A little tired. And that pain that was ruining my tennis serve? Remember that?"

Corinne nodded but didn't understand what an annoying shoulder had to do with pancreatic cancer.

"It was the first sign that something was wrong. And when I went to see Warren Olsen last week—"

"You've known since last week? And you didn't tell me?"

Lucy shrugged. "I know it sounds silly. I just thought—hoped—if I kept my mouth shut, it might go away."

"Dear God!" Corinne inhaled a deep yoga breath. "I've been blithering on about that self-consumed narcissist I'm almost not married to when you've got cancer?"

She leaned forward. "I don't understand how there can be no treatment. Maybe we should go back on that macrobiotic diet. And what about that plant in Mexico that's supposed to—"

Lucy shook her head. "It's too late." Then, when she looked into Corinne's eyes, she suddenly wanted to laugh. Her usually perfectly made-up accomplice, sidekick, confidant looked so silly. The mascara that had trickled down her face made her look clownish. Instead, she answered the question her friend didn't want to ask. "Three to six months," she said.

For the next hour they talked about how Corinne could help. "It's Ali I'm worried about," Lucy said. "She and Richard have no relationship to speak of, especially since the separation."

"Have you told her?" Corinne asked.

Lucy shook her head. "Richard's the only one who knows besides you. I called him from Olsen's office. But Allison and I are going hiking tomorrow." Her voice faltered. "I'll tell her then."

"Do you think she'll try counseling? I could talk with Paige McDaniel at the Center."

Lucy doubted whether independent, tough-as-nails Allison would see a counselor, but figured it was worth a try. "Thanks," Lucy said, then closed her eyes and pressed her lips together. She didn't want to spend precious time in tears. When she opened her eyes, she reached across the table to Corinne.

"Promise me," Corinne said, squeezing her friend's hands. "You'll let me know what else I can do? Anything," she said. "Anything at all."

They held hands until both accepted that everything that could be said—for the time being anyway—had been said. They gathered their gear. When they stood, Lucy allowed Corinne to hold her close, then stood back at arm's length. How many more coffee dates would she have with her friend? How many times would she look across a room and telegraph salacious commentary on some self-consumed academic? She felt herself wobbling then tightened her grip on her friend's arms.

"Sometimes I think I've done a little too good a job with Allison. Maybe she's becoming more independent than she needs to be."

"Oh," Corinne said. "I'm not sure a woman can ever be too independent."

Lucy paused. "We could have done better ourselves, couldn't we?"

Corrine looked away, but the fear in her eyes didn't escape Lucy. They had talked a good game these years since the Friedans and Steinems of the world began preaching independence and bra-burning and all that. They had gotten their degrees, then their jobs to support themselves . . . just in case. So, how was it, like now, when life slapped them in the face, and they took stock of their lives, they still felt inadequate, they yearned to be taken care of? Besides, they were still doing all the housework. What kind of freedom had they really achieved?

"Richard's a brilliant man, not without his charm with students and other audiences," Lucy said. "And he knows how to navigate academia's landmines." She shook her head. "But he'll be flummoxed when faced with practicalities." She braced herself. A woman like Corinne, despite all their years of training, would be delighted to take care of him. "He'll need help, too."

Their eyes locked. They hugged, quickly this time, then walked to their cars. Lucy blew a kiss to Corinne as she drove out of the parking lot.

"Namaste," Corinne called, holding her hands in prayer position. She started her ignition, then turned left toward Stewart's market for groceries. On her way, she thought of the tasks ahead of her, the ones that would distract her from Graham's pronouncement. Lucy was right. Allison had grown quite independent. Nonetheless, she would need counseling, no matter how much she resisted. And Richard . . . She parked outside Stewart's then looked at her tear-stained face in her rearview mirror. She traced the pale gray circles under her eyes. She pulled her makeup bag from her tote, then refreshed her mascara, her concealer, her lipstick.

She didn't really need groceries, she decided. She put the car in reverse, drove back to Center Street, toward Wellington Hall on the MacU campus.

⌒

Corinne breezed past Jacqueline when the young French woman motioned to her and said, "Ree-char will see you now." Before she opened his office door she took a moment to compose herself.

Richard stood when she walked inside. "Corinne," he said.

He looked unlike his usual distracted but neatly kempt self. Yes, strong and lean—he still ran five, six miles a day—but he seemed bewildered, at sea. Even his hair, his abundant, swept-back hair, graying just a bit at his temples, looked a little tussled.

"Have a seat." He waved to the chair facing his desk, then stuffed his hands in the pockets of his pleated corduroys. He suspected why she was there. And thank God. With all that work she had done. Where was it? Hospice? The Center for Hope? Wherever it was didn't matter. As efficient as she was, Corinne would know how to get Lucy the care she would need. And she had those two girls of her own. She would know how to handle Allison, too. *Good Lord, what am I going to do with Allison?*

"Lucy told me," Corinne said. She pulled the chair closer to the desk.

Richard rubbed his hand over his eyes before he spoke. "I only wanted some time away." He looked at Corinne. "I had all that work to get done," he said, motioning to a pile of apparently unfinished manuscripts. "It wasn't about women. I hope she knows that. Does she know that?"

"I'm not sure," Corinne said, though she found his admission comforting.

"I didn't want to leave forever. And God Almighty." His typically mellifluous voice faltered. "I didn't want her to die."

"Of course, you didn't." Corinne's counseling training supposedly cured her of the delusion she could fix other people. But here, now? She could at least help dispel that needy, overwhelmed look in Richard's brown eyes, couldn't she? And what about her own needs? She hesitated then edged forward. "How can I help?"

Richard shook his head. "If this were an obscure text I needed to translate, I would know what to do and how to do it. But real life? I don't know where to begin."

Corinne stood. "Yes," she said. "I can see how that might be." She walked around the desk. She held his head against her breasts. With her hand, she traced his hair, smoothing it back in place. "Don't worry, Richard," she said. "We'll get through this."

Ever since her daughter turned five, Lucy Stephenson liked to keep Allison home a day or two from school each year. From the beginning, these "Secret Study Days" required compliance on both their parts.

Dear Mrs. Tanaka, Lucy wrote to Allison's teacher the day after a visit to the Impressionist exhibit at the Carnegie in Pittsburgh,

Allison was not in school yesterday because she looked a little green around the gills.

The color green, Lucy explained after reading the note to her daughter, was a matter of interpretation. Something measurable, like fever, was not. They weren't exactly telling a lie, were they?

"Rib-it," Allison croaked, imitating the only green thing she knew that made sounds.

"Rib-it," Lucy answered. Allison giggled and rib-itted while her mother wrote Mrs. Tanaka's name in calligraphy on an envelope, tucked the note inside, and sealed it.

Even then Allison considered school as limiting as Lucy did. She was only too glad to keep their study days secret—from her teachers, her classmates, and her father. Richard Stephenson, head of MacMillan University's Department of Comparative Literature and translator of obscure literary texts, was far more likely to follow the letter of the law than was Lucy. By the time her mother took her on their first excursions, Allison suspected her father would end her days out of class if he knew about them. Provided he tore himself from his writing and publishing and teaching long enough to learn of them.

To ensure Allison understood their trips were learning experiences, not escapes from classroom ennui, Lucy insisted on home-work—a song or a poem—which she mounted in a leather-bound portfolio, filled with cream-colored parchment she bought in Italy when Richard was there, finishing his translation of *Divina Commedia*.

On the page dated Spring 1980, for example, Lucy pasted Allison's ode to an Irish girl named Kathleen, the one Allison imagined kissing her father good-bye when he and other emigrants left Ireland to build the Horseshoe Curve in nearby Blair Township. On the opposite page, Lucy pasted her own rendering of the laurel-covered hills bordering the Appalachian Trail, the vista those workmen would have seen when laying down rails. "Look how our work completes the other's," Lucy said when they leafed through the portfolio. "We make a good team."

When Allison turned thirteen, she grew tired of nature hikes or museum trips, or anything else Lucy wanted to do together. "Only if we stop at the Monroeville Mall," she said when her mother proposed one last Secret Study Day. There was that lacey negligee she had seen in the Victoria's Secret catalogue. She could more than pay for it with the money grandfather Charles gave her to celebrate the onset of her teenage years.

Early in May 1988, though, Allison was a few months from seventeen. Thanks to the fact that she skipped second grade, she was six weeks from graduating high school. The laurel in the Appalachian foothills was just beginning to paint the landscape pink, and the tulip poplars were only days from full budding. Lucy set out their backpacks as she had in years past. She packed a lunch, their *Field Guides to Appalachia*, and sunscreen. She didn't set out her easel, though, or her sketchpad. Or Allison's guitar or journal. Just a note on her daughter's room's door.

> *Meet me in the royal coach at six, before sunrise, and we'll travel west to the land of wildflowers and attainable dreams. (Just once more before you leave for college? Pretty please?)*
>
> *The Good Witch*

CHAPTER FIVE

Allison groaned when she stumbled in that night and read Lucy's note. The idea of returning to one of their secret places, one that might dredge up memories of earlier years, when her father still lived at home, when Lucy spun cotton-candy fairy-tales to cover up the family's faulty infrastructure. And when, no matter how late Richard stayed out, no matter how often he broke promises to spend more time at home, Lucy smiled and insisted everything was *fine*.

But now, Richard was out of the house, and with the wisdom of her almost seventeen years, Allison felt responsible for her mother. Lucy's marriage could end, after all, and her only child was preparing to leave for college in three months.

Allison crumpled the note and set it on her nightstand. As she wriggled out of her tube top and skirt, she figured Lucy needed this little escapade more than she did. Maybe she had always needed them more. In just her underwear, Allison slipped into bed. She glanced at her bedside table clock. One fifteen. She should have passed on the last round at the Three Bears. Or left at eleven with Suzanne instead of waiting for Robby to drive her home. Too late now. She fumbled with the dials on her alarm and set it for five thirty.

When it woke her—she had just closed her eyes, hadn't she?—
she tried to shake off the fuzziness from too many Heinekens but
couldn't rouse herself.

Lucy knocked on Allison's door a few minutes later. "Rise
and shine."

Allison grunted and pressed the snooze alarm. She pulled her
quilt over her head. "Fifteen more minutes!" When the alarm
buzzed the second time, she threw off the covers and shuffled to
the bathroom. Before brushing her teeth, she took two aspirin
to dull her hangover. She took two more after she showered and
dressed in her jeans and sweater.

She made her way to the kitchen and waved off Lucy's "Good
morning." "Too sweet," she said. "Too early."

She downed a glass of milk to settle her queasy stomach while
Lucy tidied the kitchen, set the picnic hamper near the door, and
hummed annoyingly. "Just where are you taking me today?" Allison asked.

Lucy smiled but said nothing.

Even as they packed the Jeep and drove out Center Street, then
through the tunnel at the Allegheny Front to the Appalachian
Plateau, Allison didn't know where they were going. But after they
passed streams that, even in the early light, reflected the rusty runoff
of nearby strip mines where paraffin-rich oil had been pumped out
of Pennsylvania's belly years earlier, she suspected they were headed
to Laurel Highlands State Park. If she had to endure one last Secret
Study Day, the Highlands would make for a fine destination.

Allison dozed for half an hour, then reached for the picnic
basket and served buttered banana bread and orange spice tea
from a thermos. Finally managing a smile, she fished around in
the glove box and held up a tape. "A little Joni?" she asked.

"Absolutely."

Allison popped the tape in the deck and cranked up the
volume. They rolled down the windows, their hair splaying in
the early damp air as they belted out Joni Mitchell tunes about
Chelsea mornings and circle games. But when the song came on

about how people don't appreciate what they have until it's gone, Lucy stopped singing and fixed her eyes on the road ahead.

An hour outside MacMillan, at the base of the Laurel Highlands State Park, the gray sky broke and promised a sunny spring day. Lucy pulled off the road where the Youghiogheny River Gorge formed in Ohiopyle Township and parked at the rest stop. Allison, meanwhile, pulled her hair back in a ponytail and put on her hiking shoes. When they got out of the Jeep, even though it was early for black flies, Lucy sprayed them both with repellent until Allison flailed and yelled, "Enough!"

They hiked the nearest trail through limestone outcroppings and thickets of beech and maple, then followed a hemlock-lined stream into the ravine cut by the Youghiogheny River millions of years earlier. The air was still damp and cool, so Allison kept a brisk pace, as much to warm up as to get home early enough to nap before meeting Suzanne for another night out.

"Hey, slowpoke," Allison called over her shoulder. "I thought I was the one who was too old for this." Lucy didn't respond, so Allison looked back. Her mother hesitated then smiled and waved for her to keep going.

When Allison reached a patch of laurel, she knelt, picked pink clusters, and stuck them in her hair. Lucy was still taking the hill slowly, so she gathered more laurel and wove the buds into a circlet. When Lucy made it up the hill, she placed the flowers on her mother's head. "I crown you Lady Artemis," she said. "Goddess of the hunt and laurel."

Lucy, though winded, curtsied graciously. Then they kept on their way.

Almost an hour later, they reached Butterfly Meadow, halfway up the ridge. Lucy set down her backpack and took off the cardigan she'd worn thin since she bought it on her honeymoon on Inishmore. She lifted her arms and faced the sun. Then she twirled around and around, dizzy from the smell of spring in the air.

Recovered from her hangover, and willing to share Lucy's enthusiasm, Allison spun around, too. Eventually too giddy and lightheaded to stand, they collapsed into the grass, laughing until tears came to Lucy's eyes.

Allison lay back when Lucy set out their blanket, the sun warming her face, her arms, her legs, her disposition. Then Lucy reached to her, stroked her arm, and tucked a strand of her daughter's hair behind her ear.

"Do you remember the first time we came here, Ali?"

Allison smiled. "We forgot our lunches and when we ran back to the car, we scarfed down peanut butter sandwiches and apple juice as if we'd been captive on a desert island."

"That was something, wasn't it?" Lucy laughed, then shook her head. "But, you were seven then. The first time, you were six. We sat near where we are now, but it started to rain, and we ran into that patch of pines. Over there." Lucy pointed to her right. "When we came out, a rainbow arched over the ridge, and a little mist rose up because it was so hot, and the rain cooled the valley just enough." She took Allison's hand. "You asked if this was what heaven looked like because the sky was lit up just the way it's painted behind the altar at Saint Michael's. That was when you were still willing to go to church." She turned to Allison. "You said you thought nothing bad could ever happen up here."

When Lucy lapsed into melodramatic reminiscences, Allison most often changed the subject or tuned her mother out. But her voice had turned heavy. With sadness? Fear? She searched Lucy's face, usually vibrant and innocent as a child's. Now it looked pinched, almost desperate.

"Ali, honey?"

Allison's heart raced. Something was broken that couldn't be fixed. Like when Grandma Emily died. Were her parents going ahead with the divorce?

"I have cancer."

Allison took her hand from Lucy's. She didn't speak. *I heard wrong*, she thought. *She must have said that Daddy has cancer, that he* is *cancer and she's finally divorcing him. Or maybe Grandpa is sick.*

"Ali, did you hear me?"

Allison said nothing. She didn't want to reach to hold her mother, like she thought she should. She wanted to rebuke her. *This isn't funny, Mother. Don't play games with me.* She sat up on the blanket.

Lucy wasn't laughing or chucking her daughter's chin. She wasn't saying, I was teasing. I want to prepare you for how much things can hurt.

Allison heard only snippets of what Lucy said next. "Sonogram . . . mass . . . a little bloating . . . promise me . . . regular checkups . . . once a year . . . no matter what—"

"You're having an operation?" Allison interrupted.

Lucy reached again for Allison. She shook her head.

"Chemotherapy?"

"It's too late," Lucy said. She didn't say that her doctors predicted she would make it to Christmas. If she was lucky.

"How long have you known?"

Lucy took too long to answer.

"Why didn't you tell me?" On her knees now, Allison tucked her hands under her shins to keep from jostling her mother by the shoulders.

"We don't have much time," Lucy said as she sat up. "We need to talk."

When Allison hung her head, Lucy rearranged the curls in her daughter's ponytail. "You need to do your best with your father. Ali? Honey? Look at me." Allison raised her face, tears rolling down, but resisted when her mother tried to take her hand. "He and Grandpa are all the family you have. At least for now."

Stop talking! Allison wanted Lucy to stop talking. To stop preparing her.

But Lucy continued. There might come a time, there likely *would* come a time, she said, when Richard would find another woman to anchor him without expecting too much in return. He might even take up with someone he already knew. "You'll need to try your best with her, too."

The night was still, except for the katydids, the Tettigoniidae, Lucy called them, jabbering to seduce willing mates. The same as they had the previous summer. As if nothing in their world had changed. Allison stopped halfway across the yard. She traced Orion's path overhead, rising east to west. Then she scoffed. He was hunting Merope, all the while claiming to protect her and her six sisters from Taurus, the bull. "Things aren't always as they seem," Allison remembered her mother saying when Lucy taught her that version of the Great Hunter's tale. That was years ago, before she understood the meaning of duplicity, betrayal, loss. When Lucy passed on, the world would go on spinning, the constellations would continue telling their celestial stories, and the wretched katydids would again rub their forewings together, sending mating calls into the summer night.

Those realizations might have been too much for Allison to bear, but she had smoked enough weed in the Three Bears parking lot to get a little happy-high. She kicked off her sandals. Then, steps uncertain, she made her way toward the front door, the lawn cool and damp beneath her feet.

She stopped. A car door squeaking as it closed? She turned to the street. Nothing. To the side of the house. Nothing. Maybe pot paranoia.

She started toward the front door again. As she passed the honeysuckle hedge, she feathered it with her hand and breathed in the sweet scent.

Her blouse smelled sweet, too, from the roach she tucked in her camisole, between her breasts. Ten, twelve weeks earlier she would have tossed away the remaining reefer. There's more where that came from, she would have thought, if she thought about it at all. In MacMillan, university faculty and their progeny had plenty of everything that was important—knowledge, talent, ego. There was no need for frugality, for fear.

Allison learned differently in May when Lucy told her about the cancer that was eating away at her pancreas—then her shoulder, her stomach, her liver. She became afraid she wouldn't know how to navigate the world without her mother. Afraid she would never stop feeling Lucy's illness was in some unknown way her fault. Maybe if she had been less temperamental, or if she had been kinder to her mother when her father left, maybe Lucy wouldn't have gotten sick.

"Even though I think you're the smartest young lady in the world, and one of the top ten most talented," Lucy tried to reassure her daughter, "I don't think you're powerful enough to cause cancer." But Allison couldn't chase away her suspicions. She couldn't stop being afraid. In the same way the Plateau across the Allegheny Front subsided into sinkholes where coal had been mined, she, too, would soon collapse into stark nothingness.

From the shadow behind the garage, Rusty watched.

The moon, though new and slender, shined enough light for him to see Allison get out of her car at the side of the house, walk across the lawn, and enter the front door. She turned off the outside light. Her mother must have left it on for her. That's how it was with East MacMillan parents. They cared where their sons and daughters were, who they were with, when they got in, whether they drank their juice at breakfast and mailed their college applications in on time. He laughed. If they only knew what their precious offspring were up to when they left their tidy east-side homes.

He moved slowly, closer to the house, as she reached to steady herself in the hallway. The sweet thing had enjoyed too much rum and weed at the Bears. She made her way toward the back of the house. Allison, that was her name, looked a little startled when she opened the refrigerator and the light inside glared at her. She reached for a pitcher—iced tea, maybe—and drank from it. Of course, she would be thirsty. Weed did that. He watched her walk, still a little tipsy, to her bedroom off the family room. He leaned forward when she untied the fringed shawl from her shoulders, stepped out of her gauzy skirt, and stood, all innocent and unsuspecting in her pink camisole and lace panties.

He had been watching Allison off and on at the Three Bears, mostly on Friday nights, while she nursed her syrupy rum and Cokes, or a couple brewskis, with other underage friends, the seniors, their diplomas already rolled and tied with red ribbons, waiting to be picked up as they paraded across the commencement stage, to their colleges and their futures.

Allison was pretty enough. Her longish brown hair, lightened from the summer sun, almost the color of chestnuts now. Eyes wide and deep and brown, fringed with flirty lashes. Breasts and thighs starting to stretch the limits of her camisoles and her jeans. Probably always thinking she should lose a few pounds so she could fit into a size two instead of a four.

Still, Rusty might have overlooked her if she didn't enjoy making herself so obvious. The way she tossed her hair behind her shoulder before she leaned her Salem Lite to the lit match the guy named Robby cupped between his hands. *Look at me.* When she pulled back, she drew on the cigarette in an exaggerated, hollow-cheeked, movie-star way, holding it between her middle and index fingers, the rest of her hand splayed. *Pay attention.* Then, settled back, posture erect, she perched on the edge of the bar's battered captain's chair, one leg crossed over the other, her pink-pedicured toes peeking out from high-platform sandals. She hadn't gotten enough from her famous professor daddy. Rusty could see that was true. Otherwise, she wouldn't have needed that kind of attention from those kinds of boys.

That first night he saw Allison, Rusty hadn't yet made up his mind if he would continue to do business in MacMillan. He had no family left in town as far as he knew. He'd tried to call his mother twice in the last two years. The first time she didn't answer; the second, the phone was disconnected. Nana had passed on long before he left MacMillan, and even if his father reappeared, he didn't think he would recognize Ronny Lee Jenkins Sr. if he were standing right next to him.

But he had already made connections at MacU and with the younger crowd, enough to siphon business from the only other dealer worth a damn in Central Pennsylvania. Plus, he had a day job at Charlie Miller's Gas Stop where he saw Allison once a week or so when she drove in to gas up. "Fill it," she said, not thinking, not noticing. He watched her while he fitted the nozzle into the Volvo's gas tank and while he ran a squeegee over the back window, wiping it down with a lifeless old rag.

His eyes followed her when she looked into her rearview mirror and stroked her lipstick across her lips once, then back and forth again quickly before pressing her lips together to smooth out the frosty pink color, or while she picked at the peeling nail polish.

She didn't know he felt the way she rocked in her seat, mouthing words to songs on the radio, moving with the music. Besides, if she had known, she would have liked being watched. She would have wanted the attention. Wouldn't she?

Rusty tipped his cap to her. The yellow one that had CAT written on it. "Have a nice day, miss." He handed Allison her change through her window, rolled down low enough so he could breathe her smell. Roses, he thought. A little like his mother used to smell. Wouldn't it be nice to lick the perfume off a girl like that, and taste her pretty pink lipstick, too?

When she pulled out of the station the previous Tuesday, he wrote down her plate number and checked her service records. Allison Stephenson. A brake job last October. An oil change in May. Address, 66 Tranche Street. Phone, 555-5933. He dialed the number once in a while during the day but hung up when the woman with the accent answered.

The maid, he guessed she was.

Rusty shot pool in the Bears' back room nearly every night, with other mechanics, electricians, and plumbers, all of them thanking God it was Friday—or Tuesday or whenever—by knocking back longnecks as fast as Charlene could serve them. Then came the night he bent close to the table, setting up his last shot. "Goin' in for the kill now." He laughed while other men leaned on their cues, hoping he was wrong. Until he heard a scream from the next room. Against his better judgment—he knew not to take his eyes off the table—he saw Allison, screeching, spinning around, pulling on the elastic band of the skirt that outlined her dancer's legs, tugging at the edge of her lacy top, shaking out the ice cube the laughing boy had slipped down the back of her camisole.

"Stop it, Dylan," she scolded. But of course, she didn't want Dylan to stop. *Look at me! Pay me some attention!* That's what that girl really wanted to say.

Rusty stood upright. He reached for his Bud, tilted it back, then set the bottle down. He'd had enough beer. Maybe what he needed was a little dessert. A high-class, sweet little thing. He chalked his cue, walked back around the table to take his shot from the opposite side. "This one's hardly any competition at all," he said.

Just as he planned, the seven ball dropped into the far pocket, and he slapped the back of the man who had lost. "Now what was you sayin' about whuppin' my ass?" He grinned while he took a Slim Jim from his shirt pocket and bit into it.

He stepped back after he collected another twenty, his last wager of the night. Then he turned to the next room, remembering those kinds of kids from across the Front when he was at West MacMillan High. The kind who expected life would only get better. The ones who drove into the station where he worked and didn't give him a second look when they barked over their shoulders, "Fill it. Premium."

He remembered how those boys, once they released the hood and told him to make sure he got the spot off the windshield, the one he had missed intentionally. Then they would reach across the seat of their father's car, or their own if their parents paid for one, and pull their girl close for a kiss. Or maybe just stroke her cheek or her hair.

He smiled. None of them ever guessed, when their shiny vehicles failed, that it was because he messed with them. But there were other ways to prove his point. To ruin what they thought was theirs. "See you candy asses tomorrow," he called over his shoulder to his pool-playing buddies. Then, on his way out, he eyed the boys in the next room, and the girl they all seemed to favor. Allison. Allison Stephenson. He got into his car, drove to her street, and parked two houses down. He turned off his truck, leaned back in his seat, and waited.

Now, here she was. Just a few steps away. Sugar, he thought after he crossed the yard and stood outside Allison's window. "Candy," he said, as if she was about to be served up to him on a doily-covered plate.

He had watched the house often enough to know the father didn't live there anymore, and that the mother slept upstairs in the front of the house. All that separated him from the girl—Allison—was a newly mowed lawn and a loose-fitting window screen. Even if she struggled and tried to scream—even if she begged—he would know how to quiet her, although he didn't need to hurt her, only to have her. He drank from the pint he pulled from his back pocket. He twisted the cap back on the bottle and wiped his mouth on his shirt sleeve.

⌣

When Allison bent her head toward her breasts, her hair tumbled down in front of her face. She began to stroke it with her brush, unaware he had watched her on previous nights. While she swayed and sang along with the music from the tape player next to her bed, she didn't know he was creeping across the lawn, taking a step before freezing in place, then another, until he reached the house, and his left arm sliced the heavy air and pushed the screen while his right arm hoisted him in. With two steps, before she turned toward him or screamed, he was behind her, his left hand over her mouth, his right hand bracing the knife at her throat. She couldn't see his face—her hair still hung in front of her—but she felt him against her.

Allison felt nothing else but her heart jackhammering in her chest. She batted her silver hairbrush against the man's leg where his jeans had ripped on the window frame, and cut his thigh, although she was hardly aware of this feeble little attempt at protection. She was dulled enough by the weed to not feel terror at first. But she couldn't breathe, she needed air, she needed . . . "Mommy," she wanted to say. "Mom-mmy."

When he pulled her to the bed, onto the quilt, he yanked a clump of her hair, jerking her head back far enough to see the knife just catching the moonlight. When he rotated the blade to meet her throat again, Allison gulped one shallow breath and held it. Her last? Was this her last precious breath? Was her last breath to be the smell of this stinking man?

"You scream, sugar, and I'll hurt you."

Allison still couldn't see the man's face, but she smelled him. If his smell had shape and form, it would look and feel like the mossy scum on a still pond. But something more. A meaty smell. And sulfur, like the West side on hot, humid days like this. When he wedged her legs apart and snatched her panties, tearing the lace away from her, she felt as if he had skinned her and left her bloody and raw. The zipper of his jeans caught against her leg. Then he jammed into her.

"You tell anyone, I'll be back," he said when he finished, still on top of her. "You hear me?"

She jerked her head up and down. How could she not hear him?

"Her, too," he said. He didn't have to explain that he meant Lucy. "You hear me again?"

Silent sobs. Head nodding. Up and down. Up and down.

He wrapped her shawl around her eyes. With her sheets, he tied her hands to the foot of the bed and her feet to the head of the bed. She was upside down, but she didn't know it yet.

When he hoisted himself through the window and Allison no longer heard his feet padding on the grass, she lay still. Afraid, at first, he might return. Then her tears soaked through the shawl. She moved her head around, against the quilt. Up and down again to loosen the wrap from her head. When it came off, she hesitated before opening her eyes.

The world looked the same, at least her room did. But it smelled. Like meaty, swampy rot. And Allison knew it would never feel or smell the way it had a week before, yesterday morning, even ten minutes earlier. She loosened the sheet that held her hands to the bedpost. Her tears flowing, but still silent. She reached to her feet. They were where her head should be. Nothing was in place. She focused on one thought: I cannot, I must not, tell.

She stood, shaking. The man was gone. But not his smell. The rot that penetrated her from the inside wanted to get out, to tell what she would not, could not. She went to the hallway, groped the hallway wainscot, and made her way to the bathroom. She showered and soaped and rinsed until the hot water ran cold. She rubbed the towel against her, scrubbing at the dribble down her leg. She sprayed herself with perfume from the vanity. She dusted herself with talc, all over, to try to get rid of the smell. It would not go away.

Back in her room she gathered her camisole, the towel, shawl, silver hairbrush, sheets, quilt. She rolled them into a stinking wad of shame. She stuffed them into the antique trunk at the foot of her bed. It was where she used to hide her diaries, her cigarettes, and other secrets, so small and innocent now. She locked the trunk.

Seeing that the man left the window screen open, she jammed it back in place. She fell back into the chair next to her bed, hugged her knees to her chest, whimpering and rocking. She shook. She watched Orion cross the sky, and Scorpius, The Hunter's nemesis, rising on the opposite horizon, too distant to catch her victim, already on his way out of the night.

"Morning, please come," Allison whispered, though she was certain that day or night, dark or light, she would never feel safe again.

CHAPTER SIX

The day after their trip to the Laurel Highlands Allison sat facing her mother at the kitchen table. She dawdled over her yogurt and granola, which used to be her favorite breakfast.

"You're not hungry?" Lucy asked.

Allison shook her head and pushed her bowl away.

"Can you look at me, honey?" Allison sat motionless and silent, so Lucy continued. "It's late May. I haven't got much longer," she said. "Are you sure you won't see a counselor?" Just a few visits to help you prepare?"

Allison turned to her mother. She did not want to face her feelings. She did not want to think about how she would get on in life after Lucy died.

But when Lucy stood from her chair, went to Allison, held her, and stroked her hair, Allison grabbed onto her. She shook and sobbed.

"See someone, will you? Pretty please?" Allison, still crying into her mother's arms, nodded. "Good girl." Lucy loosened her daughter's grip, went to the phone, and called Corinne.

Allison could tell from her mother's words that Corinne knew about the cancer. She wished Corinne didn't know, that no one else knew. These were her last days with her mother. She didn't want to share them.

"You can start this Thursday," Lucy said when she hung up. "Corinne's going to let us know what time." She went to Allison and held her chin in her hands. "Okay?"

Allison nodded and stood. She reached for her mother one more time. Then, her steps tentative, she went to her room and dressed for school.

After her last class on Thursday, Allison rode her bike the few blocks from school to the Center for Hope for her appointment with a counselor named Paige McDaniel. Corinne recommended her, which didn't impress Allison. Although Corinne and her mother were longtime friends, Allison hadn't, as Lucy hoped, taken to perennially perky Corinne and her equally saccharine daughters, Devon and Stephanie.

She rode into the Center parking lot and locked her bike in the rack. She grabbed her backpack, then affirmed her resolve. She would see Paige two or three times because she promised her mother. Maybe that would help Lucy feel better. Maybe they would wake one morning from this nightmare and—

A car honked at Allison, interrupting her fantasy as she stood frozen in the lot. She steadied herself, then went inside the Center and took a seat in the reception area.

When Paige entered the room and walked toward her, Allison felt relieved. She had it in her mind that if Corinne recommended the woman, she would look like Corinne, act like her, walk like her, talk like her. But this woman's smile was warm, not Miss-America-bright and white and plastic. Sincere, Allison thought. Kind. Paige seemed about the same age as her mother, but she had dark hair, almost black, with gray threading through it, pulled in a single braid in front of her left shoulder in a way that showed off her almond-shaped eyes. Blue-gray, they were. She wore a gauzy print skirt, a long loose sweater, sleeves pushed up, and crepe-soled sandals, tied around her ankles.

"Allison?" When Paige spoke her name, clearly, softly, Allison felt confident this woman wouldn't try to rob her of her sadness. She thought she might be able to tell Paige the truth without being told to feel something different.

Paige motioned down the hall to her office. Once they took their seats, she explained that anything they discussed was confidential. That she would do whatever she could to help. "Any questions?"

Allison shook her head, suddenly afraid if she spoke even a single syllable she would fall into a pit and never stop tumbling down, down.

"Okay, let's get started." Paige asked Allison how things were going at school. *Good, not great.* Was she sleeping all right? *Sometimes yes, sometimes no.* Had she told her friends about her mother's illness? *No, and she didn't plan to.*

"We'll get the most from our time together," Paige said, her voice firmer, "if we talk as specifically as possible about your mother's cancer. We need to help you rally your friends and family around you, so when your mother's time comes, you'll feel supported."

Allison looked at Paige but said nothing. Friends? Yes, she had friends. Friends with mothers. Healthy mothers. Friends who couldn't know how she felt. As for Richard—she'd stopped calling him Dad when he moved out—his support was not to be trusted. And Grandfather Charles? He'd become so distant since Grandma Emily died, as if he wanted nothing more than to join her.

Paige leaned forward in her chair, grasping her crossed legs. "Okay, we can revisit that later." From what Corinne had told her, the doctors said Lucy had a couple months, six at most. "In the time you have left with your mother," she asked, "what do you want to tell her? What needs to be said?"

Allison looked out the window, to Paige, then back to the window. She shook her head. Her lip quivered as she tried to speak and hold back tears at the same time. She stood. She steadied herself then walked to the door. Her hand on the doorknob, she turned back to Paige, but still no words came. She left, pulling the door closed behind her.

When she got on her bike and started pedaling home, she vowed she wouldn't keep her appointment the following week. What was the point? As the days passed, though, she found it more difficult to function at school and to sleep at night. She wanted to see Paige again. She wanted to hear her calming voice.

The following Thursday, Allison arrived at the Center at three thirty. She stayed half an hour that time, forty-five minutes the next. By the middle of June, she spent an hour each week. Sometimes, she told Paige, she didn't believe Lucy was going to die. Sometimes she thought Lucy was playing a cruel joke on her, or that she'd made up the whole cancer story to get attention from Richard.

Then she said how, most nights, she woke suddenly, as if a spotlight had been trained on her, and a vicious harpy shrieked inside her, inciting unspeakable thoughts and feelings. "Sometimes I want to pound my fists and hurt her for leaving me alone with my father." Other times, she said, she figured she must have done something that made her father want to leave home. And worst of all, sometimes, *almost always,* she felt it was her fault her mother got sick.

In July, after the man attacked her, Allison didn't show for her appointment. She didn't phone or return Paige's follow up calls. No one, not even Lucy, could get her to say why. She spoke to no one. Not about the rape. Not about her mother's illness.

She quit her part-time job at Metaphors, the bookstore downtown. She had qualms, of course, when Olivia, the owner, asked her to stay on. "You learned to read there," Olivia said as she pointed to the little yellow chairs in the children's section the day Allison went to the shop to resign. "You were four and so very bright. And your mother brought you here every day while she worked at the register." Olivia sniffed. "I just think it might help if you stayed close to people who care for you and Lucy."

No, Allison said, she would rather be alone. She would rather not remember how her mother taught her to read or fired up her imagination or encouraged her to become a poet. She held herself in balance between fear of losing her mother and fear of encountering the man again. The only way to keep from falling from the thin, high wire she was walking was to focus straight ahead and to say nothing. She shuttered herself in her room. She ate meals with Lucy, unless someone from Saint Michael's parish, or from Mothers Against Drunk Driving, or from Adriana's yoga class, brought a casserole or a pot of soup and stayed for dinner. But sometimes when Lucy was alone, reading or resting, Allison ran from her room and rushed at her mother. "Don't leave me."

Richard offered to move back in, but Allison would have none of that. He visited every night, around eight or nine, when Allison made sure she had either left for the Three Bears or was tucked in her room with her door closed. For the first few weeks, Richard tried to speak with her, but she refused and he let her be. The Friday after Allison stopped going to the Center, though, Richard knocked on her bedroom door.

"What?"

"It's me, Allison. May I come in?"

"Why?"

"Just to talk."

"Not a good time."

"I'll count to ten, then I'm coming in." When her father opened the door, Allison was stretched out on her bed, reading a magazine. She didn't look up as her father rested against the doorjamb, hands in his pockets.

"Your mother tells me you stopped seeing Paige."

"And you think this is something I don't know?"

He walked in the room, leaned against the bureau, and tried again.

"Why did you stop, Ali?"

She glanced toward him, thinking maybe she should tell him the truth. Then she turned back to her magazine and continued flipping through. "No time."

STARS IN THEIR INFANCY 83

"We both know you've got the time." He jingled the change in his pocket. "Paige told your mother you were making progress, then you just stopped and never called to explain."

Allison sniffed. "So much for confidentiality."

"She didn't tell anything you said, only that you stopped going."

"Oh?" She snickered. "I don't remember you explaining why you stopped being a father. Or a husband."

"Ali, I made mistakes. But this isn't the time . . ."

He seemed to be floundering, at a loss for his precious words. She rolled onto her belly, away from Richard. "I'm reading and you're blocking the light."

He hesitated, then went to the door. "Good night, Ali."

When she heard him leave the house, she grabbed her pillow. She curled in a ball and rocked herself to sleep. No, she told herself, she couldn't have asked her father to hold her, like she wanted. If he said no, she felt she would break in two.

⌣

When Lucy could no longer walk, or stand, or feed herself, when she spoke only in breathy, three- or four-word sentences, Dr. Olsen suggested she be hospitalized. Lucy mouthed a single, but emphatic "No," and Corinne arranged for her to stay at home. Corinne visited twice a day, always knowing, it seemed to Allison, when to bring Lucy soup and saltines. When to pamper her with chamomile-ginger tea. When to let her rest. She ordered groceries and re-ordered prescriptions. And since Lucy could no longer manage the stairs, Corinne arranged to have a hospital bed delivered and set up in Lucy's first-floor studio.

"It's your mother's favorite room, and it's got the best light," Corinne said, while Allison watched her move a chair here, a table there. "Open the blinds, honey, will you?"

Allison bristled. Nobody but her mother called her honey. But she did what Corinne asked. Apparently not well enough. No sooner had Allison opened the blinds than Corinne adjusted them.

When the bed arrived, Allison watched Corinne direct the deliverymen to place it exactly where Lucy would be able to see the sun set behind the Allegheny Front to the west. She watched Corinne open a new set of yellow sheets and slip Lucy's pillows into matching shams. "Your mother loves yellow," she said while she flitted around the bed, tucking corners, straightening the coverlet, emitting so much energy Allison didn't think there was space enough for her in the room. "Pull that sheet over just a hair, will you, honey?"

She watched Corinne help Mrs. Saunders, a nurse, move into the guest room, watched the way Corinne showed Mrs. Saunders around the kitchen, opening and closing cupboards. "Everyday dishes above the sink. Pots and pans to the left."

No, Allison thought, *this is Lucy's house. And mine. It's not yours to organize or take charge of.* Still, she admitted that, without Corinne's help, she would have little idea of how to keep the house running and her mother comfortable.

It was early August. Sunset came earlier each evening. Now and again a red or yellow leaf let go from a tree and drifted to the ground, hinting at autumn and endings. Allison moved a chair close to the window in Lucy's studio. She read her mother her favorites, mostly Austen and Eliot. When Lucy could no longer comment, Allison brought in the leather-bound portfolio, the one filled with mementos of their secret trips around the state. She reminisced about all those escapades she used to try to disdain. She still hoped she would wake one morning to her mother cooking French toast, calling out "Rise and shine, lazybones."

Instead, "Hi . . . Sweet . . . heart," was the best Lucy could manage, each syllable an effort. Allison didn't know if her mother slept or if the drugs just took her to a less painful place. She wondered if, when Lucy was incoherent, and her breath ran shallow and high in her chest, she got a glimpse of what death was like. Allison couldn't work up the courage to ask.

When Richard visited in the evenings, Allison either left the room without speaking or tossed an acerbic greeting his way. "Nice you could make it." "Look who's here." Even though, once the words were out, she wished she hadn't said them.

"Not now, Ali," Richard usually said, taking Lucy's hand, or stroking her cheek, or kissing her forehead. But by the time he spoke, Allison was out the door, on her way to her room where she propped herself on her bed and turned on her stereo, staring out the window with the broken screen.

Not now, she thought. In Allison's mind that meant *not ever*. She and Richard would never reconcile. And that suited her. Most of the time.

One night after Richard left, she brought nails and a hammer up from the basement to her bedroom. With too many nails, she pounded the screen into the window frame. She kept the window closed and locked, even though it was the height of summer. She sat up in her chair, facing the window, awake, except for the couple hours she fell into unsettled, unsatisfying sleep.

Most nights, she went to the door of Lucy's room. She watched the sheet covering her mother's chest. She held her breath until the sheet moved. Up and down, in and out, slowly, like a clock winding down.

On the second Monday in August, when Allison looked in on Lucy around two in the morning, she found Richard sitting by the bed. His head was next to Lucy's, his hand held hers. Allison stood at the doorway, watching. Then she pulled a chair close to Lucy's bed. All three of them slid in and out of sleep, but around six in the morning, Lucy's favorite time of day, the time when, before she got sick, she baked bread or cleaned house or exercised, she wakened Allison with a light tapping on her shoulder.

"Darling, sing . . . for . . . me?"

Allison wanted to refuse. She hadn't played her guitar or sung in weeks. Since before the man raped her, before he took her voice from her. But when her father asked, "Please, Ali," she went to her room for her guitar.

She came back, stopping in the doorway. Richard leaned close to Lucy, stroking her hair, limp and dull, away from her face. They were closer together than she had seen them in a long time. Maybe ever. Why hadn't they touched each other more? What brought them together in the first place? How did two such different people end up in each other's arms and lives, then drift so many miles apart?

She walked to the corner chair and sat down, readying her guitar and her voice. Then she closed her eyes. She rocked her sadness into her music and squeezed her eyes to keep her tears inside. No more breezy Chelsea mornings. She played her own music, her love for her mother, her sadness over their parting, the end of her childhood. When she finished, she held her fingers across the strings to silence them. She looked to Lucy.

Richard shook as he raised his head from Lucy's pillow. "She's gone, Ali." When he reached across the bed, she allowed him to take her hand.

Moments later the front door opened and closed, and Corinne came click-click-clicking into the studio in her Ferragamo flats. When Allison saw the look on Richard's face, the look that said *Thank God you're here to take care of this, to take care of me*, she pulled her hand from his. She stood, picked up her guitar, and went to her room.

On the way to the living room, where her father waited, Allison stopped to look in the hall mirror. She wiped a smudge from her turquoise eye shadow, rearranged her hair, taking long enough to let her father know she would proceed at her pace, not his. She suspected that, if Richard thought at all about what she would wear, he would expect to see her in the navy-blue suit she wore to college interviews.

But when Allison closed her bedroom door and walked into the living room, she was wearing a turquoise print shift, one Richard bought for Lucy on their last Bermuda getaway. And strappy white sandals, the ones Lucy found in her favorite little shop in

Perugia, where the owner always greeted her with arms held out as if a prayer had been answered.

When she neared her father, and he noticed the dress, the shoes, then the hair, she smiled.

Her hair was cropped close to her scalp. No longer brown, like her father's, it was caution-sign yellow, sticking up and out in spikes that she hoped appeared capable of inflicting permanent damage if touched. But no one would want to touch it. Which was why she had colored it. *Proceed at your own risk*, her yellow hair warned.

"The driver's waiting," Richard said, shaking his head as he walked outside. Allison tucked Lucy's patent leather handbag in the crook of her arm, and trailed after him, eyes focused straight ahead.

In the limousine, she looked out the window, resolute and dry-eyed, as they drove first to pick up Lucy's father, Charles, then to Saint Michael's Church. When they arrived, she checked her makeup in her compact mirror—Lucy's mirror—and declined the open hand Richard extended to help her from the limo. She walked into the church ahead of Richard and Charles, took her seat in the front pew. She sat silent and made eye contact with no one.

During the eulogy, Father Malone cited Lucy's work as a Eucharistic minister and chairwoman of the annual drive to raise scholarship money for gifted children in the parish. "Our lives and our community are richer, thanks to the many ways Lucy furthered the kingdom of God." Then a few words from Corinne about their work for MADD, and a short speech from one of MacMillan's pediatricians. "I never would have had the privilege of caring for your sons and daughters had Lucy not arranged for my scholarship to Columbia."

Allison saw everything and heard everyone's words. She wanted to feel something, anything, to be able to dab at tears like Lucy's friends in the church. She couldn't cry. At the end of the service, she mouthed words and sounds came out. "Thank you for coming." But she felt she was among strangers, not friends she had known since she was three, not their parents who had arranged playdates and sleepovers. She focused on one thought at the funeral, at the cemetery, and at the luncheon Corinne hosted afterward. *Don't tell anyone anything. Not what you think, not what you feel, not what you know.*

⁓

Allison busied herself in the kitchen the night before she and Richard left for Ithaca. She baked banana bread, as Lucy would have, the sweet scent reminding her of her mother. It also helped camouflage the almost undetectable smell of sulfur that late-summer currents west of the Front were carrying into East MacMillan. At least Allison thought they were. Since that night, since that man . . . She shuddered. His smell shadowed her. Part sulfur, part something she couldn't quite define. So strong, it seemed sometimes, that she turned and looked. Was he there, behind the bushes? Across the produce aisle at Stewart's market? In that red car that passed her twice as she rode her bike downtown?

"Just one more day," she murmured as she poured a cup of orange spice tea, another of Lucy's road trip must-haves. "By this time tomorrow . . ." Her thoughts trailed off as she considered arriving in Central New York, where the air would be clear and fresh, and she would be free of the man and his smell. She would be free of Richard, too. He would be able to work as long and hard as he wanted, publish as much as he could. He would once again be awarded the Wadsworth Prize by his enamored students. The ones who had no idea how incapable he really was of the devotion and commitment they thought they received from him.

Allison poured the rest of the tea from the pot into the thermos. Then she packed it and the banana bread into the wicker basket she set out. She put in photos, too, mostly of Lucy on their Secret Study Days. Yes, she wanted to leave Richard behind, and the man, too. But she would take her memories of Lucy with her and keep them close.

⁓

When Allison and Richard set out in the Volvo the next morning, no wind blew through her hair. Joni Mitchell wasn't blaring out open windows, and Allison wasn't singing. Not like she would be if Lucy were driving. She and Richard drove with their eyes on the road, listening to Mozart, his hair combed straight back and tidy, hers sprayed into a protective yellow helmet.

"Should I pull over," Richard asked every now and then when they passed a rest stop.

"No," she said. "I'm fine." But she wondered why he couldn't hear the unvoiced conversations in her head, the ones that blamed him. And the occasional ones that wanted him to tell her to knock off her insolence and let him comfort her. Or at least try to. *Shouldn't he know what I need?* When he didn't respond, even though she hadn't spoken, she sank further into her sullen silence.

⌒

Allison fidgeted with her sandal straps, tightening them, but not too tight. She freshened her lipstick and smoothed the wrinkles on her dress as Richard circled the campus twice, finding it difficult to navigate Ithaca's precipitous one-way streets. When he eventually drove into the Baker dorm parking area, they unloaded the car and hauled Allison's trunks up two flights to the top floor. Room 312. She cranked open the leaded window to the stuffy room to get a view of Libe Slope.

When Lucy brought Allison to Ithaca to interview a little over a year earlier, she scurried down the hill, then up again, laughing. After following, grudgingly at first, Allison yelled to her mother, "Last one up the hill treats." Gasping but giggling, Lucy bought them double mint chip cones at the student union and they sat on the Arts Quad, toasting Allison's future.

When she heard her roommate, Sallie, laughing with her mother, father, and younger brother in the hall, Allison reluctantly shut off her memories and greeted the Nickersons with her first smile of the day.

"With those hills and these stairs, you won't have to worry about gaining weight," Mrs. Nickerson said, laughing. Allison thought that, if Lucy were there, she would say the very same thing.

Allison and Sallie had written back and forth early that summer, but Allison never mentioned her mother's death, certainly not the man, or much of anything else, except that she would be studying literature with a focus on twentieth-century poetry. She never mentioned, either, that she was counting the days until she could pretend that Ithaca would be her new home.

"Hartford." Allan Nickerson shrugged when Richard asked where they were from. "Never thought I'd end up in insurance back when I was here."

"You're a Cornellian?"

"Class of sixty-eight. You?"

"Yale. Also sixty-eight."

Before long, they figured out they both went to the Dead concert at Fillmore East in 1970 and that they had an acquaintance in common. Avery Cameron, from Allan's graduating class, who now taught poli sci at MacU.

Allison looked on, wondering at the way Richard could breezily chat up other people. How was it so easy for her father to relate to them, but not to her?

While the men caught up, Sallie and her mother and brother helped Allison empty then stow her suitcases. At least, she thought, they didn't seem to care about the tie-dyed, decades-old halter dress of Lucy's she was wearing, or her lemon-yellow hair. She supposed Richard would have been happier, though, if she had chosen a cute seersucker sundress, like the one Sallie had on, rather than an outfit her mother might have worn to that Dead concert at Fillmore East.

When the unpacking was finished, and the chit chat wound down, Allison walked Richard to the Volvo. His parting words— "I'm proud of you for getting on with things"—fell miles short of what she wanted. Comfort, reassurance that the world was not as dangerous as she now believed. When he got in the car and started off, Allison stood feeling like a stick person, as if she might blow away in the slightest breeze. She wished she had asked her father for more. Then she waved, though Richard had already turned out of the lot.

Instead of returning to her room, to Sallie, her family and their affection, Allison hiked up Libe Slope in the light rain that had begun to fall. She got a mint chip cone at the student union, then sat under an old oak, wondering if the dark hole in her chest would ever fill with anything other than fear and wanting.

CHAPTER SEVEN

The next week Allison started classes: astronomy to learn more about the stars Lucy had introduced her to; anthropology and French to fulfill her humanities requirements. Thanks to Lucy's tutoring, she tested out of freshman English and earned the opportunity to write poetry with Rodney Peyton.

"Your work has an appealing rhythm," Rodney said at their first one-on-one conference. "And you have a way with metaphor." He shook his head and tapped his pen on his desk with increasing urgency. "But you need to put more of your soul on the page."

When she sat silent in response, Rodney said that limitation wasn't overly concerning at the freshman level. "But, without work, I'm afraid . . ." He waved his hand, which Allison took to mean there wasn't much hope for her. She left his office, resolved to keep her soul where it was, locked inside the hollow center of her chest.

Allison's sleeping habits—rather her inability to sleep—sent Sallie packing three weeks into the semester. When she had the room to herself, she continued dressing in Lucy's old clothes, or unusual thrift shop finds. A chinchilla wrap from the fifties. An olive-colored trench coat and brown fedora trimmed with pheasant feathers. She continued to crop and bleach her hair and did whatever else she could to keep a safe distance between her and the rest of the world.

⌒

On the second Tuesday in October, as the sun began to lower in an almost cobalt-blue sky, Allison left the Moonstone Café about four. When she stepped onto Seminary Street, she set her backpack on the bench out front. As Allison pulled her sweater over her head, a woman walked by, smiled, and said hello. She looked to be in her early forties, about Lucy's age. She was tall like Lucy, too. But Lucy had walked with quick little steps, her head turning this way or that like a curious bird.

This woman took her time. With long, fluid strides, her ballet flats crossed the cobbled street as easily as water skimming a smooth-stone streambed. She wore a gauzy, full-skirted dress, the color of a ripening peach. The scarf that danced after her was the shade of her skirt but streaked with sunset reds and pinks and corals. Her hair, somewhat darker than cornsilk, was secured with a filigree barrette, delicate as the frothy tendrils tumbling around her ears and down her neck. An unusual but pleasant scent trailed her as she continued down Seminary Street, turned into the alley, and unlocked the back door to a shop.

Without thinking, Allison followed at a distance until she saw the sign in the shop window.

Artemis
Specializing in Herbal Arts

The storefront was painted glossy white with silver trim. The windows were festooned with billowing ivory sheers, studded with rhinestone stars and silver crescent moons. Carved wooden swans, their necks coiled or stretched tall, nestled among plants and flowers on the window seat. A long-haired white cat, wearing a collar of pearls, curled in a basket in the sun. But it was the smell—cloves and cinnamon and oranges, she thought—that pulled Allison inside.

She closed the door behind her and looked toward the shop-keeper, who moved as gracefully, Allison thought, as a roving cumulus cloud.

"Just a minute," the woman said when she heard the door chimes. She was, it looked to Allison, measuring herbs and spices on scales in an alcove off the main room. Allison wondered what difference it might make if the woman placed one extra seed on the right scale or one more leaf on the left. But to this woman, proportion and balance seemed to matter.

Allison made her way through the shop, touching gauzy curtains, rubbing velvet sachet pillows that were for sale. She opened frosted glass bottles in the shapes of swans and humming-birds, holding them close to smell their bath oils and body lotions. A harp rested in a back corner, and dreamy music, a hammered dulcimer she guessed, piped through the shop's speakers.

In the center of the shop, a statue stood on a round table draped with silver cloth. *Artemis—the huntress—*the plaque read. Allison ran her hand along the sculpted doe that played beside the goddess, remembering how, on their walks through the Laurel Highlands Lucy taught her about the deity of wild places and ponds, who considered deer and laurel sacred.

"There." The shopkeeper turned around, dusting the residue from her hands. "What can I do for you?" Her voice was soft and lyrical. Like a lullaby? No, more like the Brandenburg Concertos.

Allison leaned closer. "I . . ."

Up close the woman wasn't as tall as she appeared from a distance. Only an inch or two taller than herself, Allison thought. A few freckles played across her nose, and the contrast of the brown beauty mark above her full lips, to the left, only made her skin look creamier, more delicate, her hazel eyes more brown than green. When Allison looked into them, she felt herself pulled forward, as if she might fall if she didn't brace herself.

Allison felt as if the weight that settled months ago on her chest lifted off enough so she could breathe from her belly. Like she did before her mother died, before the man attacked her. But now, in this place, or maybe near this woman, she felt she could once again draw in enough air to sustain herself.

"I'm not sure," she said tentatively. "I saw the sign." She fumbled for words. "I smelled the herbs."

"If they drew you in," the woman said with a gentle smile but a penetrating look, "they must mean something for you. Come. Sit." She gestured to a marble-topped table and carved wooden chairs. "My name is Lehanna."

Allison sat on the edge of a chair, her eyes roving the shop to avoid the woman's intent gaze.

"And you are?" Lehanna squinted as she sat opposite her customer. "Alice? No, Allison, maybe?"

Allison was intrigued that Lehanna guessed her name, but she didn't want to question her. Not yet.

"Yes. Allison."

"I'm glad you're here." Lehanna touched her upper lip with her right index finger. Then she lightly tapped Allison's hand.

"I'll be right back." Lehanna left the table and hurried off behind a purple velvet curtain, held aside by a silver rope and tassel.

Allison heard dishes clattering and water running. She looked around at the jars on the shelves, the plants in the window. She wondered why she had come in this place, but she didn't want to leave. She reached in her pocket and pulled out a cigarette and matches, then realized she didn't want to smoke.

"I'm sorry about your mother," Lehanna said when she came back, carrying a tray of biscuits and a porcelain teapot and cups.

Allison started. "My mother? My mother—"

"I'm sorry about her cancer. The pancreas, was it?"

Allison nodded, but watched warily as Lehanna poured tea, sweetened it with clover honey, and passed a cup across the table to her.

"And," Lehanna continued, "I'm sorry she needed to leave before you felt you got enough of her."

"How did you know?" Allison leaned forward, her voice a whisper. "About the cancer?"

Lehanna shrugged. "I see and hear things most people can't. And I have a responsibility to share what I know. Not every minute of every day. Just when I'm meant to help someone."

Allison took the napkin Lehanna held out, wiped her tears with it and inhaled its scent. Lavender? She began to lose her footing again and part of her wanted to run from this woman, this place. Maybe even report this charlatan to the police. But her hope that Lehanna was genuine, that she could be trusted, that she could tell her something, anything about Lucy, edged out her fear. She sipped her tea, spicy but soothing. It warmed her mouth, her throat. The churning in her stomach slowed. She smiled.

"Ginger." Lehanna said, her whisper-voice calming Allison even more than the tea. "It settles the belly." She hesitated. "Do you know your mother still has more to teach you?"

Allison searched Lehanna's face, wondering where a question like that came from.

"She wants you to know she didn't want to leave you."

As Lehanna proceeded, Allison's eyes widened.

"She wants you to try to understand your father," Lehanna continued. "That he can't really help himself—he doesn't know how. Not yet. The same with Corinne and her girls. What are their names?" Lehanna shut her eyes. She listened, waiting to retrieve the names.

"Devon and Stephanie," Allison said. Her body tightened. Corinne and Richard—during Lucy's last weeks, at the funeral—made it clear they would cling to each other in the name of griev-ing. The thought of them as a couple, so soon after her mother's death, rankled her. She put her hand back in her lap, working it nervously, then tightened it into a fist. "I will never try with Corinne. Not with any of them."

Lehanna nodded. "Your anger can help you through this. For a while, anyway." She sipped her tea, then changed the subject. "So, your name's Allison?"

"Yes."

"Like that plant over there." Lehanna pointed to a tall plant with a bulbous purple flower atop. "From the garlic family. Very healing. Spelled a-l-l-i-c-i-n but pronounced like your name." She smiled. "Yes, anger will help you survive, but eventually it will keep you from doing what you need to." She paused, gauging Allison's receptivity.

Allison, in turn, measured Lehanna. When she sensed the woman wasn't trying to siphon away her anger, she opened to hearing more.

"What do you mean? About what I need to do?"

"We're not on Earth," Lehanna said, "to muddle through. We're all called to do something bigger. Many people find that scary. They pretend they don't know any better and just go on, making money and names for themselves, never understanding. You're one of the lucky ones. With a little help, you might see that."

Allison stared into her hands.

"Allison?" Lehanna waited until the young woman lifted her head. "Your mother knows now about the man and what he did to you. She knows it wasn't your fault. And she wants to reassure you again that you certainly didn't cause her cancer or her death."

Allison froze. Spoken out loud, her secrets felt less weighty than they had when she locked them inside. Shame began to lift, if only a little, as the possibility of freedom took its place.

Lehanna finished her tea then set the cup in its saucer. "It won't help to pretend it didn't happen."

Allison trembled. How safe was this woman, this place? She wrapped her arms around herself. "He's always there." Her face contorted, pulled one way by fear and pushed another by pain. "All I got was the smell of him." Her voice sounded unrecognizable to her. It was so small. "A sulfury swamp smell. I never saw his face, but he's always there."

Lehanna came around to Allison's chair and held her to her chest. "What you need help learning," she said, stroking Allison's hair, "is that other people and other energies are with you, too. They want to help you heal." She clasped Allison's hands. There were things they could do to make the smell go away, she said, or at least dilute its power over her. "Come with me."

Lehanna led Allison to the back door then opened it. Allison expected to see the alley behind the shop. Instead, she was in a scene as colorful as those she and Lucy used to visit at Pittsburgh's Botanical Gardens. Pink and white orchids. More of the purple *allicin* that grew tall and leggy in the front window. Lacy green ferns draping from the ceiling. Velvet-leaved violets in pots on wooden shelves. And fragrant roses. Red, yellow, lavender and white.

They walked down the center row, where the herbs grew, and Lehanna named them and what they stood for. "Rosemary, for remembrance." She rubbed the short, spiny leaves of a green plant and held out her hand so Allison could smell the earthy scent on her fingers.

She went on, touching each plant. "Angelica, the angel of the garden. Lavender. Sage." Colors and smells surrounded Allison tenderly, like a mother's embrace. She closed her eyes and breathed deeply, unaware of her peaceful smile.

"Western doctors are still uneasy about using botanicals for illnesses as varied as cancer and schizophrenia," Lehanna said. "But I've been studying the science for years. Back to my undergrad days in Madagascar."

"Madagascar?"

Lehanna nodded. "That's a story for another time." She cut a sprig of a leggy-looking plant with violet flowers, then a leaf from what looked to Allison like basil. She rubbed them together in her palms and opened her hands so Allison could smell the oily residue. From the first sniff, her shoulders began to relax and lower. Then, eyes closed, she breathed in deeply and smiled again.

"You see?"

Allison opened her eyes and nodded. Lehanna asked if she would come back to the shop the next three afternoons at four o'clock. She would mix the essential oils she believed could help Allison and teach her how to use them. "You may never forget," Lehanna said. "But you won't need to be a prisoner of your memory anymore."

"Oh," Allison said. "I'll be back." She took Lehanna's arm, and they strolled back inside the shop. After a second cup of tea, Allison returned to her dorm. She slept until the next morning, when she woke feeling something she could only imagine was hope.

Allison returned to Artemis the next day at four. While she roamed around the garden out back, Lehanna got to work mixing the formulas she felt would help her new client. "We need to nourish your body and your spirit," Lehanna told her when she motioned Allison back in the shop. "Here."

Allison held up the vial Lehanna handed to her. It was the size of a small perfume bottle. She read the label's directions out loud. "Rub on the belly, twice a day."

Lehanna explained that the mixture contained essential oils of calendula and mugwort. "This is calendula." She pointed across the shop to a plant with long, narrow leaves and yellow flowers. "From the same family as the marigold. It will allow sunlight to shine over you. The mugwort—such a funny name, I know—is from the Artemisia plant. That silvery one there on the left." She waved to a collection of pots beneath a far window. "It's named after the Greek moon goddess, Artemis. You saw the statue of her?" Allison nodded. "She's sometimes called the virgin hunter and the protector of women, but she was also an herbalist."

Allison nodded again. "And deer and laurel are sacred to her," she said.

"You know Artemis?"

"Mother taught me about her. About a lot of the Greek gods and goddesses. The constellations, too."

Lehanna shook her head. "You must miss her so much."

"I do." When Allison managed that one simple sentence without crumbling, she considered what Lehanna said the day before. Maybe something or someone was protecting her. Maybe she could heal.

Early that evening, without stopping for dinner, Allison walked back to campus. She pulled the curtains almost closed, so she could block out stray glances but still see the crescent moon rising outside the window. She took off her jacket, her sweatshirt, her jeans. She wrapped herself in the pink terry robe Lucy had bought for her. Then she stepped into the matching slippers. From its little velvet pouch, she lifted the vial Lehanna had prepared. Holding it in front of her, she rotated it in the light, to see how the amber-colored oil inside glistened. Then she cupped the vial in her hands, protecting it. She walked to the bathroom and held it under hot running water to warm it.

Back in her room, she sat on her bed, loosened her robe. As Lehanna suggested, she thought of Artemis, the protectress. She opened the vial and poured seven drops into her right palm. She smelled the liquid—sweet and musty—and as soon as she took in its scent, before she rubbed the oil on her belly, unguarded tears welled in her eyes. Her belly softened. Her shoulders loosened. She realized how afraid she had been of treating herself tenderly, that only gentleness could penetrate the walls she had constructed around herself. Then she bolted up, fearful that, once the fortress began to weaken and crumble, she would be left raw and exposed, unable to stave off more hurt.

At the same time, she remembered her mother's funeral, how when friends offered consolation, she didn't hug back. She saw how the thorny distance she put between herself and the world seemed to become as comforting as a toddler's favorite blanket. *I'm afraid to let go.* Still, Allison had promised Lehanna she would try. She reclined again and reached her hand to her belly. She separated her fingers and let the oil drip onto her skin. With her hand on her stomach, she made slow circles in the oil. She remembered the man then, and the memory of his brutality grew stronger in contrast to the gentleness of her own hand. When her tears streamed to her belly, she mixed them into the oil. And eventually, there it was, delicious, restorative sleep.

"Raspberry," Lehanna said the next afternoon as she handed Allison a tiny cheesecloth bag. "To tone the uterus. Nettle to relieve stress. And yarrow to circulate energy around the pelvis."

"How much?" Allison asked, offering to pay for the tea.

Lehanna waved off her new friend's question. "Let's get you better first. Then, if you want, you can help here in the shop a couple afternoons a week. It's almost time for me to stock up for Christmas. How does that sound?"

"It sounds perfect."

When Allison returned to her room, she boiled water in the dorm's kitchenette. She dropped a spoonful of tea leaves into a mug of hot water. Then she went back to her room and set the cup on her bedside table to steep. Less gingerly than the night before, she applied the belly oil. After she drank the tea, she fell asleep for the night.

On the third day when Allison arrived at the shop, Lehanna gave her another vial. "Rose oil," Lehanna had said, "to heal the wound in your heart, marjoram to bring you joy, and geranium to relax you and help you feel safe."

That night, Allison once again made tea. She took a hot bath with rose oil added to the water. After drying herself, she used the belly oil again. That night, when she slept, she dreamed of dancing with her mother and Lehanna in a field of laurel under a waxing moon while does played around them. A wolf howled in the distance. When it approached, it knelt by her. It had no teeth, no power to hurt her at all.

When Allison arrived in Ithaca, she expected to thrive. Academically, at least. Even though she had just lost Lucy, and even though she still watched out for the man who hurt her, wondering if he—or someone like him—might be observing, waiting.

Instead, she found campus life dull and classwork boring. Nothing like the work she and Lucy had done to prepare her for college. When she and Lucy read *Pride and Prejudice*, for example, they acted out the parts of the Bennet sisters and dreamy Mr. Darcy. When they practiced their French, they did so at Jean Louis, or other bistros in MacMillan or Pittsburgh. Compared to Lucy, even Rodney Peyton could at best be called uninspiring.

As the semester drudged on, Allison finished her homework as early in the afternoon as possible. While her classmates gathered at the student union for snacks or flirty conversation, Allison hurried to Artemis to watch Lehanna mix formulas and to ask what she was sure was an annoying number of questions. Why, for example, without suspension in almond or sesame oil, could essential oils lose their healing powers, or cause rashes or burns? Why could rosemary waken pleasant memories while lavender soothed old hurts?

Lehanna answered patiently, methodically. Until one gloomy mid-November afternoon. When Allison asked why ginger was used for stomachaches and valerian for sleeplessness, Lehanna tilted her head without answering.

"I'm a pest, aren't I? With all my questions?" Allison asked.

"You're an endearing pest." Lehanna smiled.

"But?"

"You're ready."

"Ready?"

"To do more than ask questions and absorb answers. You need to start practicing."

"Practicing?"

"To learn to do what I do." Lehanna motioned to the marble-topped table and Allison sat next to it. "Before you get started, it's important to know that most people want to believe in healing, but they're not all ready to receive it. It's important not to judge, to take them as they are, and allow them to work through their doubts and insecurities in their own time.

"We can offer possibility," she said, waving her hand, "but we can't force them to believe. Even if we could, that kind of manipulation would only last a short time. Each person needs to do her own work. Everyone," she repeated, taking Allison's chin in her hand. "You, too."

Allison wasn't sure what *work* Lehanna was talking about. But, after all she'd been through, how hard could a little *work* be?

She began sitting in on client consultations. What, Lehanna asked her, might help Rhonda Carlson stay calm when dealing with her meddling mother-in-law? Would peppermint or thyme ease Arthur Rombach's shingles pain? Allison researched, then reported back with formulas, then tweaked them with Lehanna's guidance.

A few weeks into Allison's studies, Kathleen, another freshman in the dorm, came down with the flu. After reviewing the notes she had taken at Artemis, Allison brought her suggested protocol to Lehanna for review: four drops peppermint and chamomile on a cool cloth, held to the chest; alternating with two drops eucalyptus, mixed with carrier oil, in the palms, then breathed in deeply. With Allison's help, Kathleen rebounded in three days.

Once word got out around the dorm, Allison's phone rang almost nightly. Someone with exam week jitters or post-breakup blues wanted, needed her help.

⌇

"You're gifted, you know," Lehanna said early the afternoon of the first heavy snow, while they readied a Christmas display in the window.

"Not according to Rodney." Allison held a string of lights while Lehanna draped them on a miniature evergreen, decorated with silver balls and surrounded by red packages with silver bows.

"Oh, you're a good enough poet. You can probably thank your mother for that more than Professor Peyton." Lehanna motioned to a box on the floor. "Can you hand me the angel? She's underneath that tissue, over there. Careful. She's delicate." Allison took the treetop angel from her box, smoothing her yellow hair, fluffing her gold skirt, then handing her to Lehanna.

"But here, with the formulas, you're learning to look beyond symptoms to causes. You're beginning to diagnose not only by what a client says is wrong, but by observation and inspiration. Remember how, last week, you discovered Helen Stone's headaches were due to loneliness, not an allergy to milk?" It was no coincidence, Lehanna said while she lifted the angel atop the tree, that Allison's name sounded the same as one of nature's healing herbs. A signal that she had not just the capacity, but maybe the calling, to heal.

"Hmm. A calling to heal? I like the sound of that." Allison savored the sense of belonging she got from working with Lehanna, as well as her connection with the earth when she tended the greenhouse and with the girls in her dorm when she mixed their remedies. Still, she turned from Lehanna to hide her smile.

"Here," Lehanna said. "Plug this in over there, will you?"

Allison stretched the cord to the wall socket, then plugged it in. When she turned and saw the lights in the window, she nodded. "Perfect."

"Yes," Lehanna said. Allison couldn't see that her teacher was admiring her young student as much as the holiday finery and the angel atop the tree.

⌒

Even with its almost ubiquitous cloud cover, Allison figured staying in Ithaca for winter break would be more pleasant than returning to MacMillan. In their infrequent and brief conversations, Richard dropped Corinne's name more and more frequently. How they enjoyed eating at Fiore's on Saturday nights. How they spent a weekend in New York. "The girls went a little wild at Bloomie's."

Allison wasn't sure which rankled her more: the prospect of seeing her father or spending time with Corinne and "the girls." There was also the possibility of seeing the man if she went to MacMillan. Since working at Artemis, color had come back into her cheeks. The circles under her eyes faded. She walked with a lighter step, her hopes fixed on her future. Why risk a setback?

Not that she didn't still lapse into occasional despair. "If I'm so talented, why can't I heal myself?" she asked Lehanna one sullen January day while they inventoried the shop's shelves.

Lehanna came down off the ladder she used to reach the highest shelf. She sat on the bottom step, her arms around her knees.

"The journey to healing isn't only a matter of mixing oils or prescribing herbs," she said. She handed Allison a box filled with packets of bath salts to count. "And it doesn't happen just like that." She snapped her fingers, remembering how, like Allison, she used to equate being healed with being cured. "It's also about allowing the process on its own terms, in its own time, often on a circuitous path."

Allison set the packets of bath salts on the table where she sat. She wrote on her notepad the number she had counted, then looked tentatively at her mentor. For the first time since she started working with her, Lehanna sounded impatient, insistent.

"If we stay the course," Lehanna continued, "eventually the Universe, or God, or life, whatever you want to call it, has its way with us." She paused. "Do you think I was born wanting to do what I do? That I got to where I am without working? That when I was seven or eight, when all my friends wanted to be teachers or actresses or stay-at-home moms, I woke up one day and said I wanted to grow rosemary and basil in my backyard and mix potions to help women make babies or sleep at night?"

Allison shrugged. "I guess I never thought about it."

"Maybe that's the next leg of your journey. Setting aside your own hurt now and again to think of others."

Allison shifted in her chair. "I do that when I'm mixing formulas. When I help the girls in the dorm."

"Yes, you do. In a clinical way."

Allison looked away. There was no way of winning this argument, if that's what it was. Lehanna was the teacher; she was the student. "I thought you said I was talented, that I had a gift."

"I did and you do. But that's the beginning of the road, not the end."

Allison searched Lehanna's eyes. "I thought you understood."

"I understand more than you know." Lehanna paused and leaned forward. "You're not a victim anymore. You have choices."

"I know I have choices. I chose to study with you instead of wasting my time working on the literary magazine or spending winter break in Paris or Madrid."

"And did you do that because you felt called to this work or because you thought, by studying it, you could escape your past?"

"I did it because nothing else helped." Allison leaned forward. She knew her words sounded shrill. But she couldn't stop them from spilling out. "Nothing else took away the pain, not even for an hour. Now you're telling me I'm wasting my time here, too?"

Lehanna sat back against the step, with her hands in her lap. "I think," she said more gently, "you know your anger and fear are speaking for you now. And I think, deep down, you also know that learning formulas is only part of becoming a healer. Because you know what it's like to hurt and to be afraid, you know how someone else hurts, why she's afraid, and how desperate she feels thinking there's nowhere to turn for help."

When Allison looked away to try to hide her tears, Lehanna reached into her skirt pocket, then handed Allison a lavender-scented hanky. She waited until Allison looked at her again.

"I think you know, too, how we can use our pain, and anger, even our tears, to get people to do what we want. Don't you?"

Allison said nothing.

"That kind of power tastes sweet as honey going down," Lehanna said. "But after a while, that sweetness turns, and we're left with the taste of vinegar in our mouth." She paused. "It's wounds that make a healer. And the deeper they go, the more they hurt, the greater the chance the wounded one can help someone else come to some place of peace, even a—"

"That's not true," Allison interrupted. "My mother, she could help just about anyone. Not the way you do, but still. And nothing bad ever happened to her. Not until my father left anyway."

Lehanna hesitated, debating whether to tell Allison the truth about her mother. About the child she lost. About the pressure Richard had been under to marry her. About the reason Allison was conceived.

Allison shook her head. "I don't understand you." She stood, grabbed her coat from the peg near the door, and ran from the shop. She pulled her hood over her head as she slogged through the gray slush, the cold air stinging her face and her clenched hands.

In her dorm, she ran up two flights, then slammed the door to her room. *How could Lehanna—with her magical little shop and her healing gifts, the ones that came so easily to her—how could she understand how much I hurt? And what an absurd thing to suggest— that because I hurt, I could help someone else.*

⟿

When Allison's eyes opened the next day, a few foggy minutes passed before she recalled the previous day's conversation with Lehanna. Her stomach tightened as she got out of bed, reached for her robe, and shuffled to the bathroom. *At least,* she thought as she ran warm water in the sink, *I'll never need to see her again.* She splashed her face then looked in the mirror. That silly song Lucy used to sing to her, way back when Allison squabbled with other toddlers in the children's section at Metaphors, played in her head. *Make new friends, but keep the old, one is silver, the other gold.* Infantile, but probably true.

She grabbed her toothbrush, then looked in the mirror again. In just a few months, Lehanna had become more than a mentor. She was a friend. *And I don't have a lot of friends.* Allison didn't want to lose her. She couldn't lose her. She brushed her teeth quickly, energetically, then showered and dressed. On her way to Artemis, she stopped at Ramon's Florist and bought Lehanna a yellow rose.

At the shop door, she tried to quiet her racing heart. She had become used to frightening people off, pushing them away. Wanting someone close, asking for forgiveness? That felt risky, untested. When she went inside, Lehanna looked up from behind the counter where she was handing a customer her change. Allison stayed out of the way until the woman left, then walked to the counter. "I hope you can forgive me for acting like a five-year-old," she said in a small voice, holding the rose out to Lehanna. "I want to know more about you."

When Lehanna smiled and motioned for her to sit at the marble table, Allison pulled out a chair and sat. Lehanna, meanwhile, put a kettle of water on the backroom stove. While it heated, she pulled several large leather-bound volumes from the shelves and set them in front of her friend.

Allison at first leafed through the folios tentatively. They were filled with eclectic arrangements of handwritten notes, samples of dried herbs, photos and sketches, not unlike the volumes Lucy had assembled from their Central Pennsylvania ventures. Then, as the story of how Lehanna became a healer began to unfold, Allison pored over the folios, mesmerized.

CHAPTER EIGHT

The Fourth of July, 1955, Lehanna recorded in her folio, was different. For one thing, her mother didn't come to the fireworks at the high school. For another, her father didn't lift her onto his shoulders as they made their way from their Ford wagon to spread a blanket near the field, eat their fried chicken dinner, and listen to the brass band playing Sousa and Wilson before the show started.

"You're a big girl now," Mike Stanislaus said.

"I'm a big girl." Lehanna smiled as she ran to keep up with her father's long-legged stride. "But I'm still your best girl, right?"

"You betcha, cupcake." He rumpled her hair and kept on walking. "You'll always be my best girl, Lela."

Why he didn't look at her when he spoke, she wasn't sure. She grinned anyway and glanced up at him, tall and strong and "stubborn as a bull," as her mother, Regina, sometimes said. She didn't look at him sideways, like women around town did when they tried to sneak a peek at him. And not with fire in her eyes, like her mother sometimes did. No, Lehanna giggled and romped after him as fast as her brown and white saddle shoes would take her. All that mattered was that she was with her dad, the town's best-ever auto parts salesman, usher at Saint Mary's church, and softball coach at the Boys and Girls Club.

Lehanna wondered if her father didn't reach to put her on his shoulders, would she need to keep her eyes open the whole time, even when the boom-buzz-hiss scared her? When he asked, "Did ya see that one, Lela?" would she need to tell the truth? That she was too afraid to look? But, like her father said, she was a big girl this year. Maybe she wouldn't be scared.

When the show started, Mike didn't reach to put her on his shoulders. That was okay. But he didn't reach to her at all. Not to ask whether she liked the bright blue pinwheels or the fuchsia starbursts better, not to make sure she had a good view. By the time the American Flag lit up at the show's end, with all the bright-white rockets sizzling around it, Mike barely waited for the stadium lights to go on before he gathered their blanket and picnic basket, then set out for the car. Lehanna stumbled trying to catch up to him. Then the barrette fell from her hair, the one he had given her, the one with rhinestones in the shape of a star. The air was smoky-thick. She had trouble feeling her way across the grass. "There you are," she said when she found the barrette. "Don't do that again."

She fixed the clip in her sun-streaked hair, then turned back, toward the way to the car. Or was it? She spun forward, toward the field. The haze in the air made it difficult to make out anyone, even when the stadium lights blinked on, bright. She heard what she thought was the cleanup crew in the field. She walked toward them. They could help find Big Mike. Everyone knew Mike Stanislaus.

"Lela?" She turned. Her father was the only one who called her that. But that wasn't his voice she heard.

"Over here," another man called, farther to the right. She looked in his direction, but the smoke still hadn't cleared. She couldn't see far enough into the field to focus on him. "It's Jonathan," another said. "Hang on Jon-boy." She heard men running, heavy boots on the ground.

The first man called her again, "Lela, Lela," over and over. He was hurt. *He needs me.*

She spun in his direction. The smoke cleared. Jonathan's heart was pumping blood, spreading red over the field like lava. Three other men ran toward him. Not real men, more like the shadows of men. They were soldiers, dressed in fatigues and helmets, carrying guns. Jonathan called her one more time—"Lehanna," he said this time—before the others reached him.

If she hurried, she could help him. But her feet froze. Her saddle shoes would not move. "Who are you?" she called. When Jonathan didn't answer, she stretched out her hand. She wanted to help.

"Quinn." When the first man reached him, Jonathan spoke his name. Quinn ripped off his shirt and tried to bandage his fallen friend, but the blood leaked through. He sank to the ground. He curled next to Jonathan and covered him with the rest of his own shirt. He was bleeding, too, from his side. He held Jonathan's body, limp and purposeless. His legs gone from him. He put his head on Jonathan's chest and wept. Then, suddenly, he sat up. "I told you not to go there." He shook his head. "God damn you to hell and back."

Lehanna closed her eyes. She put her hands over her ears but heard her name again. "Lela." This time it was Big Mike, striding toward her. Finally, she could move. She ran to him.

"Where'd you go, cupcake?" When Big Mike reached her, he knelt and held her.

"Did you see them?" she said.

"See who?"

"The soldiers. He died. The one named Jonathan."

"Them over there? That's Jack and his crew, from town. They look like soldiers, don't they, in their green uniforms?"

"Not them," she said.

"Shh." He picked her up. "You're a big girl now. Big girls aren't scared."

No, she wanted to insist. She wasn't scared. Not anymore. She just needed for him to believe her. It wasn't Jack White and his crew in the field. It was Jonathan. And the other man, Quinn.

And there was all that blood. She was tired. So tired. She closed her eyes. She rested her head on his shoulder as he carried her to the car and tucked her inside. But when she turned back to the field and saw the men again, she said, "There he is again."

"Who?"

"The man I saw. Jonathan."

Her father turned quickly. "Uh huh. Now I see him. Clear as a bell." But when he smiled, he pointed toward the bleachers, not even close to where Jonathan had called to her, then died in the field, with his friend, Quinn, rocking him like he was a small, forgiven child.

The next morning was Saturday. Her mother usually woke her by seven, whether or not it was a school day. But when Lehanna walked into the kitchen and checked the clock, it was almost nine. Mike had already left for work. At least he should have. But his place was still set, as if he had skipped breakfast. "The most important meal of the day." At least he and her mother agreed on that.

She looked from her father's untouched plate and napkin to her mother, standing at the stove. Regina wasn't dressed in her hydrangea-print housecoat, like she usually was at breakfast. And her hair wasn't rolled up in those spongey-pink curlers. No, she wore a plain navy dress. Her hair was combed. She wore fiery-bright lipstick, like she was expecting company. Odd, Lehanna thought.

But her mother slid an egg from a frying pan onto a plate and brought it to Lehanna. Like she did every Saturday. Eggs on Saturday. French toast on Sunday. Cheerios on Monday. Lehanna repeated the litany to herself, but something wasn't right. She could tell by her mother's eyes. How red they were. And puffy. Lehanna took a bite of her egg. It tasted okay. Maybe everything else was okay, too. Just different. Then her mother slid into her kitchen chair and pulled it closer to Lehanna's.

"He's gone," her mother said as she reached for Lehanna's hands.

"Gone?"

"Last night," she said. "He carried you to bed."

She was speaking so slowly. Why didn't she talk faster? *Look at me!*

"He tucked you in. He brought his favorite cream ale to bed and then—"

Lehanna plopped her fork on her plate. She leaned forward, her foot tapping her chair. "Then what?"

"A heart attack," Her mother said. "Just like that." She shrugged as if she didn't, couldn't believe her own words. "He was gone."

Gone? No, just a few hours ago, Lehanna thought, Big Mike carried her back from the fireworks to the car. Like he did every year. "No," she said, standing so quickly and pushing her chair behind her so forcefully that it toppled to the floor. She ran to her parents' bedroom. There he was. Stretched out on the bed. Like a plastic dummy of himself. She wanted to step closer, but she was afraid. "You're a big girl now." He said that the night before. "Big girls don't get scared." *Yes, I'm a big girl. I'm not scared.* She walked resolutely to the bed. She looked at Big Mike, so tall his feet stretched over the bed's edge. She shook her head, waiting, hoping to hear words that could make sense of the previous night. And now, this morning. She heard nothing. She backed away. First there was that man in the fireworks' haze. Jonathan. Now Big Mike. Dead. Maybe she could have helped. Maybe she should have.

⁓

The day after Big Mike's funeral, after her mother left for her shift at the Star of Athens diner, Lehanna stood in front of Mrs. Connelly's desk, her toe tapping impatiently while the librarian helped the patron ahead of her. When the gentleman left, Lehanna moved to the desk. She stood tall and spoke clearly. "I want to help people."

"Yes," Janette Connelly said, "of course you do,"

When Lehanna felt the librarian's eyes on her, as if she could see deep into her, Lehanna rocked on one foot, then the other. "What I mean is, I need to learn how to help people not get sick. So they won't die."

Mrs. Connelly nodded. "I'm sorry about your father."

Lehanna pressed her lips together. She would not cry.

"So, you want to be a teacher? Or maybe a doctor?"

"Something like that."

"Okay." Mrs. Connelly reached for the cane that leaned against the wall behind her chair. "When I want to do something, I explore. Shall we?"

Lehanna nodded and allowed Mrs. Connelly to lead her around the library. In fiction, she showed her the books about Sue Barton and the ones about Cherry Ames. In research, she pointed out the Encyclopedia Britannica where Lehanna could study anybody or anything she wanted, like Jonas Salk or Madame Curie. "But if you really want to dream." She turned back to her young patron. "Do you?"

Lehanna smiled.

"Then let's go to Periodicals." When they reached the room with all the magazines and newspapers, it had a thick, flat, comforting smell, like old paper. The unlit cigar Mr. Sirotsky gnawed at while reading the sports page reminded Lehanna of how Big Mike smelled when he came in from a night at Frank's Tavern. Mrs. Connelly ushered her past the juvenile publications. "*Highlights*," she said, "are for children, not dreamers." She steered her to a row of yellow magazines, bright as the sun, on the shelves in the back of the room.

Before Mrs. Connelly finished telling her about the faraway places *National Geographic* could take her, all the places she might go to help people, Lehanna took a couple issues from the shelf. "I'll try these," she said.

"Be sure to tell me everything you learn." Mrs. Connelly waved, then walked haltingly toward her reference room desk.

Lehanna didn't hear her, though. She was already flipping through one yellow issue, until she came to pictures of Madagascar.

The island off Africa's southeast coast, that, millions of years ago, was part of the supercontinent Gondwana, until it broke off from what is now India. Eons later, she learned from the article, in the nineteenth century, the French took over what was then called Malagasy. It had another name, too—the Great Red Island—because of its rich, red soil. What did that look like? Lehanna wondered. And what about all the special plants and animals there? Golden lemurs, the size of house cats, with furry tails and crimson eyes. Fan-shaped traveler's trees, so named because adventurers tapped their trunks for much-needed water as they explored. As for the scent of vanilla that sometimes floated over the island's northwest coast? She could only imagine what it would be like to breathe it in.

⌒

"So," Mrs. Connelly said, adjusting her tortoiseshell glasses, then smoothing her wavy red hair from her face, "it's settled."

Lehanna had stopped in the library to ask for help on a biology paper she was writing, help she hadn't yet requested. She stood tall, tilted her head. "What's settled?"

"You'll be starting at Cornell next fall." Mrs. Connelly folded her hands atop her desk.

Lehanna laughed. "Mrs. Connelly, you're not one to joke." She reached into her backpack, pulled out a course catalogue, and set it on the librarian's desk. "I was thinking I would start at Seneca Community, then transfer to Syracuse."

Mrs. Connelly clasped her hands, trying to be patient with the promising young woman who didn't yet have the capacity to see herself clearly. "A fine plan that would be, if SCC had a solid enough biology program, and if Syracuse were strong in ethnobotany. No, Cornell's the place for you. Look at these course listings." She pushed aside the catalogue Lehanna had placed on her desk and edged another toward her. "Even better," she said as she leafed through the pages, "these internship opportunities in developing nations."

Lehanna bit her lower lip as she read the list of participating countries. Kenya. China. Thailand. *Madagascar*. She handed back the catalogue. "I've been babysitting. Saving up." she said. "And next year I'll check out groceries at Wegmans. That'll cover tuition at SCC. But Cornell?" She shook her head. "Plus, there's room and board."

"Which might be problematic." Mrs. Connelly leaned back in her chair.

"Might be?"

"If you didn't have connections."

Lehanna shrugged. "I don't."

Mrs. Connelly pulled out a red folder and a large, clothbound book from her file drawer. "Yes," she said, "you do." She lifted from the folder a pamphlet entitled "Women's Advisory Council." She flipped through until she came to a photo of a group of women seated around a mahogany table with a large red-and-white seal hanging behind. "You've heard of Evelyn Townsend, the second circuit judge?"

"Sure."

"What an amazing mind she has. That's her, in blue." Then, Mrs. Connelly pointed to another woman in the photo. "And Carol Crosby, who founded the Women's Action League?"

Lehanna nodded.

"And that's me, between them. Before the accident."

Lehanna forced herself to look nonchalant to keep from blurting out something desperate, like *Can you help me?* Instead, she said, "I'm sorry you lost your husband."

"Me, too." Mrs. Connelly looked away, then turned back and nodded. "But when he left, he made sure I was what you'd call comfortable. More comfortable than I need to be. So, I decided to put some money to work helping special young women. Girls who needed a little boost—like I did—to help them flourish once they got to campus.

"Carol and Evelyn and I were good friends from freshman year. But we had to work harder than most. Not because we weren't smart enough, but because we didn't have the advantages a lot of our classmates had. Private school educations, parents well-enough situated to pay for tutors and coaches. That sort of thing.

"Anyway, five years ago we agreed to help one promising young woman a year. We wanted to start preparing her, even before she applied for admission, so that, when she got to Ithaca, she could shine from the get-go and not be intimidated, like we were, by classmates who went to Choate or Rosemary Hall and learned their French in Paris."

Mrs. Connelly leaned forward and whispered, "I told them a couple years ago I had someone—you—in mind. They're anxious to meet you." She sat back again. Her young patron would need time to voice her objections. Surely, she would have them. "If you're interested, that is."

Lehanna shook her head. "There's still the money. I mean, I know I'm smart. And I work hard. But there's not much left from Mom's paycheck after she pays for food and takes care of the house."

Mrs. Connelly smiled. "We pick up the tab, at least a major portion. We do expect our girls to chip in." She picked up the yearbook and leafed through until she pointed to a photo of a male student. "It just so happens that George Swenson—he was a class-mate of ours—he's head of the ethnobotany program now. And an old flame of Carol's. We want you to meet him. He can advise you on how to prepare for his graduate program down the line."

Lehanna shifted from one foot to the other. There were too many reasons why Mrs. Connelly's plan might not work. "But I might not even be accepted."

Mrs. Connelly waved, as if Lehanna's concerns were annoying but inconsequential gnats. "Your first lesson, Lehanna, is to believe your dreams really can come true. You just need to recognize your gifts and focus."

Lehanna smiled. Someone, Mrs. Connelly, saw and affirmed both her longing to explore and her desire to accomplish. She had always felt as if her dreams needed to be kept secret. *Now, they're out in the open. Maybe . . .*

"Don't worry. Carol and Evelyn and I will get you whatever help you need. SAT prep, tutoring, everything. By the time you interview, those admissions counselors'll be so scared you'll decide on Brown—or God forbid, Yale—they'll offer you a spot before you leave campus." She hesitated. "Then comes your second lesson."

"What's that?"

"After you learn that your dreams really can come true, with the help of other women, that is, you use your gifts, time, and treasure to help others."

Lehanna pulled her shoulders back. She smiled. "That," she said, "I can do."

"Good. Now why did you stop in today?"

Lehanna reached into her backpack and pulled out the research paper draft. "I need to write more about biodiversity in Madagascar."

"Easy enough." Mrs. Connelly rose from her desk. "But one more thing."

Lehanna took a deep breath. She was almost afraid that Mrs. Connelly would shower her with more hope, more help. "What's that?"

"As of today, we're officially friends. No more Mrs. Connelly. Call me Janette."

Lehanna smiled. This gift—friendship—was the best of all the treasures Janette had helped her discover.

～

Lehanna crossed the Arts Quad the last Thursday in April. For the first time since October, it seemed, no one on campus needed to dodge raindrops, sleet, or snow. No wind to speak of, no need for students or faculty to scurry like rats from one class to another. Cayuga Lake shimmered like a bowl of sapphires at the base of campus. Most everyone behaved as if they'd been given a much-deserved reprieve from the previous six-month meteorological prison sentence. Some tossed Frisbees to German shepherds, dressed up with red bandanas tied around their necks. Others sat on stone walls outside the classroom buildings, soaking up the sun. It was the Age of Aquarius. A sweet-smelling pot-haze in the air. Love and sex were the same.

Lehanna stopped to take off her jacket and tie it around her waist. She lifted her face to the sun, deciding whether to go back to her apartment on State Street for lunch or grab a burger on campus.

The sounds of a bike, braking hard, then a scream, followed by metal scraping on cement broke her thoughts. Lehanna turned to see her classmate from biology lab on the ground, beneath the bike. "Jill!" She ran to help.

A tall, lanky guy in jeans and chambray shirt threw his books to the ground and joined them.

"You okay?"

"Fucking squirrels." Holding her right wrist with her left hand, Jill grimaced. She reached to gather the books and macramé bag that had spilled from her bike's basket.

"Here, let me get those."

Lehanna tilted her head. That voice. She knew it.

They all figured Jill probably sprained her wrist, but she was steady enough to walk on her scraped leg. She set her bike upright and got back on, declining their offer to walk her to the infirmary.

"Thanks anyway, Lehanna, Jonathan," she called as she started off again.

Jonathan? Lehanna tumbled the name over in her mind. She tried to dismiss the possibility that the young man standing in front of her was the same one she had seen on that Fourth of July, years earlier.

He turned to Lehanna and smiled. "Grey's agronomy class, right?" he asked, as if he knew Lehanna, or as if he were pretending to.

She shook her head. "No."

He narrowed his eyes, still trying to figure out how he knew her. "You look so familiar."

"I'm Lehanna." Her voice caught in her throat. "Lela."

"Lela. Pretty name. I know I've seen you before." He shrugged as if he would try to figure out how he knew her later. "Heading to lunch?"

She nodded.

"Walk you over?"

Lehanna smiled tentatively. A shiver snaked down her arm. She felt as if she were looking through a kaleidoscope, watching pieces of brightly colored glass fall into place to form a complete picture. Jonathan wouldn't understand if she explained why she looked familiar to him. That, years earlier, when she was seven, a soldier called to her across a smoky, bloody field. The same night her father died. The same night she began to feel like she was called to help. Maybe the reason they had met, right then, right there, was that she could save him from the fate she had seen awaiting him a decade earlier.

⌒

"Ethnobotany," Jonathan said when Lehanna asked what he was studying. "A year from now, I'll have my masters."

He explained how he and George Swenson, the department head, were doing research for a federally funded project to develop prescription drugs from plants. They were most interested, Jonathan said, in two drugs: one to treat childhood leukemia and another to help cure Hodgkin's disease. "We think we're on track, and that both can be developed from a strain of periwinkle grown only on Madagascar."

"Madagascar?" Lehanna hoped her voice didn't sound as overly eager and squeaky to him as it did to her. She felt weightless. Like a dandelion gone to seed, floating toward a destination that wasn't hers to determine.

Jonathan set down his burger. "You've been there?"

"No." She leaned forward. She could allow herself to trust Jonathan. She had, after all, known him a long time. "But when I was a kid—going back to the night my father died—I had this feeling

I wanted to help people. So, Mrs. Connelly, Janette—she was the librarian who set me on a journey to figure out how to do that. I knew I wanted to go to Africa. Especially Madagascar. Partly for silly, romantic reasons." She waved to dismiss her childhood fascinations. "You know, so I could see all those adorable little lemurs and run free on the Great Red Island's diamond-bright beaches. But the more I learned about Malagasy culture . . . you know, how it was threatened when the French colonized the island, then during political instability?" She shrugged. "The more I learned, the more I wanted to help preserve, not just the island's physical beauty, but its culture."

She sipped her iced tea. "Anyway, that same librarian put me in touch with Dr. Swenson, who suggested I major in anthropology and take ethnobotany classes so, when I graduated and went for a masters, or out in the world, I'd have what he called a unique set of skills."

Jonathan picked up his Coke and leaned back. He nodded and grinned. "I knew it." He took a drink, then set the cup down. "I must have seen you in Swenson's lab. Or maybe just in the halls between classes."

With only a month until finals, Lehanna and Jonathan studied together at the library or in his apartment. They made love on his worn-thin mattress in the back of his aging Jeep, on his rickety futon, and anywhere else they could. As often as they could.

They hiked the gorges just off campus and the trails at Robert Treman Park and nearby Taughannock Falls. They ate tofu and Hamburger Helper, cooked on Jonathan's cranky apartment stove, and dined by candlelight while reading to each other—everything from *Fleurs du Mal* to *Leaves of Grass* to *Slaughterhouse-Five*. The more time they spent together, the more confident Lehanna felt she could and would change the future she had foreseen for Jonathan a long time ago.

～

Jonathan rushed toward the library table where Lehanna was studying. He kissed her quickly, then sat and pulled a chair close to hers.

"He got the funding," he said in a loud whisper.

Lehanna had a pretty good idea what Jonathan meant, as much from his smile as his words, but she needed to be sure. "Who got what funding?"

"George." Jonathan went on to explain that George Swenson had been awarded a grant from Worldwide Health, an organization headed by a man named Jacques Merthin. "He's confident he's got the resources to finish developing those two drugs."

"To treat leukemia and Hodgkin's?"

"Right. From the periwinkle that's native to Madagascar." He paused.

"Which means?"

"Which means, I'll be going there this summer, working with Merthin at the university in Antananarivo. And at his clinic, north of there."

Lehanna hesitated. If Jonathan were an ocean away, how would she know he was safe? How could she protect him? "I don't know what to say."

"There's not much to say." Jonathan waved, as if saying good-bye. His voice grew louder. "Except *àu bientôt*, Ithaca."

"Hey." An annoyed student in a nearby carrel leaned toward them. "I'm studying over here."

"Sorry." Jonathan reached for Lehanna's hand. "Let's take a break."

Outside the library, they sat cross-legged, facing each other on the fieldstone ledge. Jonathan leaned forward, took Lehanna's hand. "What I meant when I said 'àu bientôt, Ithaca,' is that Merthin needs an intern to study funerary rites of the Merina population over there.

"Swenson said he had the perfect candidate. You! I wasn't supposed to spill the beans. He wants to talk to you tomorrow before he gets back to Merthin." He paused. "So?"

"So." Lehanna slid off the ledge and tugged Jonathan after her. "Let's go pack!"

They ran to their Collegetown apartment, quickening their pace when the rain started. Instead of packing, though, they peeled off their wet clothes as they stumbled inside. Lehanna lit a vanilla-scented candle. Jonathan put Fleetwood Mac on the stereo. They reached for each other, urgent and hungry, and spent the afternoon and evening and night in bed, on the futon, on the floor, imagining their future on the Great Red Island.

⌒

When Lehanna arrived at Swenson's office the next morning at ten, she paused outside his door. She wasn't supposed to know why George asked her to stop by, so she pressed her lips together to squelch her smile. She collected her thoughts, then tested the door. It was locked. She wasn't surprised. Swenson had a reputation for arriving late to classes, rushing in at five after the hour, looking like he'd been swept in on level two winds on the Fujita Scale.

She reached into her backpack and retrieved the copy of Margaret Mead's *Continuities in Cultural Evolution* she was reading for Anthro 307. She opened the book and leaned against the jamb. Instead of reading, though, she savored her memory of the scents of Jonathan and vanilla, still lingering from the night before. She imagined, too, that if this opportunity worked out, she might soon write her own book, on cultural traditions on the Great Red Island.

"Sorry, sorry."

When George rushed toward her, hefting an overloaded briefcase and wielding his office door key, Lehanna could no longer suppress a smile.

"Thanks for waiting." He opened the door and motioned for Lehanna to take the chair beside his desk. "I suppose you know why you're here."

Lehanna looked at him wide-eyed. She said nothing as she sat down and tucked a long strand of her hair behind her ear.

"You don't have to pretend he didn't tell you." George smiled and adjusted his wire-rimmed glasses. "Even though I told Jonathan to keep it to himself, I didn't suffer illusions that he could. Besides, I wanted you to have time to think about it before we met." He picked up a message that had been placed on his desk and waved it in Lehanna's direction. "Turns out, Merthin needs to find somebody—he's got a grant deadline—so I've got to get back to him tomorrow."

He leaned back in his chair. "It's a once-in-a-lifetime opportunity," he said. "But there's not much time to talk it over with your family."

Her family? It was just her mother and her now. Although her mother had been mentioning Jack White, Big Mike's friend who was Park and Rec's crew chief. First it was, "I ran into Jack at Wegmans." Then it was, "Jack drove me to church on Sunday when I got a flat." Jack this and Jack that. On the one hand, her mother's dalliance made Lehanna miss Big Mike even more. On the other, she felt less responsible for her mother and her loneliness, even if Jack was the reason for her happiness. She chased away her misgivings about the man. She was free to go to Madagascar or wherever else she chose. "It's just me," Lehanna said. "And I want the opportunity."

"Okay, then." George reached for notes he had taken on a yellow pad during a recent conversation with Jacques. "Here's all I know." He began by telling her how he and Merthin had done their undergraduate work together, then how Jacques went on to medical school in New York, while George stayed in Ithaca to earn his PhD.

"After Jacques left New York, he went to Paris and founded Worldwide Health to set up health care initiatives in developing countries. Then he returned to Madagascar, where he was raised. His pet project was a clinic. First of its kind. A place where Western-trained staff supplement and support the work of local—by local I mean traditional—healers. The malaria treatment model he developed there was so successful, he's planning to replicate it in other African countries. Latin America, too."

Lehanna tried to check her enthusiasm. She wanted this chance, but was she the right person for the job? She didn't want to plunder the Great Red Island like too many *vizana*, foreigners, had. "Wouldn't he want someone who already knows the culture? Someone from Madagascar?"

"Under normal circumstances," Swenson said, "probably. But we've been working together on the drug project a while now. You know, the one Jonathan's involved with?"

"Uh huh." Lehanna nodded.

"There may be some crossover between the projects, so I want to stay close. Plus, I've got to fill my open slot for study abroad. If I don't, I won't get funding next year." He smiled. "Besides, if I don't offer you the position, I'd need to fend off Janette Connelly's raging wrath."

Lehanna laughed. Janette did have a stubborn, or, should she say, a purposeful, side.

"I'm not kidding," George said. "Janette has a way of getting what she wants." He reached into his briefcase, pulled out a water bottle, and drank from it. "I can't tell you exactly what to expect, but you can bet your resume'll stand out with this experience on it. When you apply to graduate school, I mean."

Lehanna tapped her foot, anxious to hear the official offer.

"It's not much to go on, I know. But if you want the job, it's yours." George leaned back in his chair. "Any questions?"

Lehanna grinned. "Just one."

"Shoot."

"When do I leave?"

⌒

The following Tuesday, Lehanna called Jacques Merthin as Swenson had instructed. He explained, in his rich voice, with its hint of a Parisian accent, how he and an associate were gathering information that might lead to better treatment alternatives for a variety of conditions, based on cultural patterns and traditions. They wanted, for example, to explore whether traditions of the Merina tribe, which emigrated to the island from the Malay Archipelago thousands of years earlier, could be integrated with Western medicine without damaging local culture.

Lehanna had already researched the island's history. She knew that traditional Merina culture had been challenged when *vizana* introduced Christianity in the nineteenth century, when the French controlled the island. Although Madagascar regained independence from the French less than a decade earlier, around 1960, if data weren't gathered soon on the Merina, many traditions might go unrecorded. Her work could prevent that from happening.

The task felt daunting, but she told herself she was up to the job. Besides, she and Jonathan could tour the island that had cast its spell on her ever since Mrs. Connelly—Janette—introduced her to *National Geographic* a decade earlier. What more could she want?

CHAPTER NINE

Jonathan reached for Lehanna as their twin-engine plane lifted out of the fields around Tompkins County's airport. She tentatively took his hand in both hers. This would be her first trip out of the country, except for Sunday afternoon drives to Niagara Falls' Canadian side, the ones Big Mike sometimes took her on. As curious as she was about how she could alter Jonathan's fate, she also felt too free to be touched, as if any contact, even with him, might constrain her.

It wasn't until they made their connecting flight at Kennedy Airport, when the wheels on their jet lifted off the tarmac, banked left, then started over the Atlantic, that she allowed herself to believe that, in seven hours, they would be in Paris. After spending the night there, they would fly to Antananarivo, Madagascar's capital, where their adventure would begin in earnest.

She reached beneath the seat in front of her, checking her carry-on for her camera and tape recorder. Just to be sure they were there. She reached for Jonathan's hand again, this time holding it tight. "*C'est excitant, n'est-ce pas?*"

"I think the answer to that is *oui?*"

"*Oui, mon amour.*"

Jonathan's French was as limited as Lehanna's knowledge of the Malagasy language. But that didn't matter. She snuggled close to him. The next twelve weeks would be filled with everything they loved most: doing good, exploring, and each other.

Ten hours after leaving Paris, their plane started its descent to Ivato Airport, outside Madagascar's capital of Antananarivo. Jonathan woke Lehanna, who was sleeping in the seat next to his.

"There it is."

Still drowsy, she thought she might be dreaming when she looked out the window. She knew, when Europeans boasted they claimed they "discovered" Madagascar, they called it the Great Red Island. When she saw the water to the west, where iron-rich topsoil hemorrhaged into the ocean, staining the seawater blood-red far beyond the white-sand coast, her breath caught in her chest. From the air, the land mass looked like a blood-red organ, an exposed heart. The last time she saw blood flowing like that was the night she first saw Jonathan, fighting for his life then losing it. The night her father died. But, no, Jonathan was alive and well next to her. She reached for his hand, while the Europeans' arrogant claim that they had "discovered" the island continued to rankle her.

Closer to Ivato, they descended toward what used to be called *Analamanga*, or the "blue forest," in the Central Highlands' Malagasy dialect. No more blood-red water. Lehanna breathed more deeply. They would be safe here.

But when she and Jonathan stepped off the plane, onto the ramp to the tarmac, Lehanna hesitated. She knew enough to expect that the Central Highlands, in June, would be cool. But she shivered and reached into her carry-on for her sweater, not only to keep warm but to protect herself. From what, she wasn't sure.

Inside the international terminal, it didn't take long to pick out Jacques. He stood over six feet, with long legs and arms. His face blended his mother's Asian-influenced features with those of his Parisian father's. When he stretched his arms in welcome, Lehanna's uncertainties vanished. She was intrigued.

"You made it safely to our island," he said in English, though his accent balanced the influences of both French and the Malagasy language many islanders spoke. "Thank you for helping us."

After shaking hands and claiming luggage, they walked to Jacques's aging Renault in the parking lot and loaded their bags into the trunk. They took their seats—Lehanna in front next to Jacques, Jonathan in back—so they could drive to Antananarivo, or Tana, as locals called the capital.

"Tana sits among twelve hills," Jacques said as he pulled out of the lot and motioned to the landscape ahead. "The whole area around here is sometimes called Antananarivo-Mother Hill, or Antananarivo-Capital. It's only about thirteen kilometers from here to Tana. But the roads? Well, you'll see why it takes longer than it should to get there."

Once over the first hill, the city undulated over the remaining eleven hills. Tana, like the island itself, had a reddish cast. Not just because of the lateritic soil beneath it but also because the sun reflected off its brick buildings, their terracotta roofs, and dozens of church spires.

As they drove into Tana's center, along the dirt track that masqueraded as the country's main highway, most cars and trucks lumbered along, either because they carried too many passengers, or because they had difficulty navigating the pitted road. When Lehanna grabbed her door handle to steady herself as they drove, Jacques smiled. "Hanging on takes practice." Then he explained. "Our roads have been one of the island's greatest issues, since even before the French left in the fifties. We have a long way to go."

Much of the traffic they passed was on foot—groups of black- or brown-skinned adults and children, walking, some without shoes, carrying babies or amorphous bundles on their backs, on their heads, or in their arms. Through Lehanna's American eyes, their outfits seemed unlikely combinations. Women dressed in oversized squares of bright-colored fabric, wrapped around them like saris. Others wore what looked like thrift shop cast-offs, fancy party dresses paired with worn-through gym shoes. Men donned knitted caps, and shorts and tee shirts, or pants and dress shirts, some thin enough to see through.

"Many on the island," Jacques said, "have no home except the road beneath them." He told how the people they passed often spent the week foraging for anything they might sell—a broken vase, a plate, shoes. "When they gather sufficient inventory and energy, they walk to the marketplace. Zoma, it's called, meaning Friday, like today. They come from their camps outside of town to try to earn the next week's grocery money."

While Jacques spoke, Lehanna looked into the determined but otherwise inscrutable faces of the people they passed. Most walked with straight backs, even under weighty loads. If they felt put-upon by their circumstances, their discontent didn't show. Lehanna first felt as if she were watching a well-cast movie. A fabrication. But the people walking toward Tana were no imaginary characters. They were mothers and fathers, sisters and brothers trying to support themselves and their families under extreme conditions.

She wondered how Jacques had come from the island, escaped poverty, and become known around the world. And how it was that she was there to study this island and its people when she had never known real hunger, when she had always had a place to rest at night, while the people en route to the marketplace lived in transience, and off the discards of others. Most importantly, she wondered how she could validly, ethically document their histories when her path had so far been so different.

She didn't have long to ponder her questions. Jacques was steering the car into Zoma, off *Araben ny Fahaleovantena*. The market, the size of a couple football fields, spread out, like a living organism, trying to sustain itself. Some vendors climbed the steps on the town's perimeter to claim spaces to sell their goods—clothing, blankets, baskets, clay pots—all of which colored the market bright orange, red, yellow, and green.

On the market's fringes, people like those they had passed on the road into Tana set out more modest wares, everything from rusted tin cans to half-used pencils to worn but neatly folded blouses or shirts. Women in long, brightly colored *lamba*, wrapped around them either as skirts or dresses, toted babies or toddlers on their hips, in their arms. Some sang what sounded like lullabies. Men boasted about the used bicycle wheel they had to offer, or the dented coffee pot. All of them waited for buyers so they, in turn, could purchase food and medicine before walking home the way they came.

"It was right here at Zoma," Jacques said, "only a century or so ago, these people's grandfathers and grandmothers, their great aunts and great uncles, were traded as slaves."

Lehanna looked again to the people selling their wares on Zoma's outskirts. And now these descendants were supposedly free? How free could they be when still tethered to poverty?

She turned her attention back to Jacques when he spoke. "That's the pharmacy." He pointed to another market area on a side road.

Lehanna lingered when Jacques and Jonathan walked toward the stands where medicinal plants were sold. She wasn't raised with much, not on her mother's waitressing wages. But in these people's eyes? She had probably eaten more for lunch than they had in, how long? A day? A few days? She didn't have to wait until she buried herself in the university's library or until she visited Jacques's clinic to start her research on the Great Red Island. It had already begun. Her observations, though preliminary, were not only different than she expected, but unsettling.

She turned and hurried to catch up with Jacques and Jonathan. After a five-minute walk, they arrived at the market where remedies were sold to treat everything from malaria to snakebites. Leaves and flowers—some pale and dried, others freshly picked and vibrant—hung on wooden racks or were displayed on tables or blankets in bright-colored clay pots.

"On the island, mostly the poor are treated with natural medicines, like these," Jacques said, waving to the stalls selling the remedies. "The wealthy? They prefer Western treatments. Not because they work better. Some do, some don't. But being able to pay for pills and tests in sparkly, sterile offices? That sets them apart from those who can't afford them. At the clinic we treat patients using the best of both worlds, whether or not they can pay."

Jacques introduced Lehanna and Jonathan to a few of the sellers, who explained—most of them in Malagasy—why and how their botanicals worked. Lehanna tried to focus on Jacques's translations, though she turned now and then to the people they had passed earlier, those who sold their damaged wares at Zoma, hoping to feed themselves and their families.

After an early dinner at a café near the university, Jacques delivered Lehanna and Jonathan to their small, sparsely furnished apartment. Grateful to be in their temporary home, they fell into the narrow bed and deep, welcome sleep.

The next day, Jonathan went to the university lab with Jacques while Lehanna worked at the *Musée de l'Académie Malgache*, on the zoo grounds near the city's edge. There she began her official study of the Merina, who accounted for a quarter of the Great Red Island's population.

⁓

For the next two months, Lehanna spent ten- to twelve-hour days researching and documenting Merina culture, especially the people's funerary arts and spiritual practices. Because the Merina revered the dead and considered the afterlife at least as important as the present, funeral rituals were often elaborate and costly, even for families with limited resources. But honoring ancestors with plentiful food, music, and dance was considered vital to protect the living as well as the buried.

Long after a family member's passing—maybe because crops failed, or descendants had otherwise inexplicable bad luck, or a beloved relative fell ill—local spiritual leaders, *ombiasy,* might divine that ancestors, *razana,* were displeased. Then they would call together family and community for a *famadihana,* a ritual to appease the *razana.*

During the ceremony, or "turning of the bones," the dead were exhumed, revered, and sung to while the *ombiasy* consulted with *kokolamp*—ancient spirits—or *tromba*—immediate ancestors—seeking release of whatever spiritual imbalance was causing bad fortune. Once the bones were reburied with gifts and new shrouds, friends and relatives left the ceremony assured that the fortunes or health of the living would improve.

The more Lehanna learned about the *ombiasy* and their healing techniques, from herbalism to astrology, the thirstier she became to escape the university's confines to do her field work. Each morning she woke counting the days until she could leave Antananarivo for Jacques's clinic and its village, where she could observe and interact with the Merina who lived and worked there.

On weekends, Lehanna and Jonathan toured the island—the world's fourth largest, about the size of Texas. They knew they couldn't cover every inch in twelve weeks, so they followed itineraries planned back in Ithaca.

Wherever they explored, local legends—the ones Lehanna had read about as far back as her time with her librarian friend, Janette—came alive in their natural environments. Seeing the flora up close, touching them, intrigued her even more than reading about them had. There were the traveler's trees, named because adventurers years back tapped into the trunks' cork-like compartments for water to drink while crossing the Land of Thirst desert. And tangled thickets of didierea, called man-eating trees, because, when French colonists established unwanted settlements, like Fort-Dauphin on the island's southeastern tip, locals sometimes drove the invaders into the thorny trees, impaling them. As for the winds drifting off the turquoise water and white-sand beaches of Nose Be? Yes, they did carry the sweet scent of vanilla.

On their hikes along rope bridges and jagged limestone outcroppings called *tsingy*, they observed and wondered at the Great Red Island's unique species. Lemurs, leaping from branch to branch of unique hardwoods and bamboos, called Lehanna and Jonathan to play as well as to discover. In some places, though, they could only imagine the fauna's diversity in years earlier, when certain species, like Pygmy hippos and elephant birds had flourished, before foreign trophy hunters—as well as slash and burn deforestation—drove them off the island and into extinction.

Lehanna documented their adventures, but the pages she devoted to her experience at Tana's market, where so many lived with so little, remained blank. Even weeks after she had visited Zoma, she was unable to reconcile her observations and feelings. Yes, her motive in coming to the island was positive. She wanted her work to be of use. Eventually she could write anthropological abstracts and publish them in *American Anthropologist* or *National Geographic*. Western academics and the general public could learn from her experience and research. At the same time, she didn't want to become yet another outsider who caused the island's people, its vegetation, and its animal life to suffer in the interest of what, for too long, had been called modernization.

The morning they left Tana for Jacques's clinic, Lehanna and Jonathan reviewed a map of the Central Highlands as they waited at their apartment for Thierry, the guide Jacques had arranged to lead them to the clinic.

"It looks," Jonathan said, tracing their expected route to the interior, "like we'll drive with Thierry until we end up right here." He pointed to a spot on the map, north of Antananarivo, where the main road ended and where they would take what Thierry had said would be "a short stroll" through the hills and forest.

"We know one thing for sure." Jonathan smiled when he rolled up the map. "We're in for a rocky drive." They had driven enough around the island to know that what Jacques told them on their first day was true. Even the island's main roads were barely passable, with most pitted by deep ruts dug by cattle carts.

Thierry was a slender, agile man of about twenty, fluent in his native Malagasy dialect, but also French and English. Unlike lighter-skinned Merina from Tana, where the French influence had been strongest, Thierry's skin was darker brown, his facial features flatter and broader, like those of many outside the capital.

From their apartment, Thierry drove them inland, as planned, until the road narrowed, then ended. There Lehanna and Jonathan hefted their backpacks and prepared to hike the rest of the way to the clinic.

"The village," Thierry said as he pointed with his chin in a vague direction, "is just over the hill."

Lehanna scanned the landscape, which was nothing but hills. "Which hill?"

"That one." Thierry waved, again in a vague direction. "No need to try to get there before we're supposed to, is there?" Thierry spoke with a confidence that belied his age.

Lehanna smiled, though she suspected their hike would be more difficult than Thierry's casual manner implied. She hoisted her backpack and set out with a strong stride. "Come on, stragglers," she called as she headed in the nebulous direction of "the hill." Jonathan and Thierry followed at Lehanna's pace.

After two hours, when they had passed over many hills, she sat on the ground. "I need a break."

Thierry sat next to Jonathan, who had joined Lehanna. He picked a blade of grass and chewed on it while his companions rubbed their feet and drank from their canteens. Lehanna refrained from asking which of the remaining thousand or so hills would lead them to the village and Jacques's clinic. Then she stood, shook the dirt from her jeans, and set out again, Jonathan and Thierry following.

Four hours after starting out, they arrived at the village, a collection of twelve rectangular raffia huts with roofs thatched with palm fronds. They were built on stilts to keep pesky lemurs and rats at bay. That the huts were not round—like those on the African mainland—supported the claim that the Great Red Island's first residents arrived from Malaysia, where round huts were common.

"Dr. Merthin?"

When Jonathan asked where they would most likely find Jacques, Thierry pointed to the largest structure, a yellowish clay hut with thatched roof, situated about a hundred yards from the village center. "Follow me."

Once they reached the clinic, Jonathan and Lehanna stood in the entryway, with a clear view of the three rooms that comprised a simple ward. All beds were occupied, some by locals, others by people from surrounding villages who came for relief from everything from malaria to heart disease to head- and stomachaches. A fourth room, at the back, looked to be a small operating room, not currently in use.

"Welcome, welcome," Jacques said when they found him evaluating a new patient. "I hope you didn't fall for Thierry's 'just over the hill' routine."

"I guess we did," Lehanna admitted. "But," she said, turning to a smiling Thierry, "never again!"

Jacques laughed. "Probably for the best. If you knew in advance, you might not have come."

"Oh, no." Lehanna shook her head. "I would have come anyway," she said. "I just wouldn't have tried, like I did when we first started out, to get here before I was supposed to." She nodded to Thierry.

"First lesson learned." Jacques's smile faded. "Before you leave, there will be many more. "Now," he looked to Thierry. "Can you show our guests to their accommodations without taking the four-hour way around?"

Thierry motioned for Lehanna and Jonathan to follow him. "No more hills," he said. "I promise." Then he led them to the hut that would be their home for the next weeks.

After finishing with his patients, Jacques met Jonathan and Lehanna to give them an official clinic tour, then to share a light meal. "Rounds at seven tomorrow," he said when he left them for the evening.

Exhausted as she was, the night forest sounds—especially the shrieking sifaka lemurs and the chir-chir-chirping leaf-tailed geckos—kept Lehanna awake long after Jonathan fell asleep. After an hour or so, she slipped out of bed and went to the door. Opening it a crack, she looked to the ground, then up into the tree canopy. The stilts elevating their little house might be tall enough to keep out the wildlife that prowled at ground level, but she suspected the lemurs had easy access from their treetop perches.

When she eventually went back to bed and fell asleep, she didn't wake until six thirty the next morning, when Jonathan stood over her with a cup of rousing Malagasy coffee, fragrant, welcome, and necessary.

On rounds, Jacques explained how each patient was treated with the protocol that had the greatest chance of success—some with local methods only, some with Western medicine only, and some with a combination. "This patient, her name is Tiavina," he said when they reached a young woman in the second ward, "has malaria. Like the rest in this room. We are treating her—"

Screams outside the building interrupted Jacques. When he rushed to the window, a young woman—arms outstretched, eyes wide and desperate—ran toward them. Behind her, two men carried a child on a stretcher made of two branches with a blanket secured over them.

Jacques hurried outside where the woman, distraught, not more than twenty, pleaded with Jacques in a native dialect.

"She was cooking dinner," Jacques translated. "When she finished, she tossed a pot of boiling water out her hut's window. She didn't know her little girl—her name is Nathalie, only two years old—was playing outside the window. Not until she heard the screams."

"Inside," Jacques said. "Quickly." When he motioned, the men ushered the child into the clinic and set her on a table. Her stomach and thighs, raw and oozing, looked as red and sticky as strawberry jelly. Two village women tried to comfort the young mother while Jacques examined the girl.

"Second degree burns," he said. "Difficult to treat even in hospital settings."

When Lehanna saw the child, laid out on the examination table, she diverted her eyes. She didn't want to get sick, not on her first day in the village. Besides, she needed to help. *How can I help?*

Jacques called in Malagasy to a nurse inside the clinic. She rushed into the thicket surrounding the building and returned minutes later with a short, dark-skinned man with long graying hair. After he examined the child, the man spoke a few words and hurried off. "Haja," Jacques explained, "is the village *ombiasy*, our chief herbalist and spiritual healer."

Then, while Haja headed into the forest for plants to treat the girl, Jacques told Lehanna what he learned about Nathalie during her examination. "She is from a village to the west. Her mother and the two men walked a full day to reach us. She's lucky to have survived."

Lehanna looked to the girl, small and writhing. She was as struck by Jacques's work as she was by the men—Family? Strangers? —who brought Nathalie and her mother such a distance in the hope of helping. Whatever lingering fatigue and achiness she felt from the previous day's journey left her. Nothing mattered but helping Nathalie and her mother.

When Haja returned, he carried a slender branch about six feet long. He pulled a knife from his shorts pocket, made a clean cut at each end of the limb, and motioned to another man to hold one end over Nathalie's stomach. Haja blew into the other end, forcing its sap to drip onto the girl's burns.

While the girl wailed, Lehanna wanted to scream, too. *Hurry, can't you see the child is suffering?* Then, as the syrupy fluid spread over the burns, Nathalie quieted. She stopped writhing. When all the scalded areas were covered, Haja set the branch aside and scraped the skin off a gourd he brought from the forest. He mixed it with water and dabbed the compound on the sap-covered burn.

Within minutes, Nathalie fell asleep. The women who had been comforting her mother encouraged the young woman to rest on cushions they brought into the treatment room. Lehanna sat with them, hoping her presence was enough to comfort, to facilitate the girl's healing.

By the second day, Nathalie's burns began to crust over. There was hope.

⌒

Jonathan left the village three days later to continue researching the periwinkle's prospects for healing childhood leukemia and Hodgkin's lymphoma. Lehanna, meanwhile, settled in for her two remaining weeks in the village. She still wanted to document Merina funerary rites, but after observing Nathalie's treatment, she also wanted to learn more from Haja and the other local healers.

Lehanna accompanied Haja on his daily visits to Nathalie. Some days the *ombiasy* observed the girl for hours. Seeming to listen, but to what? Seeming to wait, but why? Lehanna knew what it was like to hear voices others couldn't, but, still, she wanted Haja to help Nathalie, whose progress seemed to be slowing. When she looked at him, as if to ask why he wasn't doing more, he simply raised his hand, as if to slow her down. He motioned for Lehanna to sit with him and Nathalie's mother. He learned that the girl's father recently left them to live with another woman and, only months later, despite his reputation as a skillful hunter, the father— Mahery—died in a hunting accident. Haja went silent then, but after an hour, he announced to Jacques and to the village that it was time to perform a *famadihana* on the girl's behalf.

"Because he abandoned her and her mother," Jacques explained to Lehanna, "Haja determined Nathalie's father's ancestors, his *razana,* are holding him responsible for the girl's condition." Until Mahery's spirit was cleansed, Nathalie could not heal.

"But he's dead." As soon as she spoke the words, Lehanna shook her head. "There I go, imposing my Western values."

Jacques smiled. "At least you're aware of your bias." Then he repeated some of what Lehanna had already learned about the *famadihana* tradition. "Physically, yes, Mahery is dead. But after exhuming his bones, bringing them back alive, they will be danced with, cleansed, then buried again. With guidance from the stars, the *kokolamp* and maybe Mahery's *tromba,* Haja will divine exactly how to appease the spirits so his herbs and remedies will be able to do their job for Nathalie."

When Lehanna noticed Haja motioning to her, she turned to Jacques to explain what the gesture meant. "He wants you to participate in the ritual."

"Oh." Lehanna hesitated. "I don't think—"

Jacques shook his head. "It's not a matter of what you want or what you think. Haja has determined, maybe because of the way you're relating to Nathalie and her mother, or maybe because he sees some connection with your own *tromba,* that you have a role to play. If you decline . . ." Jacques shrugged. "Well, let's not think about that."

The next morning Nathalie's villagers—as well as Lehanna, Jacques, Haja, Nathalie's mother, and the women who had been tending to her—gathered at dawn outside the clinic. They walked three hours to Mahery's burial site, where those responsible for the feast following the ceremony had arrived earlier to begin preparing the traditional dishes that would be served.

When they arrived at the tomb, Lehanna walked haltingly toward it, then stopped before reaching the stone building.

"You're surprised at how substantial it is?" Jacques asked. "And how ornately painted?"

Lehanna nodded. Most of the living quarters they had passed on the way were mud huts, much more modest than the tomb.

"Maybe you're trying to apply another Western construct?"

Lehanna looked at Jacques without speaking, not sure she understood his question.

"Many Merina believe that the *razana* deserve more respect, more tribute than those still walking the earth."

Lehanna tried to justify the expense of an ornate tomb when the resources it required might have been spent on more food, better health care, for those still alive.

"I know what you're thinking," Jacques said. "Sometimes I want to encourage my patients to spend more on themselves than on their ancestors, but it's not my place to do that, is it?"

Lehanna shook her head. No, it wasn't Jacques's place. Nor was it hers.

When Jacques walked toward the tomb and explained how the images carved on it were scenes from Mahery's life, Lehanna followed. "He was a zebu farmer." He pointed to carved images that looked to Lehanna a little like buffalo. "The sacred ox," he explained. "Many Merina earn their livings raising them."

Three men circled the tomb then, sprinkling rum on it, and shouting. "The day will be one to remember," Jacques translated. "No one will rest until Mahery's *razana* are pleased."

At noon, Haja, dressed in flowing red robes, led a procession around the tomb. He sprinkled rum at the western entrance, then ordered several men to open the vault and go inside. When they came out, they carried Mahery's bones over their heads and paraded them among the villagers. Then, singing, they spread the bones on the ground, dusted them off, and wrapped them in a new blue *lamba mena,* or burial cloth.

Then the party started! Lehanna joined the villagers in feasting on zebu and chicken and plenty of Malagasy wine. By sundown, when all the locals had taken turns singing and dancing with the dead man's bones, Haja motioned for Lehanna to do the same.

"Oh," she said, shaking her head, "I don't think so." Then she felt Jacques's hand on her arm. Haja had invited her for a reason, he told her, even if neither of them knew what that was. Declining his invitation would be rude but might also prevent Nathalie's healing.

Lehanna stepped forward, unsteadily at first. Like everyone else, she had had her fill of wine and rum. When Jacques saw her reticence, he motioned to Haja to ask permission to perform the ritual with her. The *ombiasy* nodded and Jacques walked with Lehanna to the bonfire. Blazing by then, it cast a smoky haze where the bones were gathered. Jacques took her elbow and guided her to the tomb. She wiped the sweat from her face. But with Jacques steadying her, she continued to the *lamba mena*. She picked it up, stepped away from Jacques and circled the fire, dancing.

She could still see Jacques through the smoke, but as she moved slowly, rhythmically, with Mahery's bones in her arms, turning, circling the fire, its flames grew taller. She lost sight of Jacques. Then she heard her name. "Lela, Lela." She stumbled. Who was calling her? The same voice she heard as a child, on the Fourth of July, the night her father died. It was Jonathan. But, no, Jonathan was nowhere nearby. She gripped the *lamba mena*. Maybe she was about to learn how to save him from the fate she had witnessed a decade earlier. But the bones she carried were so heavy now. She was so tired. And the fire. Why was it calling her closer? To reach her hand into it? She looked to Haja. *Can I please stop?* she asked with her eyes. But the healer motioned for her to continue. Where was Jacques? She looked through the fire. He wasn't there.

"Lela." Yes, it was Jonathan's voice. Then she saw him, his arms extended to her. She wanted to reach to him, to save him, but she couldn't hold him and the dead man's bones, too. She felt herself spinning, faster. As if looking down on herself, she heard herself singing in Malagasy. Words she didn't understand. Then she saw Jacques standing in front of her, smiling, his arms outstretched. He took the bones and burial cloth from her, then she fell to the ground.

She woke moments later, though she felt heavy, as if she had been asleep for hours. Jacques was holding her while Haja held out to her the leaves of a sweet-smelling plant. She started, afraid she had dropped the *lamba mena* and that Nathalie might not heal. "It is the way it is to be," Jacques said, translating as Haja spoke. What was the way it was supposed to be? Then she wept. What a fool she had been for thinking she could save Jonathan from his fate. She looked from Haja, then to Jacques as he helped her to her feet.

While Jacques assured her that he had caught the bones and burial cloth before she fell, Haja carried the bones back into the tomb. He ordered the men to seal the structure's entrance with mud. As the sky continued to darken, Haja studied the stars. Then he assured the community that Mahery's *razana* were pleased. The *famadihana* had sealed Nathalie's good fortune. It was time to return to the village.

⁓

By the third day after the *famadihana*, Nathalie's scars protected her well enough so that, when the women sang to her, she laughed and hummed along.

Later at the clinic, Lehanna motioned to Haja to ask the name of the plant he had used to heal the girl. "Liana," he said.

Lehanna said nothing. When she heard the name of the plant, that sounded like her own, she knew it was no coincidence she had been in the village to witness Nathalie's healing. She knew then, too, that her life's mission was not to dig among people's anthropological roots to document their pasts. She needed to learn more from Haja. She needed to heal as he healed.

Haja continued speaking to Lehanna in the local dialect, but her command of the language wasn't good enough to understand. Jacques translated. "You are honored by your name with the ability to speak to those present and no longer present. In return for this gift, you will bear burdens of loss and responsibility for others.

But through the pain you suffer, you will work wonders in the lives of those you touch."

Jacques turned to her. "There's nothing to be afraid of." His voice was soothing, encouraging. "We will always be here to help you."

She looked at Jacques and smiled. With his confidence in her, with his willingness to support her, she felt she could do what was being asked of her.

"Can you ask Haja if I can stay longer in the village to study with him?"

Before Jacques did so, Haja spoke to him. It was not, he said, Lehanna's time to study with him. She needed to wait and listen, to take one step and then the next. "Your path," Jacques translated, "will be made clear." He squeezed her hand, then let it go, his eyes remaining on hers.

⁓

"Let me look at you." When Lehanna returned to Tana the next week, Jonathan kissed her, then held her at arms' length. "You look different."

"What's different," she said, putting her arm through his, "is that I know what I'm going to do with my life." She smiled to prevent herself from saying what she knew—that she couldn't save him from his future.

For the remaining weeks of their trip, Lehanna tried to focus on finishing her reports, but her thoughts often drifted to the village. Not only because she felt called to do the same work as the people at the clinic, but because she felt her future was linked, in a yet inexplicable way, to the man who had founded that healing center, and who, one evening, led her through smoke and fire to see clearly.

But any link to Jacques would be in the future. What she needed to do now was walk with Jonathan through his remaining days.

When Lehanna and Jonathan returned to Ithaca, even though she knew he would not be with her much longer, they decided to start an herb farm. They studied what they could realistically grow in the Upstate soil and climate. They picked out a land parcel up Route 96 and planned how they might buy it a year later.

"Our dreams," Jonathan said every night as he held Lehanna before sleeping, "are coming true."

"Yes," she said, "they are." She knew those dreams would never materialize the way Jonathan envisioned them. All she wanted was for him to be as happy as he could, for as long as he could.

But on the day Jonathan walked from the mailbox out front into the kitchen, holding up a blue envelope, Lehanna knew he—they—wouldn't be happy for long at all. He set the mail—and the blue envelope—on the table, then pulled out a chair and sat down.

"Oh." Lehanna slipped into the chair next to his as he picked up the envelope stamped with the Selective Service System seal. She closed her eyes and shuddered.

"We both knew it could happen," Jonathan said.

"Yes," Lehanna said, though she knew that Jonathan not only could, but would be drafted and sent to Vietnam.

He pulled out the letter, the Notice to Report for Induction. "I need to report for basic training at Fort Dix, New Jersey."

She reached to him and ran her fingers through his hair. She savored the earthy smell of it, from the shampoo she made from rosemary and mint. "When?"

"November first."

She took his hand. "There's always Canada," she said, though she knew better than to think she could control his fate.

"True," he said. "But I want to be able to come home. To our little patch of land, to our dreams, to you." He kissed her. "And I *will* come home."

CHAPTER TEN

It was their first day of Weapons Familiarization. Forty-one more twenty-four-hours ahead of them until they shipped out from Fort Dix to Saigon. If he could have found a way to skip the training and get right into the action over there, Quinn Gallagher would have. He was ready to go, ready to fight, ready to do what he could to turn this lame-ass loser war around to America's advantage. Instead, he had to wait. Just like his fellow recruits. All the while knowing that a third of them would ship home in body bags. The rest maybe wishing they had been.

After lunch, Quinn and his new buddy, Sherman Whiting, were hanging outside the mess. Waiting. More goddamn waiting. In twelve minutes, at 1300 hours, Master Sergeant Gus Sanchez would be subjecting them to yet another daily dose of physical and mental abuse. In the meantime, they were shootin' the shit about nothing much when Quinn shook his head. He poked Sherm with his elbow. "Jesus, God, will you look at that."

Sherm squinted, shaded his eyes, and turned where Quinn pointed. "Look at what?"

With his chin, Quinn pointed to a tall, thin recruit a few yards away. Holding his M-16, he looked as awkward as a newborn colt struggling to stand.

Quinn grew up in rural Kansas where, by the time he was twelve, every kid had the hunt in his blood and knew how to scout, shoot, and skin anything on four legs. When he got to Dix, he figured the killing part of war would be just a matter of narrowing down the number of legs on the prey—from four to two—and substituting jungle terrain for winter wheat fields.

But this kid? His face looked peaceful as a mountain lake on a hot summer's day. He wouldn't know how to shoot anything if it was three feet in front of him. Quinn had seen that look before. His brother, Tim, had it. Such a gentle kid he was, even after their father started pounding the crap out of him. Someone with a soul like this kid—his name was Jonathan, it turned out—he didn't deserve to die in some far-off, smelly-ass shithole. Quinn decided then and there he would protect the guy, even though it turned out Jonathan was a good two, three years older than him. "Looks like he should be writin' love songs, not goin' to war." Quinn nodded as he paused. "Let's go."

"Go where?"

"We're gonna help the kid out."

"Shit," Sherm said. "We got enough to do learnin' how to keep ourselves outta body bags."

Quinn started walking toward Jonathan. He called over his shoulder. "Fine, you selfish, sorry-ass son of a bitch."

Before Quinn got that whole sentence out, Sherm had already hustled to catch up. Quinn smiled. He knew he had that effect on people. Where he went, they followed.

⌣

For their remaining time in Basic, Sancho—as the men came to call Gus Sanchez—and the rest of the brass did their best to grind the new recruits down to the point where it was hard to tell one from the other, except for the color of their eyes or skin. They found guys like Jonathan harder to break than the hotheaded cowboys, like Quinn, the ones with piss and vinegar in them. "They're like Niagara Falls," Sancho, who was from Buffalo, said. "You just harness their energy and let 'em rip." But the guys like Jonathan? The ones who seemed to let everything, including Basic's torment, roll off their backs? They were the ones that gave the brass the biggest pains in the ass.

When Basic ended, Quinn continued to watch out for Jonathan, even if his attempts at toughening the kid up mostly failed. They had a month in Advanced Infantry Training, AIT, followed by two weeks of Southeast Asia Orientation. Then they got their assignments. Quinn, with his scouting and marksmanship skills, was assigned to MACV—Military Advisory Command Vietnam. Like others on the MACV team, he was responsible for advising a South Vietnamese unit on strategy.

"What a crock that turned out to be," Quinn told his barroom friends when he returned stateside. "Imagine tryin' to tell men on their own soil how to win a war they didn't want to fight." But back then Quinn was thirsty for war and hungry to win.

Jonathan was assigned to the same unit, in charge of survival skills.

"Survival skills?" Sherm had a good laugh when he heard Jonathan's assignment.

"Well," Quinn said, "he's got that biology training, or whatever you call it when you study plants in college. He can probably tell us what's safe to eat and what'll kill us if we get stuck without food. But you're right. Survival?" What could Jonathan know about surviving in Nam, where staying alive depended more on calculating whether a man was the hunter or the hunted?

They didn't have long to ponder their questions. Less than a week later, they were headed to Saigon for two more weeks of training. Then it was on to Can Tho, the Mekong Delta's capital. And, from what they heard from men who had been there and back, the world's foulest shithole.

They were sent to replace another five-man team that had been advising a South Vietnamese battalion in IV Corps, stationed in Ca Mau. Just outside the U Minh forest, where the eighteenth North Vietnamese Division was hiding out. Or so the brass thought.

There were Quinn and Jonathan. Sherm, the radio man. Horace Washington, the medic. And Captain Richard Hoyt, with his ROTC training and some stateside filler and his railroad tracks, as the team called the bars on their supposed leader's uniform.

Not more than two weeks after the team arrived in Ca Mau, Quinn's opinion of Captain Dickie was set in stone. "Son of a bitch couldn't sniff out pussy in a whorehouse unless it was sittin' on his face," Quinn said. And even though they had only been together a short time, the other three on the team accepted Quinn's assessment. They believed what he believed.

Six weeks after Basic, they suited up, sporting their new stripes, hefting their M-16s. Except Quinn, with his six-and-a-half pound M-79 grenade launcher—they called it the blooker—and as many rounds as a man could hump. Then they made off to advise the South Vietnamese on how to win their war, in their country, on their land.

"What the hell?" On the way back from their first visit with their IV Corps counterparts, Quinn was so disgusted he didn't give a good goddamn how he addressed Captain Dickie. "Whaddya mean they don't want our advice? That they don't want to fight? It's their war, for shit's sake. They wanna win, or don't they?"

"Settle down, soldier," the captain said. "It'll take a little time to build trust."

Trust? Quinn wasn't so sure. "Any man who won't fight to save his own land and family? They must know somethin' we don't," he told Sherm on their return to camp. "Like some damned monsoon is comin' and they know the enemy's gonna be drowned, so they don't have to waste their precious energy. Or maybe there's some hocus pocus superstition in play. And if we strike, we're all gonna be laid low by evil spirits."

The team humped back to camp, gathered new intel, laid out what they figured were solid operations. "It's time to strike," Dickie again told the local higher-ups two weeks later. They listened. They nodded. They dragged on their American cigarettes. They spoke to their interpreter. Then the interpreter turned to Dickie and shook his head. "We'll wait."

The team, more disgruntled than after their first encounter, watched for another opportunity. When intel signaled the time was right, they humped back to the locals' camp. Third's the lucky charm, after all. "It's time," Captain Dickie said. But the interpreter shook his head. "Not yet."

Then and there, less than two months into what was supposed to be a yearlong tour, Quinn's agreement with the United States Army took a turn. If he wasn't in Vietnam to advise or strategize, he also wasn't there to get his johnson jerked by supposed friendlies. With the number of American fatalities exceeding twenty-five thousand, and nothing to show for their sacrifice, his new mission was to get his team back home as quick as possible.

He needed a plan. First, he needed to get Dickie in line. After observing the captain for two months, Quinn knew his superior's agenda was simple enough: he wanted to add as much color to his uniform as possible. All Quinn needed to do was lay out an op that would guarantee Dickie some serious visibility with the brass. It would take a while. And patience wasn't Quinn's strong suit. The only way he could keep his edginess in check, while sniffing out the right opportunity, was to imagine himself pounding the fields back home. Remembering what it felt like to pull the trigger on an eighteen-point white tail at just the right moment, after freezing his ass off, waiting from before dawn to just before dusk. If he stayed calm and planned things right, he and his team would be leaving Vietnam with one-way tickets to the U S of A, hopefully, with their limbs and minds still intact.

"Question for you, Captain." Quinn knew he'd already become a thorn in Dickie's side. He wasn't surprised when the captain's jaw muscles tightened as Quinn approached his tent after a noontime rain. Early May, it was. At least he thought so. Wartime misery washed each day with the same gray-blue cast.

"Another one?"

Quinn nodded and smiled. "'Fraid so."

"Make it quick."

"Yes, sir," he said. As if their fearless captain had somewhere to go. "We here to fight or get our dicks yanked by these pussies?" Quinn took one last drag off his Marlboro, then stamped it into the mud with his boot. "We keep revvin' up, then getting' told to cool our heels, sir, there won't be no fight left in us." He looked away and counted to himself while Dickie chewed on what he said. *Five. Six. Seven. Eight.* He shrugged. "Far as I can tell, that would mean no good write-ups for you."

No good write-ups? Hoyt's head snapped when he heard that.

Quinn continued even as the captain glared. "The way I see it, unless we see some action real soon, and rack up some serious enemy body count, we're stuck in this hellhole another six months. And you're wearin' that captain's uniform the rest of your days."

Quinn paused again. Dickie's nostrils flared just enough to show how angry he was. He knew Quinn was right, but he didn't have one damn idea how to remedy the situation.

"Yeah, well, when you come up with a better plan than the higher ups, let me know. Until then, shut your face."

"Sir, I do have a plan, so I'm not gonna shut my face."

There it was, the little flicker of possibility he'd been waiting to see in Dickie's vacuous gray eyes.

"So, how 'bout I lay it out?"

"Go on."

"That Hoi Chan program? Where we pay locals to wheedle intelligence out of 'em when they might otherwise not risk bein' found out?"

The captain nodded.

"You know and I know one of 'em saw an F-4 Phantom go down, not more than a day's hump from here."

"That's right," Dickie said.

American pilots, Quinn reminded Dickie, were the holy grail to the North Vietnamese. Once captured, they were paraded up and down city streets, and filmed, making for demoralizing U.S. news reports. But down in IV Corps, the Vietcong—the VC— took their prisoners undercover, moved them around the jungles and forests every day or two. Even if rescue teams got a fix on them, the pilots were whisked away before they could be retaken.

"Think about it," Quinn said. "In all our country's years in this godforsaken place, we've never recovered a captured jet jockey.

"Wouldn't it be somethin' if we formed our own self-appointed, special forces hit squad and got this one out? You'd be as much a hero as the pilot."

Quinn looked away, waving his arms, as if painting an image on a faraway television screen. "I can see your face on Walter Cronkite's show. On the front page of every U.S. newspaper from New York to Hawaii. You'd get your lettuce, and the rest of the team would get express tickets home."

When Dickie looked away, then back, his slight smile told Quinn that Captain Dickie was in, even if he wouldn't yet admit it. Quinn just needed to give him time to figure that out.

Dickie stashed his hands in his pockets and paced, stiff-legged, back and forth in front of the tent. "We've got no orders for a search and rescue."

"You're absolutely right. We got no orders. We also got no cooperation from that pack of sorry excuses for soldiers we're supposed to be advisin'. It don't take a genius to see they got no incentive to fight this war. Not when you know as well as I do, they're on the take not to.

"If we sit on our butts and wait for them to get good and goddamned ready to go after anything more dangerous than them water buffalo that's drinkin' out of that sewer, over there?" Quinn pointed to a watering hole in the distance. "We're in for a long, lonely stint here. With nothin' to show for it."

If he had a camera inside Dickie's head, Quinn knew what it would show. The captain was already envisioning himself in full-dress uniform, sitting on the back of a Cadillac convertible, waving to cheering crowds in New York or LA or even Boston, his hometown. The headline the captain saw in his brain read: Hoyt Rescues Downed Pilot.

"Point well taken," Dickie said. He looked away, as if mapping a strategy.

Quinn knew the captain would come up empty. He waited. Then he laid out his plan.

"I say we go in alone. Just the five of us. There's likely to be six men, eight at the most, guardin' that pilot. They got to travel light so they can move fast. And if the intel's correct, they'll keep headin' north from where our guy went down.

"They'll have two sentries. One east, one west. And they'll likely expect that, if anyone comes after the pilot, it'll be during the darkest hours. Between eleven and three. On a night when there's not much moonlight to speak of." He paused. "So, if I was to try to outfox 'em, I'd say our best shot at catchin' 'em unawares is two, three days from now, around the full moon.

"If you, Whiting, and Washington was to circle around to the west," he continued, "and me and Jon-boy come in from the east, about zero-four-three-zero, when the sentries are likely lettin' down their guard, maybe dozin' a little, Jon-boy and I could signal you three to attack camp while we take out the sentry on our side and come in opposite you."

"Just before first light." The captain was finding his rhythm.

"That's right."

"Then we radio back to Can Tho to come get our guy."

"And you pick up your medals without passin' go." Quinn hesitated. "Only thing is, we need to make sure there's no flyovers scheduled, nothin' that'll scare 'em into running before we get there."

"I'll take care of that." Dickie looked at Quinn straight on when he spoke, acting as if he really was in charge. "We move out tomorrow," he said. "Seventeen hundred hours. Now get the others in here so I can break the news."

"Yes, sir." Quinn saluted then left.

When Quinn rounded up the three men to take them to the captain's tent, Jonathan stumbled on his untied boot laces as he tried to catch up. "What makes you think we can do that, Quinn? No one else has been able to."

Quinn stopped and waited for Jonathan. "For one thing," he said, "knowin' if we don't do somethin' that flyboy doesn't stand a chance." He shook his head. "For another, knowin' we don't stand a chance, neither. Not unless we find a way around this fucked-up system."

"But . . ."

"But nothin', Jon-boy. Just stick with me. We're gonna save that pilot. And we're gonna save ourselves."

The captain paced the tent when the men entered, announcing he had explained their upcoming op to Quinn earlier and wanted him to lay it out for the others.

Under normal circumstances, if anyone took credit that was due him, Quinn would have laid the guy out and set him straight. In this case, Dickie's behavior affirmed that Quinn had the captain just where he wanted him. When Dickie nodded to him, Quinn took over.

He detailed the mission and all the precautions they would need to take. They would grease up their hands and faces with camo paint. Roll in the dirt and mud so they smelled like Vietnamese, not Americans. They would tape every piece of equipment—even their dog tags—so they couldn't make noise.

"The most important thing is, no one so much as scratches his ass without me tellin' him to. You hear?"

The team headed out at 1700 hours the next day, just like Quinn planned. That gave them approximately thirty-six hours—plenty of time—before they would confront Charlie, as the North Vietnamese were called. Within an hour after that, they would have their American pilot, safe and sound.

They walked through the night and set up to rest just before first light. To stay out of sight, they slept in a bomb crater, surrounded by elephant grass and filled with water as warm as a bubble bath—only it smelled like water buffalo dung and low tide.

That evening they walked again, until they arrived at their destination. They separated into two groups. Jonathan and Quinn positioned to the east, the other three to the west. They waited. Just before first light, Quinn signaled. They were ready to rock and roll.

They spotted the sentry from the right, just like Quinn planned. But the cocksucker was sitting there, wide awake, smoking. An American cigarette, no doubt. He wasn't sleeping, like Quinn expected. To minimize the risk of being heard, he would need to go in alone. He motioned for Jonathan to stay put.

Quinn belly-crawled the fifty yards toward the sentry, keeping downwind of the guy. No sound. No scent. He was the hunter back home, cradling his M-16 like he would his Remington, but his firearm would be no use to him now. If he used it, he would alert the sentry's pals. He needed his hunting knife, the one he'd brought from home, tied with rawhide around his thigh. He unsheathed it and held it between his teeth.

Two-legged prey. That's what he was after. He smelled the sentry's cigarette smoke. He ignored the sweat on his back while every tendon tightened, as he became all wet bone and hard muscle. He set down his M-16, took his knife in hand. He leapt from behind, grabbed Charlie's hair, snapping his prey's head clean back. He slashed the narrow throat. The man went rigid first, then limp. No sound, except one whisper of air exiting. Then, whoosh. He was on the ground.

Quinn stuck him again. This time up through the sweet spot at the base of the skull, deep enough this time. He ripped the head back, and left it hanging to one side, blood still pumping out of the slender stalk that used to be the man's neck. The air ripened with the smell of the man's shit and piss.

Quinn froze. He listened. He looked. There was no breeze. Even the elephant grass should be silent. Yet behind him, Quinn heard feet, running. He turned quickly, quietly. Jonathan was headed toward him. He had the kill in his eyes, incongruous on his narrow, usually gentle face. Quinn motioned for him to stay put. The kid rushed forward anyway. Until thirty yards before he reached Quinn, a Bouncing Betty sprung up, its ball bearings detonating, propelling Jonathan into the air. Half of him anyway. Somehow his M-16 was still in his hand.

Quinn heard movement from the west. Feet, but no words at first. Dickie and the other two were heading to the camp. "Motherfucker," he heard Dickie shout. "The sons of bitches are gone." All that was left? Bedrolls, a clothesline hung with smelly socks and underwear, an American pilot's helmet. Steven "Devil" Wallace was stamped across the front.

Quinn waited, making sure the landmine was no longer activated. "I taught you better than that," he called as he rushed through the smoke. He would save Jonathan, at least the half of him that was left. When he reached the remnants of his gentle friend, he dropped to the ground. "Sweet Jesus." He set his head down and curled next to Jon-boy's lifeless half-body. "Lela, Lela," he murmured. Like Jonathan used to in his sleep.

CHAPTER ELEVEN

Lehanna knelt in the dirt, pulling crabgrass and purslane that were encroaching on the rosemary and sage she'd planted out back. They were stubborn little devils, but she treated the unwanted weeds as tenderly as she did the herbs. Then she heard him. She set down her trowel. She sat up, tall, alert. He often spoke to her. Sometimes in the garden. Sometimes in the shop where she worked. Sometimes when she settled into a bubbly, lemon verbena bath. Or, at night, when all she wanted was to fall into deep, delicious sleep. Never when she expected. No. Whenever she tried too hard, or chased him, he never came to her.

Usually, when Jonathan spoke to her, she heard only her name—Lela, Lela—whispered, as if she were nestled against his chest, dreaming, hoping. But that afternoon, his voice was clear, definitive, and free of sentiment. "It's time now," he said. Her breath caught in her chest. This was the moment she had anticipated and dreaded. She pressed her dirty hand to her mouth. Jonathan wasn't going to whisper her name anymore. He was gone.

She stood in the garden, shook as much caked dirt as she could from her clogs and jeans. She wiped her hands on her tee shirt, then brushed away the dirt that had settled on her face when she touched it. She walked to the house tentatively, like a wounded raccoon, hobbling, afraid to put too much pressure on a tender leg.

Inside, she showered and changed into one of the bright print dresses she bought on the Great Red Island, one she picked out with him. She caught her reflection in the mirror, surprised that she looked the same as she did a day, a week, a month ago. No, she wasn't the same. Not at all.

She made a cup of chamomile tea, then turned on the stereo. No, Jonathan wouldn't *be around* anymore. She wouldn't *feel fine* anymore.

She curled on the couch until the doorbell rang. "It's time now," she said aloud. What it was time for, she wasn't sure. She turned the album over to play the second side. Then she opened the door. A tall, tanned, beautiful, green-eyed man stood on the stoop. His jeans and faded chambray shirt flattered his sinewy build just so. She held her hand to her face. Warm. It felt so warm.

She knew this pearl-gray Stetson-wearing man from Jonathan's letters. Quinn, his name was. Quinn Gallagher. He had protected Jonathan, then planned the mission that killed him. She also knew what he'd come to say—that Jonathan's death was all his fault. And by the way he stood in front of her, his eyes shifting left, then right, she knew he wouldn't, couldn't get the words out unless she helped him.

"I'm Quinn Gallagher." He removed his hat and ran his fingers through his thick, wavy hair.

She didn't understand why, but she wanted to reach to him and touch that luscious hair.

"I come to tell you about what a fine soldier Jonathan was."

"Quinn," Lehanna said. "Yes, Jonathan wrote me about you. How you helped him." But that was only part of the story. Quinn may have helped Jonathan, but he also put him in harm's way. And here he was, wanting expiation and forgiveness, not just the opportunity to express condolences.

She opened the door wider, though she wanted to slam it in his face. "Come in," she said. She stepped aside, motioning toward the living room. "Have a seat." When he walked past, he smelled like leather and smoky cade. She inhaled deeply.

"I can probably find you a beer, if you want one." When he nodded, she went to the kitchen and returned with two cans of Budweiser from the cupboard. "I'm afraid it's warm," she said. "I'm not much of a drinker."

"That's just fine."

She curled on the couch, and he sat in the overstuffed armchair facing her. He pulled it closer to the coffee table, set his hat there, and took a long drink.

"So," she said, "tell me."

He pulled a pack of Marlboros from his shirt pocket. "Mind if I smoke?"

Yes, she did mind. But she wanted a cigarette, too. "No," she said. "I'll take one. If you've got an extra."

When he tilted the pack her way, she took one even though she hadn't smoked since high school. When he lit it and she inhaled, her throat burned. Her stomach lurched, like she might be sick. But the dizzying swirl felt better than the anger and desolation she felt when Quinn told her how Jonathan carried her letters in a plastic bag in his rucksack and pulled them out to read at night before he went to sleep. How he told Quinn that, when he came back, Lela would be waiting. How they would start that herb farm they dreamed of and live life out of a song. They'd have a couple cats in the yard. Life wouldn't be so hard.

When he turned from her and described the day Jonathan died, she rubbed out her cigarette. She drank the rest of her beer. He told her how he made a valiant attempt to take out the enemy, how he risked his life to save the others on his team. She listened, knowing that Quinn couldn't look at her because he couldn't be honest. She had seen the truth when she was a girl, on the Fourth of July, then again at the *famadihana* for Nathalie's father on the Great Red Island. When Quinn spoke, the scene played again in front of her eyes. The only difference was that Quinn, with his Kansas cadence, smooth as cornsilk, provided the voiceover, as he lied through his teeth.

She knew Jonathan died because Quinn hadn't been able to pull off the mission the way he thought he could. What she didn't know was whether he had concocted this story and was out-and-out lying, or whether it was utterly impossible for him to face the truth: *I got him killed.*

When he turned to her and said again, "Jonathan was a hell of a soldier," she reached for a pillow on the couch and held it close. She would feel such a rush if she called him on his sin of omission. *For what I have done and what I have failed to do.* The words of the Confiteor she had rattled off as a child at Saint Mary's Catholic Church came to mind. Quinn had sinned. Didn't she have the right, the obligation, to call him on his offense? His transgression? She could taste the sweet satisfaction she would get from watching his folksy façade crumble.

But if she had learned anything in Madagascar, it was that she was called to be a healer. And that the plotline of Jonathan's death was out of Quinn's hands. And hers. Instead of going into the kitchen, pulling a knife from the butcher block, and jamming it into his lying throat, she rubbed out her third cigarette. There was no point in punishing him.

She turned and looked out the back window—to the purple lavender, the yellow yarrow, the silvery green angelica. Then she stood and walked to the chair where Quinn was—the chair Jonathan used to sit in when he strummed his guitar and sang Leonard Cohen songs, or ones he had written himself. She sat on the chair's arm, facing Quinn. His eyes shifted away and back again. His hands tightened on the arms of the chair. He was ready to spring if he needed to.

Lehanna reached for his Stetson on the table and put it on herself. Such a delicious-looking man. She ran her hand through his hair, following the waves from his forehead to the back of his neck. She stroked his face. His high forehead, his square jaw. If he wanted her, if she felt needed, maybe his passion would be strong enough to diffuse her rage, to send it scuttling off like a rat chased from a kitchen with a broom.

He pushed her hair off her face.

She ran her hand from his chin to his chest. She felt his throat contract, then loosen as he swallowed. She unbuttoned his shirt, slowly, then pressed her hand to his stomach, surprised that it didn't burn to touch his skin. Maybe by touching another man, this man, her unrelenting memory of Jonathan would leave. *It's time now.*

When she pushed Quinn's shirt from his chest, she traced with her finger the scar that ran down his left side. Where shrapnel from the same landmine that destroyed Jonathan had ricocheted and grazed Quinn from his heart to his stomach. She saw in Quinn's eyes that he was not without pain and regret over the way he won that scar, and another chance at life, while Jonathan lost his.

He closed his eyes. His chest moved up and down, faster as he breathed harder and quicker. She put her mouth to his chest, kissed it. Then, with her tongue, she traced the scar again, leaving a little stream of saliva. When she lifted her head, she saw that his tears were mixing in, his pain was blending with hers. Their sadness came from different disappointments, different failures. But they brought them to this common point. This point of moving on.

"This must be difficult for you." The words seemed someone else's, as if another's voice and feelings and understanding were on loan to her. She wondered if he could trust her compassion, if he could trust anyone again, after he had trusted in himself and found his confidence misplaced. When she stroked his face, and said again, "so difficult," his eyes focused on hers.

She stroked his cheek then brought her hand to her lips to taste. Salty, his tears were, not bitter. He kissed her fingers, then nibbled on them, hungrily. When she put her arms around him and he wept, she did, too. They fumbled out of their clothes and into each other, and he said her name, over and over—"Lela, Lela"—she knew if she could let go of her anger and hear her name, she could be called to a new place, free of judgment, where mercy roots and grows.

They made their way to the floor, taking turns cradling each other. Rocking each other into the night. Then into the next day.

Around sunrise, when Quinn was still sleeping, Lehanna got up and made coffee. She went to the back door and opened it. The air was still damp and hot, but a breeze was coming in off the lake. She wrapped Quinn's shirt around her. She poured a cup of coffee and stirred milk into it, watching the color change from black-brown to caramel. At the same time, the sun turned the sky from dark blue to rosy pink and lilac at the horizon. She and Quinn had diluted the color of their grief and their regret. Its blinding brilliance wouldn't, couldn't return.

She poured coffee for Quinn and carried the mug to the living room. He was awake when she sat on the floor, and he nestled against her. When the caffeine worked through them, they reached for each other again. Then again.

He stayed another two weeks. For the first few days, they wouldn't let each other out of sight for more than the time it took to shower. They deceived themselves into thinking that through each other they had moved on to new, permanently peaceful places in their lives. But when they hugged good-bye and looked into each other's eyes, she knew, and she thought Quinn did, too, that their reprieves were only temporary.

Lehanna opened the door and walked into the backyard. The sun had broken through the thick clouds that had stretched from horizon to horizon when Quinn left early that morning. The sky was still hazy but brightening. It was a little on the cool side for August, so she rolled down the cuffs and buttoned the neck of the embroidered blouse she had put on after taking a long, mellow bath. A flock of Canadian geese honked overhead, making their way south for fall and winter. Students would arrive back on campus in a week, bringing their hopes and ambitions and overly rambunctious hormones. Lehanna smiled. Change was in the air.

She walked to the garden and knelt to tug at a few weeds that were, once again, encroaching on her herbs and perennials. She had neglected them while Quinn had been with her. Plants, she reminded herself, like souls, needed daily tenderness and attention in order to flourish. She would spend time with her garden soon. But not today.

She stood and wiped the dirt off her hands, then walked back into the house. In her bedroom, she took her moss-colored sweater from her drawer, the one Jonathan used to say brought out the highlights in her hair and the green flecks in her eyes. She reached for the tote she had packed and set aside earlier. She headed to the kitchen, took her keys from the kitchen counter, and went out to her cantankerous Beetle. When it started, she patted the dash. "Good girl!"

She drove through town to State Street, then out Route 89. Cayuga Lake shimmered to her right. This was her favorite time of year in Ithaca. The leaves on the maples and sycamores had already begun to turn red and gold. Traffic was still manageable, though it wouldn't be once the students arrived. The summer humidity had begun to taper off. Best of all, at night, the Perseid meteor showers rained light and wonder from the sky.

Like all meteor showers, the Perseids emanated from streams of debris left behind by surging comets. But the Perseids hailed from the radiant in the constellation of Perseus, who severed Medusa's head, rescued and married Princess Andromeda. His progeny's progeny boasted Heracles, the most complete—and enigmatic—Greek hero of all. Perseus's legacy, then? Glory out of previous generations' wreckage. Celestial beauty out of that which was discarded, that seemed to have lost purpose.

We never know, she mused, how our discards, our pasts, can shape the future. She rolled down her window and let the air stream through her hair, wild and free.

When she reached the cutoff for the gorge, she turned left and parked in the lot. She gathered her tote, locked the car, and began taking the steps—carved out of sandstone and limestone and shale, once the bed of an ancient sea—to the falls. Their rushing sound called to her, even though they were not yet in sight. Halfway up, she turned back. No one was behind her. She climbed farther, and there they were. The falls. Their 215-foot plunge breathtaking, humbling. Their spray fresh, rejuvenating. She kept climbing, but when she reached the top, she diverted off the rocky steps onto a trail she and Jonathan discovered when they were undergraduates.

She found a level spot near the circle of stones someone had set there long ago to serve as a makeshift firepit. She cleared away some leaves, set down her tote, and opened it. She pulled out her small blanket and spread it next to the pit. Then she walked the nearby area, gathering kindling. When she returned, she used one of the larger sticks she had found to stir the ash in the pit where she and Jonathan, and many others, had built fires to snuggle by, to smoke weed by, to dream by. She laid the remaining kindling aside.

She reached into her tote again and removed the bundle of Jonathan's letters he had sent from Basic at Fort Dix, then from Vietnam. She loosened the red, white, and blue grosgrain ribbon she had tied around the pack and pulled out the top letter.

I got your last letter and wish more than anything you could have delivered it in person. I miss you—more every day— even though the memory of touching you and holding you is alive and well. I want you. Here. Now. Always. Everywhere.

She crumpled that letter, tossed it into the firepit's center, then reached for the next.

. . . here at Dix, I'm studying the land and vegetation of the far-off place called Vietnam. Where teak and bamboo, and roundwood for fuel, dominate the canopy. All inter- mixed, making harvest difficult, and cover easy for the VC, especially since their families have been working this land for centuries. They probably have it in their blood the same way I have Uncle Ned's pine and oak and the hills around the Tier in mine. But just because I know plants and trees and soil, and rain and sky and stars, and how to plant and harvest, doesn't mean I know how to kill . . .

Tears formed in her eyes. No, Jonathan didn't know how to kill. He was sent to do a job for which his childhood, living with his uncle Upstate, ill-prepared him. She never expected, when she saw Jonathan's demise in visions years earlier, that experiencing his death would hurt this much. She had known the ending for years. Why did it still hurt? She shook her head. The ability to see the future—what some might call a gift—was also a curse. No one should have to carry the weight of oncoming tragedy without being able to prevent it.

She wiped her eyes and continued through the letters.

> . . . *tomorrow marks the start of Tet, the Vietnamese lunar new year. That means a lull in the fighting. A lot of South Vietnamese troops are on leave and our troops are on stand-down, which we might enjoy if there were anything we wanted to do here.*

> *You are my memory and my future, Lela, my desire and my hope . . .*

> . . . *Quinn smells trouble. He thinks no one would screw with us that much without a plan in his back pocket. There's no way for us to find out, except to wait. But even when we hear, we're not sure we can believe what we're told.*

> . . . *Underground newspapers make their way to us. Last week one reported that a village called My Lai was wiped out by American troops. A massacre, it was called. To what end? Five hundred unarmed women and children were killed. Not exactly what I signed on for . . .*

> . . . *I know big chunks of my letters don't make it past the censors, but I write anyway. It helps me feel close to you, and feeling you near keeps me hanging on . . .*

> . . . *I don't know, Lela. I don't know anymore. Tomorrow I go to war. Again. But tonight, I go to sleep with the memory of the taste of you. And the sound of your name rolling off*

my tongue like the rain that falls through the night on the tent and rolls off in silence. Lela, Lela, Lela . . .

After reading each note, she balled it up and tossed it into the firepit's center. When she came to the last, she read the final paragraph three times.

. . . You're in my dreams, my love. My only hope is that my future is yours and yours is mine. When I come back, I'll write songs for you, and sing you to sleep under the Perseid meteor showers some thick August night . . .

By the time she finished the last letter, Lehanna knew, if Jonathan were still whispering to her, he'd say again, "It's time."

She set the smallest of the kindling on the crumpled letters, followed by bigger and bigger sticks, as Jonathan taught her the first time they came to this place. Digging into the bottom of her tote, she found the matches she had packed. She lit one, smelled the sulfur rising into the evening as it ignited. She touched it to the corner of one letter, then another.

She sat, mesmerized, as the flames stretched into the darkening air. She looked up. The sky was clear. A few stars glimmered. And there, from the radiant in the constellation bearing their name, the first of the evening's Perseids rained down their brilliant, affirming light.

CHAPTER TWELVE

Even when the skies were blue and the winds apparently calm, temperamental updrafts off the Appalachian Plateau, behind the Allegheny Front, often played invisible, cruel jokes on the small planes that flew above the Valley and Ridge to the east.

But the day Allison traveled home for summer break, as the sixteen-seater nosed south and west from Central New York, cumulonimbus clouds, swollen and threatening, rolled across the horizon toward the plane. The captain warned the crew and passengers to prepare for "a few little bumps," so Allison tightened her seatbelt and gripped the arms of her seat. She tried to distract herself by picking out, in the landscape below, places she and her mother had hiked. She spotted the boulder fields at Hawk Mountain Sanctuary and the hills that demarcated the Valley and Ridge province. She smiled when she remembered how, when Lucy pointed them out on their first plane ride together, she called them brontosaurus tails.

Farther west, Allison made out the Appalachian Plateau, where the atmosphere above the old mines still took on a yellowish cast. During a storm like this, the Plateau's sulfur smell would diminish, only to return when the blowing and rain stopped, and the air again hung still and heavy. The plane rattled as it dropped fast, then recovered. Sank again and recovered. Then the landing wheels groaned, fell from the plane's belly, and touched down.

"Home," she said to herself, even though it had been a while since MacMillan felt like anything other than the place she used to live. As the attendant lowered the plane's stairs to the tarmac, just as what felt like saucer-sized raindrops began to ping on the plane and splat on the ground, Allison wished that coming home felt more like landing safely in a storm. But lightning was cracking open the sky, and she felt inside as if she were breaking open, too, at the prospect of facing the memories that had been fattening up like hibernating bears before her return.

She had avoided going to MacMillan for Thanksgiving by telling her father she was behind in her schoolwork and needed to study. But when she sawed away at a toffee-textured slice of turkey in a Collegetown diner, accompanied by mashed potatoes that reminded her of kindergarteners' craft paste, she'd thought even a trip to MacMillan couldn't have been as torturous as her first holiday at school, alone. Christmas was better. She and Lehanna sang carols on the Arts Quad on Christmas Eve. On Christmas Day, they served dinner at a homeless shelter in Elmira. Still, she missed waking in the house where she had celebrated previous holidays, her mother's spirit filling the air.

On the cab ride from the airport to MacMillan, she knew that, even if she couldn't stare down the past, she needed to face the present and the changes that had been made since she left for Ithaca ten months earlier. Her mother was gone. Her father was, what? Involved? Was that how she was supposed to describe his relationship with Corinne? To her it seemed like lassoed would have been a better descriptor. But he was the Pulitzer-nominated author, the professor extraordinaire. Let him describe their liaison.

"That's it on the right," Allison said as the cab approached the house. She paid the driver a ten-dollar bill. "Keep the change." But, gripping the door handle, she sat in the taxi, staring, remembering.

The house was like many that bordered the campus on the northern edge of town: a two-story Tudor with a steep slope to the roofline and a stone chimney, built a hundred years earlier and modeled on plans approved by Mairead MacMillan. When she was little, it reminded Allison of houses in fairy tales, and Lucy told her once how it was not unlike the house where Rapunzel let down her hair for her waiting prince.

"Rapunzel's house was bigger, of course," Lucy said. "More the size of MacMillan Mansion. And it had a turret. And a moat." Minor differences, Lucy assured.

The weeping cherries, six of them, still lined the driveway. Degas dancers Lucy used to call them, because of how their frothy pink branches bowed in June breezes, begging applause.

"You all right, miss?" The driver, arm draped over the front seat, turned to face her. He had another fare waiting on Center Street.

She looked at him, disappointed that he had reeled her back to the dull gray day. "Yes. I'm fine." But she didn't move, so he pulled his cap farther over his face to ward off the rain, got out, opened the door, and held it for her.

"You want me to make sure you get in?"

"No, thank you." She smoothed her dress, Lucy's yellow linen shift, and checked to make sure her mother's seed pearl earrings were still clipped to her ears. Touching Lucy's things, feeling as if her mother were still present, she got out of the cab. "I'll be fine," she said. She picked up her bag and scurried to the front door to avoid getting too wet. When she reached the brick stoop, her stomach grabbed. She looked back for the cab. It was too late to catch the driver for a return trip to the airport.

The front door didn't open when she tried it. Lucy had always said MacMillan was the kind of place where you could trust your neighbors, so she kept the door unlocked during the day. But Richard moved back into the house after Allison left for school, and when she called home for money or to report her grades, she suspected Corinne was living there, too. The stone pot that held a miniature spruce, Lucy's hiding spot for the spare key, still sat on the porch. Sure enough, when Allison checked, the key was under it. She opened the door and went in. Maybe, she thought, she could pretend Lucy still lived there, but had just gone on vacation.

Once inside, she saw that fantasy wouldn't be possible. Too much had changed. The striped wallpaper in the hallway was replaced by peach color paint. Three smaller photographs of Corinne's two daughters and Allison hung over the fireplace where the portrait of Lucy and Allison used to be. She set down her bag and walked into her mother's studio, where almost a year earlier Lucy had spent her last weeks. The yellow walls were blue now, and pots of periwinkle-colored hydrangeas sat on the window seats. The hospital bed was replaced with a baby grand piano, and the smell of gardenia floated from a dish of potpourri on the mahogany cupboard by the door. Nothing even hinted that Lucy had lived and died in the room.

There were pictures on the cupboard, too. One of Allison at about seven, and one of Corinne and Richard in front of the decorated tree that had stood in the bay window at Christmas time. Allison walked to the pictures and lay them face down. She sat on the piano bench and looked around, feeling the unwelcome presence of another woman in her mother's house and in her father's life.

Then she stood and walked through the rest of the first floor, touching the walls, trying to get her bearings. First to the kitchen, all white now, and so bright she wanted to shade her eyes from the glare. An article from the *MacMillan Mirror* was stuck with a magnet to the refrigerator. "County Rides to the Rescue of Admitted Offenders." Reaching for the article, she read the first paragraph:

> *In many towns across America, people might have said that the problem was someone else's. But a group of concerned MacMillan citizens took the issue of rehabilitating admitted sex offenders into their own hands. The committee, headed by Corinne Kramer, social worker at the Center for Hope, is attempting to do what many municipalities have not wanted to: help admitted offenders make positive changes in their lives and communities . . .*

Allison put the article back, turned slowly and walked down the hall to her bedroom. She was getting there too fast, and not fast enough. She remembered the man and what he had done to her. She remembered how Lehanna promised that she didn't have to be a prisoner of her memory anymore. She stood back from the door, half expecting the man with the meaty swamp smell would leap out at her, *wah-wah-wah-wah*, like a gruesome, fun-house freak. Heart pounding, she opened then closed her clammy hands. Then she opened the door.

This was no longer her room. She scanned the bookshelves, full of gymnastics trophies and pictures of Devon, dressed in leotards, accepting awards. "MacMillan Girl Brings Home the Gold," one headline read. She walked in the room and lifted a trophy off the shelf where her books should have been. It felt as leaden as she did. But when she tipped it over, she saw it was hollow. Like she felt. When she heard the front door open and her father's and Corinne's voices, she replaced the trophy and went to meet them.

"You're here," her father said. Richard opened his arms and walked toward her. She stiffened but let him hug her.

"Allison, honey," Corinne reached to hug her, too, but Allison backed away.

"How was the trip, Ali?" Richard asked.

"What have you done to my room?" Her voice, crisp and cool, sounded as if she couldn't have cared less. She almost smiled when Richard and Corinne rushed to explain.

"We talked about it," Richard said, turning to Corinne for an encouraging nod, "and decided to give your old room to Devon and Stephanie."

"Your things are upstairs," Corinne chimed in. "In the guest room."

"The guest room?"

Chipper Corinne bubbled on about how they had *freshened* the room with a coat of paint and new sheers.

Allison nodded as if she were watching a Buñuel film. *Totally surreal.*

"Corinne's made it quite cozy. You remember the window seat? She's—"

"Cozy?" Allison crossed her arms when Richard and Corinne nodded and smiled. She turned and retrieved her bag from the hallway, then walked upstairs to the guest room. She closed the door behind her and tossed her bag on the bed. Before slipping off her shoes or relaxing into the admittedly comfy-looking pink-and-green-chintz chair placed just so in the corner, she sat at the desk.

She fished her address book from her purse and looked up the airline's number. The taxi company's number, too. She dialed both numbers and made reservations to return to the airport and to Ithaca the following morning. She thought about leaving the house right then and staying at the Laurel Inn for the night but decided she could bear sixteen hours in this cozy, freshened guest room that looked more like a room in a B & B than a lived-in bedroom. Sixteen hours and counting. Yes, she could do it.

She slipped out of her dress and laid it out to wear the following morning. Then she put on a pair of jeans and a tee shirt and flopped onto the bed. She reached into her purse for the lavender balm Lehanna had formulated for her. She applied it to her wrists and temples and breathed deeply.

"Ali?" Richard tapped at the door.

Now that she had a plan, she could better deal with him. "Come in."

When the smile on her face signaled that her mood had lifted, he looked relieved. "Well, you're settling in, I see."

"Not for long, actually. I'll be leaving tomorrow morning."

"Leaving? You just got home."

"This is not my home," she said. "Not with all this *House Beautiful* coziness." She waved her arm around the room, her face scrunched in displeasure.

"We wanted you to have space to yourself. And Corinne—"

"What's with this 'we' business? You're wondering why I'm leaving? Why this place doesn't feel like home when you've allowed her to strip it of anything, anything at all reminiscent of Lucy's quixotic charm?" As her words came out louder and sharper, Allison felt tears stinging her eyes. There was something behind her recalcitrance she could not say. A throbbing rage stuck in her chest and throat. *This is the place he raped me. And you weren't here to protect me.*

"I don't know what to say," Richard said. "We—I—wanted you to feel comfortable."

"Well," she said, calmer now. "I don't."

"Where will you go?"

"Back to school."

"What about money? Do you have enough?"

Lucy had left Allison a decent amount of what she called "fun money," which Richard apparently knew nothing about. "Oh," she said, not wanting him to know about her stash, "I'll eat Ramen noodles. And get a job."

Richard shook his head, suspecting Allison would do neither. But he had never been able to endure Allison's obstinacy for long. He reached for the doorknob. "Dinner's at six thirty," he said, closing the door behind him.

⌣

"We'd really like you to stay," Richard said when they sat down to the roast chicken dinner Corinne placed on the table. "We hoped you and the girls would—" He caught Corinne's glance that said *no-no-we-talked-about-this.* "Well," he shrugged. "You're certainly old enough to make your own decisions, and we'll respect your choice."

"We're disappointed, of course," Corinne said as she passed the spinach casserole.

Then why, Allison wondered, are you smiling? She took the dish and passed it to Richard while Corinne continued.

"Tell us all about your schoolwork. Is Rodney Peyton as compelling in person as he is on the page?"

Their plural pronouns grated on Allison. In her mind, in this house, "we" should stand for Richard and Lucy, not Richard and Corinne. And when Corinne said "we," she should mean her and her daughters. At least the girls were, blessedly, visiting their father and not "home" to further annoy her. Fortunately, Lehanna's formula had calmed Allison sufficiently so she could manage to tell them about her classwork and how Rodney Peyton had encouraged her to submit a poem to *Ploughshares*.

"That's a very good sign," Richard said, wiping a telltale green-spinach glob from his lip. "A very good sign, indeed." He sounded pleased, even enthusiastic. What Allison really wanted to tell him about was her work with Lehanna, but when he reached for Corinne's hand, her desire dissipated. Besides, she suspected they would question why she was monkeying with aromatherapy and herbs when her talents were in the literary arena. Instead of sharing much more of her life, she listened while Richard and Corinne flattered her too obviously, their encouragement as grating as it was synthetic.

"Dessert!" Corinne announced after she and Allison cleared the table. She carried a baking dish to the table and set it on a strawberry-shaped hot pad. "Your father loves his blueberry cobbler."

Allison looked to Richard. He always hated blueberries. They stained his teeth. But he smiled as he reached for the plate Corinne passed him. "This is delicious," he said when he took a spoonful.

"You're sure you don't want to stay for a few days, Ali? Just to catch up and spend a little time together."

Allison knew Richard was crossing the boundary Corinne and he had agreed to, but he proceeded anyway. At least he had the guts to try, she thought. But she said, no, she would rather not. She excused herself, went upstairs, and read until midnight.

The next morning, when Richard knocked on the guest room door, Allison pretended she was asleep. After Corinne and Richard left for work, Allison packed her bag, went downstairs for breakfast, and waited for her cab to take her back to the airport. On her way out the door, she took the article about Corinne's work with sex offenders off the refrigerator and put it in her purse.

⌒

"What a surprise!" Lehanna looked up from her paperwork when she heard the shop door open. "I thought you were in MacMillan."

"I was. For about a minute and a half."

"What happened?"

Allison looked at the basket of violets on the counter, stroked one downy leaf with her finger, then sighed, setting the stage for her dramatic recollection of her trip. "Okay," she held both hands out, palms up. "I know they're both adults, and they don't have to check with me before they get on with their lives. But she's living there. In my mother's house. In my house. And they gave my room to The Girls!

"They stuck me in the guest room. Which, I might add, is right down the hall from their room. I had to listen to them chasing after each other like teenagers in hormone heaven before they went to sleep last night. But what really made me sick was this."

Allison reached in her purse and held out to Lehanna the article she had taken off the refrigerator, the story of how Corinne was developing a program for treating sex offenders.

Lehanna took the article, read the first couple paragraphs. Then, with her head tilted in empathy, her eyes soft and a little sad, she looked up at Allison. "You're being asked to grow up very quickly."

"I'm not sure growing up means I have to lie in the room down the hall from theirs listening to their mattress squeak all night long." She made a sour, self-satisfied face. "But what really set me off was their plural pronoun usage. We this, we that. If I hadn't had that ginger formula you gave me to settle my stomach, I would have vomited."

Lehanna knew Allison was serious, mostly serious anyway, but she couldn't help giggling. Allison laughed, too, and minutes later they were both still blotting away happy, girlfriend tears.

"How," Lehanna started as she caught her breath, "how would you like a summer job at Artemis?"

Allison's smile signaled she was interested, very interested.

"Of course," she cautioned, "the pay will be only slightly better than what you'd get at a fast food place."

Allison waved. The money didn't matter. Lucy had seen to that. Learning more about the herbal arts and spending time with her mentor and friend—that's what she cared about most.

⌣

Late in July, one thunderous Monday afternoon, after a meeting with George Swenson, Lehanna breezed into Artemis, beaming. "Good news," she whispered as she just about floated past Allison, who was behind the counter, ringing up her customer's sale. When the woman left with her purchases, Lehanna held her arms out wide and wrapped Allison in a delicious hug.

"It must be very good news," Allison said, stepping away. "I haven't seen you this ebullient in a long time. Make that never."

"Ebullient." Lehanna repeated the word, playing with it as it rolled off her tongue. "I love that word."

"Okay," Allison said, taking Lehanna's arm and leading her to a chair at the marble-topped table. "I can't stand the suspense."

Lehanna sat on the edge of the chair, her gestures animated, her words rushing like a creek in spring thaw. "I don't know if I ever mentioned it, but Dr. Swenson was thinking about a fundraising event for Worldwide Health. Did I tell you that?"

Allison shrugged. "Not sure."

"Did I tell you he was hoping to get Jacques Merthin to participate?"

"No, that I would have remembered." Allison motioned to Lehanna to continue.

"He's the head of Worldwide Health. And founder of a ground-breaking clinic in Madagascar. Where I studied, back in college."

"I know, I know. Get on with it, will you?"

"Well, the symposium is scheduled for August twenty-sixth and twenty-seventh. First week of the semester. Jacques will be here on the twenty-fifth and leave on the twenty-eighth."

Lehanna had told Allison about Jacques's clinic in his native Madagascar, and that he and George Swenson were bringing new drugs to market, based on centuries-old botanical treatments. She also knew he had a reputation for manipulating people into feeling responsible or guilty enough to contribute to his efforts.

But looking at Lehanna, she knew the rosy blush on her friend's face wasn't just because Worldwide Health would be many thousands of dollars richer after Jacques's visit. "That's great," she said. "But why all the—" She stopped mid-sentence. "Ah ha." She nodded. "You're smitten."

Lehanna leaned back. "What do you mean?"

"Okay, now I'm hurt. Am I just another worker bee here at Artemis? If I were running around with a full-faced grin, getting a little too excited about some, quote, business associate, unquote, would you want to know what I was up to?"

"Well, I would, but it's not like—"

"It's not like what? You think I didn't suspect something when you told me about your visit to Madagascar?"

Lehanna shook her head. "Now you're totally off base. "I was crazy in love with Jonathan."

"Maybe. But that was then, and this is now. And this woman," Allison said, reaching for an antique hand mirror on a nearby shelf. She held it up to Lehanna. "This woman is enamored *today*."

Lehanna patted her hair. She bit her lower lip.

"It's not a crime to be infatuated, you know," Allison added, still not understanding why Lehanna seemed so reluctant to talk.

"Maybe not a crime, but it can be inconvenient. Under certain circumstances."

"Oh. Inconvenient, as in halfway around the world?"

Lehanna shook her head.

"Married?"

Lehanna nodded.

"Yes." Allison put down the mirror. "That makes things more complicated."

⁓

At the on-campus dinner for Worldwide Health Symposium volunteers, Lehanna hurried toward Allison.

"What's up?" Allison asked when she reached her.

"I want you to meet Jacques."

"Then why are you looking at me like my mother used to when I exceeded my after-school snack limit of two cookies?"

"Because," Lehanna said as she ran her hands down her velvet skirt to straighten it, "I know you. You're going to appraise him as if he's a prize-winning steer at the county fair."

"Come on," Allison said. "I'm not that bad. Here." She reached into her purse for her lipstick. "You need a touch up."

Lehanna stroked the Paradise Pink across her mouth, then handed the tube back to Allison. "Just don't ask him to open his mouth so you can check his teeth." She nudged Allison forward and led her to the other side of the room, where Jacques was holding court with a half dozen awe-struck student volunteers.

"It's a pleasure to meet you," Allison said after Lehanna introduced them.

Jacques smiled and took her hand. "Lehanna's told me how she can't decide whether your future lies in poetry or herbalism." He shrugged. "Either way, I suspect you'd make a fine addition to our team at Worldwide Health." Then he released her hand.

Allison crossed her arms. Something in his voice, or maybe it was the way his gaze had already shifted to a nearby group of donors, struck her as false, patronizing. Yes, the man was charming, brilliant, and the acknowledged leader in his field. But sincere? Capable of commitment to someone, something other than his work? Of that, she wasn't sure.

Her thoughts were interrupted when George Swenson arrived to escort Jacques to the head table on the dais.

"Very good looking," Allison whispered to Lehanna when they sat down in the audience. "But I'm wondering—"

"SHHhhh."

"Okay, okay."

Jacques took the podium, then, sparing his audience any preliminary jokes or soft introduction, got right to the point of his speech: the need to sacrifice for the sake of better health care outside developed nations. "There's no denying that jobs in developing countries often pay less than those in the States or Europe," he said. "But the impact we can make? The number of people we can help? The possibilities are limitless."

While he spoke, Allison looked from Lehanna, leaning forward in the seat next to her, to the man walking from one end of the stage to the other, engaging students, faculty and guests alike. He seemed quite comfortable with his celebrity and with what she imagined was a sizable salary. How many similar egoists had she been introduced to by her own self-consumed father? Allison leaned back, wondering whether Lehanna might sacrifice too much of herself in a relationship with this man who seemed like he hadn't sacrificed much of anything at all.

⁓

Allison looked up from her lunch menu when Lehanna swept into the Moonstone, not bothering to settle into the booth before talking.

"I have extraordinary news." Lehanna sat, shrugged off her cape and leaned across the table.

Allison stiffened. Her friend was altogether too chipper. She was trying to soften some important but hard-edged news. Just like Lucy on their last trip to the Laurel Highlands, when she promised a Secret Study Day for old times' sake, then told of her cancer and how little time they had left together.

When Allison leaned away, as if anticipating a blow, Lehanna tempered her enthusiasm. "You've come too far, haven't you?"

"Maybe not far enough. Tell me."

Lehanna reached for her napkin and smoothed it on her lap. "Swenson's arranged for me to work for a year, give or take, with Jacques. At the clinic." She paused to let Allison absorb the news. "They're close to another breakthrough in how plant-derived compounds can be used to formulate new drugs. Remember how Jonathan worked on the vincristine project when I went with him to Madagascar, way back in the sixties? And how he and Swenson discovered a way to extract the periwinkle's alkaloids to treat leukemia?"

Allison nodded but said nothing. She knew she should be happy for Lehanna, and excited about the possibility of new drug therapies. But as she looked across the table she felt as if Lehanna and their friendship were already floating away over the Atlantic.

"Well," Lehanna continued, "the plant with the most promise now is a shrub called *Sutherlandia frutescens*. It's traditionally used for diabetes, but now seems to have potential to treat AIDS."

Lehanna paused when the waitress came to their table. "We need a few minutes," she said. Then, after the young woman poured water for each of them, she continued.

"Anyway, George feels that, if I'm on site, working with local herbalists—*ombiasy*, they're called—work will proceed faster and we can move forward with other drugs, too. If Swenson can get patents approved, the university will make a lot of money, which means more jobs here and, more importantly, thousands of lives saved or improved. All around the world."

Allison leaned back against her seat while she tried to assimilate what Lehanna was telling her. Of course, saving lives was important. Especially with AIDS running rampant. And, of course, Lehanna should continue to use her skills and learn new ones. But her body tensed. She'd done months and months of her own work, but now she felt that, without Lehanna, she would slip away into her former, wounded self. That she was a child again, incapable of caring for herself. *I should be better by now, stronger.* She felt as if a hazy scrim were lowering between her and her friend.

Lehanna continued to explain why it was important to gather the data quickly, before the big pharmaceutical companies stepped in and threatened relationships with Haja and other local *ombiasy*. "That's what happened in India," she said. "Swenson was on the verge of a breakthrough in the Ayurvedic treatment for schizophrenia. Then Jackson and Winterberg sent in a research team that exploited local practitioners and the whole project fell through. Haja wants to cooperate, but only with Jacques and Swenson. And me. He trusts us."

"I trusted you," Allison barely whispered.

"And I trust you. Present tense." Lehanna folded her hands on the table in an attempt to tamp down her enthusiasm, to try to address Allison's disappointment, her fear. She had come a long way since they met and began her treatment. It would be important for her to continue her inner work and her herbal remedies when Lehanna left. Otherwise? Lehanna didn't want to consider the possibility that her friend would once again fade into a shadow of herself. "I'll only be gone about a year," she said. "And when I come back, you'll have a better idea of what you want to do and how you want to use your talents."

"I know what I want to do," Allison said, dismayed that Lehanna needed to be reminded. "I want to study with you. And do what you do."

"That may very well be. But no matter what you think now, when I go away you can test whether that's true or whether you're just trying to please me."

Allison glanced at the menu in front of her, then edged it away. She wasn't hungry. Not anymore. "I could go with you," she said. It was a long shot, but worth a try.

Lehanna leaned forward. "I didn't hear you."

"I could go with you."

Lehanna hesitated. "Madagascar is halfway around the world," she said, knowing she was speaking too slowly, as if repeating a lesson to a child who refused to listen. "It's not like saying you'll follow me to Chicago or Boston."

"I know where Madagascar is," Allison snapped. "You went when you were my age."

"I'm sorry. I didn't mean to sound patronizing. I'm wound up. It's just that I went to Madagascar with Jonathan. That was like going with family."

"You're my family. Almost, anyway."

"That's true. But you have your father, too. And your grandfather. Even Corinne and her daughters."

Allison shook her head. "I hope you're kidding. About the interlopers, I mean."

Lehanna reached to her friend, but when Allison pulled back, she saw how the awakening young woman was losing ground to the child inside her, hurt and scared. Still, she planned to accept the opportunity Swenson offered her. She tried again. "You sound as if people—me included—are punishing you, trying to hurt you, by following their own paths. People move on when they're called to, just like you will."

"I'm meant to be with you."

"That's been true for a while now." She shrugged. "In time, it may prove true again. Right now, though, I'm going to Madagascar, and you need to finish your studies."

Allison braced herself. "When do you leave?"

"In two weeks."

"So soon?"

Lehanna nodded, her foot tapping against her chair. "Like I said, we need to act quickly."

"Take your orders?" When the waitress returned to their table, Lehanna smiled, relieved to have a break from explaining herself to Allison. She wanted to get to her apartment to begin packing. "I'll have the Italian wedding soup," she said, though she no longer felt hungry. Allison ordered the same.

"This isn't something I'm doing to you," Lehanna said when the waitress left. "I'm doing it for the good of a lot of people, including me. You might discover—"

"What about Artemis?" Allison interrupted, uninterested in what she might discover or how she might grow or change when Lehanna left.

"I'll close it and set up again when I get back. Or I'll do something else. I'm not sure."

Allison leaned forward. "Do something else?" She shook her head. "That's just plain silly. And if you're only going for a year, why can't I run the shop for you?" She smiled as if she'd come up with a perfect solution. "I'm good enough with the formulas now. I bet I could manage Artemis with my eyes closed. Especially if you'll only be away for a year."

When Lehanna shook her head, Allison sat back. "The truth is," Lehanna said, "Artemis isn't as profitable as it used to be. A lot of people don't have the patience to wait for herbal remedies to work. They want speedy answers and speedier results. So, it's not only a possibility that I'll need to do something different when I return, it's a probability."

She leaned across the table and took Allison's hands. "Besides, the most important thing is that you have to find your own path. You've worked hard and you're strong enough to do that now. You'll be shown the way. I know you will."

Allison said nothing but sat taller. If Lehanna believed she could do what was being asked of her, then she could. She would.

If she had a chance at moving forward, she needed to remember what Lehanna taught her: she had a choice. She could choose fear, or hope, the past or the future. It was important for Lehanna to go to Madagascar. She knew that. And as much as she wanted to be, she wasn't the center of her mentor's universe.

"I've only got two weeks to get ready," Lehanna said. "I need to close up the shop, put some things into storage and get rid of others. And the most precious things, I'd like you to keep safe. Will you help me? Allison?"

"Okay." Allison's voice was steadier, her smile sincere. At least she had fourteen more days with her friend. "When do we start?"

Every morning for the next week and a half, Lehanna and Allison sorted inventory. The "Store Closing" sign on Artemis's front door drew in faithful customers and inquisitive new ones. When most of the merchandise was sold or donated, they hauled furniture and fixtures to the hospital thrift shop.

On the store's last day, Lehanna handed Allison two leather-bound folios. "Will you keep these safe?"

Allison knew they were Lehanna's most prized possessions, containing formulas and instructions for their use.

"They're too bulky for me to take," Lehanna said, "and they contain all you'll need to know if you really want or need to know more about my work."

Allison leafed through the first volume, reverently, touching the samples of plants, or photos of them, pasted or taped next to instructions for cultivating or harvesting them. Then she closed the folio and held it protectively. She looked up and smiled. "Of course I'll keep them."

When Allison drove Lehanna to the airport, she packed her a loaf of Lucy's banana bread and a thermos of orange spice tea. She kept her tears at bay by helping with Lehanna's bags, her last-minute passport- and ticket- checks. She hugged her friend and assured her she would study hard and safeguard her folios. Then she wished Lehanna well on her return to the Great Red Island across the Mozambique Channel from the African continent.

CHAPTER THIRTEEN

It didn't happen often. Maybe once a month or so, when Quinn was back in town for a weekend, or when he was between jobs for Lester, and he and Sherman went to the Bowl-A-Rama or to shoot pool at one of the dozens of bars that dotted the county's towns and back roads. Every now and again, someone got under Quinn's skin, and he took it upon himself to teach that someone a little respect. It might be a young punk who moseyed into a barroom and tried to force some girl's affection. Or someone new to town who figured he could help himself to a slight advantage at the pool table when he thought Quinn wasn't looking.

It happened again the night a heavy snow was making its way from Lake Erie in the west toward the center of the state—a newcomer came into the Elm Grove Tavern when Quinn and Sherm were shooting the breeze and some pool with a couple other regulars. He was looking for a game, the stranger said, and while he navigated his way toward the table, on thick, unsteady legs, Quinn judged that the man had a little too much to drink wherever he'd stopped before the Grove.

"Only problem is, me and my friends already got a game goin',"

Quinn told the man, whose gut swelled out enough over his jeans that he couldn't button his sheepskin coat.

"Well, the hell with you sonsabitches then." The man turned from the table, muttering as he set his course toward the bar.

Already restless because the late-night air hung too still as the snow approached, Quinn felt another storm brewing. Inside him. "What's 'at?"

"Guy's tight, Quinn, leave him be." Sherm took Quinn by the elbow and tried to steer him back to the table, but Quinn broke away. He set his cue against the wall, fixing to call the man back to reconsider his manners.

"I said, Fat Man, I didn't hear you. You wanna come back here and tell me again what it was you said?"

The man was already at the bar, signaling for the bartender to set his Rolling Rock and a shot in front of him. He elbowed Jared Johnston, standing next to him, and motioned to Quinn. "Guy must have a hearing problem." He laughed. Jared picked up his glass and made for a table near the back corner. If he hadn't turned quick before he sat down, he might have missed the action.

Quinn was already at the bar. He had the stranger by the throat, pinned against the pine-paneled wall half a foot from the dartboard. The man flailed his arms and tried to barrel his way past Quinn, but Quinn's rage was talkin', as Sherm liked to say when Quinn got in these situations. The man gasped and turned as red as his plaid flannel shirt. Then Quinn reached his right hand to the dartboard, picked a blue-feathered dart from it, and drew it across the man's throat.

"You're thinkin' I can't hear too good?" The man responded with a shallow, desperate gulp. "I ask you a question, Fat Man." The man couldn't make words, couldn't even nod as Quinn wedged his head against the wall, then brought the dart in front of his face. "Well, I'm thinkin' you might not see too good, once I accidentally jab your eye out. You still think I don't hear so good?"

The man tried to shake his head, but by then, Sherman had summoned help from a couple other regulars, and they pulled

Quinn off. "Get the hell out!" Sherm yelled while the men pinned Quinn against the bar. "You got ten seconds."

By the time Sherm counted out loud to eight, Jared signaled that the man was making off in his Ridgeline. Sherm dropped a twenty on the bar to cover Quinn's tab and escorted his buddy out the door. After they settled into his pickup, without saying anything, Sherm drove out Route 220 and pulled into the Denny's parking lot. Once inside, Darlene, the hostess, seated them in the booth nearest the door and poured their coffee.

"We'll think about orderin' afterwhile, hon," Sherm said. As soon as Darlene turned from the table, Sherm lit into Quinn. "You can be a stupid-ass son of a bitch." He stirred extra sugar in his coffee and looked across the table at his unrepentant friend, who was lighting a cigarette, acting as if he didn't know what Sherm was talking about.

"Don't look at me like I'm the one with the problem here." Sherm pointed his spoon at Quinn, then set it on the table. "You ever gonna do somethin' about this?"

"'Bout what?"

"'Bout what? You idiot. I'm talkin' 'bout not lettin' go of what happened nine thousand miles away over twenty years ago."

Quinn shook his head. "Quit your bullshit."

Sherm lit a cigarette, inhaled, and blew out an insistent stream of smoke. Then he pointed his finger across the table. "Look, I know you now since sixty-seven. Right?"

"Yep."

"And we been through some tough shit together. Right again?"

Quinn gave a grudging nod.

"The way I figure, if I can't shoot straight with you, I can't with nobody."

Quinn dragged on his cigarette to distract himself from Sherm's rock-hard gaze and the discomfort of what he suspected his friend was about to say.

"You can avoid the matter all you want, but you ain't gonna avoid me, 'cause I'm tellin' it like it is, man. I seen too many guys ruin their lives or somebody else's 'cause they was sufferin' and not doin' nothin' about it except takin' their pain out on their wives or their kids or some poor fat bastard in a bar. They got so much anger and hate built up inside they let it out where they got no business doin' so. You hear me?"

"Hell, I hear you." Quinn drank from his coffee mug. He looked out the window to his right, at the green and yellow Holiday Inn sign next door, to try to hide the sadness gathering in his eyes.

"Well, if you hear me, you got to do somethin' about it, and then you got to get on with your life."

"I'm over it all I'm gonna be. Like you said, it was twenty years ago. Give or take."

"Well, if the way you act is over it . . . Will you *look* at me?"

Quinn faced Sherm.

"If the way you act is over it, I don't know what the hell *not* over it looks like. We all did shit we're not proud of, man, but we had no choice. But you keep goin' on like there's somethin' you might'a done to keep that boy from followin' you. And you know damn well there wasn't."

"That's where you're wrong, soldier." Quinn pointed at Sherman, while the cigarette he held swirled smoke between them. "I coulda prepared him better."

"Maybe, maybe not. But his life wasn't under your control, any more than any of the rest of ours was. The sooner you start believin' that the better off you're gonna be."

Quinn straightened his back against the leatherette bench. He wasn't used to people calling him out. He was usually the one doing the calling. And he wasn't used to asking their opinions, because, for the most part, he didn't think they amounted to much. But Sherm wasn't most people.

"So, what you suggestin' I do?" Quinn swiveled his body from the table when he spoke and mumbled so Sherman wasn't sure he heard right.

"What's 'at?"

"I said, *damn it,* just what are you tellin' me to do?"

"Thank you, Sweet Jesus." Sherm raised his eyes to a heaven he wasn't sure existed. "The man actually can admit he walks and talks just like the rest of us humans." When he looked at Quinn again, he wasn't smiling. "I'm tellin' you to get yourself over to the Center for Hope. They got a program down there for vets. I know guys who benefited from it. You get yourself a counselor to talk to till you come to some sort of peace with what happened over there."

"You gotta be kiddin'." Quinn screwed up his face. "Sounds like the lamest-ass thing alive, talkin' to a counselor."

"Maybe, maybe not. But I'll take lame over bloodthirsty any day. I went over to the Center once or twice myself. Made a difference." Sherm yanked a napkin out of the metal dispenser, then scribbled a phone number on a scrap and passed it across the table. "Give this here number a call. Ask for Paige."

The next day Quinn picked up the phone to call Paige at the Center for Hope, then set it down again. He did the same thing three, then four times before he dialed the number and let it ring. When the receptionist answered, and he asked to set up an appointment for the following week, he swore his heart was pounding hard enough for the girl to hear it clear across town. His voice didn't sound right either. It vibrated, like the words weren't working hard enough to get out of his throat. When he hung up, he wiped the back of his hand across the sweat bubbled on his upper lip. "Pansy ass," he muttered, unsure if he was thinking of Sherman, for suggesting this, or himself.

⌒

On the following Tuesday, when he pulled his pickup into the Center's parking lot a little past four thirty, Quinn sat for ten minutes, tapping the steering wheel with his left hand, lifting a Marlboro to his mouth with his right. He forced himself out of the truck, walked to the lobby, and worked his way to the receptionist's desk. "How can I help?" When the receptionist spoke, tears stung the corner of Quinn's eyes. He wanted to run from them as desperately as he would have if a grizzly had snuck up on him.

"Darned if I didn't leave that insurance paper in the car." Quinn managed to smile at Shoshawna as he turned from her desk. "Back in the blink of an eye." He winked at her, then barged through the door, shutting it hard and loud behind him. *Can't do it,* he said to himself as he strode across the parking lot and got back into his truck. Then, out loud, pounding his steering wheel, "Jesus, God, I can't do it." He ripped off his hat and slammed it on the seat next to him.

The tears started in earnest then. He looked around to make sure no one could see him. He wiped his eyes. He had no choice. If he didn't get out what was stuck inside, he might as well have a cancer in his stomach. Besides, Sherm wouldn't steer him wrong.

He lit another cigarette, took one long drag on it, flicked it out the window. Then he set his Stetson square on his head and vowed he wouldn't cry again. When he walked back into the lobby, he asked to see Paige.

"First door on the left." Shoshawna smiled. She said nothing about the insurance paper Quinn supposedly retrieved from his truck.

He went where she pointed, even though his legs felt less reliable with every step. Then he knocked on the door to Paige's office.

"Come in."

He stepped forward, then froze in the doorway.

Paige rose from her chair and extended her hand. "Quinn?"

"That's right." He nodded and took off his hat, holding it in front of him with both hands. "I guess you're Paige." He had expected a counselor to look different somehow. She was in her forties, most likely. Not a bad-looking woman, with a gentle smile and a strong handshake for someone so petite. He couldn't pinpoint how he thought a counselor should look, but it shouldn't be like just another person going to work, doing her job. Should it?

"Yes. Paige McDaniel. Have a seat." She waved Quinn toward a couch. "I'm glad you're here."

"Thank you." He felt like a yellow school bus was parked on his chest. How could he breathe, much less carry on a civil conversation? Or, worse, reveal his secrets to this stranger, no matter how sweet and trustworthy she looked?

"You're a friend of Sherman Whiting?"

He nodded.

"Good. What can you tell me about why you're here?"

He opened his mouth but gave a self-conscious little laugh when words wouldn't come out.

"You said when you called that some things are troubling you from your time in Vietnam."

"That's what I'm told." Another nervous laugh.

"What you're told, or what you know?"

"Both, I guess."

"Good. Because if you're not here for yourself, because you want or need to be, there's no sense in wasting your time or mine, is there?"

He bristled. He expected Paige would be as easy to pick off as the little print flowers that circled the hem of her skirt. That it would be her job to coddle him into feeling better, not pull him up short.

"Is there?" she asked again.

He tried to get comfortable in his chair. He couldn't. "No, I guess not."

"Good." Her eyes softened, but her voice stayed steady and direct. "So, tell me what brought you here to talk about the war, now, when it ended two decades ago."

"I got in one fight too many. Or that's what Sherm says." He looked at Paige after he got the words out and knew there was more to say. "I . . ." His voice cracked. He swallowed hard and looked away. "I'm not sure," he stumbled, unable to make another complete sentence.

She leaned forward in her chair, clasping her hands around her knees. "I hope you know you're not the only one who's just now starting to face what he was made to do in that war. It was a terrible time in a terrible place."

When she threw him this lifeline, he breathed deeper and raised his eyes to look at her. But he needed more relief, and any words he might have spoken were stuck inside.

"Wherever you can start is fine," she said. "There's no right or wrong about how to do this."

He felt like he was stepping on a landmine with a kick as powerful and potentially destructive as any Bouncing Betty he had launched in Southeast Asia. Yet he knew if he didn't take the risk, knowing he had failed would be more painful than any loss he might incur, any limb he might lose, any death he might suffer. He took a deep breath. "He . . . he was just a boy."

"Who was a boy?"

"Jon Boy. Jonathan."

"What about Jonathan?"

He told the story. Of how he met Jonathan in Basic. How he and Sherm decided it was their duty to look after the kid. Then how he got the idea to rescue the captured pilot. How the strategy was his, the plan was his. And, damn it, the fault was his.

Paige listened to every detail, about the mission, Jonathan's death, his trip to visit Lehanna, his nightmares, his barroom brawls. "It was an awful war."

He squirmed. *Say it, damn it.* He wanted to yell it out loud. He wanted to get it over with—the certainty that this woman and anyone else would condemn him for not just masterminding the plan but, worse, for failing to execute it properly. But when she looked at him without recrimination, just a sideways tilt of her head that seemed to say nothing except *tell me more*, Quinn felt the weight on his chest lift a little. It didn't go away; it just eased up enough for him to breathe deeper. He clenched his hands and released them. Clenched them and released them.

"When you were planning the mission," she asked, "did you ever plan Jonathan's death?"

His look questioned her sanity, but he said nothing.

"So, you didn't intend for him to die?"

"'Course not."

"Did you plan on the fact that he would admire you so much that he would want to be as good a soldier as you?"

"But I wasn't—"

She cut him off before he could finish. "That's not what I asked. Did you have any way of knowing how much Jonathan wanted to please you, and how he might endanger himself and the rest of your team by doing what you did? What you told him not to?"

"No."

"And when you look back, from here, today, is there any way you might have prepared for that?"

Quinn shook his head. "What're you after?"

"For just a minute, try to imagine that Sherman planned the mission. That he came up with the idea to get you guys out of that hellhole. And try to imagine that he was still as torn up as you are today. Can you do that?"

He nodded.

"If the mission had been Sherman's idea, would you condemn him the way you're condemning yourself?" Quinn looked away. "Would you?"

"'Course not."

"So, if you wouldn't punish Sherman, why do you keep punishing yourself?"

Quinn looked at Paige without answering. He blinked back tears. A little yelp caught in his throat. A pathetic sound, he thought. When he tried to swallow it, it had a vile taste, and still no words would come out.

"I can't hear you," she said gently.

"Because it wasn't the first time." He turned his eyes from Paige and propped his elbow on the arm of his chair. With his forehead in his hand, he lowered his eyes as the tears ran down his face and arm.

"What do you mean, it wasn't the first time?"

"It wasn't the first time things was my fault," he spit out, then silenced himself abruptly. He shouldn't say anything more, but the storm rumbling in his chest was too powerful and impatient to contain. He closed his eyes and folded his arms across his chest.

Paige waited until he stopped shaking, then asked him to explain.

He told her about his younger brother, Tim, and how, when they were growing up in Kansas, their father came in after drinking, looking for someone to take his bourbon rage out on. How, when his mother was home, she tried to get between his father and Tim. Then how, when he was big enough, Quinn tried to fend off his father. But if his mother was out working, Glenn Gallagher usually went straight for Tim, because he didn't fight back, not like Quinn.

The last time Quinn saw his father weaving up the front sidewalk, his mother wasn't home. He took off out the back door and ran, not bothering to take Tim with him. He spent the day in the fields shooting crows, and when he went back home late that afternoon, he found Tim hanging from a rafter in the basement, swinging from a rope, still wearing the Batman cape his mother made him for Halloween. The note read *Don't let him hurt Momma no more, Quinn.*

"But I never had to worry about him hurtin' him no more 'cause I never saw him again. None of us did." He hesitated.

"I cut Tim down. Then I did things to myself, so anyone would think my daddy beat me, too, and they wouldn't think I just stood there and let Tim take it. When my mother come home from work, I told her how we both got beat somethin' awful and how I was knocked out, and when I come to, Tim was swingin' in the basement."

That was the day, he told Paige, he figured it would be best if he kept his distance from most everyone he met. To spare them the certainty that he would choke when the chips were down, that for sure he would fail them.

"I see."

"You don't look convinced."

"I'm just wondering," she said. "You were how old when Tim died?"

"Twelve, I guess."

"You were a boy. Maybe a little older than Tim, but still a boy."

"But I was supposed to—"

She held up her hand so she could continue. "And how old was Jonathan when he died?"

"Geez, I don't know. Twenty, twenty-one?"

"Older than you were when you were in Vietnam."

"A little older maybe, but . . ."

"But what?"

"He just wasn't prepared like I was. He was just a kid."

"So, Tim was a boy, Jonathan was a boy. But you were supposed to be a man who took care of everybody when you were twelve. Certainly, when you were nineteen."

Quinn shrugged.

"Why do you suppose that is?"

"'Cause . . . Just 'cause."

She nodded. "How about you think that over before we meet next week." Then Paige told him their time was up for the day.

He pulled himself out of the chair, relieved to have the ordeal over, but not sure he wanted to leave. Somehow the world was going to be different when he stepped back into it. He hesitated then went to the door.

"And Quinn?"

He turned back when Paige spoke.

"Our appointment starts at four thirty next time."

"Right. Yeah. Next week. Four thirty." He closed the door behind him, hustled through the lobby and into the parking lot. He got into the cab of his truck. It felt familiar, snug around him. He sure as hell felt different, though. Lighter. Like he wanted to listen to the Eagles instead of George Jones. "Next week, my ass," he said to himself. "I got this licked."

He lit a cigarette, inhaled, and reached for the door handle. But instead of closing the truck, he leaned out and wretched into the parking lot. Then he rested his head on his steering wheel, wishing he could sleep right there, for a long, long time.

It took a couple months for Quinn to believe what Paige tried to help him understand that first day: he was a boy as much as Tim was when their father ran roughshod over their family. And when he tried to assume responsibility for his unit's care in Ca Mau, he was even younger than Jonathan, who chose to disregard Quinn's plan.

But by the following spring, when Quinn headed to Scranton to work on a new library at Immaculata College, he understood that Jonathan and Tim weren't the only boys who had been abandoned. There was that little kid named Quinn, who worked so hard at taking care of everybody else he never noticed nobody was taking care of him.

CHAPTER FOURTEEN

Business boomed for Rusty in Pittsburgh when he landed there. Students at the 'Burgh's twenty-nine colleges and fans of the city's three championship sports teams proved to be faithful customers. But as May rolled in, students began heading home for summer break. The city started to feel too hot and humid and close around him. It was time to expand.

He set out with no destination, crisscrossing the state's highways and back roads—a day in Scranton, maybe two in Erie—careful not to travel the same route twice. The last thing he needed was some Terry Sullivan–wannabe sniffing him out, forcing him to shutter his operation on his way to the state pen.

With the help of a few greenbacks to grease the palms of like-minded individuals along the way, he changed vehicles every two or three weeks. But wherever he ended up, his customers all knew him as Red. And even as the denim jacket he wore faded to a ghost of itself, it still bore the name RED MAN on its back.

Once his operation spread across the state, as invisible yet functional as a spider's web, he hooked up with the owner of Miller's Gas Stop on Route 22, outside Duncansville. Working with Charlie Miller, he figured he could eventually set up a chop shop of his own instead of paying someone else for new vehicles every few weeks. In the meantime, Rusty set a cot and phone in the back of Charlie's garage. He stocked the refrigerator with Bud. Pumped enough gas now and then to give himself a legitimate look and laid low the rare times he wasn't dealing.

A few weeks later, on his way out of town for what he referred to as one of his sales calls, Rusty's Ram headed out Cedar Street, through MacMillan Tunnel. He sat forward in his seat as he turned onto Hemlock, then lit a cigarette when the truck, of its own mind it seemed, crawled onto White Ash. Part of him expected Susie, Hank Roland's collie, to dart out at his car and trail him, nose in the air, roopf-roopf-roopfing behind a cloud of dust, like she used to when he pedaled his Schwinn up and down the road a dozen years ago. He almost thought he might see Annie Roland, too, hanging out her sheets, a couple clothespins at the ready, calling, "Git back, Susie-Q, you hear?"

But when he reached the Rolands' place, Susie didn't run out and Annie wasn't hanging wash. A shiny silver mailbox glistened on its post out front with the name Johnson in red letters. Parked where Hank's pickup used to be was a Ford Taurus, with a self-satisfied looking tabby curled on its hood, sunning.

Rusty drove past and parked in a grove of pines across from where he and Lorraine lived before he left for Kansas, even though he had a pretty good idea his mother wasn't there anymore. He tried calling last Christmas, and on her birthday once. No one answered the first time; the second time the phone was disconnected. Still, he looked around at how nothing much had changed. Not for the better anyway.

The rhododendrons Nana bought for Lorraine—to try to give the place a little color, she said—still hadn't been pruned, and their gnarly brown branches knotted like accusing fingers of old hags. The mailbox still leaned to the left on its post, and the screen on the front door was still duct-taped in the upper right corner. The house's foundation had cracked again, proof the mines to the west were still settling even though most of them had shut down. The driver's side door panel was rusted out of the light blue station wagon under the carport, giving Rusty the surest sign Lorraine was long gone. Even if she'd hit hard times, there was no way in hell she'd be driving a car that wasn't red. Still, he waited. He wanted to know for sure.

Ten, fifteen minutes went by before the door opened and a young woman, about nineteen or twenty, came out. She was heavy-set, with long, stick-straight brownish hair, and she was toting a yellow plastic laundry basket under one arm and a baby dressed in pink in the other. A toddler, sucking one thumb, pulled at her mother's skirt with her free hand.

Rusty knew he should drive away. Instead, he watched them hobble to the car. Slow motion it was, the mother balancing that basket, that baby, the other child aiming to pull her momma off balance. Then the woman strapped her girls in their seats, set her laundry in the back, and drove away.

Rusty sat a few minutes more, then got out of his truck and walked to the stream behind the house. The water was orangey-brown, like when he lived there, and the sulfuric acid in it seemed to still be sucking the green life out of the grasses and weeds that lay dull and dry around its banks. He looked across the Plateau at how its surface was pocked with sinkholes and how the land beyond the Rolands' property line hadn't filled in with the scrubby little pines that had been planted there after the coal was stripped from it.

He started for the Ram, then picked up a stone near the creek and wiped its orangey residue on his jeans. He turned back and threw the stone. Glump! The creek was running low, the stone settling quickly, leaving no trace. Rusty walked back to his truck. When he turned off White Ash Road, he didn't look back.

⌒

After his crew left the site of the future library for Immaculata College, Quinn fixed himself a bed on the pullout couch in the construction trailer. He kicked back with a couple brewskis. The trailer was far enough from the dorms and the apartments in town that he could crank his stereo and not have his Willie Nelson or

George Jones infected by the god-awful stuff the college kids played. Besides, if he woke early, he could get to work an hour before the crew showed up at seven. And all he had to worry about anyway was work.

After Lorraine, Quinn tried again with a couple women. He even got as far as buying a ring for Roseanne Carmello. But in the end, he didn't want to hurt again, and he didn't want his anger to get out of control again, the way it had with Lorraine. Every so often, when the loneliness got so heavy he couldn't carry it anymore, he started thinking that a night or two with a woman couldn't do much damage. But when he looked into the eyes of someone who wanted him too much, when he smelled her coming on too strong, he ran for cover in his work, or into the fields he hunted or the streams he fished. When anyone asked wasn't it time he settled down, if he answered at all, he said that saving to send something every month to Cheryl and her kids was all the commitment he wanted or needed.

Lying in the trailer at the Immaculata College site, trying to get comfortable, Quinn debated whether it was time to break away from Lester Craig's operation and set up on his own. He folded his pillow in two and stuffed it under his head; running through the numbers of such a deal, he heard the rumble of early April thunder. He hoped to high heaven the rain would fall, then dry up by seven so his crew could start on time. But when he heard the rumble again, he felt something knocking against the trailer, shaking it a little. He sat up, reached for his Levi's, and hobbled toward the door while pulling up his jeans.

Quinn was still zipping up after he opened the door. It took a while to figure out if the shape up against the trailer was one body or two. But when a young guy turned his way, then ran, Quinn saw that a woman, maybe a girl, was on the ground, holding the side of her face with one hand, trying to straighten her clothes with the other. He rushed down the steps to see what happened, then scanned the area around the trailer. The kid who left was already out of sight.

When Quinn reached the girl, even in the mottled light that

filtered from the closest streetlamp, he saw that her face was bruised. Her dress was torn at the waist.

"What the hell? Here let me help you." He held out his hand, but she kept her face turned away. When he got closer, he saw that her hair had been cut halfway on one side.

She tried to get up and run, but Quinn caught her arm and steadied her. "No one's gonna hurt you. You're gonna be okay." The girl struggled until she figured she would be safer with this stranger than if she ran into the man who hurt her. When Quinn knelt to carry her into the trailer, he spotted a hunting knife sheath on the ground. QMG. Those were the initials carved into it. It was the one that went with the knife he left for Rusty that November, years earlier. He picked up the sheath, stuffed it into his back pocket, then carried the girl inside.

Even before he set her on the couch and covered her with his blanket to help her stop shivering, she started to whimper. "I can't . . . can't tell anyone. They'll send me home. Don't tell anyone."

"No one's tellin' anyone nothin'. How far'd he get?"

The girl looked up, not sure how to respond.

"Did he rape you?"

She shook her head.

"It's important I find who did this to you. I got reasons, more than I can say. You understand?"

She nodded.

"How'd you know him?"

"I can't . . . tell . . . you. I . . ."

Quinn saw a small plastic bag, filled with weed, stuck into her pocket. "You was buyin' dope?"

Her eyes looked as scared as a doe's, trapped, with nowhere to run. "It's for a friend. She made me promise . . ."

"Okay." He put his hand on her arm to steady her. "Let's me and you get somethin' straight. I don't give a damn whether you been smokin' reefer or not. I care you got hurt and that this guy might hurt someone else. I want to get him before he does. You understand?"

"It wasn't for me."

"I don't care who the drugs was for, and I'm not gonna tell the nuns or your daddy or anybody else. You gotta believe me, okay?"

She nodded.

"You know this guy?"

She shook her head. "I ran into him at Curley's Tavern, just off campus. He said if I met him out here at the trailer, he would sell me some good stuff at a fair price." She started to cry. "I paid him, then he grabbed me and wouldn't let go. When I tried to run, he cut my hair."

"Jesus." Quinn shook his head. He didn't want to believe the truth he already knew. "What'd he look like?"

"Red hair. Straight. He hadn't seen a barber in a while. Scraggly little beard. Skinny. Strong though."

"That's all I need to know." He knelt next to her and took both her hands in his. "You're gonna be okay. You just gotta clean up and get yourself a pretty new haircut." Quinn reached into his wallet and took out four fifties. "Now I'll make you a deal. You don't want no one to know about this, right?"

The girl nodded.

"Neither do I. So, early tomorrow you put some makeup over that bruise on your cheek there. Tie up what's left of your hair so as nobody sees what happened. Then you go get yourself a new hairdo and a new dress. Take this." He handed her the cash. "And stay away from that bar from now on, while I find who done this. I don't tell the school about the drugs, and you don't tell no one about that man. Deal?"

She nodded.

"Good. Now where you live?"

"Eagle Street."

"Okay. Not far. You get yourself home. I'm gonna be right behind you, far enough so as not to be seen, but close enough to do serious damage if anyone tries to hurt you. You hear me?"

The girl nodded again and brushed away her tears. She rearranged her clothes and her hair, then got up and walked out the door.

After closing down the site the following day, Quinn paid Curley's Tavern a visit. If he'd seen and smelled and heard one backwater barroom, he thought, he'd seen and smelled and heard a thousand. And this one, with its malt- and smoke-saturated haze, its salty chatter, and its honey-pine paneling, looked and smelled and sounded no better or worse than any other.

The crowd looked predictable, too. A mix of men who may or may not have scrubbed up after getting off from the nearby anthracite mines or gas stations. Linemen from Penelec. A few construction guys. Women who worked in grocery stores and dry cleaners and beauty salons, hair teased out, as if big meant beautiful, sprayed stiff and sticky as cotton candy. And those eyes! Made up extra thick with peacock-colored blues and greens, better left for exotic birds than humans, Quinn thought.

Then there were the college kids, shiny-haired and bright-eyed compared to the locals. Still too young to drink in Pennsylvania, legally anyway, most not seasoned enough for whatever trouble waited for them down the road.

Quinn ordered a Budweiser at the bar. Then he took a seat in the far corner, one that offered a view of anyone who came in, what they did once inside, and when they left. At twelve, he called it a night. He would come back the next night for as long as it took to find Rusty.

Two weeks later, around one in the morning, Quinn was in his truck in Curley's parking lot, getting ready to head back to the trailer, when he saw a young girl leave the bar with Rusty six steps behind her. Quinn sat forward. The boy had grown some—to about five-ten—but what he noticed most was how Rusty still walked with the same stiff gait he had when he was a boy, with his neck stretched out in front of him a little too much, as if that would help him get where he was going sooner. He was lean and taut and looked as ready to spring as a mountain cat. He wore a red bandana as a headband around his long hair. An attempt at a beard feathered his chin. His jeans sagged in the seat where his ass should have filled them out, and RED MAN was painted on the back of his faded denim jacket.

The girl walked to her car and Rusty went to his. When each of them took off down Main Street, Quinn followed. A mile or so from the center of town, the girl pulled over at the entrance to Highland Park. When she got out of her car, and headed up the hill, Rusty trailed and met up with her in a grove of lilacs, not yet in bloom. Quinn took a path to the right, then hid in a patch of holly, farther down the hill, but with a good view. As the girl took money from her purse to pay Rusty, Quinn threw a small rock toward them. Rusty pivoted, crouched close to the ground, and crept to the edge of the path.

The girl froze at first, her eyes momentarily fixed where the rock landed. Then she ran to her car and drove off.

Rusty worked his way deeper into the park and nestled in a pine grove, between two boulders, one big enough to shield him, the other low enough for him to see over. He listened. The gears of a diesel working hard to make it up the boulevard and a westerly wind, threading its way through the treetops, were the only sounds he heard. He waited.

By the time the moon started to lower behind the ridge, when he figured it was safe, Rusty circled to the left through a thicket of holly and juniper. Then he stood upright and walked back down the street, as casually as if he were heading to work an early shift at the bakery downtown. He made his way up Jewel Street, checked over his shoulder as he neared his car. No one there. He opened the door.

"Are you early or are you late, Red?"

Rusty spun around, saw Quinn, and froze. The muscles in his jaw tightened. His hands started working. He said nothing.

"Cat got your tongue, Rusty? I ask was you early or late?"

"What you doin' here?" He was one part incredulous, two parts defiant.

"Curious is all. What brings you to this part of the state?"

"I asked you the same."

"Well, it ain't dealin' drugs to college girls. Or gettin' in their pants uninvited."

"None of your business. That's what brings me here."

"I saw you two weeks ago at that trailer over to the college library site. Found my sheath where you left that other girl. The one you give a haircut to."

Rusty said nothing. His arms hung at his sides, his hands working.

"I don't see as how what I do has nothin' to do with you. You made that clear when you left years ago. And I wouldn't've known how to cut that girl's hair if you hadn't showed me how."

"What I done or didn't do don't make it right for you to hurt young girls."

"I didn't hurt no one. Now I got to get on, and you're in my way."

Quinn grabbed the car door and slammed it shut before Rusty could get inside. "You forget who you're talkin' to."

"I know exactly who I'm talkin' to, and that's why I'm gettin' as far from you as I can."

Quinn stepped closer, clenching his fists. "You leave and I'll report you. You hear me?"

"I hear you loud and clear." Rusty barged past Quinn, tripping him as he passed. "Like I said, that's why I'm givin' a wide berth." Rusty opened his car door and climbed inside. "Y'er the one that left." He started the car, then sped off toward Route 81.

When he looked back, he saw Quinn limping toward his truck. "Serves the bastard right," he said. South of Wilkes-Barre he picked up Route 80. Then he drove. All night. He took a break at a rest stop outside Bloomsburg. Then he drove farther, until he was so strung out, he no longer saw Quinn every time he blinked his eyes.

Back in his trailer, Quinn poured a glassful of Johnny Red. Rusty was right, damn it. He was the one who left. He could very well be the cause of Rusty's bad ways, no matter what Paige might say. But now he had a chance to do right by the kid. How that would work, he wasn't quite sure.

Reclining on his couch, he figured he had three choices. He could go to the police, try to find Rusty's mother, or hunt the kid down and beat the crap out of him. He was partial to that third option, which, unfortunately, might land them both in jail. He finished his drink, then checked the clock. Only a few hours until his workday started. Before he tried to sleep, he left a voicemail for Paige. If he could get an appointment to see her the following Saturday, maybe she could help him figure out just how responsible he was. Then he could make a plan. Meanwhile, he needed a little shuteye so he could keep his mind on business.

Quinn drove into MacMillan a little before ten, smiling as he remembered how his heart used to pound when he went to the Center. How afraid he used to be that, if he told the truth about what was going on inside him, the sky would fall, or the earth would crack open and swallow him up. Those days were over. Now he knew if he could keep his cool and talk things out, he would find a way to deal, not just with Rusty, but with the ranting doubts and screwball talk in his head.

When Paige walked into the reception area, Quinn rose from his chair and greeted her with a smile. "Good to see you," he said. Then, seemingly without reason, his stomach clenched. This was a mistake. He wanted to run.

She was already leading him down the hall to her office, but he figured he still had time. He didn't need this anymore, did he? He was old enough and wise enough to figure out why he was feeling what he was feeling, wasn't he? And damn it, he could make his own decisions.

When they reached her office door, Quinn hesitated. Paige was talking about the PTSD conference she just attended in New York. "The panel was terrific," she said. "And the new treatment modalities are going to help a lot of people. Have you ever been to New York?"

"What's that?"

"New York. Have you ever been?"

"Sherm and Jonathan and I made a trip in when we were stationed at Dix." He shook his head. "I guess I'm a little foggy bein' here." He laughed to try to shake off his jitters as he sat down. "This don't get easier, does it?"

"Simpler, hopefully. But easier? Not always." Paige pulled her chair to her desk. She pressed a button on her phone to forward her calls to the receptionist.

When she turned back, Quinn saw that look again. Like she had all the time in the world to listen to what he had to say. "What's up?"

He took off his Stetson, placed it on the table next to him, leaned forward, and got down to business.

"What I say in here's private, right?"

"Yes."

"I got your word on it? That anything I say stays between us and no one else?"

"That's true," Paige said. "With one exception. If what you tell me involves a crime, and you name the people involved, I need to notify the police if I feel someone might be in danger. But if you don't use names, and if you're not the person who's a threat, you've got my word."

Quinn looked away. He didn't want to see Paige's reaction while he told her his history with Lorraine—he didn't use her name—and her boy. How he felt like a father to the kid, so for a long while he was willing to overlook even the fact that she was running around with other men.

He turned back to Paige. "That was until the day she decided I shouldn't be teachin' the boy to hunt." He shook his head. "When she said that, the rage took me for a ride again. That's no excuse, I know. I went after her with a kitchen knife, roughed her up, and give her a haircut." He caught himself before making light of Lorraine's new hairdo. "When I came to and saw what I done, I packed up fast, as if my ass was on fire—excuse me—and left."

He told how he never went back, how he left the boy his knife and a rifle. And how, just a few nights ago, on his site up in Scranton, he came across the boy—"Hell, he's a man now"—and how the kid was messing with a girl and selling drugs.

"I coulda maybe saved him from endin' up where he is if I stayed. That's what's eatin' me up." He looked out the window again, at the parking lot where one car was coming in and one going out. "I want him to know he's responsible for what he done—just like I am. But I don't want him to end up in jail, neither."

Paige waited. When Quinn didn't continue, she spoke. "So, what is it you're thinking? That you failed him, the same way you felt you failed Tim and Jonathan?"

Disgust rose from his gut and out through his words. "Yeah, that's what I'm thinkin'." He almost shouted as he pounded his fist on his thigh. "I did it again," he said, his voice softer.

This, Paige thought, was the part of the job that nearly killed her sometimes. When she wanted peace and truth for someone so much she wished she could measure its ingredients as easily as if she were baking a cake. Mix them together, bake them, and hand them over on a platter to enjoy, digest, and be nourished by. What she told Quinn earlier—that the work often gets simpler, but rarely easier—was true for her, too. She crossed her legs, clasped her hands around her knees, and leaned forward.

"I can sit here and tell you that it wasn't the same with this boy as it was with Tim and with Jonathan. But where you are right now? I don't know if that's even important. The difference with this boy, this young man, is that you may be able to find him and plant a seed and hope that something grows out of it. And you can hope and pray that he'll want to change as much as you want him to. If that doesn't work . . ." She shrugged.

Quinn knew it was either find Rusty and get him help or go to the police. "Exactly what'll I do once I find him?"

"There are programs for people who want to straighten up," she said. "Even people who dealt drugs or committed sex offenses. If he signs up voluntarily, and stays clean, that would be considered. If he ever goes to court, I mean." She opened her desk drawer and rummaged through her files.

"One's been started here in town based on a program in Philadelphia. I thought I had an article about it in here somewhere, but I can't put my hands on it." She pushed the file drawer closed and turned back to him. "All I know is that it works for guys who want it to. And I mean really want it to. How about you let me worry about getting information, and you worry about getting your friend to come clean?" She made a note on a pad. *Corinne, program info for Quinn.* "Okay?"

He nodded. "Okay."

She smiled as the tension melted from Quinn's face. *Those green eyes. That killer smile.* She said nothing.

"There's somethin' else?" Quinn asked.

"Just that this may not be easy. Getting your friend into treatment, I mean. Like I mentioned, I'm not the expert in that field. But I know that for every hundred offenders, only three accept help unless they're forced to."

"You mean unless someone turns 'em in?"

"Right." She leaned forward again and nodded. "But that doesn't mean you shouldn't try. As long as you feel it's the right thing to do. Not because you think you can control what *he'll* do."

There, you're wrong, Quinn thought. He had ways of bringing the kid around. "I gotta try."

"I believe you do."

Quinn put on his hat, stood up, and started to the door. "I'll let you know as soon as I run into him. And I *will* run into him." He turned back, leaned against the door. Whatever he wanted to say was caught in his gullet, waging battle with pride, trying to work its way out. "I don't know exactly how to say this . . ." He looked down at his feet. *Damn, words can be ornery gettin' said sometimes.*

She tilted her head and smiled. "Are you trying to say thank you?"

Quinn blushed. "I guess I am."

She waved her hand, minimizing her part. "You're doing all the work. All I do is show up."

"That's all I ever wanted to do. Show up. But it never came easy to me. Not when people was involved."

"You started the day you walked in here and showed up for yourself. The next step is to show up for that young man." She wanted to touch him but checked herself. "Now get the hell out of here and find him."

~

Quinn whistled as he got in his truck. He popped a Patsy Cline tape in the cassette player, then started on his way out of MacMillan. But when he got to Route 220, he decided to circle back and stop at Lorraine's house. It was a long shot, but maybe, by some miracle, she had changed. Maybe she could muster enough concern to help save her son. When he drove through the tunnel to West MacMillan and turned onto Hemlock, his heart worked harder the closer he got. What if Lorraine *had* changed? Maybe they could work things out.

At the end of White Ash, though, his hope withered. The place looked pretty much the way it did when he moved in, before he fixed it up. It needed a paint job and more patching around the foundation, where it had cracked again. The rails along the porch were rotting now, too. And the side gutter hung down like a skeleton's long, bony arm. It wasn't likely Lorraine was driving the big old Ford wagon that was parked under the carport. She must have moved on.

He sat there for a few minutes, then he put his truck in gear and drove back toward the Three Bears to ask for word about Lorraine.

"Last I seen her," the bartender, said, "she was chasin' after a dude from Harrisburg. Sold insurance, I think was what Lorraine said he done for a living. Must've been two, three years ago now."

Quinn finished his beer, then left the bar and tried calling Helene Somers, Lorraine's best friend. Helene's mother answered, though, and said her daughter had married and moved to Florida. "Her Brian's playing football over to Jacksonville State," she said. "Quarterback."

Quinn humored the woman a while, then got off the call. He dialed Jackie Hochenberg, another friend of Lorraine's. "Last thing I heard," Jackie said, "Lorraine was up at Millertown. A wet brain is what she got."

A wet brain? That killed any possibility that Lorraine could help Rusty turn around.

Quinn hung up and rooted through the phone book for Millertown State Hospital's number. He dialed and when he asked to speak to Lorraine Jenkins's doctor, the receptionist told him that only family members could inquire about locked ward *guests*. "Guests?" Quinn caught himself before he laughed. He drove by the hospital many times on his way up to the Scranton site. The building was a hulking old brick place that looked more like a prison than a hospital. So, captives seemed like a better word than guests for the people that were locked up there. "I *am* family," he said. "Only family she's got except for her son. And I come all the way out from Kansas to see my cousin." When the receptionist transferred Quinn to the administrator, she agreed to let the slow-talking man speak to Lorraine Jenkins's doctor.

"It's called Wernicke-Korsakoff Syndrome," Dr. Crawford said. "Commonly known as alcoholic wet brain." The symptoms were memory loss, confusion, and uncoordinated gait, and in severe cases like Lorraine's, the patient's limbs became unusable. "Sometimes the dementia and amnesia improve with thiamine and abstinence from alcohol," he said. "But when they're advanced, as they are for Mrs. Jenkins, I'm afraid there's no hope."

"If money's the problem, Doctor—"

"Like I said, Mr. Gallagher. There's no hope."

CHAPTER FIFTEEN

At five, Quinn drove to Sherman's house, the little ranch that seemed more like home than any other he'd had. Always there when he showed up, in good times and bad. Before he was out of his truck, Sherm hustled out on the concrete steps.

"Man, you keep showin' up like a bad penny. Why aren't you on the site?" He held the storm door open and waved Quinn in.

"I gotta have your word you won't tell none of this to no one." Quinn tossed his Stetson on the couch and slumped down next to it. "Turn that down, will ya?" He nodded to the stereo.

"Must be plenty important if Patsy can't be in on it." Sherm reached for the remote and lowered the volume. "What am I not supposed to tell?" He spoke in an exaggerated whisper, trying to lighten Quinn up, but his buddy looked like he was trying to dead-lift the Allegheny Front. Sherm sat in his recliner and leaned back.

"I mean it now," Quinn said. "Not a word."

Sherm raised his right hand. "On my honor."

"I run into Rusty the other night."

"Lorraine's boy?"

Quinn nodded.

"And?"

212

"He's got himself sellin' drugs to college kids. Girls mostly. And tryin' to take payment any old way he feels like it."

"Now ain't that somethin'." Sherm hooted. "You the poacher takin' the high road. And if I'm not mistaken, you been known to smoke a little weed yourself."

"It's not the fact he's doin' the weed, damn it. It's that he's dealin' and tryin' to take advantage. He gets caught he could go up for quite some time."

Sherm shrugged. "You play, you pay."

"Yeah, but if I'd stayed and helped the boy, he might'a had a chance at makin' somethin' of his life."

"We talked about this years ago and decided whatever happened to the kid wasn't your fault. It was the mother's job."

"Maybe so. But now she's locked up at the state hospital with a wet brain. Had I stayed, I might'a made a difference."

"If I was you," Sherm raised one eyebrow, "I'd get back on the highway headed east and finish the job you started at Immaculata. Then get on to the next."

Quinn looked at him in a way Sherm had seen before—eyes hard, jaw set, eyebrows nearly touching. No matter what anybody said or did, Quinn would find Rusty. Sherm shook his head. What the hell, he'd go along for the ride. "If you ain't gonna listen to me, you can at least buy me a drink. Let's go over to the Millbrook and think this through."

They got in Quinn's pickup and headed out MacMillan Ridge, toward Hollidaysburg. At the Millbrook Tavern, they planned how they would go about tracking Rusty.

Then, for the next week and a half, every night, they drove the western part of the state, asking around about "Red." They got a few leads, but whenever they got to where Rusty was seen last, he'd already packed up and moved on.

⌒

"Pull in over here to gas up." Quinn pointed to the gas station, Charlie Miller's, that sat at the base of the Front near Duncansville.

Sherm steered his truck up to the pump. They'd driven through the night, north and west of Pittsburgh and back again, looking for Rusty, or at least trying to catch word of him. The last they heard, at a Goth bar in Johnstown, he was most likely headed for the MacMillan area, so they drove back east.

A light was on behind Miller's shop. Sherm pulled up near a banged up old Mustang and beeped the horn. No one came out, so Sherm got out to pump his own gas. When the pump didn't work, he called out to see if whoever was in the back of the station would come out. He got no answer. He jammed the nozzle back in the pump, headed around to where the light was shining, and banged on the door. Still no answer.

"Tryin' to buy some gas," he yelled.

"Closed," was all he heard in return.

"Can't you just turn the damn pump on?" Sherm reached into his wallet for a twenty, then opened the door to give it to whoever was inside.

"I said we was closed." When the door opened, before it slammed shut from the inside, Sherman saw the blade of a knife catching the light from overhead and the red hair of the man who was holding it. He saw the plastic bags of weed, laid out on the table at the far end of the room. And he saw the jacket, the one Quinn described Rusty wearing, hanging on a chair facing the table.

"Sorry." Sherm went around the building and got back into the truck. He started the engine, then told Quinn to slide down on the seat. "Looks like this here's your boy's headquarters."

"What you mean?"

"Unless there's more than one red-haired dealer in his twenties out this way, with a jacket says RED MAN on the back of it, we found your boy."

"No shit."

"If you was lookin' to give him a reason to see the light of day, you got all the evidence you need layin' out on his table back there. I'd guess his little stash—at least what I could see of it—is worth thirty grand or so. Now get down on the seat so he doesn't see you."

Sherm put the truck in gear. "I'll drop you off in that stand of pines just beyond the station. Then I'll drive farther up the road and park while you work your way back. After I circle to the right, you come in from the left. He's got a knife and I don't know what else."

"Well, I just happen to have one, too," said Quinn, adjusting the rawhide strap on the sheath Rusty had left outside Lester's trailer. "You take the Winchester."

Quinn stepped from the truck and slipped into the pines, moving just inside the shadow of the trees. Meanwhile, Sherm eased his truck down the road and parked. He got out, closed the truck door quietly, and circled back. When they were both in position, Sherm signaled to Quinn. They closed in on the station, Sherm from the right, Quinn from the left. Ten feet from the building, Sherm shot out the yard light and Quinn charged the door, ramming it with his shoulder. It didn't give, but he heard movement inside. Quinn went around to the front of the building while Sherm knocked out a rear window. When Rusty ran to the front and tried to get out through the garage door, Quinn jumped him from behind and wrestled him to the ground while Sherm came around from out back.

"What the hell?" Rusty tried to squirm away, but Quinn was already tying his hands behind his back while Sherm worked rope around his ankles. "You get your sonsabitchin' hands off me."

Quinn held his knife against Rusty's neck. "You're comin' with us, or we call the state police." The knife cut below his ear and a thin red line slid down to Rusty's collarbone. "Your choice."

Rusty spit. He said nothing. Sherm went for the truck while Quinn stood guard. They propped Rusty in the cab and bound him to the gun rack behind him.

"I'll go find his keys, pack up the weed, and get that Mustang to Salvatore's shop so he can chop it tomorrow," Sherm said. "Meet me there in ten." Tomorrow, he figured, he would call Sal and tell him to dispose of it and any evidence inside.

"You ain't takin' my car," Rusty called, squirming to try to undo the ropes that bound him.

"'Fraid we are," Quinn said as he started the ignition in Sherm's truck. "The easiest thing for you to do now is just settle down and accept the fact you're not in charge here."

After Quinn picked up Sherm at Salvatore's, they drove to Sherman's house. They shuffled Rusty inside, setting him on a kitchen chair with his hands and feet still tied. Sherm poured Wild Turkey, double shots all around.

Quinn pulled a chair up to Rusty's and drank down his bourbon. "We're gonna make you a deal," he said. "We know what you're up to, and we figure you got two choices. One is to do what we say. The other is for us to turn you in."

Rusty looked from one man to the other. "What you done with my money?"

"Your money?"

"The pile of it on my table back at the station."

"Oh, that money." Sherm laughed. "We figured that was our tip for gettin' you out of the hole you gone and dug for yourself."

Rusty eyed the door.

"So," Quinn said, "now that you don't need to worry about your money, maybe you wanna think a while about your choices." Quinn turned toward Sherm. "We got time while he thinks, don't we Sherm?"

"Hell, yeah. How about a ball game?"

"Sounds good to me," Quinn said.

Sherm went to the living room and turned on the television. "Bulls is up by six."

"How much time left?" Quinn asked.

"Five minutes to the half."

Quinn turned to Rusty. "Knicks got plenty of time, too, don't they?"

Rusty kicked the floor with his boot. He said nothing.

Sherm rifled through a cupboard over the counter and pulled out a cellophane-wrapped packet. "How about I microwave us some popcorn?"

"You got the natural or butter flavored?" Quinn asked.

"Natural."

"Good. I don't like that fake butter. I like to melt my own on it." Quinn turned to Rusty. "Rusty, you care for popcorn?"

Rusty glared.

"Guess he don't want none, Sherm. Just make up the one pack."

Sherman pressed the buttons on the counter microwave. "Says not to leave this unattended while cookin'. You'll keep an eye on it, right?" He looked toward Rusty. "Unless you got plans to go somewhere."

When the popcorn stopped popping, Sherm poured it into a bowl. Quinn and Sherm ushered Rusty into the living room, watched the rest of the game, then decided they'd take shifts guarding their captive through the night. Sherm sacked out first. While Quinn grabbed a beer and turned on the late news, he heard Rusty mumble, so he pointed the remote at the TV to lower the volume. "What's 'at?"

"I said I went lookin' for you."

"Where to?"

"Kansas."

"Where at in Kansas?"

"Chautauqua County. Figured I'd find you huntin' whitetails."

Quinn shook his head. "I stayed right here in Pennsylvania. Except for when I first left your mother's house. I went back to see my sister and her kids." He tilted back his beer. "You get anything to speak of?"

"I got plenty. One rack the size of your pickup. Woulda won me a national record had I got it legal."

"That so? How long you out there?"

"Just long enough to avoid that sonofabitchin' warden."

"Who's that?"

"Terry stick-it-up-his-ass Sullivan, that's who."

Quinn sat forward. "So, the Sullivan boy's walkin' in his father's footsteps." He shook his head. "His father was a helluva guy. Woulda made a good friend if he hadn't sent my father to jail. And if we saw eye-to-eye on certain legal technicalities.

"Truth is, Rusty, I never got half the trophies I told you I did. I made 'em up so you'd think I was some big shot I wasn't."

Rusty's eyes narrowed.

"So, here we are, lookin' each other—and the truth—straight on." Rusty glared when Quinn stood and pointed a finger in his face. "You got a chance to do somethin' with your life. Here and now. You hear me?"

Rusty said nothing.

"I ask, did you hear me?"

"Hell, I heard you." Rusty turned away when he heard his voice go soft. "I went after you all those years."

Quinn put his hands on his hips. "I admit it. I was wrong to leave you when I knew your mother couldn't care for you. But I can't do nothin' about the past. Like I told you when we was huntin', you miss a shot, you can't go pissin' and whinin'. You set yourself up for the next. The way I see it now, we got an opportunity here, both of us, to make a new life." He hesitated. "You willin' to try?"

When his lower lip trembled, Quinn knew which way the boy would go. But he needed to make sure Rusty knew he meant business. "Sit and think about it a while." He turned and went to the kitchen for another beer. "And just so you know, you double-cross me, I go straight to the authorities and you go up."

⌒

The next morning, Quinn made breakfast while he told Rusty about the program at the Center for Hope. "It's called Viewpoint," he said, "and it's part of our deal."

Rusty knew Quinn would turn him in if he didn't go straight, but that didn't mean he was about to do every damn thing the big-shot bully wanted. He took a couple sips of coffee through the straw Quinn put in his mug, so he could drink without being untied. "I admit I done what you said," Rusty told him. "Some of it anyhow. And I'll stop."

"And just how is it you plan to stop?"

"By not doin' it, that's how. Now, untie these damn ropes."

Quinn had planned on some back and forth before Rusty gave in. Both Paige and Corinne Kramer, from the Viewpoint sex offender program, warned him about that. Just because Rusty felt up against it, they said, didn't mean he could change unless he got help.

"Maybe I didn't make myself clear the first time," Quinn said. "You don't do the program, we got no deal."

"Okay," Rusty said while he tried to wriggle free of the ropes that held him. "I'll go."

"Go where?"

"To your damned program, that's where."

Quinn smiled. "That's good. Real good. And just to make sure you're certain, why don't you think about it overnight. In case you got any doubts."

The next morning, when Rusty told Quinn once more that he would go to the program, Quinn brought the phone to him and dialed the Center's number. He told Rusty who to ask for, then wedged the phone between his ear and shoulder.

"I want an appointment with Corinne Kramer," Rusty said into the phone. When Quinn took the phone back, Rusty said Corinne would see him Monday afternoon.

Quinn untied him, and after Rusty rubbed his hands to get circulation back, he scowled while he shook Quinn's outstretched hand.

"You up for a hike?" Quinn asked.

"Where to?"

"Hawk Mountain."

"I guess," Rusty mumbled.

"Well, don't do me no favors."

"I said I'd go, now I gotta take a piss."

When Rusty left the room, Quinn caught the boy's smile, the first hint that their arrangement really might work.

Quinn packed a couple meatloaf sandwiches, a few apples, and a six pack in his Coleman cooler. Then he and Rusty hopped into the Silverado and headed toward Altoona.

"We goin' out 220?" Rusty asked.

"Till we pick up 80," Quinn said. "We got a good three hours ahead of us if you want to catch a snooze."

Rusty shook his head. "I ain't tired."

Rusty looked out the window, Quinn thought, as intently as when he was a kid. When they used to drive east to Hawk Mountain Sanctuary to see the raptors catch the updrafts over River of Rocks Trail.

"Feels good, don't it? Gettin' out on the road, I mean."

Rusty kept his eyes on the landscape. "I guess."

"You know," Quinn said, "there's a history to this place we're goin' to."

"The sanctuary?"

"That's right." Quinn pushed in the lighter on the dashboard. He reached into his vest pocket and pulled out a pack of cigarettes. "Care for one?"

Without speaking, Rusty reached for a smoke and lit it. "It used to be, way back, in the twenties and early thirties," Quinn said, "the eagles, falcons, hawks—even the red-tailed ones that was your favorite when you were a kid—they was considered fair game."

"They wasn't protected like now?" Rusty looked across the bench seat when Quinn shook his head. "Why's 'at?"

"People thought they was pests, when they was just doin' their job, keepin' down rodent and insect populations. Anyway, back then if a man shot one down, he'd get paid five bucks."

When Rusty shrugged, Quinn figured five dollars meant nothing to a kid who was used to taking in thousands a night dealing weed. "Doesn't sound like much now, but back then, when folks was sufferin' from the Depression, five dollars meant a man could feed his family for a couple days.

"Anyway, a woman out of New York—her name was Rosalie Edge—she got wind of what was goin' on. And she come up with enough cash to lease fourteen thousand acres where the birds was gettin' killed. Later she bought all twenty-six thousand acres." Quinn shook his head. "That's some woman, huh?"

Rusty nodded but warily. Quinn was about to make a point.

"The birds're safe now, doin' what they're supposed to do, not strayin' from their purpose. They're at home."

Rusty rolled down his truck window and tossed out his cigarette. Maybe Quinn would say that he was home now, too, that they could be a family, like he always wanted. He looked to the hills so Quinn wouldn't see the hope in his eyes.

"All I'm sayin'," Quinn said, "is you wasn't meant to be no predator, Rusty. You made some real bad choices along the way. Nobody taught you right. But that's no excuse." He handed a pair of binoculars to Rusty. "Here," he said. "Take a look."

Rusty took the binoculars.

"What I mean is you're home now. Just like those raptors." He pointed to a vee formation of red-tails, coming back to the sanctuary. From the Carolinas, no doubt. "So long as you get in line and stay there. Just like those birds." He pointed overhead. "You with me?"

Rusty shrugged. "Maybe, maybe not." He kept his eyes on the red-tails.

"Gimme those damned things." Quinn grabbed the binoculars. "Well, I'm sorry for tryin' to help you make somethin' of yourself. Now look at me. You with me or not?"

Rusty dug his hands into his jeans' pockets. "I guess," he said.

"Okay, that's a start. Now let's figure out how you're gonna cut loose of that connection in Minnesota."

⁓

As Rusty cleared the kitchen table Monday after lunch, Quinn called over his shoulder. "I'll drive you soon as I clean up."

Rusty stacked the dishes in the sink, then ran a wet rag over the table. He would go to the damn appointment, but he didn't want company. It was humiliating enough to go in the first place. "I'd rather handle this myself." He threw the rag into the sink. With his decision made, he went to the hall closet and took out his jacket.

Quinn tucked his clean shirt into his jeans, zipped his fly, cinched his belt. "Well, I think I'd rather you don't handle it by yourself."

Rusty threw his jacket on the kitchen table, set his hands on his hips, working up to a standoff. "You sayin' you don't trust me?"

"I absolutely don't trust you." Quinn stopped at the hall mirror, ran a comb through his hair. The subject was not open to negotiation. "No use workin' yourself up over this. We both got a good bit of past to undo between us. Until then, I'm gonna do my share to make sure you get off on the right foot."

"Well, shit, Quinn, I don't trust you, neither." Rusty pulled on the new denim jacket Quinn bought him and stormed out the door. When Quinn yelled after him to quit acting like a child, Rusty kept on going. He'd walk if he had to. He took off toward the tunnel. When Quinn caught up to him a few minutes later in the truck, Rusty kept on walking while Quinn idled. "Git in."

"I'm not a damn infant," Rusty yelled back, ashamed he couldn't even drive himself across town. But when Quinn continued to follow, Rusty grabbed the door handle while Quinn kept driving. "You can at least slow down enough for me to hop in, you bastard."

Quinn stopped the truck and Rusty jumped in. Once they turned down Midland Avenue and he saw the Center up on the right, Rusty thought about what getting into treatment might mean. And when the knot in his stomach tightened up even more, he decided it wasn't so bad having Quinn along after all.

"What kind of program is this exactly?" he asked when they pulled into the parking lot.

"Not sure." Quinn kept his voice cool. Even. Like they were driving to the grocery, deciding whether to buy hamburger or hot dogs. Deep down he was in knots, too. "I just heard it's helped other men who got your same situation."

"My situation?"

"Men with problems takin' advantage of women."

"Hell." Rusty lit a cigarette. He thought about bailing out of the truck, catching a train out of town. He could set up again in

Pittsburgh or back in Minnesota. Anywhere but this place where everything was pressing in so close. But he knew Quinn would rout him out, or worse, turn him in. When he considered that the state pen was the next stop after that, he thought maybe it wouldn't be so bad, getting into a program. So long as Quinn was around.

Inside the lobby, Rusty asked the receptionist if he could see Corinne Kramer. Then he flopped into a seat next to Quinn. He leaned back and stretched his legs out in front of him, nice and casual, not a care in the world.

When Corinne walked in, Rusty sat up. Maybe, he decided when he felt his heart pounding, he had to go to the men's room. And maybe if he just hung out there, she'd get tired of waiting for him and move on to the next poor bastard, someone who really needed help.

"Ronny Lee Jenkins?" Corinne held out her hand to Rusty, the bracelets on her wrist tinkling, her blue eyes sparkling. She might as well be wearing a fluffy pink ballgown, carrying a bouquet of roses. Miss Mental Health. What she was doing with men like him, he had no idea.

Quinn stood and nudged him to get out of his chair and shake the woman's hand, but Rusty gave them both a puzzled look. He wasn't used to shaking any woman's hand. He felt his jaw working, the way it always did when he got riled. Eventually he stood and held out his hand to Corinne.

Quinn put his hand on Rusty's shoulder. "I'm waitin' for you right here."

How much worse, Rusty wondered as he trailed Corinne down the hall, could the state pen be? No more humiliating, that's for sure.

Once in her office, Corinne turned down the volume on the stereo. Some high-pitched Irishwoman's voice ooh-ing to harp music. Rusty figured it was supposed to be relaxing, but it grated on him. And those posters! Overgrown pictures of sunsets and footprints in the sand.

He took one of the cushy chairs then listened to her go on about how she understood he had a history of what she called sexual violence. He wanted to get everyone, including her and Quinn, off his back, so he nodded when she spoke. When she asked how many women there had been, he said one or two. "'Course there's others who've wanted to be with me." He didn't want her thinking he had been with only two women his whole life.

She nodded, waiting for him to say more. When he didn't, she told him about the Viewpoint Program, how each week for a year he would meet with a counselor and attend a group as well.

"A group of what?"

"A group of men like yourself who have offenses against women. Most have served time in prison." She hesitated. "You're one of the lucky ones, Mr. Jenkins."

Lucky as a pig in shit, Rusty thought.

Most offenders, she went on, didn't have someone like Quinn who cared enough to help them before they were facing five or more years behind bars. "So, we help their friends and families, too."

Rusty wondered how, if turning someone in was caring about him, what was not caring. "I don't mind speakin' to one person." He leaned forward in his chair. "I admit I done some things, and that I don't care to go up on account of 'em. But I don't see how talkin' with a bunch of sick sonsabitches'll help."

Corinne waited until Rusty went on about how it was the girls' fault anyway, how he wouldn't have done anything to hurt anyone if he hadn't been provoked, and how he didn't plan on doing anything anymore.

"Ron," she said, that high school prom-queen smile still pasted on her face like a postage stamp. "May I call you Ron?"

Rusty gave a grudging nod.

"If a man with a problem doesn't understand why he did things to begin with, and if he doesn't learn new ways to act, the behavior repeats, the damage gets worse, the stakes increase, and so do the prison terms."

Rusty figured Miss Mental Health had a point. "Still and all," he conceded, "I'll talk to one person, but not to any group."

He could start with three counseling sessions, she said. After that, when he took a polygraph test, he could decide whether to attend the group.

Rusty got the distinct feeling she didn't really mean it when she said he had a choice. He'd have to put his foot down but not get too pushy. The last thing he needed was Quinn leaning on him for that, too.

"Polygraph tests is for criminals."

"That's true," she said. "But, in this case, they're for men who want to stay out of prison. Sometimes it takes a while for men in treatment to uncover everything they did in the past. The polygraph helps them remember. And it gives us a baseline to work from."

Baseline! What was this, the World Series? Rusty shifted in his chair. "Look." He stood up, stuffing his hands in his pockets. "I'll sign on for the three sessions with the counselor." He rocked back on his heels, then forward again. "Period."

She kept smiling. "Your counselor's name is Vance Carmichael." She wrote the time and date of Rusty's next appointment on a little white card, handed it to him, then glanced at the clock on the table next to Rusty. "We still have a few minutes. Would you like to sit or stand?"

"Stand."

She told him about the family program and how the success rate for offenders with family involved was higher than for men who tried the program on their own.

"Only family I got is sittin' in the state hospital over to Miller-town. Her brain's pickled in Four Roses and Chardonnay."

"Your mother?"

He nodded.

"What about Quinn?"

"He ain't family."

"Family doesn't have to mean blood relatives. You'll learn how to create a new one while you get on with your life."

When he didn't respond, Corinne changed the subject. "What do you do for work?"

He slumped back into his chair. "When I was in Kansas, I poached whitetail deer and sold racks on the black market. Other than that, all I done was deal weed and pump gas."

"I see." She nodded and smiled when she saw Rusty's brashness begin to fade. "We think structure's important. A job. Volunteer work. Anything constructive that will help a man set down roots and keep busy."

What did she expect him to do, volunteer at the YMCA teachin' kids how to poach or deal?

"How are you at fixing things?"

He shrugged. "Long as it's made of metal, I can make it work."

"Good." Corinne reached for a pen and paper then leafed through her Rolodex. "We know employers who help men get started when they're trying to turn their lives around." She wrote a name and number on a paper and handed it to Rusty. "Give Bud Johnson a call. He'll be waiting to hear from you." Then she told him their time was up for the day, and that he could meet with Vance the following week.

Rusty sprang out of his chair. He stuffed the paper and business card in his pockets. He'd toss them out later. Then he tore out of the office and through the reception room without so much as nodding in Quinn's direction. He bolted through the parking lot. When Quinn caught up, he was already in the truck, window rolled down, his arm propped out the door. "Don't even ask."

CHAPTER SIXTEEN

A week later, when Rusty walked into Vance Carmichael's office, he met his counselor's handshake with wary eyes and a lukewarm grasp. From the size of the guy, Vance looked to be a past-his-prime lineman who hadn't made the cut at the Steelers' training camp. Rusty didn't ask if that was the case. Who the man was or wasn't didn't matter two cents, except that he might help Rusty get the world off his back.

Vance motioned to a chair in front of his desk. Rusty sat, propped his forearms on the chair's arms, and leaned forward, positioning himself to run like hell if the next fifty-nine minutes felt too close or confining. At least there wasn't any of that sugar-sweet harp music in this guy's office like there was at Corinne's. And no pastel posters. Just a gray metal desk, a couple of chairs, and a big old clock on the wall. Tick tock. Tick tock.

"This your first time in this kind of situation, Ron?"

"If you mean was I ever in a counselor's office, the answer's no."

"Well, I can assure you it's a heck of a lot more comfortable than prison."

Rusty's jaw muscles worked while he felt the screws being put to him.

"I know from experience," Vance said in an off-the-cuff way as he took a form from his desk drawer and clamped it to a clipboard. "Before we get started, I'm gonna ask you to fill this out." He handed Rusty the board and a pen. "While you're doing that, I'm gonna get some coffee. Care for some?"

"No, I don't care for none."

"You're welcome."

Rusty looked up, wondering why Vance said that when he hadn't thanked him for anything. "You want somethin' from me?"

"What I want," Vance said, "if you plan on joining our program, is for you to think about brushing up on your manners. We're big on the important things, like please and thank you."

Rusty didn't care much for this big shot, but given the size of the man, he wasn't about to refuse him. "No, thank you."

Vance smiled and left for the kitchen. Walked with a limp, Rusty noticed. Serves him right.

Meanwhile, Rusty worked on the form. The first section—name and address—was okay. He and Quinn were living at Sherman's house until they found a place of their own. But when he got to job history, he came up empty. Pumping gas probably didn't amount to much to these folks. And then there was the poaching and the dealing. "Salesman," he finally wrote on the line that asked for his occupation. Then he put the pen down and picked at a hangnail that had started bugging him something fierce the minute he walked into Vance's office.

"Mind if I take a look?" Vance asked when he came back in the room, closing the door behind him.

Rusty shook his head.

"I beg your pardon?"

"No, I don't mind." He hesitated. "Thank you."

Vance smiled as he took the clipboard and sat at his desk. Rusty watched him make a few checkmarks on the paper as he read. Hell, he wouldn't have agreed to come if he knew there would be a test. He looked at the clock on the wall behind Vance and wondered if they made the damn things work slower in this place to add to the torture of being there. He stared at the minute hand, willing it to speed up, but the clock just kept ticking loud as a locomotive and moving slow as a Sunday sermon. He would have been happier to rip it from the wall and smash it under the heel of his boot. Besides, he needed a smoke.

"Well," Vance said, four and a half minutes later, "this looks like good news, bad news as far as I can see, Ron."

Rusty didn't respond and Vance said nothing. Based on the earlier please-and-thank-you incident, Rusty figured the guy expected something from him. Conversation, maybe? He shrugged and gave it a try. "Why's that?"

"The reason this is a good news situation, Ron, is that your escapades to date haven't landed you in court or jail. That's correct?"

Rusty nodded.

Vance waited.

"Correct."

"And the reason this is a bad news situation, Ron, is that your escapades to date haven't landed you in jail."

Sonofabitchin' comedian!

"Are you at all curious why not going to jail is bad news?"

"Never thought about it."

"Well now's your chance to think about it, Ron." Vance set the clipboard on his desk. "Let me give you some facts." He clasped his hands behind his head and leaned back. "Less than three percent of all men who commit sexual offenses come into treatment. And less than half of them make it two years without a repeat offense." Vance gave Rusty a while to absorb what he said, then he folded his hands in front of him and leaned forward in his chair. "Those aren't very good odds, are they, Ron?"

"Guess not."

"Well, they get worse. That's because the highest rate for repeat offenses of all those convicted for violent crimes is for sexual offenders. Even among guys who did time and vowed to never commit a crime again.

"What that means is that this demon we're dealing with, this devil called sexual offense, is a mean bugger. Even when a man comes into treatment and learns to behave different than before, that darn desire to revert to old behavior is out in the parking lot doing pushups and wind sprints, watching and waiting. And when that desire sees a guy letting his guard down, it pounces."

Rusty flinched when Vance slammed his right fist on his desk, but Vance didn't miss a beat.

"And before that man can yell 'it's all her fault,' or 'the devil made me do it,' or anything else he can think of to try and blame somebody else for his own behavior, he hears the clang of that big steel door closing on his cell and he's got five, six more years behind bars. This time without any chance of parole." Vance settled back in his chair. "So, can you see why we focus our attention on men who really want to stop? And not smart alecks who just waste our time?"

Rusty nodded. Corinne had said some of this the previous week, but it sounded different coming from Vance. He talked like a man who knew what it was like to feel that desire, that need, bearing down on him like a Peterbilt eighteen-wheeler that's lost its brakes. It would take some pretty fancy dancin' to pull anything over on Vance Carmichael. He could respect that.

"What we like to do when we interview a man is make sure he's not wasting our time. Or his. There are plenty of guys out there whose illness—yes, we call it an illness—has knocked them down more than yours has. And if you don't want the privilege of what we offer, I guarantee you one of them would take your place in a heartbeat."

Vance glanced at the form again. "Your job history's a little spotty."

Rusty nodded.

"I beg your pardon?"

"Yes, sir."

"And you've got no wife or kids. Nothing tying you to the community."

Rusty shook his head.

"So, you can see how, on paper, you don't look like a heck of a good risk."

Rusty looked at the floor, at Vance, at the clock, at the floor. This used up old jock strap didn't need to tell him that the sky was blue and the grass was green. He already knew he was a worthless piece of cow crap.

"That's why I need to find out how committed you are to turning your life around." Vance picked up a piece of paper from the table behind his desk and handed it to Rusty. "Read this," he said. "Please."

VIEWPOINT
Program Contract

Before he is admitted into the Viewpoint Program, each participant agrees to:

1. Attend and participate actively in one one-on-one counseling session per week for the first 52 weeks of enrollment.

2. Attend and participate actively in one group counseling session per week for the first 52 weeks of enrollment.

3. Complete in a timely manner all assignments assigned by the counseling professionals responsible for his treatment.

4. Refrain from using and/or selling illegal drugs, or illegally obtained prescription drugs, while in the program and from associating with anyone selling or using illegal drugs.

5. Take periodic polygraph tests as required by the counseling professionals in charge of his care.

6. At the end of his first 52 weeks of treatment, renegotiate his program contract and agree to do what is required of him to remain a program member in good standing.

I, _____, agree to the rules listed above and understand that if I break any one rule listed above, I may be eliminated from the Viewpoint Program and not permitted to return.

Rusty squirmed. First the manners lesson, and now rules. Hell, he hadn't followed rules of any kind since he was twelve.

"Does that look like something you can agree to, Ron?"

Rusty looked at Vance, at the ticking clock, at Vance again, and out the window. A rabid animal was stuck in his chest, scratching at his insides, making them bleed. The only thing he knew to do when he felt like this was to run. Or to lash out and try to hurt someone else as much as he hurt.

When Vance spoke again—two and a quarter minutes by the clock—Rusty heard a different, kinder tone.

"I won't sugarcoat what you're up against, Ron. And I'm not picking on you. I'm just laying things out square. If you want to turn your life around, you have to change. Everything. From the way you earn your living to the way you tie your shoes. It won't be easy. I know because I did it myself."

He did it himself? Rusty looked straight into Vance's eyes.

"Uh huh." Vance nodded, affirming that Rusty heard right. "Another thing I know is you don't have to do it alone. In fact, you can't. Just like any junkie or drunk who wants to get clean and sober, you've got to ask for help and take it when it's offered. Then, when you get your bearings, you need to put out your hand to the next guy." Vance set a pen on the desk in front of Rusty and sat back.

Rusty figured he could ram Vance's damn clipboard down his throat and storm out of the room. Or ask him for a cigarette. Or tell him the truth, which was that he didn't know what the hell to do or what was expected of him, even after reading the contract. But he knew if he walked out without signing on, he'd be walking out on Quinn, too.

Rusty picked up the pen and scratched the ballpoint in the paper's margin to get the ink flowing. His heart pounded so hard his hands shook, but he signed his name, Ronny Lee Jenkins, Junior. When he handed the form across the desk, he felt as helpless as a downed doe. But a little relieved, too. Maybe there was hope for him.

Rusty took his first polygraph test at his session with Vance the next week. They spent the rest of the hour talking about how, as he grew up, Rusty felt like he stood outside of his own life, watching. That he'd wanted from the time he could read to go to MacMillan University like the kids from the other side of town, unless they wanted to go to college somewhere else. But he felt different from them. Not only because he lived on the other side of the Front, but because he had secrets. About how much his mother drank, and how many boyfriends she had, and the things she did with them.

He learned life could be different when Quinn moved in and taught him how to hunt deer. Catch trout. Hell, even how to cook a meal. But eventually, Lorraine started drinking too much again. Seeing other men. And treating Quinn the same as she treated Rusty. Like a spot on the wall on the good days. Like a chewed up old shoe to be kicked out of her way on the bad ones.

Even before the blowup, he knew Quinn would leave. He just thought Quinn would take him with him. Out to Kansas. Anywhere. When he didn't, Rusty went to the only safe place he knew, deep inside himself.

At his next appointment, Rusty told Vance about the first time he forced a woman to have sex. Or at least tried to. It wasn't her so much that made him do it, as her husband. "If he hadn't acted like such a stick-up-his-ass game warden," Rusty said, "I'd've let her be."

Vance pushed back in his chair. He knew this game. Holding everybody but himself responsible was the place every sex offender in treatment started from. It would be a while before Ron stopped blaming a game warden and his wife, his mother, or anyone else for the fact that he was an offender. But everybody had to start somewhere. "Time's up," he said.

Rusty looked at the clock. Then at his watch to make sure the clock was right. It hadn't felt like a whole hour had gone by.

"Your first group meeting's next Tuesday," Vance said. "Seven o'clock. Second floor conference room."

Rusty's right knee pumped like a piston.

"Nervous?" Vance asked.

Rusty stilled his leg by shifting his foot. "No."

"I hope you don't think you're the only guy who's wanted to vomit at the thought of sitting around with a bunch of guys talking about the most intimate parts of their lives."

"I guess I did figure everybody else'd know how to do it, and I wouldn't."

Vance laughed. "There's not a man walks in there without wishing he was almost anywhere else. It never gets to be a day at the beach, but it gets easier." He told Rusty how the group was nothing more than six other men like him who met once a week to talk about what's going on in their lives. "Sometimes their past problems with sexual offenses, or what it's like to be an offender in a world that doesn't know what that means. Mostly they talk about everyday events." Vance shook his head. "Like how an old man doing thirty-five on a two-lane stretch of Route 22 could set a guy off cursing and ruining his day and everyone else's who had the misfortune of running into him. Or how, when he came up against a tough job at work, a head gasket change, maybe, he threw a tantrum if he couldn't finish it in a few hours, instead of the full day he—and his boss—knew it should take."

Rusty squinted. He didn't see what getting mad or scared had to do with women.

"In other words," Vance continued, "what we're trying to do is unlearn whatever made us think sexual violence was okay, then learn how to act different."

"Yeah, okay. I get it." Rusty moved to the edge of his chair, his leg bouncing again. He felt like an unfortunate brookie, skimming the surface of Sinking Creek from the wrong end of a two-pound test line, trying to wriggle free of the fisherman's fly he'd mistaken for an afternoon snack.

When Vance stood, Rusty split, full speed, out of the office, through the reception area, stuffing a cigarette in his mouth before he pulled the Center's door shut behind him. He lit his cigarette. Took a big, deep drag. Then he galloped to Quinn's truck, borrowed for the appointment, and settled in. He started the ignition, turned on the radio full blast, and drove to Lester Craig's construction office where Quinn was waiting.

⌣

With his hands tucked into his jeans' pockets, Rusty moseyed into the Center's second floor meeting room, his eyes roving the place like they would in any barroom he had ever done a deal. He ran through the questions he always asked when he went someplace new. Who could be trusted? Who couldn't? How would he get out if he needed to? All he saw, besides the table and chairs, the flip chart, a thirsty old snake plant, and the blinds pulled closed over the windows, were three men standing in the far corner around a coffee pot, laughing. The hum from the fluorescent lights was all he heard, except for the damn hyenas over in the corner.

Despite his efforts to sneak in unnoticed, when he walked up to the table and pulled out a chair—the one closest to the door—it *screeeech*ed on the floor. One of the men turned and waved. Rusty nodded, then sat down, telling himself not to get comfortable. When one of the coffee guzzlers worked his way over to Rusty, he stuck out his hand, like the welcoming committee for a church social. "Name's Bill. You're new?"

Rusty nodded.

"It's tough the first few times. It was for me anyhow."

The other two men came over and introduced themselves, then took their seats. Not that much different, Rusty thought, from a bunch of guys getting up a game of pool.

Vance came in a few minutes later, followed by three other men. At seven on the nose Vance told everyone to sit down so the meeting could start. He introduced Rusty, then, as if following a recipe he made every week, Vance said it was important to maintain confidentiality, that what they said in the room was private and nobody else's business. When he finished, he pushed back from the table, like he was getting comfortable. "How'd everyone do this week?"

No one spoke for what Rusty thought was a long time. Then Mitchell, across the table, started to talk. Tried to anyway. *Poor bastard's in rough shape*, Rusty thought when he saw how the guy shook. But Rusty wasn't prepared for what Mitchell said. How his girlfriend, the first woman he dated seriously since starting treatment, told him she was leaving for three months. "Out to California to visit her sister. A change of scenery, she said, while she's between jobs."

Rusty crossed his arms when Mitchell told his sad sack story. Anyone the guy's size—maybe six-two, two-twenty—wouldn't bawl his eyes out. But that sure looked like what Mitchell was about to do.

The group acted like what Mitchell said was natural as stars in the evening sky. Worse, they egged him on. "Get it out, man," Bill said. "That's what we're here for."

Rusty was dumbfounded. *He's scared his girl is leavin'? Let her go, man, and find yourself two more.*

"I'm afraid she's not comin' back," Mitchell said. "And I don't want to be alone again." The other guys nodded like they knew how he felt. The one next to Mitchell even put his hand on the guy's shoulder.

"One at a time," Vance said, "let's remind Mitchell of the tools he can use to get through this rough patch without acting out. Frank, you start, and we'll go around to the left."

"You can call any one of us, day or night."

"Keep yourself occupied while she's away."

Rusty wondered if he was the only one in the room who had any sense. He wanted to spit out his opinion, but another guy name Stuart started talking. About how he got so peeved at his boss at the railroad yard he darned near told him where to put his job and how to shove it.

When everyone else around the table laughed, Stuart laughed, too. Rusty shook his head. *These are the sickest sonsofbitches I ever seen.*

The following day, Rusty fished the paper Corinne gave him out of his jacket pocket and dialed Fresh Air's number. When Bud got on the line, he sounded decent enough. "Come down on Thursday," he said. "We'll see what we can work out."

Thursday morning, after Rusty showered and put on clean jeans, he borrowed Quinn's truck and got to Fresh Air about ten to nine. After they talked awhile, mostly about things Rusty didn't think had anything to do with a job—like whether he was from MacMillan and if he liked to hunt deer or preferred pheasant— Bud said he had a fleet of vans that Fresh Air repairmen used when they made calls. "Busy season's coming up and every vehicle needs to be tip-top before then."

Rusty felt Bud looking him over like he wasn't sure he was up to the job. "Hell," he said, "I can have your fleet runnin' smooth as silk. Two weeks, tops. Provided you got the necessary tools."

"Then let's step out back." Bud gave him a tour of the garage's three bays and full set of Snap-on tools.

Now this, Rusty thought, was somewhere he could fit in. Anything was better than sitting around every Tuesday night with that bunch of whiners.

"So," Bud said, "we'll see you next Monday? Seven thirty sharp?" Rusty grinned while Bud told him he'd have a lunch break from eleven to noon and he could plan on leaving around four, unless an emergency came up.

⁓

In his group the next week, Vance asked Rusty to introduce himself. Rusty shot a dart-sharp look across the table to make sure Vance knew he didn't appreciate being thrown that curveball.

Vance shrugged. "Everyone's got to do his share of the work. You part of the group or not?"

Rusty glanced around him. Seven pairs of eyes were looking back at him, waiting. He'd let his guard down. Hadn't gotten there early enough to get a seat near the door. Odds were, he couldn't get out without a couple of the men intercepting him. And the bastards all looked prepared to wait forever if it took that long for him to come up with something to say.

"I had a couple girls," Rusty said, his eyes on the table.

"And?" Mitchell said.

Rusty looked up. All eyeballs still on him. "And what?"

"None of us got here just because we took a girl out for an ice cream sundae and left her with a little kiss goodnight."

Rusty wedged himself into the corner of his chair.

"You could start with what you told me the other day, Ron."

Rusty figured Vance was referring to the story about Terry Sullivan's wife. He cleared his throat. "I lived a couple years out in Kansas," he said, his eyes back on the tabletop, not sure he was saying the right thing. "There was a warden there. He had a fine-lookin' wife. And she knew just how fine she was. Workin' those pretty pink dresses she favored when she welcomed her husband home." He looked up and saw everyone listening and figured he must be on the right track. "One night, after I was at the Plainview a while—it was a couple nights after the son of a bitch—"

"You can lose the foul language, Ron."

Rusty shot Vance another razor-sharp look, then continued. "Okay. So, I decided I wouldn't mind havin' a little of pretty Carolanne Sullivan for myself." He stopped. What he was saying sounded so lame. "But I didn't do nothin' really. Just got into the house and roughed her up a little."

Rusty looked around. The men were still listening. A couple nodded. *See,* he wanted to say to Vance, *they don't think I did nothin' so bad.* But eventually the silence felt ten times worse than anything they could have said.

"Sounds like you're thinking she made you do it. That's what you're saying?" It was Bill, the guy to his right, who eventually spoke.

"Well, yeah! If she hadn't've . . ."

Mitchell interrupted. "From the way you tell it, seems the guy opened his front door, handed you a beer, and said, 'Oh, by the way, how'd you like my wife, too?'"

Rusty's face flamed when the other men laughed. He pushed his chair back, then stood, not caring that he would need to work his way around three of them to get to the door. When he slammed his chair against the table and stomped out, the meeting went on without him.

CHAPTER SEVENTEEN

Rusty entered Vance's office and sat down. His jaw worked while he prepared to defend himself for storming out of the group earlier that week.

Vance got right down to business. "We let each guy have one chance at acting the way you did on Tuesday," he said. "After that, they're out of the program."

"What the hell kinda way was that for him to talk to me?"

"First, his name is Mitchell. Second, you know we don't favor cursing."

Rusty turned away but Vance continued.

"Mind if I say a few words, Ron? Before we get to you?"

Rusty shook his head. He'd been seeing Vance going on a month. He learned early on that when the man turned on his honey-roasted voice, he would prevail no matter what. Rusty folded his arms and leaned back in his chair.

"I've got a visual aid today." Vance pushed his chair back and stood to open the blinds covering the window behind his desk.

Why he bothered, Rusty couldn't figure. All they could see was the Allegheny Front. In your face and imposing, just like Vance.

"She's somethin', isn't she?"

Rusty checked the clock. Five ten. When Vance started off on one of his rants, it might be a good three-quarters of an hour before he made his point. Then it would be time to go. Rusty had to admit, though, the mountain looked pretty. With the laurel almost full from the rain they'd had the last three weeks, the blossoms just about covering the escarpment like pink snow. And the sun lowering behind, big and bright and yellow-orange against a red and purple sky. Okay, he'd give the big guy that. The mountain looked good.

"I don't mean disrespect by calling the Front 'she.'" Vance was still looking out the window. "I just think anybody, anything, that beautiful has got to be female." He turned from the window to Rusty. "You know how that mountain got formed, Ron?"

Rusty figured the answer must be stashed in his brain some-where, the section labeled "high school science class." He remem-bered something about continents colliding, millions of years ago, but he couldn't recall more. He shrugged.

"I'll get to that in a minute. Like I said, I wanted to talk a little about me today." Vance opened a drawer, rummaged under a stack of papers, and pulled out a framed picture. He set it on his desk where Rusty could get a look. Penn State Nittany Lions—1973, the caption read. "A little before your time. You probably never heard what a hotshot I was back then. I went there from seventy to seventy-four, by way of Greenville, east of Pittsburgh. My father worked the mines there, but I never met him. Just in case you thought you're the only one who grew up without a dad.

"The difference between you and me was I had a mother who would've cut off her right arm for me or any of her kids." He shook his head. "But, you know, she could've done that, and I still would've been the same angry young man. Living in that dead-end town. So damn quiet a guy had to go to Pittsburgh just to make a drug connection, if you can imagine that major inconvenience."

Rusty figured Vance had forgotten his high and mighty rule about no swearing. But why point it out and prolong this agony?

"Despite my bad habits, the football coach, a guy named Sam Redmond, was willing to give me a shot. Before I knew it, I was voted all-state, then all-American offense and defense, three years running. Just for doing what I did best. Getting mad and getting even. Recruiters from all over—Michigan, Iowa, SMU—started buzzing around even when I was a sophomore. And that was back when it wasn't twisting the rules too much to sweeten a scholarship with a car, a little allowance. Tutors. You name it.

"But I wanted to play for Paterno. I figured he was the best, and I knew I was. And when I hit State College, there was nobody except him who was gonna even suggest I do anything I didn't want to. Even so, I knew to at least show up for class now and again, to keep my grades out of the sewer. I bet you didn't know you could earn college credits for courses called Business Communication and Rocks for Jocks. You still with me, Ron?"

"Still here."

"Good. Real good. 'Cause here comes the best part. So, I arrived on campus with an ego that could've filled Three Rivers Stadium. I started as a sophomore, still playing offense and defense, and even that year led the division in quarterback sacks. I'm a damned hero, Ron. I got girls, I got drugs, I got my picture in the paper. All for knocking the shit—excuse the language—every Saturday out of guys as big and dumb and ugly-mean as I am.

"Only trouble was, I was having a tough time controlling myself off the field. Once a clerk at the bookstore—a guy one-third my size—decided to question my God-given right to walk out without paying for a couple blue-and-white Nittany Lion sweatshirts. Hell, I was earning the place tens of thousands in television rights, wasn't I? So, I worked him over. You know, to teach him some respect."

Rusty wasn't sure whether Vance wanted an answer, but he knew he would've done the same. Some punk questioning him like that.

"Then there was a cashmere-sweater sorority girl who decided to question my right to take what I wanted from her." He shook his head. "By the time I'm a senior, I'm in and out the athletic director's office on a revolving-door basis. What's everyone's problem, I keep asking. Because by then, the pro scouts were swarming thick as flies in August. I couldn't've swatted them away if I wanted.

"But like I said, I did make it to a class now and again. And in that course Rocks for Jocks—otherwise called Earth Science 101—I read about something called tectonics. How geologists started thinking in the sixties that the earth is covered with giant plates, always slipping and sliding around over the planet. And how three, four hundred million years ago, there were only two continents. Big ones. Neither with the sense to move out of the other's way. And one day, those two uglies collided, and they were so big and mean they didn't let go. They couldn't let go. Letting go wasn't in their nature.

"Only thing is, they got a little banged up in the process and got all crumpled. That's how the Valley and Ridge was formed east of the Front. Then west of the Front, where there was less impact, the land stayed pretty flat. But where the continents hit the hardest, the Appalachian Mountains were formed, including the Front, all the way from the southern states to Canada. Some say the Appalachians were higher than the Rockies then, before they wore down over time."

Vance looked at Rusty, who was sneaking a look at his watch.

"You got somewhere to go, Ron?"

Rusty pulled his shirtsleeve back over his watch. "Restless is all."

"I'm heading for the home stretch."

Rusty nodded.

"I didn't think much about that lesson at the time. I was too important, remember. By then, the spring before I graduated, I had my contract with the Steelers under my belt. But my girlfriend's starting to get a little pushy. She doesn't like it when I come in late, when she smells some other girl's perfume on me. Imagine that."

Rusty nodded again but said nothing.

"So, I decide I better remind her how it is she's wearing that pretty diamond ring. And who's paying the rent. I tell her if she doesn't like my being late, I won't come home. Period. That keeps her quiet for a while. Until I miss her birthday party. And when I come in and she's heaving my clothes out the door, I get a little testy. 'Leave the shit alone,' I tell her. But when she pitches my new Bose speakers, I decide that was no way for the mother of my child to be acting. Oh, did I mention she's pregnant by then?"

Rusty shook his head.

"Well, I figure I won't hurt her too bad. Problem is, I'm on a run. I'm having trouble drawing the line between bad and not too bad. The next thing I know I'm up for manslaughter. The death of my own child, who would have lived if I hadn't crushed her skull while trying to teach her mother a little respect."

Rusty leaned forward. "You mean you killed your own kid?"

"I did. And once I'm convicted, I'm looking at the world from behind steel bars over at the state correctional facility. I don't have to worry about reporting to training camp that summer. But even that didn't wear me down. I figured I was still young. I could do my time and still get out and play ball. That was until one of my roommates—that's a joke, Ron—cut my hamstring to teach *me* a little respect. That's where I got the limp from. And for the next five years, I got to watch that mountain every day. Winter. Spring. Summer. Fall. Knowing that the life I planned on, the one I felt entitled to, wasn't gonna happen.

"That's when I started looking at my life different. And don't you know, I remembered how all those millions of years ago, those continents were up against each other, pushing their weight around, just like I had. And there was the result." Vance looked toward the Front. "A mountain. The Clint Eastwood type. Strong and silent. It didn't matter ten cents how that mountain was formed. Only that it was there. Changing every season. And it didn't matter anymore how I was formed. Whether I had a father or not. Whether I could catch a ball or sack a quarterback."

He leaned toward Rusty, his voice soft, his eyes sad. "All I'm trying to say is, once you know you've crossed the line from man to beast, and you pay the price, you get a chance to look at things different. Whether it's a mountain, or a lost love, or a dead child."

Rusty looked away, embarrassed. Vance had a point, but the guy looked like he was gonna cry.

"So, you see, Ron, why we named this program Viewpoint? How it's all in the way a person looks at things?"

Rusty set his jaw. He felt his face muscles working. He knew what Vance said when he first met him was true, that the desire, the need, was always there, patient, pumping iron, staying strong. He swallowed. Then he looked at Vance, not through him or around him, but into the hope in his eyes.

"Yes, I see."

Vance smiled. "Now let's go back over your first offense."

When Rusty stood to leave that day, he wasn't sure his legs would work.

At the group meeting the following week, when Vance signaled it was time for him to talk, Rusty leaned back in his chair. "Okay," he said. "That little incident I told you about last week? It didn't have nothin' to do with sex. I made up that part about how Carolanne pranced around in pretty pink dresses. I went after her because her husband was somebody I could never be, a college guy, a warden, and I was a lowly poacher from West MacMillan P-A." Rusty looked down at the floor. "I wanted to take the guy down a peg or two."

When Rusty looked up, he saw the men nodding like he'd done something right, something good. "That was one big step you just took, Ron," Mitchell said across the table.

A few days after starting at Fresh Air, Rusty had all the vehicles checked out and cleaned. "You ought to consider rotatin' the tires on a more regular basis," he told Bud when he stopped in the office. "Saves on gas and tires both in the long run."

Bud put out his cigarette, then sized Rusty up. "You've got initiative, Ron," he said. "Have a seat."

Rusty took the chair facing Bud's desk, his heart pumping. He was about to get the axe. He could feel it.

"A couple fellas went out of their way to say how you're making their jobs easier by keeping the vans shipshape."

But?

"The way I see it," Bud continued, "you've got a future in this business if you want." He reached behind his desk to the credenza. He filled his coffee mug and pointed the pot in Rusty's direction. "Care for a cup?"

Rusty nodded. "I mean, yeah, I'll have a cup if you don't mind. Please."

Bud poured a paper cup full, handed it to Rusty, then continued. "You've done a first-rate job getting the fleet ready for the busy season, and I suspect if you put your mind to it, you could learn the rest just as easy."

Rusty flushed then lowered his head to hide his smile. He knew from the other guys in the shop Bud wasn't afraid to point out a job done well, and one done not well enough. But to Rusty, praise scratched like sandpaper. He was sure it would backfire somewhere down the line. Besides, any monkey with a set of wrenches could have done what he did.

"The only thing I want to point out is the way your temper flares when something doesn't go as easy as you think it should."

Rusty put down his coffee cup and gripped the chair's seat. *Here it comes.*

"Take as an example Jake's van—the one with the axle that was nearly split in two. There's no reason you should have expected to do that job in one afternoon, even if it was the first day of the busy season. I sure as heck didn't expect you to."

Rusty looked at Bud and screwed up his face when he couldn't understand why Bud wasn't chewing him out.

"Some things just don't go as fast as we like, and even the best of us make mistakes."

Rusty shifted and tightened his hands on the chair, hoping Bud was finished and he could get back to the garage where he felt like he knew his way around.

"What I'm getting at, Ron, is that, if you want, I'll train you to get into the heart of the business. To make calls and do on-site repairs."

Rusty stared at Bud. Maybe he hadn't heard right.

"Is that something that might appeal to you, Ron?"

"Learnin' the business?" Rusty repeated what he heard, just to be sure he understood.

"That's right."

Rusty had a hard time hanging onto his chair. Except for pumping gas, this was his first real job. He never had a boss to speak of, and never one who told him he did a good job and could do a bigger one if he wanted. "Well, yes, sir, I would be interested."

"Good. Tomorrow I'll take you on a couple routine calls. Regular customers I check on personally every year. Then I'll send you out with Jake and a few other guys to watch how they make a call and what the proper way to handle customers is. If everything works out—what I mean is, if you like the work and we like you doing it—we'll set you up with a van and a route."

Rusty looked at Bud with an unfamiliar feeling in his chest. The man knew who he was, how he got sent to his shop to begin with, and he was still willing to take a chance on him. Rusty got up. "I'd like that, Bud. I'd like that very much." His smile felt too big for his face.

They shook hands, and as Rusty was leaving, Bud called to him. He turned around, still smiling. "We like our men to have a certain appearance when they call on customers. Hair trimmed, beard cleaned up."

"Yes, sir." A small price to pay, Rusty thought. He was getting sick of looking like he climbed out of a sewer anyway. On his way out, he caught sight of the small crucifix that hung above Bud's doorway. It reminded him of something his nana said years ago. How He died for our sins. How if we repented and did our best, we could hold our heads high and walk free.

He'd never quite understood how that could be. But there was something in the way Bud looked at him and trusted him to do a good job. Maybe the way he felt after that was the kind of freedom Nana was talking about.

He stopped at the barbershop on the way home. When Smitty handed Rusty a mirror so he could see the back of his hair, just touching his collar, he decided he wasn't such a bad-looking dude after all.

It was Saturday, and the sun shone brightly. The October sky was almost too blue for Rusty's eyes. At least that's what he told Quinn when he reached in his shirt pocket and put on his Ray-Bans.

"Leaves turned early this year." He scanned the landscape. "Looks to be a good season for whitetail."

Quinn agreed. "Only a couple weeks and we'll be out poundin' the fields."

Rusty couldn't think of anything more to say, so he kept his focus on the road ahead and off the fear of seeing his mother again.

In its day, before labor costs sent its three biggest employers looking for cheaper operations down south, most people in Miller-town made their livings in the town's fabric and clothing factories. But when Quinn rounded the curve at the base of the Appalachian foothills, and the town presented itself below, it seemed to Rusty that nothing about the place would convince a visitor that it hadn't always been desolate, gray, and without prospects.

As Quinn drove off the highway onto Elm Street, they passed boarded up storefronts and the weedy patch that used to be the town's green. He continued up the boulevard toward the looming brick building on the hill, enclosed by an eight-foot-high chain link fence. Then he pulled into the parking lot, turned off the truck, and set the parking brake.

"You okay with this?" He slid his Marlboros from where they were stowed on his visor, then replaced them before he lit up. He was smoking too damned much.

"What you mean?" Rusty avoided Quinn's eyes. He took a cigarette from the pack in his pocket and lit it.

"With seein' your mother."

Rusty inhaled, then blew a stream of smoke out the truck's window. "I'm not okay with it, and I suppose I never could be. There's too much, or maybe not enough, gone on between her and me." Rusty kept his gaze straight ahead. "But they told me in the program, if I want to get on, I got to come to terms with the past. So, that's what I'll do."

"Just remember, I'm right behind you. We can leave any time you want."

Rusty tossed his cigarette out the window. He adjusted his cap, opened the truck door, and got out. "Let's go if we're goin'."

In the lobby, Rusty looked around at the peeling paint, the scruffy linoleum floor, the faded aerial photo of the Valley when it was a place where a man could earn a decent living. How people were supposed to get to feeling better in a dingy place like this was more than he could figure, but that wasn't his to worry about. He walked to the front desk, with Quinn following.

"We're here to see my mother," Rusty told the receptionist. "Lorraine Jenkins." Rusty's foot tapped while the woman ran her finger down the patient list in front of her.

"Jenkins," she said. "Here she is. On three."

She handed each of them a visitor's badge. "Through the second set of double doors to the elevators on your right. Go up to the third floor and check in with the guard. He'll see to it you get on the ward."

Quinn and Rusty clipped their badges to their shirts, then set out down the hall.

"Damn quiet in this place," Rusty whispered. The only sound besides his voice and their rubber-soled boots squeaking along the floor was the ding of the elevator when its doors opened to let them board.

When they got off on three, they found the guard seated behind a gray metal desk, hat tipped down over his eyes, arms folded across his chest, legs stretched in front of him.

"'Scuse us." The guard showed no sign of life when Rusty spoke, so Quinn jostled him awake. "We're here to see Lorraine Jenkins."

The guard ran his hand over his face to wake himself up. He reached for the set of keys hanging from his belt, picked one out, and led the men down the hall. He unlocked the double-steel doors, held one open for Quinn and Rusty to walk through, then locked it behind them. If not for a muffled moaning from farther down the hall, Rusty thought, and the antiseptic smell that covered up the possibility of any other odor, the place would feel like nowhere at all. At Lorraine's room, the guard unlocked the door and swung it open.

"One at a time." He motioned toward Lorraine who sat on the only chair facing the only window. Rusty's chest tightened. His arms stiffened. His hands clenched.

He looked to Quinn, then back to his mother. When he felt Quinn's hand on his shoulder, he was aware of his feet moving toward her before he was sure he had decided to walk into the room. "Go see your mother," Quinn said.

Rusty walked in front of the chair, looked at Lorraine, then up at Quinn and the guard. "That's not her." His face scrunched as if asking a question. "That's not my mother."

Quinn nodded. "It's her." Rusty still didn't move, so Quinn prompted him. "Make your peace as best you can."

Rusty walked toward the chair and the little person in it. Lorraine had never carried much weight, but this woman, who couldn't check in at more than ninety-five pounds, looked like an old little girl. Too small and too pale to match the vivid memory Rusty had of his mother. Her hair, gray mixed with barnwood brown, barely reached her chin. Her bangs were cut straight across her forehead. Everything about her was faded—her hair, her skin, her apron, or whatever that washed out blue rag was she was wearing.

Rusty took two silent steps and stopped, two more steps and stopped, as if approaching a strange animal. He paused about ten feet from this woman, this stranger, close enough to see that, although everything else about her was dull or slow, her eyes smoldered. They darted side to side in their sockets, lightning bugs looking to land.

"Momma." Lorraine looked toward Rusty, but past him, through him, as if he weren't there. "It's me, Rusty." When she turned away, he walked around in front of her chair so he could look at her straight on. "I come with Quinn. To tell you where I been, why I come back."

Nothing moved but Lorraine's eyes. Rusty leaned closer. Maybe she couldn't hear him. When he started to speak again, her arm shot out and her hand, frozen into a claw, rapped him across his mouth. He flinched and held the spot where she hit him, then leaned away, stunned, like that little kid on White Ash, always trying to figure out what he did wrong. "I come to say I'm sorry."

"Sonofabitchin' liar." Lorraine's voice was mean and flat, slurred now by whatever drugs she was on, like it used to be by alcohol.

"I'm tellin' the truth now. I come to try to—"

She kicked at him, but he was too far away for her skinny, dried out leg to reach. Rusty froze. Then Quinn was at his side. Rusty thought back to the day when Lorraine threw the cast iron skillet at him at breakfast. The day Quinn went after her with the knife, then left. This time, Rusty knew Quinn wouldn't take after Lorraine. He knew, too, that Quinn wouldn't leave him.

"It's the booze that done this to her, Rusty. You just say what you need to say. Then we'll leave her be."

Rusty looked from his mother to Quinn. He felt small enough to crawl into the old barrel under the carport where he used to hide from Lorraine when she was on a rampage. But he wanted to punch a wall, or kick out a window, or gulp down a six-pack of tallboys fast enough to get a decent buzz. He wanted to rise far enough above his hurt so he could look down on it and say it didn't matter one mouse turd what his mother thought of him.

Instead, he stood still, feeling something shift in his chest. He could breathe better. "I would've done things better if I could've. Now I know better." He turned and walked out of the room, with

Quinn by his side. The guard followed, then locked the doors behind them.

———

Rusty proved to be a quick study, as far as the mechanical aspects of the job went. Bud said he needed to relax a little more around the customers, but that he expected that Rusty's nervousness only meant he wanted to do a good job. Aside from the time he swore a blue streak after he cut his hand on the rough edge of a duct at Eleanor Frain's house, he acted like a pro. Later, when Rusty went on calls with the other men, both the Fresh Air guys and the customers gave Rusty good marks.

The third week in October, Bud handed him the keys to the van he would drive on calls each day.

Rusty smiled. "You won't regret this."

"I suspect I won't."

Rusty turned to go inspect the van he'd been assigned. He wanted it in perfect shape.

"One more thing," Bud called. "Beginning next week, you'll see an extra hundred in your check."

That night, Rusty ran into the house yelling out when he didn't see Quinn in the living room. "Where you at?"

When Quinn came out of his bedroom, he again noticed Rusty's haircut and clean-shaven face. Since he'd cleaned up a while back, the kid looked darned good. Had a smile that could turn anyone's day sunny, when he made his mind up to. Still a little thin, though. "What's all the fuss about?"

"Quit askin' questions and get on a clean shirt. We're celebratin' tonight."

Quinn did as he was told, and an hour later at Fiore's, he and Rusty feasted on all-you-can-eat linguini with clams and fried calamari, then spumoni for dessert. The others at the family group he was attending at the Center taught him how important it was to recognize and comment on new behavior, but from the smile on his face, Rusty already knew things were working out better since he started the program. He was about to suggest Rusty get some new clothes when Rusty said he was going down to Sal's Men's Shop on Saturday for some new shirts and jeans. "Might even get me a sports jacket."

Quinn smiled and reached for the check when the waitress offered it, but Rusty grabbed it. "This one's on me." He put down two twenties, then smiled at the waitress. "Keep the change, miss. You done a real fine job." He sat back, draping his arm across the back of the leatherette booth. Living straight might not be so bad after all.

CHAPTER EIGHTEEN

When Lehanna stepped off the plane, she hesitated at the top of the ramp. She looked beyond the Central Highlands' hills to the setting sun, its light reverberating off the terrain's red soil, as it had twenty years earlier. She put her sunglasses on, then stepped down toward the tarmac.

As she approached Ivato's international terminal, she saw Jacques inside, leaning forward, arms open wide, palms pressed against the window. Lehanna smiled, waved, and quickened her pace. Then she stopped suddenly. A stiff-legged guard in military uniform blocked the terminal entrance, his rifle rigid and accusing across his chest, while another guard ushered passengers through the door. "One at a time," the guard called, first in Malagasy, then French, as he looked each passenger up and down, tugging occasionally on a shirt sleeve or a carry-on bag to slow the procession, or to inspect someone more carefully. Lehanna's steps became more tentative. Things *had* changed on the Great Red Island.

When she walked inside, Jacques embraced her. "Let me help with that." He motioned to Lehanna's carry-on bag. It wasn't until he wiped tears from her cheek that Lehanna realized she was crying.

"So sad to be back?"

"Not sad at all." Lehanna fumbled in her bag for a tissue, dabbed under her sunglasses, waved the tissue in the air, then stuffed it back in her purse. "They surprised me." She motioned to the entrance. "The guards, I mean."

"They're part of the landscape now. I'll tell you more later." Jacques took her arm and led her to his car. "You must be exhausted."

"More wired than tired, I think." She told him about her stay the previous night in a hotel near Charles de Gaulle Airport and how the planes whining overhead kept her from sleeping much. She didn't say that even if the hotel had been quiet as a cathedral, her anticipation about returning to the island and seeing him would have kept her awake anyway.

"Not the best introduction to *La Ville-Lumière*," Jacques said. "We'll have to make sure you get a better one."

Lehanna looked away, uncertain whether Jacques's invitation to visit Paris was serious or simply casual conversation.

"For now, though, you get to decide whether I take you to your apartment on campus. Or, if you're up for it, we can have dinner. Anything from *achards* to *zebu*." He smiled. "Your choice."

"Dinner," she said. "But you pick the restaurant. My decision-making abilities went on autopilot a few time zones ago."

After stowing Lehanna's bags in Jacques's car, they drove to the parking lot exit where another soldier was checking identifications at the gate. When they pulled up, he inspected Jacques's driver's license and Lehanna's passport before waving them through.

"It's been like this for months now," Jacques said, eyeing his rearview mirror as they drove off. "After another attempted coup on President Ratsiraka's regime in May." Most people, he said, had had a taste of democracy after the French gave up control in the sixties. They wanted it to continue and spoke privately against military interference. "But the guns are doing the talking now. They have been since nineteen seventy-five when Deba took over. That's what people call Ratsiraka. It's Malagasy for Big Man. And nothing will change unless someone rallies enough grass roots support to openly confront him."

Gripping the steering wheel while still speaking of Ratsiraka's regime, Jacques steered his Renault over the brick-paved street, managing to squeeze it into a tight parking spot between two other small vehicles. "The number of cars in Tana," he said as another driver shook his fist at him for taking the spot, "has probably tripled since you were here last." When Jacques spoke about the city's challenges, he focused as intently as he did when examining a patient with a difficult-to-diagnose condition. "The air quality is suffering, too. Look over there to the west. That gray haze means more asthma, especially for children and the elderly."

"The air does seem dense," Lehanna said, though she suspected the tightness in her chest resulted as much from anticipation about her next months with Jacques as from Tana's pollution.

He turned off the car, then looked across the seat at Lehanna. "Somehow that all seems a little less pressing now that you're here."

She smiled but said nothing. Then she opened her door and stepped out, taking a deep breath of air, no matter how polluted it was.

"Over there." After locking the car, Jacques motioned to a pink stucco building. "*Etoile Tana*," he said. When he reached for her hand, she had already turned toward the stairs leading to the second-story restaurant.

"Dr. Jacques." As they entered the small, dark-paneled room that held about a dozen tables, each covered with bright red, yellow, and orange cloths of different floral patterns, a woman called out. "It's been too long!" As she approached them, the round, middle-aged woman opened her arms to welcome Jacques as if he were a younger brother. He responded with a warm hug and engaging smile.

"Correct as usual, Nadine. But I hope you'll forgive me and say hello to my guest. This is Lehanna," he said, "a friend and associate from the United States, back after a long absence to work at the clinic."

Nadine welcomed Lehanna as graciously as she had Jacques. "So glad to see you. Both of you. You prefer a table inside or out?" Jacques looked to Lehanna.

"Outside, I think."

"Then outside you shall have." The woman steered them to a small table, covered with a scarlet cloth, at the edge of the second-floor roof garden, laden with potted white gardenias, rich green ferns, and red cyclamen. "This is good?"

Lehanna smiled, and Nadine held out a chair for her on the terrace overlooking the street below, where the setting sun was throwing fiery light on the nearby buildings. The church spires especially seemed to vibrate against the surrounding hills.

"Perfect," Jacques said. "We'll start with some *gris*, please."

Nadine nodded. "Yes, yes. I'll send Claude right away. The *ravintoto* stew is especially good today." She turned away, her thick hips swaying, to find the waiter.

After Claude poured each of them a glass of *gris,* the grayish wine from nearby Ambalavao, Jacques ordered from the menu of native dishes. Then he gave Lehanna more background on how the island had changed since she last saw it. How Philibert Tsiranana and the Social Democrats had tightened their grip on the country in the sixties, but how, in the early seventies, the army staged a coup and Chief of Staff Ramanantsoa took over. A few years later, another military faction, headed by Ratsiraka, gained control, and named the country the Democratic Republic of Madagascar.

"Like I said before, Ratsiraka suppressed another coup this spring, so we're back to limping along. Every time the party in power makes headway in building better roads or giving the economy a boost, things get better for a while." He shrugged. "Then another party challenges, and the cycle begins again."

Slowly, he said, the roads were improving, and the Malagasy were beginning to realize that slashing and burning the rainforests to plant rice fields wasn't an effective long-term solution to hunger. "But a lot of people still go to bed without enough food and the health of most—unlike the wealthiest—continues to slide. Now that AIDS is on the scene, there's a whole new set of challenges. Malaria, at least, is treatable. But this new beast?" He shook his head.

As Jacques talked, Lehanna watched his gestures grow more animated. His political concerns, and his commitment to improving health and eliminating hunger, were as much a part of him as his long limbs and intense brown eyes. So far, he hadn't once mentioned Celeste or their children. She shooed away her desire to hear about them. Instead, she tried to bolster his flagging hopes, his apparent frustrations that he wasn't working hard enough, seeing sufficient results.

"Well," she said, measuring her motives. Which did she want more? To do good or to please this man, to lighten his burden? "That's why I'm here, isn't it? To get to work on the *Sutherlandia frutescens* project? To further hope, if not to find a cure?"

Jacques picked up his *gris*, held it for a moment, looking off toward town reflectively, then set it down again and smiled. "You're correct. That's why you're here." He drank from his glass. "And I'm glad you are."

When he held her gaze, she needed to know more, not about their project, but about him and her prospects with him. "So, what's going on with you? Celeste? The children?"

He sat back, waved his hand to dismiss his personal problems, and laughed. "Me? It's much easier to go on about the problems of the world than to look at ourselves, isn't it?" Celeste, he said, had taken the children to Paris a year earlier to protect them in case political unrest became more aggressive. "But even before that we knew our marriage was breathing its last." His daughter, Marie-Christine, was at the Sorbonne, and Jean-Paul was in private school. "Ironic, isn't it, that Celeste, the island native, wanted to leave, and I, the expatriate, wanted to stay?" Jacques again picked up his *gris*, drank, and looked down at the table. "She's filed for divorce."

Lehanna nodded and bit her lower lip to keep the sudden lightness she felt in her hands, her arms, her chest from showing in her face. "You were together a long time," she said.

"It was a long time, but not always a good time." Jacques hunched over his wine glass, twirling its base as he spoke. "Looking back, it's easy to see this, but even in the beginning, we were rarely on the same path. Hopeful, sure, but we were always drifting and searching, each of us.

"It was okay at first because at least we weren't picking each other apart. The truth is," he said, his eyes still on the table, "my work always came first, Celeste a distant second. And I was too wrapped up in other children's well-being to take care of my own. They deserve not to be stuck here if they don't want to be. But I can't give up on the clinic. Not when this model is beginning to work in other places around the world." He paused and looked at her. "There, you see?" An embarrassed boy-smile brightened his face. "I haven't learned my lesson. I'm still thinking all about me and my dreams and schemes when I should be asking about you."

She noticed him admiring her lavender outfit, her hair, her skin. She lowered her eyes, even though they were still hidden behind her sunglasses. She hoped he would shift his gaze to the pots of coral-colored hibiscus spilling over the terrace or the street bustle below. But he persisted.

"How are *you*, Lehanna?"

She looked out over the balcony, then her eyes drifted back to his. It was easier to talk about him, even Celeste and the children, and keep her needs and wants sequestered. "I'm . . ." She smiled. "I guess I'm fine."

"Fine?" Jacques laughed.

She usually enjoyed watching him toss back his head, his smile almost overtaking his face. This time her stomach tightened. He was about to say something she didn't want to hear. She could feel it.

"Fine," he said, "is a small word with little substance. And you are many things, but not without substance."

She smoothed her skirt and removed her sunglasses. "Searching? Does that have enough substance?"

He reached for her hand. "It's not what I would wish for you, but yes, searching has enough substance."

When she looked down toward the street, she saw the unlikely outfits of the poorer people who roamed Tana. Faded pink party dresses paired with worn loafers or sensible, low-heeled pumps. Running shorts with pin-striped dress shirts. Fuchsia print tops with orange plaid pants. Her unsettled emotions seemed as incongruous as those mismatched ensembles, observed through her Western eyes and judgments. Then she saw two khaki-clad soldiers, mingling, stopping people occasionally, prodding others to move along. In the distance she spotted another soldier, his camouflage uniform silhouetted against the darkening sky, pacing the roof of the capital building. Sometimes, she thought, life might feel safer with a guard on patrol, with defenses secured. Not now.

The waiter arrived, providing Lehanna the opportunity to withdraw her hand and shift her attention to the *romazava* beef, *ravintoto* pork stew with manioc greens, and the curried vegetables known as *achards*. She inhaled the aromatic spices slowly and smiled as the waiter also placed a complimentary *trembo* at her plate. When she lifted the coconut palm wine to taste it, Jacques proposed a toast.

"To a successful research effort," he said, tilting his glass to hers. But before she could steer the conversation to the idea of how wonderful it felt to have her first good meal in days, he proposed a second toast. "And, to you, Lehanna. Welcome back."

Jacques went on to the village the next day. Once she collected the necessary research at the university, Lehanna followed with Allain, the student Jacques hired to guide her. They traveled the route she and Jonathan had taken in the sixties, which proved Jacques right: the roads were only slightly easier to negotiate than they had been two decades earlier. But the hulking, recalcitrant *taxi-brousse* she and Allain rode in, easily twenty years old, was at least partly responsible for the slow and rocky trip. When they reached the foothills and prepared to hike the rest of the way, she knew in advance the trek would take longer than she felt she could endure. She also knew she would arrive at the clinic exhausted but exhilarated.

As Lehanna and Allain rounded the steepest and final hill, and the clinic came into view, the sight immediately ameliorated the aches and pains and fatigue Lehanna had felt during their trek. The simple thatched-roof shelters would have been considered primitive by Western hospital standards. But here, the line of patients waiting for treatment regarded them with awe and respect. She had written fundraising brochures and grant applications to elicit support for the clinic and had seen photos of the new structures. But the images didn't impact her the way the hope in the faces of the people waiting for help did. Some, she learned later, had come farther than she had from Antananarivo, and most of them on foot. Wide-eyed, thumb-sucking children with broken limbs or fevered lips were cradled in their parents' arms. Older people were carried on makeshift pallets of planks tied together with rope or vines. The most able-bodied transported themselves, despite bandaged heads or arms in slings of scarves, red, orange, or yellow, some with limbs slim as storks' and bellies distended and taut. No matter their infirmity, they proceeded as if on pilgrimage, searching for respite or reprieve from whatever pathogen or injury prompted the trip to see Dr. Jacques.

While Allain struck up conversation with friends on staff, Lehanna threaded her way through the line to the main building and asked for Jacques. He was making rounds in the AIDS ward in the next building, a young nurse said, so Lehanna went there.

In the treatment room, one of three in the single-story building, Jacques was seated on the bed of a man Lehanna guessed to be about thirty, although his reed-thin body might have been five years older or younger. Jacques was wearing what he always wore to work: loose-fitting shirt, khaki pants, Nikes. He held his patient's hand, a sight that reminded Lehanna of a photo she saw in *The Times* of a young boy being sent home from a Philadelphia school because he was diagnosed with AIDS. Since no one yet knew how the illness was transmitted, most everyone was afraid to touch those afflicted. Jacques was not.

"New drugs," he said in French, "are coming along all the time. You must not give up hope." His voice was crisp, not plaintive. "To help me do my best for you, *you must not give up.*"

The man smiled, at least his lips parted as if he wanted to smile, and Jacques patted his shoulder. Lehanna stood at the door and watched him with the next young man. His message was the same. *I'm helping you, and you must help me. I'm not giving up on you, so you must not give up on yourself.* But it was spoken with such conviction that the man nodded as if he, too, were convinced—or at least hopeful—a cure would come along any day.

"Good," Jacques said. "Now keep your thoughts on how strong you'll feel when you're back on your farm, raising zebu, feeding others so they are strong and healthy, too." When the man nodded and managed a weak smile, Jacques turned to the door, where other clinic staff were welcoming Lehanna. "You're here!"

He waved her over and introduced her to the nurses and other doctors on duty. "Not that there's such a thing as being off duty. They work hard, these men and women. They get an hour or so during the day to rest, to take care of themselves, then maybe five or six hours of sleep a night." All the staff, he said, except for a U.S. doctor named Charles, were from Madagascar.

"Judged by U.S. standards, the medical school at Tana—that's where all these people were trained—probably wouldn't win many awards. But whatever they may lack in training, these men and women make up for in compassion, dedication."

He took her through the thin-paneled wards, most of which were outfitted with what seemed decades-old metal beds and side tables. He knew all the patients' names, except those admitted that morning, and those lined up for treatment or medication outside the day clinic. Even the most emaciated or desperate smiled when Jacques spoke their names or held their hands. Some spoke in French, some in Malagasy, a couple managed a few words of English. But Lehanna suspected they all repeated some version of the same message. *We need your help, Dr. Jacques. We appreciate you.*

Returning to the main building, Jacques waved to a nurse on her way from the staff residence. He motioned for her to join them. The woman looked to be in her early twenties, Lehanna guessed. She was slender and walked with a graceful, loose-limbed stride. Her skin was light brown, her hair long, dark and straight, and her eyes so large and alive, Lehanna at first didn't notice the scars that marked her left arm. Lehanna was puzzled that Jacques didn't introduce her.

"You don't recognize her?" he asked.

Lehanna covered her mouth with her hands. "Nathalie? Can this be Nathalie?" Lehanna looked into the woman's eyes. Yes, this was the young girl Haja had healed years ago with the liana vine and the *famadihana*.

"Nathalie, you've heard your mother talk about Lehanna, yes?" Jacques asked.

Nathalie said yes, of course, there were times when her mother still mentioned her. "She is convinced you were the reason for my cure. That the vines and even Dr. Merthin's healing were released when you participated in the *famadihana*. That's what Haja told her, and she still believes him."

"I did nothing," Lehanna said as she reached for Nathalie's hands. "I was just there."

"You're quarreling with Haja? And with the words of a mother who knows her child like no one else could?" When Jacques spoke, Lehanna wasn't sure whether he was teasing or criticizing. She said nothing.

"It's especially rare," Jacques said, "for women to leave remote villages and get even a little education. But Nathalie received the first Worldwide Health scholarship for studies in health care." He turned toward her. "Now we're working on her to consider medical school."

Nathalie shook her head and spoke before Lehanna could comment. "I don't want to go back to Tana or anywhere else. Someday, maybe, but not now."

"I'm not letting you off that easily, Nathalie," Jacques said.

She smiled, though Lehanna sensed Nathalie's conviction couldn't be shaken, even by Jacques. "What lies ahead," she said, "I don't know. But now I must get to my patients." She and Lehanna hugged and promised to meet the following evening for dinner at the staff residence.

"It's true," Jacques said when Nathalie left. "She would make a fine doctor. Maybe you'll talk to her about it before you leave?" It was a directive, not a question. Lehanna didn't welcome the idea of pressuring the woman, but when a chill passed down her arms, she saw a fleeting image of Nathalie doing great things, whether Jacques got his way or not.

After showing Lehanna around, Jacques told her that Haja would meet her at the clinic the following morning and would work with her as long as she needed to take notes, collect rainforest samples to send to George Swenson, and longer term, to work on the *Sutherlandia* project. "I'm leaving for Tana tomorrow," he said. "Then I'm off to Paris." He took her hand. "We'll catch up when I get back next Thursday?"

She resisted the temptation to ask whether he was going to Paris on business or to see his family. It was none of her concern. She knew that, which didn't mean she could squelch her curiosity.

⌇

While Jacques was gone Lehanna collected specimens from the forest beyond the clinic. With Haja directing and Allain interpreting, she recorded required growing conditions, harvesting times and techniques, and how and why each species should be used to heal, or at least temper, maladies as wide-ranging as angina, muscular sclerosis, and arthritis. In the evenings, she spent time with the clinic staff, especially Nathalie.

After only a few weeks Lehanna understood, at least in some way, how Nathalie felt about the clinic and how difficult it would be for her to leave. The place and people reverberated with energies that matched her own: the desire to help, to heal, and to create. It began to feel like home, and Lehanna wasn't at all sure she would want to return to the States when her year was up. Still, she needed to follow through on the job she came to do. That meant cataloging the information Haja shared with her, passing it along to Swenson so he could file patent applications, and delving deeper into the possibilities for *Sutherlandia frutescens.*

Lehanna wrote to Allison weekly when she first arrived in Madagascar. But after the first month, she received no cards or notes in return. Several weeks later, the letters Lehanna thought she sent to the States came back to her in a single bundle. With the latest political instability, delivery on non-government mail had been postponed.

She tried to call Allison at her apartment in Ithaca. "The number you have reached . . ." Allison's phone had been disconnected. She contacted the dean of the Arts College and learned that Allison had withdrawn.

In her next call with him, she asked Swenson to write to Allison in care of her father at MacMillan University, explaining why she had been unable to communicate. After jotting down a note, Swenson tucked the reminder in his blotter, along with all the others he left there, none of which got tended to.

Lehanna met Haja every day, as he requested, outside his small concrete block home on the village's edge. For the first month, they roamed the nearby landscape, collecting samples, with Allain interpreting between them. But by the time Allain needed to return to Tana, Lehanna and Haja understood each other well enough to cobble together, with words and gestures, what each wanted to know from the other. After they established a routine of meeting at dawn, Haja explained that Lehanna needed to do more work, different work. When he asked her to meet him on the night of the new moon, at midnight, she agreed, though she didn't understand how they could work in the dark.

When she arrived at his home, Haja invited her to sit on the front step, a simple concrete slab. He motioned for her to turn off the flashlight she used to help guide her to his place. Then Haja motioned above. When Lehanna looked up, she wondered at the sky, which, with no ambient light, appeared grander than it did even in Ithaca. Haja pointed to the Dipper and Cassiopeia, then he looked back to her. "Your home is not here," he said. "Not now."

Lehanna tried to smile, to nod, to show Haja the respect he was given by others in the village. Instead, she turned from him to hide her determination to prove him wrong.

"You're pleased with your progress?" When Jacques looked across the simple wooden table as he and Lehanna ate dinner after his return, she smiled. She was pleased, not just with her work, but the fact that—despite Haja's message—she had become immersed in the clinic's mission and the land, flora and fauna of the place that was beginning to feel like her own. "All I know is that I feel like I'm in the right place, at the right time, that my work matters."

"And you matter. Not just to Haja or Nathalie or the rest of the staff," he said.

He didn't say what she wanted him to—that she mattered *to him*—but since his return from Paris, he seemed freer when he touched her arm to thank her for helping a patient, when he looked into her eyes long enough to see into her, she thought. It would be only a matter of time—Days? Weeks?—before she knew if her imaginings were real.

CHAPTER NINETEEN

Allison picked up the last note she received from Lehanna. It was breezy, short, and littered with exclamation points, as if excerpted from an adolescent's diary. She apparently felt she was thriving in her work and in her relationship with Jacques.

Allison set the letter on her desk and leaned back in her chair, trying to come up with an equally airy message—one that was honest and didn't dwell on her disappointment that she hadn't heard from Lehanna in, what was it? Six weeks? Eight?

Dear Lehanna,

Late autumn in Ithaca. Warm days, sunny skies and . . .

Okay, let me start again. With the truth this time. November in Ithaca and I'm freezing my ass off every dark, dank day—how's that for alliteration? —except when it's out-and-out raw and either drizzling or pouring. The sun? I think I saw it a week and a half ago for five, maybe ten minutes while walking through Collegetown. It's no wonder the first jumper of the year—a second-year architecture student— took a header off the Thurston Avenue Bridge last week. She broke her back, her femur, and cracked her skull. It was touch and go for a while, but she's the first to survive that jump. Anyway, enough of that.

I can only imagine how busy you are, and how much you're learning at—and contributing to—the clinic. I hope you're happy, too, and that you and Jacques . . .

Allison sat back and studied the letter as she would an essay for a composition class. Were her words credible? True? She shook her head. Except for the words *dark*, *dank*, and *drizzly*, the answer was "No. Not at all."

Even more incredulous to Allison than her note was that when Melissa Warner was interviewed for a news story, she said she wanted to return to school after rehab. Allison understood what it was like to consider ending things. But she was certain that, if she ever tried, she wouldn't come back. Not to school. Not anywhere anyone knew her.

She looked out her window where, yes, it was raining. The truth was, she didn't hope Lehanna was thriving in her work and with Jacques. She wanted her to come home. Where she belonged. She wadded the note into a ball and tossed it into the trash basket next to her desk. What was the sense of writing to Lehanna anyway? She either had no time to respond, or no interest in doing so.

When Lehanna first left the States, Allison continued taking the remedies her mentor formulated for her. She meditated. She studied Lehanna's folios. She figured if she immersed herself in them, she could work with Lehanna when she reopened Artemis, or started a new business. By then she'd be qualified to be an assistant manager, or a specialist in diagnosing or treating students. The title or job wasn't important. What mattered was that she would be back with her friend, doing something useful, learning more about how to heal herself and others.

But when she stopped hearing from Lehanna, Allison began to lose faith in the remedies. She took them if she remembered.

She felt too busy to meditate and lost interest in treating her classmates' afflictions and anxieties. She turned to her poetry, and Rodney Peyton congratulated her for putting more of her soul on the page, but she lost interest in her writing, too. She woke each morning admonishing herself: *Pull yourself together.* But like the pots of catnip and savory and sage she set on her windowsill, without daily care, she dried up and withered.

She stowed Lehanna's folios, already gathering dust, under her bed. She began to drift.

Later that month, when darkness came earlier, and loneliness filled her from throat to toes, she stopped going to classes and began to wander, searching for the feeling that seemed to leave with Lehanna. She needed to hear that sweet whisper deep inside. *You matter, you belong.*

She meandered around campus at first, especially when she couldn't sleep. After midnight, she had the hills to herself except for cruising security guards or pre-med students en route to the genetics lab to check whether their fruit flies had mated and produced progeny. She stood on the Thurston Avenue Bridge more than once, listening, wondering how the whooshing falls seduced Melissa Warner into tumbling down, down, into their roil and certain harm. When she got no answer, she wandered into bars downtown. Then, after convincing Richard to send money to buy a car, she traveled east, or south, or north, hoping to find a town, a spot where she could plant herself and grow.

When no place called to her, she attached herself to men, like moss to rocks. She rooted her affection to the curve of this one's upper back—the stained-glass maker from Elmira—or that one's inner thigh—the vintner near Seneca Falls—and stroked her finger along the topography of another's arm. She embedded in the company of any man who drank or raged too much, too often. Excess, she came to believe, felt better than the empty expanse that ran the length of her chest, the width of her ribs. *Fill me,* she wrote in one poem that fall. *Hurt me if you must, but don't ignore me. Whatever you do, don't leave me.*

⌣

Allison downed the shot the bartender at the Speedway on Route 89 placed in front of her. She swiveled on her stool, raised her hands over her head, then clapped as the band started their next set. She blew a kiss to the bass player, then grinned when she almost slipped from her seat.

The bearded guy on the stool to her left—his name was Carl, or Curt, maybe Kirk—leaned toward her. "Easy there, sweetheart."

"Easy?" She tried to steady herself.

Curt or Carl or Kirk shook his head. He reached into his flannel shirt pocket, and offered her a white tablet. "This'll help."

Allison turned the pill over and over trying to read the numbers or letters stamped on it. Her eyes couldn't focus.

CurtCarlKirk tapped the bar. "Another round." The bartender shook the vodka and triple sec and lime juice, then poured the Kamikazes. He edged one toward Allison, the other to her bearded friend. "Bottoms up."

Allison tossed back the little white pill, then the shooter. She shivered as the drink worked its absolutely splendelightful magic. Was splendelightful a word? Of course not, but it had a Disney Princess buoyancy about it. Like the word alacrity. Or reciprocity. Words that skittered across the page. She would use splendelightful in a kids' poem sometime.

Her creative intention was interrupted when CurtCarlKirk reached to her and kissed her. From a distance he had an earthy appeal. But up close, he smelled like sweat and cigarettes. His beard grated her face.

"Easy." She pushed him away. When he glared, she laughed again.

Allison didn't remember much after that. Not until the dream, the nightmare, of those falls at the Thurston Avenue Bridge. They called her. *It's safe here.* Her eyes started open. She felt for the bed beneath her. The worn sheets, dark blue, not her own pink sateen bedding.

She tried to steady herself, because the room—wherever it was, whose ever it was—was spinning. She rolled to her left. She wretched, then wiped the vomit from her mouth with her bare arm. She was naked. With a tall and lean, clean-shaven man next to her. She had downed the last Kamikaze, then the little white pill bearded CurtCarlKirk gave her at the bar. After that? She had no idea. She swallowed. Her throat was scratchy-dry. She blinked. Once. Twice. She felt wet between her legs. Yes, they had had sex. And no condom. *Oh, God, help me!*

The man—the bass player from the Speedway?—woke, rolled to his left, and leaned over her. So thin he looked spectral, and as ready to strike as the snake tattoo that wound its way up his arm. *Live free or die.* She reached the covers around her.

"You puked on my floor?"

Before Allison could respond, a hand, no, a fist, struck her jaw. Hot yellow light flashed in her head. A hand clamped around her wrist and pulled her from the bed. Allison struggled to get her feet under her, but the man dragged her before she could find her balance. A door opened. Cold. It was so cold. Then she was hurtling down metal stairs, landing with a fleshy slap against numbing concrete.

The cold revived her. Her face throbbed, and her hip. What was wrong with her hip? She tried to sit up. A boot hit her on the shoulder, followed by a ball of clothing.

"You weren't worth it anyway."

When the door to the apartment above the Speedway slammed, Allison vomited again. *You weren't worth it, anyway.*

She struggled into her clothes, found her car keys in her jeans' pocket and hobbled to her car. She drove back to Ithaca, past her apartment, to the bridge. She could tumble, tumble into the gorge, like Melissa Warner had. When she splattered on the rocks below, it would no longer matter that she *wasn't worth it, anyway.*

She could be with her mother again. She would be important to someone again.

"Mommy." Then she thought, no. If she were with Lucy, she would need to explain herself, what happened that night in their home, what happened with that man, and now others. Besides, if she jumped, she might live. Like Melissa. She turned the car around and drove back to her apartment.

⁓

Richard took the stairs to Allison's apartment two at a time. He glanced at his watch. Three fifteen. Only an hour later than he'd promised. At the top of the landing, he knocked on the door, slicked back his hair, adjusted his tortoiseshell glasses, tugged on his Donegal tweed jacket's sleeves. He tried to slow his breathing after taking three flights as fast as his legs, no longer in competitive condition, let him. He leaned close to the door. "Ali?"

Instead of getting up from the couch where she had fallen into a much-needed afternoon nap, Allison stayed where she was. She pulled the afghan Lucy had crocheted close and waited until her father jiggled the doorknob then entered the apartment. This was, after all, his idea.

Richard walked toward Allison as if his legs, like his concern, were untested. "Hi, sweetheart." He had struggled the entire drive up to assimilate what his daughter told him about the fact that some barroom bass player had roughed her up. Things like this happened to other people, less reputable people. Or on television. For his sake as much as hers, he wanted to tell her none of it had happened. Except that it had.

Allison allowed him to hug her but didn't hug back. She accepted the fact that he was there, and that maybe, as Richard suggested, she ought to get away. That she ought to come home for a while. But for Allison, MacMillan wasn't home anymore.

She wasn't disappointed that her father was late, again. Some obscure manuscript, of interest to approximately point zero zero three percent of the world's population, probably had compelled his attention. Besides, she had pretty much forgotten the whole incident. Except when she touched the reddish-purple bump on her cheek where The Beast, as Richard called him, hit her. Or when she forgot to roll her weight to the left side when she sat down—it was her right side that hit the concrete when The Beast pushed her down the stairs.

She smiled while Richard fumbled, dangling like a participle or a misplaced modifier. She said nothing.

"You okay?" He reached his hand toward Allison's face. Afraid to touch the bruise, he traced the length of it in the air.

"I'm fine."

"You look good. I was worried about how you would look." Richard stuffed his hands in his pockets.

"I'm fine."

"You straightened out the lease?"

"The landlord said he'd send the deposit after he checked the place over."

"And the dean?"

"I have until January to let him know about next semester."

"Good. Good. Okay." He looked around for her bags, and she pointed to the hallway. "Let's go then." He opened the door, grabbed his daughter's things, and followed her down the stairs.

After loading the bags and boxes into the Volvo, they set out down State Street, out of Ithaca. He gassed up at the Mobil station and got coffee at the 7-Eleven. When he started toward Route 80, he turned down the volume on the Mozart and reached for her hand. "There's nothing wrong with taking a little time off," he told her. "Nothing at all."

"Uhm hmm."

"More than a few of my students do. In six months, a year, they come back with different perspectives. Maybe," he continued after reflecting, "your mother and I shouldn't have let you skip second grade." Richard paused again. "And don't forget you were only seventeen when you left for Ithaca."

"Sixteen."

"You were sixteen?" He glanced at her, but she was looking out the window, counting Guernsey cows in their pastures. "Well, you can go back to Cornell whenever you want. Or to Brown. Andrew Cunningham heads the MFA program there you know."

"Uh-huh."

"In the meantime, you can write. Get a novel going maybe. Have you ever thought of trying a novel?"

Allison looked across the front seat. He was being too agreeable. "Is there something you want to tell me?"

He sat taller and adjusted the rearview mirror. He had rehearsed what he wanted to say with Corinne, after she pointed out that Allison was at a critical stage. "We used to talk about this, Lucy and I," Corinne had said. "The challenges of raising girls in a world where, if we weren't careful, they could fall right back into roles that women worked so hard to get free of in the sixties." Sure, she told Richard, it would be tough to let Allison find her own way. But good parenting brought a plethora of difficult choices—she knew this from experience—and avoiding them didn't help the parent, the child, or, in this case, the young woman. "She's almost twenty years old now, honey. She's ready." Then she suggested he speak with Stanley Klein in the psych department. "He wrote that book on parenting."

Richard wasn't surprised that Stanley agreed with Corinne or even when Stanley plucked from his bookshelf a tape he made from his book. *Separations*, it was called, *The Parent's Guide to Growing Healthy Adult Children*. "Have a listen," he said as he handed Richard the tape. Richard thanked Stanley and offered to take him to lunch the following Thursday. Then, with his hand on the doorknob, ready to leave the office, Richard turned back to ask about Stanley's son, who had left for Harvard Law the previous fall.

"Jeff's doing great." Stanley smiled. "Really coming into his own. But law school's not for him. He's coming home to get his feet on the ground. Three months max."

Richard suspected there must be a reason why it was okay for Jeff to live at home and not Allison. But he was running late for his next class, so he thanked Stanley again and walked out the door.

"Now that Corinne and the girls are in the house," Richard continued, reciting from the script he and Corinne had crafted. "Maybe you'd prefer a little space to yourself." He glanced over, hoping he could read Allison's reaction, but she was still looking out the passenger side window. "There's plenty of room at your grandfather's house. And he could use a little help, even though he'll never admit it." The stroke, he said, hadn't damaged Lucy's father's cognitive function, thank God.

"He's got Marie. Remember, the nurse who helped with your grandmother?" He explained how Marie stayed overnight when she wasn't taking care of her grandchildren, but that she wasn't always there when Charles wanted to get back and forth to the library. "And of course, she's of no help writing letters to his retired faculty buddies." He waved his hand in the air. "Not that he wants the help. Still, he could use it."

Allison kept her eyes on her father long enough to shake her head at the way he strained to sound casual, authentic. "Fine." She acknowledged him so he might stop trying so hard to expiate his guilt. Then she turned away.

CHAPTER TWENTY

Driving into MacMillan, with the sun beginning to set big and orange behind the Allegheny Front, Richard pulled up to Charles's brick colonial on Maple Street. Charles and Emily, Lucy's parents, moved there in 1982, when they'd been married forty-six years, and Charles had retired from thirty-nine years at Saint Francis University, twenty-seven as history department chair.

As Emily's Parkinson's progressed, Charles thought it best for her to be near her only daughter and close to MacMillan University Hospital, where neurologists were developing promising treatments. A fine move it was until, after three years of progress, all the research and all the doctors and all the experimental treatments couldn't stop, or even slow, Emily's deterioration. When she started mistaking Charles for the mailman and Lucy for the cleaning woman, Charles reminded himself that he had commanded a fine history department, that until the last two years he taught, his classes were waitlisted every semester. He re-read the books he had written on Roosevelt and Kennedy, regretting only the most egregious copyediting. Yes, he had accomplished a good deal, though not enough to save his dear Emily.

Since the early forties, when he earned his PhD, Charles hadn't spent a night apart from his wife, except for her hospital visits to give birth to Lucy and to recover from two miscarriages. After Emily was moved to the University Adult Care Center, and then to her grave, he needed to master how to sleep alone. Without Emily to turn to, he learned something new about history, too: how much it could hurt for a man to watch his past slip away, and how, with enough disappointment and loss, it could begin to feel as if the past never existed at all.

Richard dropped Allison at her grandfather's house and left before Charles wheeled himself into the living room from his first-floor bedroom. Richard hadn't detailed the damage from Charles's stroke, so Allison wasn't prepared for the way her grandfather's face had lost its reddish color or the way the left side drooped, like melting putty. What shocked her most, though, was the way Charles's words tripped and slid over each other.

"H-h-howw did y-y-ou do th-th-this sem-ess-ter?"

Allison couldn't understand him, so after he repeated himself twice, he waved his hand, spun his chair around, and wheeled back toward his bedroom. She didn't know if he was disgusted with her or himself. When he slammed the door behind him, she took her bags to the second floor and settled into the room at the back of the house.

She hung her three dresses—two of her mother's—in the closet, then arranged her sack of books on the shelves. She plugged in her portable stereo and turned up the volume to fill the emptiness she felt in the house without Emily. When she could no longer avoid the way Charles banged his cane on the floor—"Quiet!"—she turned off the stereo and snuggled into bed. No, she thought, this wasn't home.

Allison needed to escape Charles's rancor at least a few hours a day. And she needed cash. She suspected Olivia, owner of Metaphors bookstore, was most likely to hire her. Not so much because Allison had been a good bookseller when she worked at the shop during high school but because Olivia and Lucy had been friends. And it was, after all, while Allison read and played in the little yellow chairs in the children's corner of Metaphors, that Lucy introduced her daughter to Giovanni and Stevenson and Blake and Frost. It was there Allison decided she wanted to be a poet.

Before she picked up the phone to call Olivia, Allison tried to imagine returning to the bookstore now that Lucy was gone. Of course, she would read the new releases faithfully, yet she would brush up on the classics. And not make the mistake of assuming that bestsellers made the best choices. But without Lucy, who would advise her on which books would please which customers? Who would invite her to dinner at the Emerald Palace for their favorite dumplings and miso soup? Still, Metaphors seemed her only alternative. She reached for the phone and dialed.

"Metaphors."

Allison hesitated before responding to Olivia. "Hello?"

"Olivia. It's Allison. Allison Stephenson."

"What a lovely surprise. How's school?"

"Actually, I'm taking a break. And I'm wondering, do you need help at the shop?"

When Olivia paused, Allison figured her former boss might be recalling how Allison could be a little quick-tempered with customers and needed to be reminded—sometimes weekly—to be more pleasant, especially with Metaphors' regulars. On the other hand, Allison was trustworthy, never balked when asked to work Sundays or evenings, and was, of course, Lucy's daughter.

"Prayer answered!" Olivia replied. "My wonderful Letitia gave her two-week notice on Monday. I was dreading the possibility of putting an ad in the *Mirror*."

When Allison heard the question she was waiting for—"When can you start?"—she took a deep breath and smiled.

~

It was Wednesday, Allison's day off from Metaphors. Not a bad-looking January morning. She looked out her bedroom window to the backyard, covered with a light dusting of snow. She changed into her jeans, put on her mother's old cable-knit sweater-jacket and planned her day. After picking up Charles's prescriptions at the pharmacy, she would take his almost indecipherable grocery list to the market to do his shopping. Then she would walk a couple laps around Wonderland Lake and return home to read. Keeping up on new releases—even *A Thousand Acres* and others she was anxious to read—took time.

She checked the clock. Almost nine. She grabbed her keys, headed downstairs, then out the door. She needed to be back by eleven, Charles's breakfast time. Halfway to the pharmacy to pick up his medications, she realized she had forgotten his grocery list. She decided not to turn back. The important thing to remember was that he was out of cereal. If he didn't have his Kix-fix, as Allison called it, there would be hell to pay.

~

Allison buttoned her jacket to her neck and walked to the water's edge. The view was the one most often featured on postcards of MacMillan. The one where wedding party photos were taken. Why wouldn't it be? With its charming stone bridges, swans paddling along the water's surface, the boathouse where rowboats and canoes were rented by both visitors and townies. All set against the backdrop of the Allegheny Front.

It was a man-made lake, dug on the grounds of what used to be called Wonderland, the amusement park Martin MacMillan built in the 1860s to give MacMillan residents a place to forget the ravages of the war just ended. But the lake's history was not as placid as the water looked that morning. There were rumors about how Martin's son took advantage of a young woman there, then gave her an arsenic overdose before tossing her into the lake.

Details of the girl's death were never made public, but according to local legend, she sometimes called to passersby and confided her secrets. Allison dawdled after circling the lake twice. She knew what it was like to "be taken advantage of," a far-too-innocuous term for rape. She stood still. Waiting. Maybe the young woman would speak. When she heard nothing, she checked her watch. Quarter after eleven. She hurried to her car and drove home to Charles.

~

"Whaat tooook you so looongg?"

"I stopped at the lake."

Charles bristled.

"I know, Grandpa. Sorry."

She pulled the Cheerios out of the grocery bag.

"I ss-said Raisin Bbbran." He banged his cane on the floor. "Thaat's whaaaat I wrrrote on-on the list."

"I forgot the list." She set out the remaining groceries on the table. Two green apples rolled to the floor. "I'm sorry. Again."

Marie ran to the kitchen from the laundry room, hands on hips. "He's irritable enough when he gets what he wants," she said. "And plain impossible when he don't." She picked up the apples from the floor and spotted a colony of ants beneath the cupboard, feasting on remnants of Allison's late-night salsa and chips. "I just mopped this floor yesterday," she mumbled.

Allison had already left the kitchen and tossed her jacket to the living room couch. "And don't throw your coat there, young lady. Closets was made for a purpose."

Allison stopped. She gave Marie a disdainful look, even though the woman was a room away and couldn't see her. Or so she thought.

"And don't give me none of those looks." Marie, a dripping sponge in hand, white nurse's shoes squeaking, marched to the living room. "I'm carin' for one patient here, not two."

Allison glared when Charles called to her.

"You ca-can't treeeat MMMMare-ee tha way. Iiit's ruuude."

Allison returned to the kitchen. "Rude? That woman wrote the book on rude."

"Emm-mily insissted the help be re-re-re-spected."

Allison shook her head.

"Don't get sss-sanctimmmmonious with me. You were tr-trouble from the ver-rey first, aaa-and your mother shou-should have ggott-gotten rid of you like she did the f-f-irst one."

"Gotten rid of me?" Allison's eyes narrowed. "Is that what you said? What other one?"

Charles waved at her without saying more.

Allison started imagining the story Charles wasn't telling. Secrets lurked behind his reluctance to talk. She smelled opportunity.

Allison pushed the brass bar to open Wellington Hall's heavy wooden door. She remembered laughing at the sound of her heels cuh-lunking along the marble floor when Lucy brought her to visit her father there years earlier. The soft yellow glow from the overhead lights still made it feel like twilight all the time. Her father's office secretary, May, had always kept butterscotch candies on her desk and she let Allison spin around and around on her rickety swivel chair.

That was more than ten years ago. The new department secretary, Jacqueline, wore her blonde hair piled on top of her head, tentatively secured by the silver spike jammed into it. Jacqueline was from the outskirts of Paris and fond of short leather skirts and fishnet stockings. She kept a pack of Players where May's butterscotch candies used to be, and she squeezed a glop of vetiver lotion on her hands, rubbing it in, when she told Allison she was "not so seertain when Reeshar" would return. So, Allison pulled a copy of *Remembrance of Things Past* off the shelf and made herself comfortable in the worn-leather waiting room chair.

When Richard rushed into the office half an hour later, Jacqueline flipped her hand toward Allison to draw his attention. "Ali," he said, rushing to his desk. "I'm between classes. Just stopped to get my lecture notes for this graduate seminar." He was going to say he was due all the way across campus in ten minutes, but she strode into his office.

She didn't sit but told him that Charles had been particularly cantankerous that morning. "He said I should have been gotten rid of, like the other one." Richard looked away—like a child caught in a not-so-white lie. She smiled, knowing she would get what she wanted. A new place to live.

A couple weeks later, on a Thursday evening, after Marie stalked out of Charles's study, he called Allison in saying he'd "had qu-quiite enough" of her "sh-shenanigans." She would need to be more considerate of Marie, or she should pack her bags.

Allison figured it was probably the load of wash she had ruined by putting her red cotton sweater in with Charles's white sheets that set Marie off. Without a word, she left the room and scurried upstairs to pack.

After he heard Allison dragging her bags to the driveway, Charles picked up Emily's picture from his desk, stroked his finger along the line of his beloved's chin, then held the picture to his chest. "Sooooon," he told Emily as if he were cradling her in his arms. "I'll bbb-be ww-ith you ver-ry soon."

Richard closed the family room doors, then sat in his leather chair as Allison curled under an afghan on the couch. "You need to apologize to your grandfather," he said, reaching for his brandy. "Then you need to find another place to stay."

"I did nothing wrong. And I'm going to stay with you."

"You can't stay here, Ali."

"Why not?"

"Because Stephanie and Devon will be home from school soon for break. There isn't room for all of us."

"They have a father." She fished in her purse, pulled out a cigarette, and lit it. "They can't stay with him?"

"Corinne doesn't allow smoking in the house."

Allison looked at him through half-closed eyes, blew a petulant curl of smoke at the ceiling.

"Do you have to smoke?" Unable to sit, Richard downed his brandy then paced the room, his hands shoved deep in his herringbone trousers' pockets.

Allison nodded. "Jacqueline smokes."

"Not in the office," Richard said. "The girls' father," he continued, trying to control the timbre of his voice, "is on sabbatical, and he's rented his place to a new lecturer in the history department. Besides, you're almost twenty, and Steph and Dev are just teenagers."

"But it's my house." Allison rubbed out her cigarette in a small porcelain dish on the coffee table as Richard rushed toward it. She debated whether to remind her father that she wasn't yet nineteen. But if she did, he might be tempted to treat her like a child, like "the girls." And with what she'd been through, the term "girl" no longer applied to her.

"That's not an ash tray."

Without apologizing, Allison went on. "Well, it may not exactly be my house, but it's certainly more mine than Steph's or Dev's or Corinne's."

"Ali, it *was* your house. You grew up here. But you're an adult now. It's time—"

"For what?" She raised her eyebrows.

Richard wanted this conversation, this situation, taken care of, sooner rather than later. "What if we look for a place for you? One of your own?"

"A home of my own." She played with and tasted the idea as if it were dessert. "Very Virginia Woolf. But how do I pay for it?"

"You'll have to ask Olivia for more hours at the bookstore. Save more of what you make. In the meantime, your mother set aside some money for you."

Allison dawdled, hoping Richard wouldn't think he was getting off too easily or too quickly. She stifled a smile.

"There will be rules," Richard went on. "And we should get them out on the table. You'll need to keep up with the mortgage payments, and make sure the place stays in good repair." Allison nodded and smiled. Then she nodded and smiled again.

That afternoon, Richard called Nina Whyte, the realtor who helped Charles and Emily find their place. He asked her to pick out a few houses for Ali to look at the next day.

<hr>

"Out of your room *now!*" Richard yelled to Allison, then hurried back to the kitchen. If he hadn't been running to flip the French toast, he would have heard, "You mean Devon's room, don't you?"

When Allison padded out five minutes later, knotting the belt of her pink terry robe around her waist, Richard waved his spatula while he spoke. "Nina called. She's got a couple houses in Penn's Woods for us to look at and one on Grace Street. Then, at eleven, we're meeting Michael Sullivan at the bank. It would be good for you to wear a dress."

Allison picked at her breakfast, then showered and changed. At 8:20, she emerged wearing a turquoise flower-print shift, a yellow mohair cardigan, and a spray of baby's breath in her hair.

"Lovely," Richard forced himself to say, though it still rattled him when Ali dressed in her mother's clothes. Was it her way of holding him responsible for Lucy's death? He wasn't about to ask. He looked at Allison's feet and back up at her face. He set the frying pan and spatula in the sink and went to get a sweater. "You'll need shoes."

"Details." Allison drank a glass of juice, then stacked her dishes in the sink. In her room she pulled on a pair of knee-high white vinyl boots, then walked past Richard to the car in the driveway.

⁓

"I think you'll like any of these," Nina said as she handed Allison and Richard copies of property listings with pictures and descriptions of the houses she wanted to show that day: a clapboard Cape on Grace Street; a cottage with no basement on Elm Street; something brick of squarish, indeterminate style—Nina called it a bungalow—on South Avenue.

When Allison didn't look impressed, Nina handed her a stack of other listings, which she separated into piles—some no, some maybe. When she came to the pictures and descriptions of half a dozen ranch-style houses, Allison set them down. She crossed her arms and turned to stare out the window.

"I think we can skip anything ranch-ish," Richard said.

"Even these on the west side? The ones with such appreciation potential?" Nina asked.

"Even those."

They left the office with three listings to consider.

Nina took them into each house, waving her arms to show how Allison might, seemingly without funds or effort, move a wall here to get more light, or add a closet there to improve resale potential. Allison sped through each house, then waited at the door for Richard to chat with Nina as she pointed out a pull-down attic or a newly installed central vacuum unit. He didn't like the houses any more than Allison did but felt obligated to try to compensate for Allison's glacial chill.

By the time they reached the third house, Richard acquiesced and asked Nina to take them back to her office. They were driving down Silvermine Road, toward the tunnel and the center of town, when Allison blurted, "Stop." Nina gasped and braked suddenly, afraid she'd run over a skunk or a stray tabby, but Allison had rolled down her window and was pointing toward a house with a For Sale sign out front. "I want to look at that one."

The diminutive Victorian was set back from the road, almost invisible behind neglected wisteria and rhododendrons. Nina pulled over and backed up to the stone path to the house. If it made Allison happy, Nina was glad to oblige, even though the house had been on the market—with good reason—since Mrs. Kramer's death eighteen months earlier.

"I don't know, Allison." Richard enumerated problems with the place just from looking at the outside: peeling paint, missing roof shingles, overgrown shrubbery.

But Allison was already out of the car, unlatching the corroding iron gate. She felt her way along the stone pathway, almost visible beneath the belligerent weeds and matted leaves.

The narrow little house, with its stained-glass window in the front hallway and second floor turret, reminded her of the cover of *The Miracle Garden*, the story her mother read to her when she was a toddler. She imagined the house had once been painted a peach color, that the shutters on the nine-foot windows had been green, and that the scalloped trim and the gingerbread around the porch probably had been ivory.

Nina, meanwhile, explained that, although the house needed "a little TLC," and maybe some work on the heating system, it was a steal at sixty thousand. "It's one of the places Mairead MacMillan designed," she said. "It'll not only appreciate in value but qualify as a town landmark."

Allison ignored Nina and pushed through overgrown juniper and milk thistle to the back of the property. What was that smell? Working her way through the thorny tangle, she saw Miller's Pond. In a squared off area that was less densely overgrown than the rest, the scent became stronger.

"Rosemary." Allison heard Lehanna's voice. "For remembrance. And lavender to overcome distrust." She knelt on the moist soil and began clearing the prickly overgrowth and the flattened leaves, uncovering other herbs and perennials beginning to peek through the early spring soil. Eventually she saw that a square brick walk marked off what used to be a garden the size of a tapestry rug. "Tarragon for selfless sharing. Chervil for sincerity. Chamomile to make every dream come true." Yes, Lehanna was guiding her.

"Don't worry about that mess back there." Allison stood when she heard Nina calling. "Jack Farley's landscapers at the nursery can have this place looking like a park in no time. Just put some pachysandra over there. And some azaleas in front of—"

"This is the house I want."

Richard turned to Allison. He thought, at least he hoped, she was joking. It needed so much work. And wasn't the zoning board reviewing plans for a strip mall down the block?

"We haven't looked inside," he said. But when he turned to her, the fix of her gaze, the set of her jaw told him she was serious, and her small, sweet smile also suggested—for the first time since Lucy died—that maybe Allison could be happy again. How could he get her to see what a dump the place was without discouraging her? He tried to recollect what Corinne had told him about boundaries. How, if he couldn't set them, Allison would continue to demand her way, all the while resenting him for conceding.

"Nina says it's only got two bedrooms, Ali. That's not great for resale," he added. "You have to make sure you could get back the money you put into it. When you sell. Down the line."

Allison continued pulling weeds in the grass. "This is my house," she said.

Hope for further discussion, Richard knew, was over.

As the scent of a sale wafted her way, Nina fiddled with the lockbox on the back door. When it opened, she and Richard started in while Allison lingered in the yard. "Will you humor me and just come look inside? Ali?" Richard called. "Just to see what we're dealing with here?"

Allison wiped her hands on her dress, then reluctantly went inside, catching the heel of her boot in the cracked concrete step leading to the back porch.

"You okay?" he asked.

"Fine." She regained her footing and walked in to look around, ignoring both Richard and Nina.

"The kitchen looks a little tired," Nina said as they went into the small, dark room. The former owner apparently hadn't lived by the legend on the needlepoint sampler hanging over the sink. "Cleanliness is next to Godliness."

"Comatose is more like it." Richard breathed in short, shallow draughts of the greasy air. The wallpapered walls, the icebox, the red Formica counters with the metal strip along the front edge, all were covered with a sticky gray film. He ran his index finger along the stove, then held it up to show Allison—and Nina—the grime he collected in one little swipe.

"It's what happens when older folks end up alone." Nina motioned Allison to the living room, but she was admiring the yellow plastic-covered chrome chairs pulled up to a silver-gray Formica kitchen table, and the flamingo-shaped salt and pepper shakers. On the wall hung a clock that looked like Felix the Cat, with a tail that used to swing like a pendulum, stopped at 12:20. Allison felt she couldn't have decorated it better had she hit pay dirt at a full year of yard sales and flea markets. "Can I have the table and chairs, too?"

"They're part of Mrs. Kramer's estate," Nina said. But when she saw Allison's disappointment, she promised what she wasn't sure she could deliver. "I'm sure we can work something out."

Allison smiled. When can I move in?" She looked from Richard to Nina.

"Whoa, we have to talk to Michael Wright at the bank," Richard said. "And then make an offer to Mrs. Kramer's son."

"They want sixty thousand dollars, right?"

"It's not like buying shoes," he said. "There's a process."

"A process?" She tilted her head.

"You make a bid." With one hand in his jacket pocket, the other motioning in a circle, Richard tried to impress on his daughter that wanting a house wasn't the same as buying one. "You negotiate."

"Negotiate?" Allison liked the sound of the word. "Well, then." She slipped her arm through her father's and led him out the back door. "Let's negotiate."

⌒

Michael Wright looked warily at Allison. He understood she was very bright and wouldn't hurt a fly, but would she make her mortgage payments?

"You're offering fifty-five?"

When Richard nodded, Michael shuffled the application forms and assessed whether Allison's earnings at Metaphors justified the mortgage she was applying for. "This is a tough one," he said to Allison. "We figure out how much a person can afford each month based on income and credit history." He paused, turned the application to face Allison and Richard, and pointed to the lines showing Allison's estimated earnings for the year.

"I'll cosign," Richard said before Michael went further. "And we're willing to put twenty, even thirty percent down to get the monthly payments to a reasonable amount." Richard checked his watch. He knew Corinne wouldn't be happy that he acquiesced, but he had a class to teach in an hour and a half.

"Okay." Michael thought the loan was a stretch for Allison, but if Richard was willing to increase the down payment to help, who was he to judge? "Allison, if you'll sign here. And Richard, you sign here." He slid the loan application across the desk. "I'll take these to the approval committee this afternoon, and you should hear back by end of business tomorrow." Richard and Allison shook hands with Michael, then left the bank.

"I've got a class at twelve," Richard said on the way to the parking lot, "so I'll drop you off at the house on my way back to school."

"Sure," Allison said, but she was already dreaming about next spring in her garden and the butterflies that would make themselves at home there—Sleepy Dusky Wings among the lilacs, Painted Ladies in the asters, Silvery Checkerspots among the phlox.

She would put a light in the garden so she could read there at night, while the constellations changed with the seasons. She inhaled the scent of the honeysuckle and climbing roses she would plant there, to shelter the lavender and sage.

During lunch breaks from the bookstore, even before the title for the house was passed to her, Allison walked to the end of Center Street and crossed over to Elm, then turned down Silvermine, following the aromatic scent to number 173.

Sometimes when she unlatched the gate, she got so excited about having her own home, her own garden, she took off her shoes so there would be no barrier between her and the earth. Then she held her arms out wide and breathed deep into her chest. She wished she could share the place with her mother and Lehanna.

The feeling of belonging was beginning to root. For half an hour, sometimes longer when she lost track of time, she raked the carpet of soggy brown leaves. Without wearing gloves, she broke dead branches off bushes and tugged on overgrown vines until they pulled up from the ground, some with such force they sent her reeling backward. And sometimes, when she missed her mother and Lehanna most, she just knelt and kneaded the dirt, feeling that if she wanted them enough, they would come back to her.

When it was time to return to work, Allison wiped her mud-caked knees and dusted off her blouse and skirt. Then she rinsed under the spigot behind the house, pushed her hair back with a wide elastic band, and walked to Center Street.

Back at the bookstore, she did her best to dispense with customers efficiently and somewhat cordially so she could leaf through gardening books. She often laughed at their simplistic, naïve, or even false information, pitying the authors who hadn't had Lehanna for a teacher.

Allison moved into the house three weeks later. She brought her duffels of clothes, her journals, her books. From the shed in Corinne and Richard's yard, she took Lucy's old clippers, an edger, a shovel. That same day, she stopped at the animal shelter and left with two cats: a year-old tabby that had reached his paw out of the cage and petted Allison as she passed and a six-week-old fluffy orange kitten. She named them Mugwort, the protector, and Calendula, the sun.

Allison didn't clean much or paint when she first moved in, and she postponed patching walls and fixing dripping faucets. But she blessed and protected her house by lighting stems of sage and letting their smoke ease out any discomfort that was stored in the eaves. She tucked sprigs of pennyroyal in the kitchen cupboards to get rid of the ants and mint in the pantry to keep mice away.

She worked in the yard every day. At its own pace, the garden began to reveal its shape and history to her. She began to uncover four egg-shaped borders of lavender that faced toward the center, where a square border of rosemary enclosed silver thyme, bay laurel, and tree rose. Inside each of the four egg-shapes were plantings of mint, lovage, dill, and angelica, and at each outside edge, a small border of yarrow, filled by marjoram, verbena, valerian, and violet. After she thinned the perennials, fed them bone meal, and protected them with peat moss, she planned how, over time, she would fill in with basil and borage, tarragon and coriander. In the center, where the ovals intersected, she would plant allium—otherwise known as allicin—to make the garden her own.

When she heard the knock, Allison turned off the oven, grabbed a dishtowel to wipe her hands, and went to answer the front door.

"It's you." She felt as surprised to see her father on the porch as he looked uncomfortable being there.

"Yes," he said, "it's me."

"Well," she said. "Come in."

He walked into the living room noticing how Allison had not only cleaned it but made it look almost cheery with the new curtains and Lucy's sketches she had hung. "You've done a nice job with the place."

"I like it more every day." She knew her father must have stopped by for a reason other than to compliment her or the house. "What's up?"

He reached into his jacket pocket and held out a letter addressed to him. "It's from George Swenson—remember? The head of Cornell's research department, the one your friend Lehanna worked with?"

"Yes." Allison took the envelope, wondering why George Swenson wrote to her father. They didn't know each other, so his reason must have been important. "What happened?"

"It's all in the note," Richard said. "Apparently mail's not being delivered from Madagascar, at least not overseas. Lehanna tried to reach you by phone in Ithaca, but your number was disconnected. She's been able to keep in touch with George through university channels and asked him to get in touch with me." He shook his head. "Not unlike the rest of us who bury our heads in our work, George forgot until a few days ago. Then he wrote that." He motioned to the envelope.

Allison took out the note and scanned it. She smiled. No, Lehanna had not forgotten her. Even better, she would be back in the States in a matter of months.

CHAPTER TWENTY-ONE

Once Rusty started in the Viewpoint Program, Quinn moved out of Sherman's house and bought a three-bedroom ranch on MacMillan's west side, big enough for both of them. As soon as Rusty began earning enough at Fresh Air, they split the mortgage and chores. Most weekday evenings they ate pizza and drank Rolling Rock for dinner, or they grilled burgers or steaks on the Weber. After cleaning up, Rusty drove to his program group or his one-on-one counseling in the truck he bought at the Car-O-Rama. Quinn went to family night sessions, or puttered around the house, or met Sherm for a beer or game of pool.

On their nights off, they watched football or rented movies. Weekends they hunted whitetails or fished for rainbow trout, depending on the season, rode the rapids at Ohiopyle, or hiked the trails on Laurel Mountain or Blue Hill. Once in a while, when a gray film spread on the bathroom floor and sink, and when the dishes piled up, they thought about getting someone in to clean up after them.

"Wouldn't hurt to have a woman's touch around here," Quinn said one night while they finished off the large double cheese Rusty brought home for dinner.

Rusty looked at Quinn like he wanted to say something, then picked up the half slice of pizza left on his plate and kept eating.

"I struck a nerve?"

Rusty shook his head, reached for his beer, but set it down before he drank. "How am I ever gonna have a chance with a girl? After what I done."

Quinn crumpled his paper napkin, set it on the table, and pushed back in his chair. "I'm not the best man to answer that, seein' as I don't have much luck with ladies myself. But I know one thing. The girl you find is gonna be someone special. Someone who knows the past is the past. She's gonna see you got a good heart and that you're man enough to admit a problem and do somethin' about it."

Rusty tilted his chair far enough back so he could reach behind, open the refrigerator, and grab a can of Coke. He popped the top, still balancing on the chair, looking to Quinn as eager to please as the boy he took hunting when he first moved in with Lorraine.

"It's not so much her reaction I'm worried about." His words caught at first. "How can I be sure I won't hurt her? Or that I won't go back to what I was?"

Quinn pushed his plate toward the center of the table. His family group had warned him this subject would come up and he wished he could see the future and promise the kid everything would be okay. Instead, he said what he had been told to say by others who had gone through the same thing. "You're gonna practice everything you been taught at the Center, and you're gonna let people you trust help keep the demons away."

⌒

The next week, Rusty dropped off their laundry as usual at the Suds 'n Duds on his way to work. The clerk, a new girl, rummaged through the sheets and sorted the darks from the lights so she could give him a receipt. "You got here just in time."

"Say again?"

"I said," the girl spoke louder, "you got here just in time." She continued sorting darks from lights, socks and underwear in a different pile altogether. "You waited any longer to bring this stuff in, the health department mighta come after you."

Rusty smiled but didn't look up. He couldn't take his eyes off her hands, her slender fingers, with nails perfectly rounded and polished the color of cotton candy. "We're not much on keepin' house." Then he looked at her face as she sorted the clothes, imagining how her hands would feel unbuttoning his shirt, unzipping his jeans, tossing them off the couch or the edge of the bed, then running her pink painted nails along his neck, his back.

"Who's 'we'?" she asked, bringing her ring finger to her eye to remove a stray lash.

He wanted to help her find the eyelash and get rid of it, or anything else that might hurt this pretty girl or make her sad. "What you mean?"

"I mean who's the 'we' that's not much on keepin' house?"

"Quinn. He's . . . my stepfather."

"Well, you're right. Neither of you's too domestic." She piled the clothes on the scale, wrote a receipt, and handed it to Rusty. "I've always wondered how God created men, so sure of how smart they are, but so helpless they can't figure out how to run a washing machine."

Rusty smiled again. "I guess if we could read them directions, you'd be out a job."

"Oh, no." She shook her head. "This here's not my job." She leaned against the counter, tapping her long pink nails on the Formica, letting Rusty know that running a Laundromat did not play a big part in her future. "I'm just helpin' out my mother is all. But you are right about one thing, Mr. Jenkins. Your name is Jenkins, right?" Rusty nodded. "If it wasn't for men like you, my mother wouldn't have been able to support us with this place. So, I guess I got you to thank, in part."

"Well, I'd accept your thank you, but I don't know your name."

"Jolene. Jolene Cummings."

"And what is it you do when you're not helpin' out your mother, Jolene?"

"Study." She twirled a strand of sun-streaked hair around her index finger. "Over to Altoona. The school of cosmetology."

"You a hairdresser?"

"Not yet. A salon stylist is what I'm gonna be."

He studied her hair while she gazed off, still twirling, giving Rusty time to admire her uninterrupted. "I can see what a fine advertisement you'll make for your services."

She smiled, adjusting the bow at the throat of her ruffled blouse.

"But," he continued, "how is it you're gonna keep your customers from gettin' all mad at you, thinkin' they can't never look as good as you?"

Jolene picked a dirty tee shirt out of Rusty's laundry pile and tossed it at him. "Don't you have nowhere to go?"

"As a matter of fact, I do." He picked up the shirt and set it back on the pile of laundry, smiling all the while. "But I'll be back," he touched the bill of his cap. "Yes, I will, Miss Jolene Cummings."

⌒

"I think it's time we washed them sheets again." Rusty walked into the kitchen to grab a cup of coffee before he went to work. He set down the plastic laundry basket that was filled past its brim and took a mug from the cupboard.

Quinn looked up from the morning paper, wondering what brought on this sudden interest in domesticity. "Just did 'em a week ago."

"Still and all, they could use it."

Quinn folded the paper, set it down. "Since when you become so conscious of clean sheets and towels?" He had a fair idea of the answer, judging from the blush on Rusty's face.

"Like I said . . ." Rusty started. Then he decided, why not, he'd tell Quinn about Jolene. He'd been hoping over the last few days that Quinn would somehow, without him having to say anything, know enough to ask about her. "Since a pretty little blonde named Jolene Cummings started workin' over to the Suds 'n Duds."

"Jolene?" Quinn saw how the sound of the girl's name brought a smile to Rusty's face. "Pretty name."

"And she's ten times prettier than her name."

Quinn carried his cereal bowl to the sink. "You ready for this?" He spoke while he rinsed the dish, hoping Rusty would hear a casual tone in his voice.

"For what?"

"A girl."

Rusty turned from Quinn. He hunted through the fruit on the counter, looking for the right apple to take for lunch. "I don't know for sure. They say give it two years or so, and I'm almost there now. I figure if I don't try, I might never know. And this girl's worth tryin' for."

There was no discouraging him. Quinn saw that. "Then go for it, young man." He switched to a subject with less of a charge to it. "You thought of puttin' new tires on your truck? Them in the front's a little worn."

"I just might do that," Rusty said, tossing his apple in the air, catching it, then picking up the laundry basket under one arm. He opened the kitchen door. "Provided I got enough left of my paycheck after I buy the roses." He grinned at Quinn and walked out, whistling and carrying the basket like laundry was no chore at all.

~

One warm spring Sunday, Rusty was up by eight, though Quinn had heard him come in around three. Chugging down a mug of black coffee, he said he was taking Jolene and her mother to church, then back to Nancy Cummings's house for breakfast.

Quinn set down the morning paper, pausing before he spoke. "You must be pretty serious about the girl if you're takin' her and her mother to church."

"I love her."

Quinn hesitated. "She love you?"

"She says so. And I got no reason to doubt her." Rusty spoke with a confidence Quinn knew went deeper than wishful thinking. "But I feel I got to tell her."

"Tell her what?"

"About my past. My treatment."

"That's a decision you got to think long and hard about. If you've shown her enough of the man you are today, things'll have a chance of workin' out. You just got to be ready for the possibility they might not."

Rusty didn't say anything. But from the set of his jaw and the way his eyes focused straight ahead, Quinn knew Rusty was determined that things would work out with Jolene.

"It's your first time in love?" Quinn asked. Rusty nodded. "Well, young man, I suggest you buckle your seat belt and hang on for the ride. Now get your butt in gear and get to that girl's house on time. One thing women can't stand is a man who's late." Quinn turned to pour some coffee and asked over his shoulder, "When can I meet her?" But Rusty had already left the kitchen and turned on the shower.

⌣

Jolene showed Rusty in the house and led him to the kitchen where Nancy Cummings was setting things out for the breakfast she would serve after Mass. "This here's Rusty," Jolene said with a smile.

"A pleasure to meet you, ma'am." Rusty nodded to Jolene's mother and handed her the flowers he'd bought on his way. "These're for you."

"Why, there was no need for you to bring anything, Rusty," Nancy said. "But I'm pleased you did." She smiled when she admired the tulips and daffodils.

"I figured I owed you for all the times you done up my laundry so good."

"Well, it's nice to be appreciated." Nancy motioned Rusty into the living room. "I hope you're gonna be hungry."

"Yes, ma'am."

Nancy told Jolene to pour Rusty a cup of coffee, then hurried back to the kitchen with the flowers, calling over her shoulder for her daughter to find a vase in the breakfront. Before Jolene followed her mother into the kitchen, she hugged Rusty. "I can tell she likes you," she whispered.

"Did I dress all right?" He hadn't been to church since Nana took him when he was eight or nine. He was anxious about how to act and was relying on Quinn's advice to just watch and do what everyone else did. He had put on the white shirt and khaki pants he bought a while back at Sal's but borrowed a tie and sport coat—a little big in the shoulders—from Quinn.

"You did just fine." Jolene gave Rusty a quick kiss before she picked out a crystal vase from the breakfront and rushed off to the kitchen.

When Nancy came back into the room, dressed in her spring coat and hat, she held up her car keys and asked Rusty if he wouldn't mind driving her Impala, so they didn't have to squeeze into his truck.

"They all moved on," was all Rusty said in the car when Nancy asked about his family, relieved when she didn't press the issue. But he knew by the way she perked up when he mentioned working at Fresh Air that she was pleased.

"Bud's an usher at the ten fifteen," she said. "Maybe we'll set in one of his pews."

Jolene looked across the front seat to smile and let Rusty know he'd won another point with her mother. But Nancy was already going on about how when they got through with breakfast maybe Rusty could check out her furnace and see why it had been rattling so.

After church, Nancy set out scrapple and pancakes and muffins and eggs. Rusty didn't have to pretend he enjoyed the spread. Even though he spilled orange juice on Nancy's good white tablecloth, he knew she was glad he was there by the way she fussed over him, making sure he had seconds.

When they finished eating, while Jolene cleared the table, Rusty tightened the two bolts that had loosened around Nancy's furnace ducts. Then Rusty and Jolene changed into hiking clothes. With Nancy smiling and waving from the front door, they got into his truck and set out for a drive.

"You be careful now," Nancy called as they backed out of the driveway. "You got precious cargo in that truck."

"Yes, ma'am, you're right about that." They both waved as he turned the truck to Route 220, south and west, toward Ohiopyle State Park. Every once in a while, Rusty raised Jolene's hand to his lips or held it to his cheek. The air was warm against their faces and the scent of white pines so thick, they didn't notice the sulfur smell that still hung over the Plateau.

They left the truck at the base of the Laurel Highlands Trail and hiked up the ridge toward the summit where the Youghiogheny rapids tumbled below. "Know this trail like the back of my hand," he said as he led her to a ledge where the falls sent spray all the way up the ridge. As they sat dangling their legs over the sandstone edge, he told her how he and Quinn had run the rapids ten, maybe fifteen times.

"That's Devil's Truth." He pointed to the sharp bend where the water swirled most furiously. The Devil, as he told her the rapids were known, was the only Class Five run in the state. "Just about the most dangerous white water in the East." He didn't say that, in all the times he and Quinn had run the Devil, the turbulence below was nothing compared to the roil in his stomach as he searched for the words to tell her about his past.

"Your Mom's a good cook," he said instead. The right words were inside him. He just needed to settle down for them to come out.

"She worked her butt off to take care of us kids."

"Done a fine job, too." He pulled her toward him, kissed her, and she wrapped around him. He stroked her shiny hair, her manicured hand, then leaned away. "There's somethin' you got to know about me, Jolene."

"Oh, I already know plenty."

"What's that?" Rusty hoped her answer would assure him he was on solid enough ground for the admission he needed to make.

"That you got a big heart." She was wary now. "What else matters?"

"That I done things in the past I'm not proud of. Things that were wrong."

She pulled her hand away and set it in her lap, studying him while she imagined the worst he could tell. "You been in prison?"

"No, but I oughta been." He looked away. He'd rather dive off the ledge without a life jacket than tell the truth. "I just didn't get caught." Could the churning rapids below be any more threatening than the fear of losing her? "It was a while ago." He was close. So close. His heart raced. Then his stomach grabbed. "I sold drugs."

Jolene was silent. The whitewater whooshed below. Her voice tight, she braced herself. "You still sellin' drugs?"

He shook his head. "I been in a program for going on two years now. I don't use drugs and I don't sell 'em."

"You got plans to?"

He reached around her waist, bringing her close. "Only plan I got is to marry you and be the best husband I can."

"That's the only plan that matters to me." She nestled close. "And I want it carved in stone." She smiled and pointed to her ring finger. "The shiny kind that goes right here."

Then her smile faded. "I got a past, too." She told him how her father messed with her when she was young, until Nancy found out and threw him out. "Even though he died a couple years back, I never felt safe with a man. Not like I do with you."

When she finished, Rusty kissed her long and hard. Whatever chance he had of finding the right words to tell her the worst of his past floated away like a lonely leaf on the rapids below. "Don't you worry about a thing, Miss Jolene Cummings, soon to be Mrs. Jolene Jenkins. You're safe with me."

⌒

On the Fourth of July, before Rusty and Jolene knew she was pregnant, smoke from the fireworks still swirled in the humid air as the rest of the crowd left the WestMac High School field. Rusty reached for her hand as she gathered leftovers from their fried chicken dinner. "Let's hold back awhile," he said. She set aside their picnic basket and nestled into his arms under the stars and the nearly full moon.

"Now," he said, "close your eyes and make a wish." She did as he asked, knowing—or at least hoping—what was coming next.

"You're not peekin', are you?"

She shook her head while he pulled the little velvet box from his pocket. "Can I open 'em now?"

"Not just yet." He took the ring from the box, then reached for her left hand. "Now," he said.

When she saw the diamond—bigger than she hoped—she hardly heard him as he slipped the ring on her finger.

"Will you marry me, Miss Jolene Cummings?"

She threw her arms around him, so he took her answer to be yes.

She held up her hand, rotating it left then right so the stone caught the field lights, not taking her eyes off it as Rusty spoke. "Sparkles like a damn firecracker, don't it?"

"Yes, it does," she said. Then all the plans she had made in her diary tumbled out. When they should set the date. Where they should have the reception. How many they should invite.

The prattle only stopped after he checked to make sure everyone else had left the park. He settled her back on their blanket, unbuttoned her blouse, and told her how he never wanted to forget how she looked just that minute.

It was after one when they left the park, one thirty when they got to Nancy's house. Jolene knocked on her mother's bedroom door anyway, and Nancy rushed out of her room, tying her robe. "What happened? What's wrong?"

"We're gettin' married, Mom."

Once Nancy got the sleep out of her eyes, she wrapped her baby girl in her arms. She hugged Rusty, too, before she remembered the spongey rollers in her hair. "Oh, my word." She ran back to her room. "We'll talk about plans in the morning."

Around seven, when Nancy found them curled around each other on the couch, she made breakfast. They told her they had decided on next Valentine's Day, a Saturday, for the wedding. "That's fine with me if Father Malone's available."

When Jolene called the church, Father Danny congratulated her and confirmed the date. "You'll bring the young man by for prenuptial counseling?"

Jolene knew his question wasn't a question at all. "Yes, Father."

⁓

Not long after Labor Day Rusty pulled his truck into the driveway, then hustled into the house toting a six-pack in one hand, a couple stogies in the other. "Anybody home?" He popped two cans and set them out on the table while Quinn yelled from the basement. "Be right up."

When he came into the kitchen through the basement door, Quinn tried to figure out what looked different about him. "You got a bug or somethin'?"

"Nope." Rusty handed over a beer with one hand, a cigar with the other. "But I got a pregnant soon-to-be-wife."

"You two're havin' a baby?" Quinn reached for the beer and lifted the cigar to the match Rusty held out.

"That's what I said." Rusty bumped his beer against Quinn's for a toast.

"Damn! I'm gonna be a grandfather before I ever got to be a father."

"You excited?"

"'Course I'm excited." Quinn blew smoke rings into the air. "You're not?"

Rusty shrugged. "I'm only nervous 'cause I didn't tell Jolene yet."

"Didn't tell her what?" Quinn reached for an ashtray, set his cigar in it, and leaned against the table.

"About Viewpoint."

Quinn paused, trying unsuccessfully to control his dismay. "Where in the hell does she think you're goin' every Tuesday and Thursday night?" He pulled out a chair at the table and sat down, motioning to Rusty to do the same.

Rusty remained standing. "I told her I go for counselin' to keep away from drugs." He snuffed out his cigar, so he didn't have to look at Quinn.

"And how'd she take that news?"

"She said it didn't matter much. Long as I stayed off the stuff and didn't deal."

"Why didn't you tell her the rest?" Quinn heard his accusing tone but barreled ahead. "Isn't that what they advise? Your group, I mean. That you get these things out in the open with important people once you have enough time in Viewpoint?"

"Yeah, but there's other circumstances involved." Quinn's smirk told Rusty his excuse was lame, so he explained. "It's because of her father."

"Her father's dead, I thought you said."

"Yeah, he's dead. And she couldn't be happier. But he done things to her." Rusty didn't say what "things" meant, and Quinn didn't have to ask.

"And you're afraid she'll associate what you did with what her father done? That she'll leave you if she finds out?"

Rusty nodded. "And now she'll take my baby with her."

Quinn thought about what each one in his family group said about whether Rusty should or shouldn't tell Jolene about his history. Some may not have wanted him to tell too much too soon, but with the wedding coming up, and now the baby, Quinn figured they'd all agree Rusty had gone too long without speaking up.

He would rather walk on fire than say anything more now, when Rusty was so upset. He tilted back his beer, then set it down. "Well," he pushed away from the table, "I guess you got to handle it the way you feel's best." Then he went to his bedroom, took a red gym bag from his closet, and carried it back into the kitchen.

"This here's yours." He set the bag on the table. "Go ahead," he said. "Open it."

Rusty unzipped the bag. He reached inside, took out a handful of bills, then looked at Quinn. "Mine?"

"From the garage where Sherm and I found you that night," Quinn said. "And don't think I condone the way you come by it. But I can't think of a better cause to give it to than the little girl you're gonna have. Or," he smiled, "the boy."

CHAPTER TWENTY-TWO

When Eamon Malone walked out of the chilly March rain into Metaphors bookstore, the first thing he noticed about Allison—the first thing everyone noticed about her that day—was the green feather boa draped around the neckline of her otherwise unadorned black dress. He nodded and smiled as he approached the rack of new releases near the door. Though he got no response from the young woman, he kept his eyes on her while he pretended to give the bestsellers a cursory going over. She was working awfully hard to discourage him, or anyone else, from attempting to cross the moat she had dug around herself and filled with off-putting disdain. Still, she intrigued him.

Bent over an inventory list, checking it against the books that had arrived in the previous day's shipment, Allison acted like she didn't notice Eamon, even though Olivia had just last week reminded her to express a little more curiosity about her customers.

"You do a fine job of tidying the shop," Olivia said. "You're to be commended for that."

"But?"

"But people don't come here just to stay current or to expand their horizons. They come here to connect. Like E. M. Forster wrote in *Howards End*."

"The epigraph."

"Yes." Olivia smiled. "Our customers come here to make friends with characters between the covers and with us, too. They all—we all—just want to be heard."

Allison tried harder after that, striking up a conversation with Mrs. Lewiston after her third re-read of *Persuasion*. And with Mr. Silverstein, who enjoyed all things Doris Kearns Goodwin. But as often as not, she still preferred listening to the makings of a poem in her head. She had read that Eudora Welty often heard the tone of a book, like a tuning fork's vibration, deep inside her before a character or a plot started taking shape. If such internal music-making was good enough for Ms. Welty, it was good enough for her, too.

The Metaphors customers who knew Allison—at least friends of her mother, the ones whose children she'd played with when she was small—mostly figured Allison's distance resulted from her mother's death. Others muttered while counting their change about why Olivia kept her on, or how Richard, with his command of the English language, could have fathered a daughter who spoke so few words.

Eamon, though, on that rainy day in mid-March, was curious about the way Allison dressed—her bright yellow hair, her emerald eyeshadow, the same shade as her boa. If he wanted to know what made her so interesting, yet so scared, he would need to proceed slowly.

"See you next Thursday, Mr. Groves."

When he heard Allison say good-bye to the only other customer in the store, Eamon took off his hat and chased the rain from his slicker. He walked toward Fiction and leafed through *The Pelican Brief*. Then he took it to the cash register, where Allison was busy ignoring everything except the work spread open on the counter.

"So, you're celebrating the feast of Saint Patrick, are you?"

Allison looked up at him over her glasses, which she wore as extra insulation between herself and the rest of the world. She tilted her head sideways. Then her right hand reached for the very pointy edge of her black-plastic frames, where the rhinestones were set. She looked at him, his black hair stuck to his head because his hat had smooshed it down, and saw a blue-eyed pup caught in the rain. If she had a bone-shaped biscuit, she would toss it to him and watch him catch it mid-air. Then, as he licked his mouth and wagged his tail and circled back, looking for more, she would pat his head. "Good boy." She wanted to smile.

Her brown eyes were so vague, so uncomprehending. Maybe she was slow. "You're wearing green." He pointed to the boa. "Today's the seventeenth of March. I thought you might be celebrating."

"No," Allison said, suspecting this foreigner, of what she wasn't sure. "No," she said again, with so little invitation that most would have turned from her chill, as raw as the day's rain. "Today," she said, "I'm celebrating the fact that in only sixty days, give or take, the lavender plants in my garden will be in full bloom, and the air there will be fragrant and full."

"Well, then," he said. "There you are." Eamon smiled. "A feast day after all. And it's a sure thing Saint Patrick wouldn't mind sharing his day with as worthy a cause as your garden."

Allison suppressed a smile. The man had a quick wit. And those eyes, those white teeth, with just a little space there in the center, enough of a flaw to make him almost too endearing. She took the book Eamon held out to her, scanned the price. "Sixteen dollars and twenty-one cents." She slipped the book into a plastic bag. He pulled out a twenty, then fiddled with coins from his pocket. "Here, give me two of these and one of these." She reached for two dimes and a penny from his handful of change. She put the coins in the cash drawer, plucked out four dollar bills, then handed them to him with the receipt that spit out from the register. She heard Olivia in her head reminding her to be cozier with customers. Usually she ignored that voice, but today? She had promised she would try harder. She picked a yellow pencil out of the holder near the register, then tapped it on the counter.

"What brings you to MacMillan, all the way from Ireland?" She adjusted her glasses once again. "I assume you're from Ireland, anyway." She chewed her lower lip in a sulky little pout that she hoped showed she really didn't care whether he answered.

"And a fine assumption it is," Eamon said with more than enough enthusiasm to compensate for Allison's lack. "My brother's one reason. Danny Malone. The priest at Saint Michael's." Allison's disinterest told him that mentioning the Church didn't buy the approval it would from some girls in Ireland. "Back home I'm studying at University Galway, astronomy and literature. But this semester, I'm doing independent study with Richard Stephenson, then teaching."

Allison stopped her pencil tapping. She rolled her eyes. "Don't let him know you're reading Grisham."

Eamon laughed. "You know Professor Stephenson?"

Although secured by a dragonfly of too-blue rhinestones, the boa on Allison's shoulder began to slip. "He's my father." She adjusted her finery. "He didn't mention you," she said. "Then again, we don't talk much."

Her tone told him that the reason she and Richard didn't speak wasn't open for discussion, so he changed course. "I'm staying with Danny till I find an apartment." Eamon picked up the bag that held his new book. Then he put on his flat woolen cap and tipped the brim toward her. "A pleasure to meet you, Ms. Stephenson. What is it your friends call you?"

"Allison." Was it her imagination, or did her voice squeak a little when she spoke to this Eamon Malone? And her heart. Was it beating faster than it had before he started chatting in that adorable accent?

"Have a lovely day, Allison, celebrating your future lavender harvest."

When Eamon smiled, Allison felt a little ache in her chest. Not a pain. There was nothing sharp about it. Just a tiny tug that seemed to loosen her ribs and let her stand a little taller and breathe more deeply. She smiled, too.

He turned and walked out of the store, and she again focused on the inventory list Olivia had asked her to review. Until she heard the door close. Then she stole a look at Eamon through the window as he secured his new book on the back of his bike. The rain had stopped. He took off his slicker and tied it around his waist. He waved to her, but she pretended not to see him. When, out of the corner of her eye, she saw that he had pedaled past the store and was riding uphill toward the university, she closed her eyes. She breathed in long and deep, savoring the fresh scent of possibility that was left in his place.

For the next three days, Allison took extra care when dressing for work. No, she wasn't doing it for *him,* she would have told anyone who might have asked. Not that anyone would ask.

Yet her memory of his scent—she could only describe it as woodsy and minty at the same time—sent a tingle down her back when she got ready in the morning. It seemed to pull something dark and foul out of her, or at least dislodge it enough to make way for a little light. She sprinkled less rose oil in her bath. She didn't need as much. When she stepped from the tub, she dropped her towel and looked at herself in the mirror. Maybe she had let herself get a little too thin these last three years. Since that man changed her life. She decided not to apply lavender oil to her damp skin as she used to when Lehanna first gave it to her. Whatever was left of the swamp smell she had been trying to cover up seemed not so much to have disappeared, but to have lost significance.

On the fourth day, when Allison was about to abandon hope of running into Eamon again, she wondered what it would be like to not maintain such distance between her and the rest of the world. She reached for her drapey blue skirt, the one that floated a little when she walked. She chose the white blouse with the round neck and tiny tucks in front and the black ballet flats. She admired herself in the mirror, then tied a purple ribbon in her hair.

She took Lehanna's folios from under her bed and leafed through them to find a formula she vaguely remembered. A medieval wedding night boudoir, it was called, made by strewing verbena, marjoram, mint, thyme, valerian, and violet, all sacred to Venus, on the floor of the bridal chamber. A potpourri of these herbs in a bowl near the door was suggested, too, so anyone entering the room could stir the preparation with the fingers to release the scent and "enhance nuptial ardor."

~

Allison shelved a new shipment of paperbacks and thought how she might go home over lunch hour to work in the garden, when out of the corner of her eye, she saw Eamon ride his bike to the front of the store. After he locked the bike in the curbside rack, she made a quick and desperate dive for her purse under the cash register. She held her compact mirror close, touched up her lipstick and patted her hair. Before grabbing the special order list she had been compiling, she took off her glasses and stowed them in her purse. When she heard the door open then close, she pretended she hadn't noticed him for as long as she could. Then she looked up and smiled.

Eamon smiled, too, as he walked to the counter carrying a small white box tied with a pink ribbon. "I'm a bit late to be celebrating Lavender Anticipation Day, I know."

"Oh," she said, as she smoothed her hair again, "it's not so much a day as a season, anyway." She wished she could look at him directly, but her eyes roamed the store. "There's the mild winter to be taken into account. Then the cold snap two weeks ago. With that combination?" She shrugged.

"Still, I brought you a little something to see you through till harvest." He held out the box to her.

She looked at the package, then at him. She tucked a strand of yellow hair behind her ear.

"Well, thank you." She moved and spoke slowly. She didn't want to look as anxious as she felt. "Thank you."

"You can open it," he said, when she seemed to freeze.

"Oh, yes. I can. I will." She fumbled with her words and with the package's ribbon. When she opened the box, she leaned close to breathe in the scent of the lavender sachet. "It's lovely," she said. "Just lovely."

"There's a story behind it, you know," he said. "In Ireland, there's a story behind everything, of course. But tradition has it—and I've been told this has been going on for centuries now—that the giver of a lavender sachet is owed the honor of the recipient's presence at dinner."

When Allison hesitated, he continued, looking, she thought, very, very sad. "Of course, if she doesn't accept," he said, "there's no telling what might befall either of them."

She laughed and said she couldn't bear the burden of believing herself responsible for breaking a centuries-old tradition. So, yes, she would join him for dinner, would Saturday do? She wrote her phone number and address on the back of a sales receipt and handed it to him. "If I'm not home, just leave a message on my machine," she said, suddenly worried she might miss his call.

He said he would be in touch by Thursday, then told her he needed to get back to campus for class. This time, when he took his bike from the rack and looked through the window at her before pedaling up the hill, she smiled and waved.

⌇

Wednesday evening, when Allison came in from work and found no message on her answering machine, she spoke out loud to herself. "Just accept the fact. He's not going to call." She fed the cats, tore a head of lettuce into salad for herself, then set out the ingredients for double-fudge brownies. She creamed the butter, the sugar. She stirred and tasted. Beat the eggs, the water, the oil. Sifted the flour. Added the baking powder, melted the chocolate, and stirred again. She tossed in a handful of chocolate chips and a little peanut butter, then stirred one last time. After she put the pan in the oven, when she was rinsing the beaters under the faucet, the phone rang. Wiping her hands on a towel, she rushed to answer, but let it ring three times before picking it up. She braced herself against the wall. "Eamon who?" she asked when he said who was calling.

After agreeing he would come to her house at six on Saturday, they hung up, and Allison ran to her bedroom, pulling outfits from her closet and considering what she would wear. She held up this dress, then tried on that skirt with three different tops. She smooshed her breasts together to see if a push-up bra would look better than no bra at all.

When she smelled smoke from the kitchen, she ran downstairs, tripping on the dress that she was pulling on. She took the brownies from the oven and emptied them into the trash. She wasn't hungry after all.

In her garden before dawn on Saturday, Allison pruned and edged and weeded by the light of torches she set out around the brick walk. She looked up from her work in time to watch night leave the sky. She didn't need Lehanna's folios to tell her the new moon could portend fortuitous beginnings.

She worked through the day without stopping, raking up limp brown leaves, soggy sticks, and other winter remnants. When she went inside around three that afternoon, she set a pot of water on the stove for tea, then slipped into a tub full of fragrant bubbles. She removed the deep red polish from her nails, replacing it with pale peach. After she washed her hair, she blew it dry, imagining how it might look if she let the natural brown color grow in.

When Eamon arrived at six, he wasn't wearing his hat, and his hair wasn't matted down. Allison noticed for the first time how it curled around the sides of his ears and how a lock fell in a playful wave in the center of his forehead. She told herself not to stare but couldn't take her eyes off it. She wanted to put her hands through it, to tousle the curls, then to hold this man close and listen to his heart.

"Come in," she said. "Please." When she tried to open the screen door, it scraped against the porch, like it always did, and got stuck half open. She tugged at it, trying to open it farther, until Eamon reached for the door from the outside, lifted it a little, opened it all the way, and stepped in.

"You might need a little taken off the bottom there," he said, motioning to the door. "I could do that for you."

She felt weak at the prospect of him fixing her door and of waking next to him and not wanting him to leave.

"You look lovely, as always," he said when they went inside. Then he looked around the house and smiled. "I like your place. Very homey."

"It's not perfect." she said, sweeping her arm toward the living room, thinking she might have dusted or vacuumed, or at least picked up the pile of newspapers and books by the couch. "But it's home." Home? Did she just say it was home? "Have a seat while I get my coat."

But, as always when Eamon first entered a room with bookshelves, he gravitated toward them and ran his finger along the books' spines. Joyce. Chekhov. James. And Austen, of course. Then he picked up a picture and stood holding it when Allison came back in the room.

"Your mother?" he asked. "You look like her," he said when she nodded.

"Not really," she said. "Mother was beautiful."

"She's passed on?" Allison nodded again, and he set the portrait back on the shelf. He resisted reaching for her, telling her he couldn't imagine anyone more beautiful, more perfect than she was. But he hesitated, because he saw in the way she diverted her eyes that she would run like a baby rabbit if he offered too much comfort or praise too soon.

"Maybe it's the mirror you've been looking in." He tucked his hands in his jacket pockets.

Allison said nothing. She put on her coat, standing far enough across the room so Eamon wouldn't try to help. Then they went out the door, down the stone path, and up Silvermine toward the center of town.

—

"Three sisters," Eamon said at dinner, when Allison asked about his family. "All of us raised on the farm in Connemara. Until Danny and I were sent away to study."

When he went back to Ireland, he said, he planned to teach, to offer other children of modest means a chance at a good education—like he had. He talked about the land, and how there was no place as green and, especially in the west, as invigorating. "Topographically, it's not unlike the land around MacMillan," he told her. "But we've got the ocean there, of course, and the rain." He smiled. "Have you ever been?"

"To Ireland?"

Allison shook her head. She didn't know she had been born just weeks after her parents' honeymoon there.

"Well," he said, "that's something easily fixed with a plane ticket."

Was he inviting her? Of course not. Way too soon to think of anything more than what it would feel like the first time he stroked her hair, the first time he leaned close, then lingered, for what would seem an interminable few seconds, before brushing his lips against hers. No! Too scary. She reached for her purse. She needed to leave.

"Don't go," he said.

When he took her hand, she withdrew it, but set her purse back down.

"Tell me about you."

She hesitated, emotions playing tug-of-war inside her, then started slowly. About her mother. How Lucy used to incite her imagination but died the summer before she left for college. She told him about Lehanna and how, when she left for Madagascar, Allison felt she had nowhere to go but to MacMillan, even though it no longer felt like home.

"And why is that?"

Why was that? How could she tell him about the man who robbed her of the freedom to call anywhere home? How could she explain the men after him? And Richard and Corinne and their impetuous rush to each other, so soon after Lucy died? She swallowed. It was inconceivable that she could tell him not just the facts of her life, but the truth. "There isn't much more to tell," she said.

He smiled and shook his head. "Of course, there is. You've got goals and dreams, don't you? Maybe you want to pick up where you left off in your studies? Or learn more about what Lehanna taught you? Or maybe you just want to grow the most abundant, fragrant garden of lavender?"

Allison fumbled with her napkin. Goals and dreams? Were they still possible?

"Mud pie to finish up?"

Allison looked to the waiter when he approached and proffered dessert menus. "No pie for me," she said. "But maybe ice cream. Chocolate chip?"

"Chocolate chip it is."

Allison looked across the table to Eamon. She smiled. Chocolate chip ice cream versus mud pie. She still had choices. Maybe, with a little more time, she could have hopes and dreams again, too.

⌒

A few Sunday afternoons later, Allison made fried chicken, fruit salad, and banana bread. She brewed iced tea from peppermint and nettles and packed everything in the wicker hamper Lucy used for their trips through Pennsylvania's countryside. It was warm for early April, perfect weather for the pond-side picnic she planned for Eamon.

"Watch out for those rascals," she said when she handed Eamon the hamper. She pointed to Mugwort and Calendula, who were flirting with Eamon's shins, hoping a little leftover chicken might be tossed their way.

As they walked along the stone garden path, Eamon stopped. A slow smile came to his face. "Your garden's the shape of a Celtic knot." He turned to Allison. "Did you know that?"

She shook her head. "I only followed the pattern Mrs. Kramer laid out. I cleared the brush and gave the perennials some breathing space. It doesn't look like much now, but it will in a month or two when the perennials wake up and I add some annuals for color."

"None of that self-deprecation, now," he said. "It's a fine job you've done."

When they had eaten their fill, and after Eamon read to Allison from a book of Seamus Heaney's poetry, they picked up their plates and napkins, stuffed them into the hamper, and shooed the cats ahead of them. He hesitated before starting back to the house.

"I wish I could stay longer," he said, "and watch the stars come out with you." He started to reach for her but put his hands in his pockets instead. "But I've got to prepare for class tomorrow."

She smiled but said nothing. If she told him she wished he could stay, too, all the desire and need she felt since her mother died might overtake Eamon like a rowdy ocean swell. It might sweep him up and carry him off, while, smaller and smaller, he waved from a distance, eventually melting into the horizon. She clasped her hands in front of her. "Maybe you could come another time," she said.

Eamon placed his hands on her upper arms. He tried to urge her toward him, but she resisted. Instead, he ran his hand over her hair, then smoothed a strand from her face. "Whatever it is that makes you so scared, Allison, I hope it's something you can put aside. I want to know you. Even just a little."

She looked down, away from Eamon, then back again. "I . . ."

"You what?"

"I hope so, too."

He grazed her cheek with his lips. It wasn't a kiss, Allison thought, so much as a tender promise. *I won't hurt you.* She reached to the warm spot on her face, then stroked her hands down her dress.

"I'll call you this week?"

She nodded. Without touching her again he smiled and waved as he went out the door, down the sidewalk, and up the hill toward school.

⌒

For the next months, Allison and Eamon spent most Sunday afternoons together. He built a garden bench, facing the pond, and installed lights so she could read there at night. He shaved off the bottom of the front porch door, so it no longer scraped the floor when it opened and closed. He repaired the backdoor screen so Mugwort and Calendula couldn't weasel their way to the yard and maul the catnip Allison planted under the maple tree, mulched with cedar chips and eucalyptus, to keep fleas away.

"Time to start working inside," Eamon said once the garden was established and the house exterior repairs completed. "If you want, that is."

"Yes," she said. "Of course." And maybe, she thought, maybe . . .

They painted the kitchen a creamy color and wallpapered the living room in a navy William Morris print. Some Saturdays they combed antique shops in Tyrone and Hollidaysburg for Eastlake Victorian chairs and mirrors, and Empire marble-topped tables, so the living room looked as it would have when the house was built. They hired a painter to do the outside of the house in peach and cream, but they painted the shutters themselves. When they hung them again—forest green—Allison put gauzy sheers in all the windows.

One steamy Saturday night in August, after a movie in town, they sat in the garden, drinking lemonade, when Eamon sat forward on the bench. "I haven't told you much about me and my family, have I?"

She shook her head. She hadn't asked him much because she thought that if he told her about his family, she would need to reciprocate.

"I'd like to."

She set her lemonade on the side table and curled in the corner of the bench. "I want to hear."

He told her how, with five children in the house, there wasn't enough money. Danny was sent to seminary and Eamon to Dublin with his mother's sister. "I was glad for the education I got in the city, but"—she had never seen sadness in his eyes or heard it in his voice— "I missed my family. Danny especially." He chuckled. "Even my sisters' constant chattering.

"I missed the deer in the fields and the Aran Islands across Galway Bay, too. But most of all, I missed having a place to call home." He reached to her and stroked her arm. "You know that line from Robert Frost. How home is where, they have to take you in, no matter what?"

She nodded.

"There was nowhere to go where they could—or really wanted to—take me in."

Allison said nothing at first. But she knew why she felt safe with this man. He knew what it was like to drift. She turned to him, pulled her legs up on the bench, and hugged them toward her.

"I would like to hold you, Allison," he said. "You don't have to tell me what makes you so scared, only that you're not afraid when you're with me." She inched her way across the bench. He put his arm around her. Then she curled in his lap, leaning her head against his chest, and listening to his heart. She heard her own heart, too. She felt at once small and protected and powerful and free. It was time to try.

She circled her arms around his waist, and Eamon told her the story of the monks of Skellig Michael, and how one dark night they witnessed, almost ten centuries earlier, a spasm of light that—for just a moment—lit the whole sky. "It was the death of the star in Taurus," he said. And when she looked sad that a star could die, he told her she needn't worry. New stars were in the making.

"See the sword in Orion?" He pointed to the three stars descending from the great warrior's belt. "How the middle one looks fuzzier than the rest?" She nodded. "It's not a star at all. Not yet anyway. If we had a telescope, you could see a swirling cloud of gas, heated to fluorescence, filling out Orion's whole body. It's called the Great Nebula, an ocean of infant stars."

He told her then how Apollo sent the deadly Scorpio to kill the great hunter Orion because he had designs on Apollo's sister, Artemis. Orion escaped but Apollo tricked Artemis into killing the hunter with an arrow. When she swam into the sea to claim her victim, and realized she had killed her lover, she begged her father to bring Orion back to life. Zeus refused, so Artemis placed the great hunter in the sky, where he remains to this day, just out of the scorpion's reach.

While Eamon talked, Allison remembered the different tale of Orion her mother taught her. How Lucy said he was a hunter, with suspect motives, and how the scorpion was always at his heels to chase him away. She thought a while about which story to believe but fell asleep before she could decide. She wakened an hour later, with Eamon's arms still around her.

"Stay," she said when he woke.

The next day, Eamon brought over his duffel. The following week, his backpack and steamer trunk. His only requirements, he said, were a bookshelf all his own and her as much as possible. She swept out the back bedroom. The cabbage roses on the wallpaper had faded, and the ceiling occasionally dropped a piece of plaster on his work as he studied into the night, but Eamon hung a picture of his brother and sisters on the wall, stacked his books on the shelves, and made himself at home.

The next week, Allison stopped bleaching her hair, except with lemon juice. By late summer, it fell around her face in soft, caramel waves.

CHAPTER TWENTY-THREE

Eamon flailed at the clock from his groggy half-sleep until his hand landed on the snooze alarm. Mercifully, the buzzing stopped. When it sounded again ten minutes later, he groaned, leapt from under the quilt, and hurried to the bathroom in the underwear he slept in. When Allison heard his footsteps crossing the tile bathroom floor, then the hardwood in the bedroom, she threw the covers open to make room for him to jump back into bed.

"For the love of God, it's cold in here, even for October," he said, diving under the blankets, circling his arms around her waist, and pulling her toward him. Only half awake, she murmured that the furnace hadn't gone on the day before, but her words melted into dreamy little moans when he whispered he would show her how men kept women warm in Ireland.

After they made love, Eamon showered to get ready for school. Allison went to the kitchen to make tea and toast. She tried to adjust the thermostat in the hall after setting the water on the stove to boil, but when Eamon came out for breakfast, the furnace still wasn't working.

"Best to have someone come take a look." He brought her close to him on his way from the refrigerator to the table. "Heating, unless it's between the sheets, is beyond my abilities."

Giggling, Allison disentangled herself from Eamon's arms. "I have no idea who to call for above-the-sheets heating management." She reached to salvage a burning piece of toast from the toaster.

Eamon had already grabbed the phone book and was thumbing through while Allison handed him a cup of tea. "Heating and air conditioning," he said, running his finger down a column of ads in the yellow pages. "Here's what we need. This place called Fresh Air. Bud Johnson, owner, it says. One of Danny's parishioners, I think." He dialed the number and left a message on the answering machine. "Eamon Malone's the name, 555-4639." He hung up the phone, finished his tea, then kissed Allison before bundling up and riding off on his bike to campus, half-eaten piece of toast in hand.

Later that morning, Bud from Fresh Air returned Eamon's call as Allison was stepping out of the shower. She wrapped a towel around her, left a trail of wet footprints on her way to grab the phone, and made an appointment for a service man to look at the furnace late that afternoon.

⌒

Allison came home from Metaphors at four, as she usually did on Thursdays. She was making tacos for dinner when the doorbell rang at five. She wiped her hands on a linen towel at the kitchen counter.

She opened the front door. The man who stood on the porch—slender and not too tall, clean-shaven, with closely cropped red hair—nodded and smiled. "Fresh Air, ma'am." He wiped his feet on the mat. She returned his smile and showed him in. "You done some work on this place." She smiled again, glad her efforts were recognized. "Paint job looks real good."

"Thank you." Allison looked more closely at his eyes. Pale and blue, they sparkled like crystals of new-fallen snow. Pretty, but icy, too.

"Where's your thermostat at?" When she led him to it, he fiddled with it, but nothing happened. "She won't kick on, that's the problem?"

Allison nodded. "It started acting up late last spring, really, but we haven't needed it until now."

"Better take a look downstairs," he said, and Allison turned to point the way. But as she led the man to the basement door, she stumbled. She coughed once, then put her right hand to the side of her head, reaching with her left to steady herself against the hallway wainscot.

"You all right, Mrs. Malone?"

"Just a little woozy," she said, still holding her hand to her temple. "A cold coming on maybe." Something was wrong. Her stomach lurched. The smell of this man—a boggy, swampy smell— stirred up emotional rubbish she thought had been buried and decomposed. Startled, she turned toward him. His blue eyes looked indecipherable, limitless. They were not to be trusted.

"Get you a glass of water, maybe?"

"No," she said. *It can't be him.* "No, thank you." She continued to the basement door. She turned the key, then the knob. When she pulled the door open, it groaned as it always did. Usually, she took comfort in the predictable sounds of her little old house. She turned to lead the man into the basement, then stopped. She motioned for him to take the stairs first. When she followed, the wooden steps creaked beneath her. *Watch out.* At the bottom of the stairs, she reached for the chain on the single overhead bulb.

Allison turned to face the man, who was taking off his jacket. Embroidered in red over the pocket of his denim shirt, where a couple of Slim Jims were stowed, was the name *Ron.* While Ron opened his tool chest and pulled out a screwdriver, a hammer, and a pair of pliers, Allison looked around the basement, past the washer, the snow tires, Eamon's boxes of books. The smell of the place—no, the smell of *the man*—was making her sick. How would she escape if she needed to? The little windows were too high, too small. Could she get to Eamon's workbench to grab a hammer maybe, or something sharp? Mugwort wound around Ron's feet and arched his tail in a question mark. When Allison reached to shoo him away, his tail straightened into an exclamation point. He hissed and ran upstairs.

"He gets a little excited around strangers," she said while looking more closely at the man named Ron. "I'll be in the kitchen." She glanced over her shoulder before starting up the stairs. "Just yell if you need anything."

"Thank you, ma'am."

She ran upstairs, closed the door behind her, and leaned against it, trying to steady the breath that escaped her chest in quick, loud spurts. She wondered if Ron could hear her all the way downstairs. She wanted a shower, a bath, to scrub the smell off her. She ran upstairs to the bathroom, slammed and locked the door behind her, then turned on the water to fill the ball-footed tub and to drown the sound of her breath. She started to unbutton her sweater but was afraid to take off her clothes. She pushed aside the lace curtain and opened the window. She turned off the water, then stood at the pedestal sink, kicked off her shoes, and felt the cool tiles beneath her feet. She opened the wooden medicine cabinet and reached for something to take away the fear, but knew that aspirin, camphor salve for cold sores, even eucalyptus balm wouldn't work.

When she closed the cabinet and looked in its mirrored front, she ran her hands over her face, then under the water. She rubbed them with soap, then scrubbed them with her nailbrush. She reached into the closet, grabbed the cleanser, shook some on her hands and scrubbed again to get rid of the smell, then scoured her face and legs. She splashed water on her hair, her feet, and toweled them dry. Leaning forward suddenly, she retched into the sink, but she had nothing to vomit. She shivered, then went to the little vanity that she'd brought from her mother's house. She sat on the stool, covered with pink-and-white chintz. When she started shaking, she wrapped her arms around her torso to steady herself. *Get up,* she chastised her frightened reflection in the vanity mirror. *Get up and get rid of the smell.*

She stood and went back to the kitchen, pausing to put her ear against the basement door, listening to the man banging on pipes, and the scraping sounds of metal on metal. From the closet, she pulled out a mop and a plastic bucket. She filled the pail with water, added a half bottle of ammonia. She scrubbed the walls, then the fake brick linoleum floor. She sprayed the appliances and wiped them down. The clock in the shape of a cat. The yellow plastic-covered chairs. The microwave on the counter. Cleanliness is Next to Godliness. She wiped the glass over the needlepoint and repeated its message to herself. Over and over. *If I get rid of the smell, I'll feel safe again.*

In the basement, Ron continued rattling and hammering. The vibrations passed through the pipes and right on through Allison. She shook as she washed, mopped, and scrubbed the same surfaces again and again.

When the clattering stopped, she heard the man named Ron packing up his tools, getting ready to leave. Watching the basement door, she used the kitchen phone to dial Eamon's office, but the department secretary said he was in class. She left a message. "I need to hear your voice." She called her father, but he wasn't in his office. "No message," she told Jacqueline.

She opened the front and back doors, even though the crisp autumn air sent a chill through the house. When she heard Ron's footsteps on the stairs, she grabbed a knife from the block on the counter. She went into the living room so she could get out easily and quickly if he tried to hurt her. She stowed the knife behind the oval-backed lady's chair she bought in Duncansville a few weeks earlier. Then she grabbed tight to the carved roses at the top of the chair's frame. And when Ron came through the basement door, a muck-dredging phantom rising out of her past, she braced herself.

"Looks like your blower motor needs repair, Mrs. Malone." He knew for a fact the part was back ordered, so most likely he wouldn't be back with it until next Monday or Tuesday. Meanwhile, he put in a new filter to replace the dirty one that he held up to show her. "Till the motor comes in, I suggest you keep these doors closed." He smiled. "Cold came on sudden this year, didn't it?"

Allison nodded, her jaw clenched, her eyes unblinking. She shivered.

Ron said something about how most years MacMillan got another week or two of Indian summer and wasn't it a shame they didn't get that extra time to enjoy the outdoors? "Mind if I toss this in your trash?"

She shook her head and Ron carried the old filter out the back door. She hugged herself from the cold but didn't move from behind the chair. When he came back in, he walked toward the front door, toward her. "Tuesday's all right for me to come back?"

She took two steps away from him. The smell again. She clutched her stomach. "Tuesday. Yes. Tuesday afternoon would be good. Call first, to make sure I'm home." He smiled, tipped his hat, and walked out the front door. Once he was on the porch, Allison shut the door and secured the dead bolt. She ran to the back door and locked it, too. Then she hurried to the living room window to watch Ron load his equipment in the van, light a cigarette, get in, and drive off.

She closed the window blinds and sank into the chair near the door. She didn't want to move, but she knew she must do something. She peeked out the window again, making sure Ron had left, that he was driving down the street. She ran to the bathroom, rummaged under the vanity, and found the hair color she had stopped using months earlier. She mixed the formula, inhaled its ammonia smell until she gagged, hoping its pungency would drive away the man's smell, or at least cover it up so she could think straight. She spread the paste on her hair, waited the thirty minutes for it to work. She made tea, valerian and kava. Not strong enough. Could anything slow her heart and calm her thoughts? She patted Mugwort, then picked up Calendula and rocked her. She rinsed her hair. Without drying it, she went to bed.

She didn't get up that evening, even when she heard Eamon close the front door. When he came into the bedroom, and asked if she was all right, she told him she had been making dinner when the man came to fix the furnace, that she felt faint and chilled. He sat on the edge of the bed.

"Your hair." He reached toward her. When she turned from him, he leaned away. He had no idea why she had retreated into her fear and her yellow hair but suspected the worst thing he could do now was to ask her to explain, to try too hard to comfort her. "How about dinner?"

No, she said, she just needed to rest. When he went back to the kitchen, Allison gathered the comforter and blankets around her, struggling to feel warm.

⁓

Friday was Allison's day off. She was still in bed when Eamon left for school. As soon as she heard the front door close behind him, she shot out of bed, ran to the bathroom. Without showering, she put on makeup. She gelled her hair and sprayed it into meringue-like peaks, the way she wore it when she first met Eamon. She pulled on a long black skirt, a bulky black mohair sweater, and wrapped a blue challis scarf around her neck. She put out extra food for the cats, stuffed her black leather bag with a notebook, a sandwich for lunch, a thermos of tea. She went to the attic and opened the trunk she had brought from her mother's house. She took out the quilt and the hairbrush, the ones from that night. She gagged as she stuffed them into a shopping bag. Then she called Eamon at his office to say she was feeling better and was going to the Carnegie Gallery. Did he forgive her for being so cranky and cold the night before?

"Of course," he said. "You're sure you're okay now?"

For a moment, Allison thought of telling him about Ron, but first she needed more information. She needed a plan. "I'm okay."

Allison drove west to Pittsburgh. But when she turned onto the expressway toward the center of town, she headed up Front Street to the library instead of going to the Carnegie. She parked across the street and put on a pair of dark glasses and her wide-brimmed black hat with the pheasant-feathered band. As she walked toward the square, gray building, pigeons fluttered near her feet. The library's solid, reliable appearance calmed her like she imagined a kindly aunt would. When she walked through the revolving door, into the lobby, she remembered how she always loved the attic-smell of the place when Lucy brought her there. She loved the librarians, too, and their purposeful confidence when searching for answers, no matter how obscure the question.

Allison walked past the reception area to the research desk. The woman seated there asked in a thick Slavic accent how she could help. The librarian's name, according to the plaque on her desk, was Hedviga Huryz. She looked to be about sixty, with short graying hair crimped into tight curls. She wore a white blouse, a straight brown skirt, and serviceable rubber-soled oxfords, and Allison found herself wanting the woman to hug her, to comfort her in those round, fleshy arms. But even though Hedviga was a stranger, and Allison would never see her again, she didn't want to tell her—or anyone—the truth.

"I'm working on a report for a social work course. I need to know how long a woman has to bring a case against a man who raped her when she was young."

"How young?"

By the tilt of the woman's head, the narrowing in her eyes, Allison wondered if Hedviga suspected the truth.

"Sixteen."

The woman nodded slowly, still eyeing her. Allison wanted again to confide in her. But Hedviga rose from her desk. She led Allison past students studying in carrels, and gray-haired men reading sports pages and financial news, to a corner where the musty, library smell was strongest.

"Aye." Hedviga strained to the lowest shelf and pulled out a couple hefty leather-bound volumes. She set the books on a nearby table and put on the glasses that hung from a chain around her neck. With her left hand on her hip, she flipped through the first book, then the second. She hesitated about halfway through. Using her index finger, she navigated through a page of tiny type. "Dis is vhat you vant, yes?"

Allison smiled and thanked Hedviga. When the woman turned and walked back toward her desk, Allison pulled a pen and pad from her purse. She sat down to read and take notes. She skimmed the text, then sat up straight in her chair when she found the pertinent paragraph. The statute of limitations for rape in the state of Pennsylvania, the reference stated, was five years after the victim turned eighteen for a criminal case. But the victim had the right to file a complaint for damages in a civil case beyond the five-year limit, provided sufficient evidence was presented. After she made notes, she glanced down the list of phone numbers for the district attorneys' offices around the state. Her index finger followed the alphabetical listing until she reached Tyrone, the office closest to MacMillan. After she wrote down the number, she returned the books to the shelf, went to a phone at the back of the library, and dialed the number.

"I want to speak to the district attorney." Her voice was steady, but quick.

"In reference to what?"

Allison winced at the sound of the woman's sour voice. "I have a friend," she said, figuring a half-truth was the most expeditious route, "who was raped. She wants to take the man to court." Allison spoke clearly and directly now that she had a plan. The law, at least, would be on her side. She felt less afraid, less ashamed. She could punish the man who harmed her. Ron would never hurt her again.

The receptionist said she would put Allison through to the assistant district attorney in charge of the regional sexual violence unit.

"Elizabeth Reedy." When the woman announced her name, quickly and with no hint of humor, Allison felt she was in competent hands.

"I have a friend," she said as she began her story again, "who was raped three years ago in MacMillan. She knows who assaulted her and she's got evidence."

"And?"

"And she wants to file charges against him."

Elizabeth asked how old the friend was when she was raped and what kind of evidence she had. Allison answered, then asked questions of her own.

"Can my friend come see you? In about two hours?"

"Unfortunately, I'm leaving for Harrisburg in about half an hour. I won't be back for a couple days, so I can refer your friend to another assistant DA—"

"No." Allison trusted this woman's voice. She would wait. "What about next Tuesday?"

"Five o'clock?"

"That's good."

"Does your friend know how to get to the Tyrone Municipal Building?"

Yes, Allison said. Her friend knew Tyrone and would be there by five.

"Tell her I'm on the third floor."

When Allison left the library and got in her car, she needed both hands to steady the key so she could insert it in the ignition. She started the car and put it in gear to pull out of her parking spot. But she saw Ron's face. She heard his voice. She smelled him. She slammed the car into park again. She grabbed a tissue from her purse, wiping away tears, wishing she could as easily wipe away her memory of him. Then she fixed her eyes on the rearview mirror. There was no need to cry anymore. She knew what needed to be done. She tossed the tissue into her purse, pulled out of her parking spot, and drove to the Carnegie Museum.

That night over dinner, when Eamon asked her about the Post-Impressionist exhibit, she said she was partial to Gaugin's revolutionary use of color, but that she still favored Van Gogh.

CHAPTER TWENTY-FOUR

Tuesday morning, Allison waited until Eamon left for school before she called Olivia. "Just a twenty-four-hour bug. That's what my mother called this kind of thing," she said, confident that if she alluded to Lucy, her boss wouldn't consider coaxing her to come in. After hanging up, she cleaned the house. Windows. Doors. Floors. Furniture. She sprayed and scrubbed and mopped and wiped. She opened all the windows, but the acrid smell of ammonia and bleach blotted out the scent of the crisp autumn air as well as the sage growing on the kitchen windowsill, the lavender sachets in the drawers, and the rosewater spray she usually used to freshen the bathrooms.

"Mrs. Malone?" Later that morning, Bud Johnson called to say Ron would be by at about two o'clock.

"Looking forward to it," Allison said, glad that Eamon had used his last name, not hers, when booking the service call and that Bud assumed they were married.

When she finished cleaning, Allison dressed in her long pink corduroy skirt, the one with three tiers that made it look like a rosy wedding cake, the one with the extra deep pockets sewn into the side seams. She went to the kitchen and took a knife from the block on the counter and tucked it in the right-hand pocket of her skirt. She wedged a hammer on the ledge behind the cross panel on the basement door. Under the sink, she stowed the hatchet she used to cut back stubborn holly bushes. She moved her car out of the driveway and parked it a few houses down. And, just in case anything went wrong, she wrote a note to Eamon and set it on his pillow on the bed.

About one thirty, when everything was in place, Allison sat in the rocker near the front window and waited for the red-haired man named Ron.

When the doorbell rang, she slipped her hand in her pocket to feel the comfort of the knife. Before opening the door, she took two deep breaths, trying to calm her queasiness.

"Afternoon." Ron tipped his hat, then looked at her closely. "Your hair," he said. "It's different."

For a moment she didn't know if he meant it was different from the last time he saw her or different from the night he barged into her bedroom. She forced a sliver of a smile, standing aside to let him in. "Yes," she said. "It is."

Her eyes followed him, studying him like she might an old film, frame by frame by frame. She noted how he held his toolbox in his left hand, the new blower motor tucked under his right arm. How his pants hung a little low over his narrow hips. How his boots were laced, the left one looser than the right, looking like it might come undone sometime soon. "Nice day," she said, hand in her pocket.

"Not for long," he answered. "Storm's headed over the Front. I can smell it."

Allison's chest tightened. If he could smell a storm, could he smell her fear? She put her hand to her mouth to stifle a cough but couldn't stop it.

"You okay?"

Still coughing, she nodded and pointed to the cellar.

"That bleach smell gets in your lungs. It's a wonder you can even breathe."

She nodded, keeping her eyes on his face. She wondered where he was raised, if he looked like his mother or his father, if they knew what a beast they had spawned. She wondered if he'd hurt other women, other girls.

"I can breathe just fine." But the air she took in felt like it hadn't gone farther than the top of her neck. Her chest was too tight to let it pass.

She flipped on the kitchen light, and Ron headed toward the basement.

"This won't take but a few minutes," he said as he thumped down the wooden stairs.

She listened to each footstep and heard how the third step from the bottom creaked when he landed on it, just like it did when she stepped on it, or when Eamon did. She was sure Ron was the man who raped her. But his smile? His cheerful conscientiousness? They were incongruous with the actions of the monster who had hoisted himself through her bedroom window that dark night and irrevocably stolen her security.

She kept the basement door open but stayed upstairs. She checked to make sure the hammer was still in place. She reached into her pocket one more time to check the knife's blade.

At the stove, she turned on the front burner. She filled a kettle to boil water for tea. She rattled around in the silverware drawer. Anything to make noise. He couldn't know how she was waiting, prepared if he tried to hurt her.

"Mrs. Malone?" Allison looked toward the basement door when Ron called. She was glad Ron thought she was married. Someone would miss her if she were taken away. Someone would care if he hurt her again.

"Yes?" Her heartbeat was too loud now, too fierce. She was sure Ron could hear it marching across the kitchen floor, parading down the steps, announcing her fear, her terror. She breathed deeply.

"You got mice down here, you know."

"Mice?" The sound of her voice—high-pitched, tight, strained—shocked her.

"Yeah. I'll show you where they're comin' in if you want."

"No," she called down the stairs. "I'm afraid of mice. But thanks for telling me. I'll have someone get rid of them."

"No need to call anyone." His voice softened as he walked up the steps. She grabbed the knife hidden in her skirt. When Ron reached the top step, she began to chop the chives she had set out on the counter. *I can get him now*, Allison thought. *If I just turn, quickly, I can slam this in his chest.* Her hand tightened around the knife handle as Ron entered the kitchen, a few leaps away.

"Just put some mint leaves down there," he said. "Especially around the far wall. You got some mint out in your garden. I saw it last time when I tossed out the old filter." Allison wanted to make some guttural sound that would give shape to her rage. She couldn't. "You want me to go get some and take care of it?"

"No!" She caught herself when she responded too quickly, too forcefully. "No, thank you."

"Put some tansy down there, too, if you got any."

"Tansy?"

"That's what my grandmother taught me. 'Course, your cats'll help, too. Have a heck of a time stalkin'."

Stalking. Like she was doing now. If he only knew. Still, she wondered how he, the vermin more dangerous than those in the basement, could sound so sincere, so helpful. And he had a grandmother who taught him about tansy. Why didn't she stop him before he took his twisted sense of entitlement out on anyone? *On me?*

"Do I pay you now?" Her hands shook, so she stuffed them in her pockets and patted them against her thighs. Touching helped her know that, even though she felt separate from her body, she was still intact. Physically anyway.

"No, Bud'll send your bill," he said. "If you'll just sign right here."

She took the pen he offered and signed. A. Malone. Just in case he knew her name back then.

"You let him know if you have any problems." Ron tipped his hat. We want our customers happy."

"Yes," she said. "I'll call if I need to." She leaned back against the counter to steady herself. "But I'm sure everything's fine."

"You wouldn't have a Band-Aid, would you?"

"A Band-Aid?"

"Cut myself on that front panel." He held up his index finger. "Those edges can be nasty."

Allison went to get the first aid kit from the bathroom. When she returned, Ron was wiping the floor with a paper towel. "Got a little blood on your floor," he said when he walked to the trashcan and tossed in the paper towel.

"That's okay," she said as she handed him a Band-Aid. "You're sure you're all right?"

"Just a small cut." He smiled. He bandaged his finger, picked up his tools, and walked to the front door.

"Is this your last stop today?"

He turned back to look at her as he reached for the door, then hesitated. Had he noticed something familiar about her? "Uh huh." He spoke slowly, turned the doorknob cautiously. "Done for the day." He walked onto the porch, down the stairs, along the path.

Allison closed the door behind him. She locked both locks. At the window, she pulled back the curtain to watch Ron stow his gear in the van, light a cigarette, then look back at the house before he got in and drove away. From the trashcan, she fished out the paper towel with Ron's blood on it, stuffed it in a shopping bag with her quilt and her mirror. She raced to her car and followed the route Ron would most likely take back to Fresh Air: Silvermine to Center Street, through the tunnel, then west to Walnut.

From a block behind, she watched him pull into the 7-Eleven on Walnut, gas up the truck, then go inside to pay. From across the street, she saw him buy what looked like a half gallon of orange juice, some beef jerky, a lotto ticket. He smiled and tipped his hat to the counter girl. Then he drove the truck to Bud Johnson's shop, parked, and went inside. Bud gave Ron a "good job" slap on the back. When he came out the door again, smiling, Ron sat on the bench out front, guzzling the juice and tapping his left foot to whatever tune he was hearing in his head. She felt her jaw clench, so hard that her teeth hurt. Had he followed her this same way? The way she was following him now? Had he watched what she ate, drank? Were there other girls? A lot or a few? Would he watch her again?

Five minutes later, a blue Buick Century pulled up. A woman was driving. No more than twenty, twenty-two, Allison guessed. She had long movie-star hair, highlighted and shiny, curled at the ends, teased a little on top. She got out of the car. When Ron came around to take the driver's seat, before the woman walked toward the passenger's side, Allison noticed how she leaned back, a little off balance. It wasn't until the woman turned sideways that Allison saw how her stomach filled out the loose sweater she was wearing. How she smiled. Happy to be pregnant. Ron held her. She stood on her tiptoes, and he kissed her. Then he let her go and she got in the passenger's seat. From across the front seat, he turned toward her, smiled, patted her belly. She smiled again, too.

Allison's thoughts raced. *Don't you know who and what he really is? Or do you know and not care? Are you a victim, too? Should I warn you about what danger you could be in? Or are you a co-conspirator worthy of the same contempt as Ron?*

When Ron drove the Buick from the Fresh Air lot, turned left down Center Street, then right onto Fifth, Allison followed. Halfway down the street, he pulled into the driveway at number seventeen, a trim white vinyl-sided Colonial with green shutters. A grapevine wreath on the door, with bittersweet branches winding through it, a little plaque at its center. *Welcome.* Ron got out and opened the car door for the woman, closing it after her. With his arm around her waist, they walked into the house telling each other about their days, maybe how she felt the baby kick, maybe how many blower motors he replaced.

How, Allison wondered, could he have this tidy little life? A girlfriend, or maybe the woman was his wife? A child? Shouldn't he live under a bridge and drink rotgut gin from quart bottles? Cook over a camp stove? She sat in her car, across the street, for almost an hour. She got out once, and with her coat wrapped around her and her hood pulled over her head, walked by the house, close enough to see them through the kitchen window, eating an early dinner.

When Ron left the house again, he had traded his work uniform for jeans and a Pittsburgh Steelers sweatshirt. He took the front steps quickly, whistling. When he got in the car and drove away, Allison followed as he worked his way downtown, then into the Center for Hope parking lot. After he went inside, she turned around and drove east, out of town toward Tyrone.

Looking straight ahead, focused and purposeful, Allison walked through the glass doors into the Tyrone Municipal Building. She carried her shopping bag in her right hand, her purse in her left. She stepped into the waiting elevator and pressed three on the panel of buttons. When the elevator doors opened on the third floor, she turned left down the hallway decorated with sepia-toned photos of Tyrone when it was home to the previous century's railroad tycoons. She walked past the assessor's office and the public works office, then followed the sign pointing toward the district attorney's office. She pushed the milky white glass door open and approached the reception desk.

"Elizabeth Reedy, please."

The receptionist—Cornelia, according to the sign on her desk—reluctantly took her eyes from the document she was proof-reading. "You have an appointment?"

"She's expecting me."

Cornelia picked up her phone, pressed four buttons, then looked up. "Your name?" Allison said nothing. "There's a young woman here to see you," Cornelia said into the phone. "I don't know. Fine."

"She'll be about twenty minutes. Have a seat." Cornelia motioned toward a bank of scruffy, fake-leather chairs. Allison sat in the one closest to the woman's desk. The walls, metal desks, and partitions that separated the space beyond into a dozen or so work cubicles were all the colors of a stormy sky or cream of mushroom soup. She peeked inside her shopping bag to reassure herself. The brush, the quilt, and towel were still there.

At five thirty, Cornelia set aside her work and placed her pencil in her top desk drawer. She dusted her desk, straightening her blotter and phone. After gathering her purse and her thermos from her credenza, she assured Allison that Elizabeth would be out shortly. "Restroom's down the hall to the left." Allison nodded, though she hadn't paid attention to what Cornelia said.

Ten minutes later, a woman in a blue suit walked briskly from one of the cubicles to the reception room. "Elizabeth Reedy," she said, her hand extended to Allison. She was shorter than Allison imagined, not much over five feet, round and efficient, like her voice. Her full, squarish face was clear, with no makeup, except for a hint of rosy lipstick that apparently hadn't been freshened all day. Allison guessed her dark brown, chin-length curls were natural. Elizabeth Reedy didn't look the type to fuss with her hair or anything else. Not when there was work to do.

"My friend called you last week," Allison said, shaking Elizabeth's hand. "She told me to come see you." Allison talked faster than usual. She didn't want to waste time. From the looks of Elizabeth, neither did she.

"Third cubicle on the right." Elizabeth motioned down the hall. "Coffee?"

"Just water, please."

"Get yourself settled. I'll be there in a minute."

Allison took the one available chair in front of Elizabeth's desk. She set her shopping bag in her lap. The rest of the cubicle—the desk, the other guest chair, the floor—was heaped with files. They were neatly stacked but didn't leave room for anything extraneous.

Elizabeth returned, handed Allison a bottle of water, and threaded her way through the piles on the floor. She set her coffee on a coaster, then sat in the chair facing Allison. "Let's start with your name."

"Allison. Allison Stephenson."

"Two Ls in Allison?"

Allison nodded and Elizabeth made a note on her pad. "Stephenson. With a P-H. No V."

"And you want to report an incident that happened how long ago?"

"Three years ago. I was raped. And now I know who did it." Allison sat straight in the chair, responding in kind to Elizabeth's efficient manner. "I want to see him punished."

"So, the victim, or the survivor as we prefer to say, is you and not a friend?"

"Yes."

"And you were how old? Did you tell me sixteen?"

Allison nodded again. She diverted her eyes from Elizabeth's while she told the rest of the story. "I was living with my mother then. A man broke in our house. He had a knife."

For the first time she told the story from beginning to end. Even Lehanna had heard it only in bits and pieces. As she spoke, the words felt like they belonged so far in the past that they didn't make sense. *Did this really happen to me?* She started to sweat. She remembered the sticky, steamy heat of that night, the man's smell, and his voice, ragged and as steel-wool-rough as the way he plowed up against her, then inside her. She shook, but her voice was clear, steady.

"My mother was dying that summer, and my father and I weren't on good terms. We still aren't. I went away to school that fall, a few weeks after my mother died, and never told anyone. I tried to forget."

Elizabeth observed her for a lapse in concentration, a twitch of her eye, a skipped beat, any signal she was lying. The young woman, Elizabeth Reedy believed, was telling the truth.

When Allison finished, she noticed that tears had fallen onto her hands, clasped tightly in her lap. Elizabeth held out a box of tissues. Allison took one, wiped her hands then her eyes. She looked up, her voice almost a whisper. "Do you think he remembers?"

"We can try to find out." Elizabeth set the tissues within Allison's reach. "But first, tell me why you're coming to me now, three years later?"

"I saw him."

"The man who attacked you?"

Allison nodded. "He came to my house to fix my furnace. Last week and again today."

"You're sure it was the same man?"

She nodded again. "I knew by the smell."

"The smell?"

"The swamp smell. Mixed with something meaty. Like beef jerky. Or Slim Jims. Ever since that night, the smell of him on me was as thick and real as if it were an old coat I wore every day. One I couldn't take off. There was his voice, too."

"Did the man recognize you?"

"He didn't act like he did. I weighed more back then. And my hair was long and brown. When my boyfriend made an appointment to have the furnace fixed, he gave his name, not mine. I guess the man—his name is Ron—assumed I was Eamon's wife. So, even if he knew back then my name was Stephenson, he thinks it's Malone now."

Elizabeth wrapped her hands around her mug, turning it this way and that. "You're not the first woman who's come to me because she remembers her attacker's smell. But that's not evidence that stands up in court."

She hesitated. "I'm not saying I don't believe you, but we need to support what's called probable cause. That means we have to establish that a reasonable person would suspect the man of the crime you believe he committed." She leaned forward. "Ultimately, if the case goes to trial, we need strong enough evidence to persuade a jury of his guilt beyond a reasonable doubt."

"I don't just *believe* he raped me." Allison reached down beside her chair for her shopping bag. She pulled out the quilt. Then the hairbrush. "This quilt was on my bed that night," she said. "And this was on my bedside table. When I hit him with it, I caught him on his leg." She held up the hairbrush and showed Elizabeth the rough edge where a drop of blood dried on the silver. "And today when he was at my house, he cut himself on the furnace. This is his blood, too." She held up the paper towel. "I *know* he raped me."

Elizabeth looked from the items Allison laid out, back to Allison. "Good," she said. "We might just have a chance."

She confirmed what Allison read at the library. "Since you were sixteen at the time of the assault, and a minor according to state law, a jury would be required to assign a mandatory sentence of five to ten years. If the accused is convicted, that is." Even if the man were exonerated in a criminal case, she said, a civil case could be filed within ten years of the offense. "For damages."

"You mean money?"

Elizabeth nodded. "For a case like this, somewhere around two to four hundred thousand dollars."

Allison gathered the quilt, the hairbrush, and the paper towel and put them in the bag. "I just want the smell to go away," she said, her voice wavering. Then she sat up straight and spoke with a clear edge that Elizabeth hadn't yet heard from her. "And I want him to know what it feels like to be afraid."

"I'm sure you do." But there were things Allison needed to know, Elizabeth said, about rape cases in general and about her case in particular. "Even though you have forensic evidence, nothing you've told me so far would preclude a judge or jury from thinking you might have had a relationship with the man. That the incident might have been consensual."

Allison winced. She started to ask how anyone would possibly think she would invite a man like that into her life. Then she remembered the other men she had spent time with—no, *wasted* time with—in Ithaca. It was, she decided, better to keep quiet about them.

"Sexual assault cases are never pretty," Elizabeth continued. "Not for the accused, but especially not for the survivor. She—"

Allison sat forward when she interrupted Elizabeth. "Can a trial be worse than the fear that someone who ripped my life in two might hurt me again? That he might hurt someone else?"

Elizabeth paused. She knew it took time for any sexual violence survivor to trust her and the legal process. She picked up a pen and turned it end over end. "I just want to prepare you. The process takes time, and it won't be like going to traffic court. Before you go ahead, I want you to think about how you'll feel about opening your life to the public. On the news, in the papers."

"I've thought about this for three years. I don't need more time."

"Okay." Elizabeth pulled out a yellow pad and readied her pen above it. "Let's start at the beginning."

While Allison told her everything she remembered about that night in July, Elizabeth made notes, then asked questions. Was Allison aware while she was at the Three Bears, or on her way home, that she was being followed? *No.* Was she aware before that, that anyone might be following her? *No.* There were no phone calls? *No.* Threats at school? *No.* Was she forced to have sex? *Yes.* Other than the evidence, did she have any way of identifying the man? *I know him by his smell. And his voice.* Did the man use a weapon? *A knife.* Do you know anything else about him? *He works at Fresh Air on Walnut Street, in West MacMillan. He's got a pregnant girlfriend.*

How could her words, Allison wondered, her weak-kneed little words, convince Elizabeth what that night was like? And the years since? She thought of Rodney Peyton. *You need to put more of your soul on the page.* What syllables, what sounds—grunts and screams and nighttime forest noises, maybe—could she reach inside for and pull out to tell this tale? Still, when she finished, she knew by the look in Elizabeth's eye, the nod of her head, the set of her jaw, that she had heard Allison. That she believed her.

Elizabeth flipped through her notes to be sure she'd asked everything she needed for the time being, then set down her pen and pad. When she asked if Allison had family in the area, Allison told Elizabeth about her father, his connection to the university. Her grandfather. Eamon. And Corinne Kramer. "You mean Corinne Kramer from the Center for Hope?"

Allison nodded.

"Have you told them yet?"

"No."

Elizabeth turned and looked out the window at the last of the red and yellow leaves dangling from the maple trees, how precarious they looked as they hung on, reluctant to let go. She knew it was partly because she had never married, and never had children, that she felt so protective of the sexual violence survivors who were placed in her path. And partly, too, because when her father had been violent with her mother, she knew what it was like to feel helpless, scared, and ashamed. Since she organized the Blair County Survivors Unit almost a decade earlier, she had prosecuted dozens of cases. Her conviction record was more than respectable. But a conviction never came without a price.

When she turned back to her client, Elizabeth explained the process they would follow if Allison decided to move forward. "First, I'll call Chet Mullen, the police investigator who's usually assigned to sexual violence cases." Chet would pick up Allison's evidence, have it examined and tested, and begin the investigation. "He'll verify that the accused was in the MacMillan area at the time in question and that he could have committed the crime." If Chet gathered sufficient evidence, he would present the accused a warrant requiring a DNA sample to compare to the fluids on Allison's hairbrush and quilt. She would be required to give a blood sample, too, to make sure her fluids were also present. The testing, Elizabeth said, could take a few weeks.

"If the DNA of the accused matches that on the evidence, Chet will issue an affidavit of probable cause and file a complaint. Then he'll present him with a felony arrest warrant, and bail will be set—probably a hundred thousand or so, depending on whether he's determined to be a flight risk."

"He won't be locked up?"

"That depends. If he can't come up with the required amount, usually ten percent of bail, he'll be taken into custody. If he makes bail, he'll be released."

Allison grasped the arms of her chair. "He'll still be out on the street? Even after he knows I've filed charges? Even though he knows where I live?"

"Like I said, it's a process." Elizabeth continued, telling her how, a week or so after the arrest warrant was served, they would attend a hearing in front of the district magistrate. The accused and his attorney would be present. Or, if he couldn't afford counsel, the court would assign representation. The next step would be a preliminary hearing in front of a judge.

Allison listened to the language Elizabeth used—all cool and tidy—about filing a complaint, as if someone were whining about a restaurant meal that had arrived cold or overcooked. About the accused being present, as if he would have been invited for cocktails. That was probably for the best. Her own words and feelings were dry tinder waiting for a match.

"Then," Elizabeth said, "the case would go to trial."

Allison reached for the water Elizabeth had given her. She took a sip then set the bottle down. "When?"

Elizabeth sat back. She crossed her arms and swiveled in her chair. "Depending on the number of cases in the pipeline, anywhere up to six months."

"Springtime maybe?"

Elizabeth nodded. She stilled her chair. "Sooner if we're lucky. In the meantime, I think it's important for you to tell your family about the case and to see a counselor in the rape crisis program."

"I'll tell them. My family I mean. But I've thought about this as much as I want to. I don't need a counselor."

Elizabeth looked over her coffee cup rim as she drank from it. "The cold, hard reality," she said as she set the cup down, "is that, from this point forward, what *you* think you want or need isn't all that important. Everything you do needs to be consistent with the reasonable actions of a woman who wants to win a court case against a man who raped her.

"Especially because the incident occurred a while ago, our case needs to be meticulous. That means you get counseling." Elizabeth handed her the card of a woman to call from the County Social Services Department. "Besides, you just might find, once we get into this, that you want some extra support."

Allison saw it would do no good to argue. She nodded and tucked the card in her purse. Before she left, she gave Elizabeth the shopping bag that held the quilt her mother had bought for her in Bucks County, the hairbrush that had belonged to her mother and grandmother, and the paper towel with Ron's blood on it. As she held them out, she hoped she would feel lighter by turning over the remnants of the man who had stolen her safety and security. But when they were out of her hands, she felt discomfited, not relieved. There were parts of herself in that bag, too. And parts of Lucy and Emily. The best she could do to compensate for those losses, from now on, was to make sure she lost as little else as possible and to make *the accused* pay as much as possible.

She stood, shook Elizabeth's hand, and turned to leave. But at the doorway, she stopped and looked back to make sure Elizabeth was still there, that she was on her side, that there was hope of justice. Their eyes met. They each nodded. Then, straightening her shoulders, Allison walked out and closed the door behind her.

Elizabeth reached for her phone and dialed. "Chet? Elizabeth. I've got a late report on a rape charge. . . . Yeah. . . . She's got what she claims is DNA evidence. . . . Three years ago. . . . In my office."

CHAPTER TWENTY-FIVE

Eamon left school earlier than usual. He stopped at the florist shop to pick up a pink rose for Allison, then bought chicken and veggies to grill so she wouldn't have to cook.

When he walked in the house, he called to her but got no response. Before he went up to the bedroom to check on her, he set the groceries on the counter and opened the windows. "It's no wonder you're under the weather, what with this smell." Still no response.

After stashing the groceries, he went upstairs and opened the bedroom door, trying to keep it from squeaking like it usually did. He didn't want to wake Allison if she was asleep. When he went in, she wasn't there. The bed was hastily made, and her nightclothes and towel were strewn on the bed and floor. When he picked the towel off the bed to take it to the hamper, he found a note from her, set on his pillow.

I needed to be free of him. Finally.
Ali

Eamon reread the note. Was Allison playing some sort of scavenger-hunt game? Was he supposed to guess who this *him* was she wrote about? He checked the bathroom, his upstairs office, then called again for her as he raced downstairs. When he opened the basement door, a hammer fell from behind it and thudded down the steps. He ran downstairs, picked it up, then climbed the stairs again, two at a time, to the first floor. He looked out to the garden, then for the car. It was gone and so was Allison. No, this was no game. He called his brother and read Danny the note.

"She's been acting distant the last week. Scared. And she bleached her hair again, like she used to when I met her." He said how Allison hadn't felt well that morning. "At least that's what she said."

As Danny tried to calm his brother so they could make a plan, Eamon heard a car out front. He looked out the window, then slammed down the phone.

"Hi," Allison said as she strolled up the front steps. She gave him a little kiss when he met her on the porch, then smiled. "I was feeling better, so I went out for gas."

"Gas?"

He had never spoken to her with that edge in his voice, nor glared at her, like now. "I felt better," she repeated. "I went—"

"I found your note." He held her arms and turned her to face him.

"The note?" She'd forgotten she'd left it on the pillow when she followed Ron. "What note?"

"What note?" His hands tightened on her shoulders. "You're lying to me."

She broke away, ran into the house, up to the bathroom, and locked the door. She turned on the water in the bathtub and in the sink, hoping the rushing sound would clear her head and help her decide what to tell Eamon. By then he was pounding on the door, shouting.

"Allison! Come out. Now."

She breathed deeply, counted to ten, and opened the door.

She walked past him and sat on the bed, eyes straight ahead. She needed to be free of Ron more than she feared Eamon might be angry with her or, worse, leave her. She told the truth about how Ron attacked her and how she had seen him a week earlier. And again that day. "Here, in my house. He came to fix the furnace." She told him she had met with Elizabeth Reedy and that she was going to take Ron to court.

Eamon sat next to her. His anger dissipated, his voice softened, though his heart still raced. "Why didn't you tell me?" He took her hands in his. "I would have done something."

She shook her head. "*I* needed to do something."

"But what happens to you, or what happened to you, that's my concern now, too. You know that? Allison? Look at me."

"I was afraid. That if you knew, you would leave."

He sat back, better understanding the way she was when they first met. And why she had slipped away from him this past week. She needed to be comforted, not chastised. He reached to her, rocked her in his arms.

"I won't leave you, Allison. Especially not when someone's hurt you." He released her and took her hands. "You're sure you want to go to court? To drag up the past?"

She nodded.

"Then will you talk to Danny?"

⌣

Allison hesitated when Eamon opened the door to Saint Michael's rectory for her. She hadn't been in the church since her mother's funeral, when the cloying scent of incense and too-perfectly arranged spider mums and lilies and roses hung in the air.

"You ready?" he asked.

She nodded and took his hand as they entered the cream-colored stucco building, with its chocolate-brown trim and rusty-orange clay tile roof.

When Allison was small, her mother often brought her there when Lucy worked on the annual bazaar or chaired committees overseeing everything from religious instruction at the elementary school to selecting contractors to remodel the church. *Bless me, father, for I have sinned.* Allison dismissed the confessional prayer that came to mind. She had no need to confess. She had done nothing wrong.

As they stepped into the vestibule, Allison felt comforted that the place hadn't changed much. The stained-glass windows, still amethyst, amber, and rose, depicted each of the seven sacraments, from baptism through anointing of the sick. The wall sconces cast a soothing glow on the ominous dark-paneled walls. The carpet, thick and mossy green, muffled their footsteps. So quiet, the place felt almost safe.

When Danny came out of his study, he and Eamon hugged. No one could look at the two men and miss how much alike they looked. Both slender. Both medium height. Both with waves of shiny black hair, though silver strands dignified Danny's temples, as Allison supposed they would Eamon's in a few years. While both their dimpled smiles were engaging, Danny's was less spontaneous than Eamon's. When Danny reached to Allison, she took his hand, then released it quickly as she looked, not at his eyes but his clerical collar. A barrier, one that seemed to divide good from bad, him from her. He could never understand.

Eamon brushed Allison's cheek with a kiss, then looked from her to Danny and back again. "You're in good hands," he said. "I'll be back at seven."

Danny closed the vestibule door behind Eamon, then led Allison through the double doors to his study. From first glance around the room, she saw that Danny shared Eamon's love of books. No space was left unoccupied in the glass-door bookcases, and still more volumes sat atop the cabinets, on a table to the left, in stacks behind his desk. Her eyes traveled up the walls to the ceiling edged in molding that looked like whipped cream piped around a cake. At the center, from a rose medallion, an iron and glass lantern-shaped chandelier emitted sleepy yellow light.

Eventually, her eyes rested on the crucifix, set on a standard, centered at the bay window that bowed out behind Danny's desk. Less than two-foot tall, painstakingly carved, it caught the soft overhead light directed to the cuts in the Christ figure's side. *It's wounds that make a healer.* Allison heard Lehanna's words but could only respond with the same question she wanted to ask her not long after they met, but never did. How could you possibly know how I feel?

Danny motioned for her to sit in one of the armchairs facing his desk. He told her that Eamon had called when he found her note. "We'd both like to help." He was encouraging, and she was resolute, so Allison started her story, the same one she told Elizabeth Reedy that afternoon, and Eamon that evening.

When she finished, her eyes lowered and cut away from Danny's until he spoke.

"That's a terrible thing that happened to you."

Allison's lip trembled. She said nothing.

"Especially when your mother was ill, and her passing and all. It must hurt very much."

When she didn't respond, he reached for one of the photos on his desk. "Has Eamon showed you where we were raised?"

She shook her head, relieved that Danny didn't want to further probe her past. "Just pictures of the family."

"It's a beautiful place, Connemara." He handed a silver frame across his desk, but Allison only glanced at it. "May I tell you a little about it?"

She nodded.

He told her that, by the time he was nine, he had begun to shine like a bright light in the village school. The teacher praised him for his way with words, for the fact that he could look at a map and point to just about any country around the world and recite the capital city and the names of animals that roamed the wild in each one. Australia. Sydney. Kangaroo. Wallaby.

As he continued, Danny's wistful voice and its sad undercurrent calmed Allison.

After learning the names of faraway places and their four-footed inhabitants, Danny went on, he started spinning tales about them. How a herd of buffalo roaming the American plains ruined the crops of a family of homesteaders called the Nicholsons and how, as a result, they moved to Florida to grow grapefruit. How a priest and nun in a Madagascar rainforest, filled with screeching sifaka lemurs, saved thousands of villagers from mosquito-borne malaria.

But his finest stories, he told her, were about the life and the wildlife in the Inagh Valley, where fields of heather—white or purple or pink, depending on the season—waved in the wind. Where foxes and rabbits fed on blackberries and hazelnuts. It was the deer that young Dan liked most, though. "Freedom, Danny. Freedom," they seemed to call when they scampered by, beckoning him to follow.

When Danny's mother didn't force herself out of bed after the birth and death of her sixth child, even the neighbor women's ministry couldn't rouse her. Yes, we know what it's like to bury a child. We know what it's like to hear a voice that's dark as night, yet somehow more friendly than life itself. But you must not give yourself to the voice, Ellen. You must hear us instead." The women sang and prayed and cooked and eventually breathed spirit back into Ellen Malone, but she never gave up that distant look in her eye. The one that seemed to pin her hopes on a place just over the hill and out of the valley of never-ending toil and pain.

A few months later, Danny's father took him for a walk up the mountain, to the ledge with a view of the entire valley. Where the soft purple carpet of heather and violets rolled gently in the wind and the Twelve Bens rose past Clifden, beyond the bogs, like a dozen docile sheep.

"The teachers tell me you've a gift for the language, Dan," his father said. "That if you want to work hard, you can be a teacher. Even a priest. And wouldn't that be an honor for us, to see you in the pulpit preaching the word of the Lord?"

Danny smiled when he remembered how he wanted to please his father. "I'd rather be preaching from this pulpit here," he told his Da, jumping up on a rock, spreading his arms. "To the deer and the foxes."

"That's a worthy thing to do, but maybe the Lord wants more from you than to be preaching to the rabbits. What deer needs to learn the law of loving his neighbor, after all?" He ruffled Danny's hair. "It's humans who have the beasts in them. Am I right?"

"I guess." But Dan's smile wilted when his father's voice began leading him somewhere outside the fields.

"Your Auntie Moira's arranged for you to be going to the good school in the city, Dan. Father Sullivan's put in a word for you there, and that's an honor to be proud of now, isn't it?" He didn't tell Danny that, with Ellen sick, she couldn't care for the lot of them and, with as little work as he was getting, he couldn't feed them.

Danny wanted to make his father proud, but he didn't have to leave, did he? Couldn't he stay? "No, Dan." His father's hollow voice, and the fixed look in his eyes, told him there was no sense pressing the matter.

The day he left for Auntie Moira's, his mother packed him biscuits and cheese for the trip to her sister-in-law's. "Be a good lad, there now, won't you?" Her voice was kind. But why, he wondered, did she turn from him? Not seeing her tears, he imagined her glad to have him gone. That morning he left Heaven on Earth, his parents, his brothers, his sisters, the deer in the fields, the trout in the stream. "Make us proud, Dan," his father said when Danny boarded the bus, and the boy smiled and hid his own tears so as not to disappoint his Da.

Two years later—what an honor!—Auntie Moira read the bishop's letter to him. Danny had been chosen to attend minor seminary on Inishmore, the largest of the Aran Islands. "You've done your Da proud, now haven't you?" Danny smiled, as if pleased to be uprooted once again. On the day he was to leave, his aunt and uncle took the bus with him to Rossaveal and waited in line to put him on the ferry across Galway Bay. They carried his books, his bags, his lunch. "We're proud of you, lad," they said. He suppressed his smile. It was a sin to be proud, he was beginning to learn.

But after five months, maybe six, Danny didn't worry about hiding smiles. It no longer occurred to him to laugh, to run with the wind at his back. At first, he thought it an honor that Seamus O'Connor, the theology teacher, singled him out from the rest of the class because of Danny's devotion to the Blessed Mother.

He told Danny to report to the lower classroom and helped Danny with early Church history, particularly the study of Augustine. He explained why women were rightfully relegated to positions of servitude in the Church, on account of Eve's transgressions, and the Magdalene's, and so on. And how, in the eyes of the Church, the only good woman was an untouched woman, such as the Blessed Mother herself, although any other virgin could at least hold a place for herself in heaven. Still, man had needs. If defiling a woman was out of the question, what was a man to do? Especially a man chosen by the Lord himself to do the Church's work? He was to tend to his own needs and that of his fellows, wasn't he?

"You wouldn't want to be shaming your Da by being sent home from the seminary," Seamus asked, "now would you, Dan Malone?"

"No."

"And you won't be telling them about your extra studies, here with me?"

The following spring, Seamus didn't show at prayer one Tuesday morning. His class was taken over by Brother Francis, and no one spoke of Seamus again on Inishmore. A year later, when Danny left the seminary, he loaded his canvas bag onto the ferry headed for Rossaveal. As he left, he turned back to look at the island one last time. The bay was calm and flat that day, unusual, even in May. The clouds were full-bellied and laboring, it seemed, to split open and spill the makings of new life. The two seminarians who walked with him to the dock cupped their hands around their mouths. "We'll be wanting to hear from you, Dan," young Kevin called. "And don't be forgetting us now," Sean yelled.

Danny raised his hand to his forehead to block the light so he could see the young men on the dock. But with the sun's blinding angle, he could only imagine they were standing where their voices came from. He raised his left hand and waved at the brightly lit void. He smiled, then turned from the rail and sat on a ferry bench. In his heart, he wished the two young men well. He prayed for their futures, for their protection. And he vowed to himself and to God he would never again set foot on Inishmore.

Danny told Allison how he eventually took charge of a small parish in Wicklow, then a bigger one in Dublin, and then had the opportunity to come to America. It wasn't an opportunity so much as a necessity, he told her, because in the vise grip of his own anger and unforgiveness, he was of little use to his parishioners. Sure, he preached a fine sermon with all the right words. Love. Forgiveness. Kindness. They skated off his tongue like sharpened blades on ice. But they left the taste of cold metal in his mouth.

It wasn't until he came to Pennsylvania that a parishioner pointed out to the man behind the collar what should have been said long ago. The messenger had lost movement in both legs in the Vietnam War and given himself to helping other veterans whose spirits or bodies had suffered in that steamy faraway place. "You're in good hands," he told Danny, casting his eyes skyward to show confidence in whatever plans his Creator had in store. And judging by the peace on his face, and the calm in his eyes, Dan saw that the man believed what he said.

"How is it," the man asked weeks later, when Dan himself knew he had delivered a sermon without conviction, "you've got the look of a prisoner in your eye, Father?" The look, he said, he had seen in the eyes of men held captive in jungle prisons or in decimated bodies for years, decades even. Was Danny not a free man?

No, Dan admitted. He was no freer than any man in chains, though his captors were his own past, his anger, his fear.

"Walk free, Father Dan," said the man whose legs didn't work. "Walk free." In time, with that man's ministry, Dan unbound his shackles and did just that.

As Danny finished his story, a response to the question Allison hadn't asked, he turned to her. "No, I can't know exactly how you're feeling, but a little maybe."

So, Allison figured, that was why he told her that sad sack story. Not because he wanted her to know him, but because he wanted to soften her, to take away her rage, her fire. "I'm sorry you suffered," she said. And I'm glad you feel better.

"But I'm not a saint or a nun," she said, gathering her coat around her. "And I don't want to be." All she really wanted, she told him, was to not be afraid anymore. "To make sure that man hurts as much as he hurt me."

Danny nodded. He knew better than to expect a different response right now. Maybe something in his story would speak to her in an unexpected moment, when truth most often did its work, *His* work. Maybe she would someday see that if she wanted to run free, she would need to knock on the door she had closed to forgiveness and ask to have it opened. "Will you come back then? And speak to me again?"

"I'm not sure." She kept her eyes on Danny's. Just as Lehanna told her years earlier, no one was exempt from hurt. And if wounds really did make a healer, Danny Malone was in the right business.

"May I pray for you?"

Allison stood and nodded, as if Lucy were there, urging her, though she froze in place.

"Heavenly Father," he began. As Danny asked for her protection and peace, she imagined he really wanted to ask God to help her learn to walk free, in the same way he had been taught. But she was convinced she would only feel liberated when Ron Jenkins was locked in a cell, unable to walk free for at least five years.

<hr />

After Eamon arrived at the rectory to take Allison home, Danny returned to his study. He sat in the chair Allison had taken when she was there, hoping she would find something in his story to help her realize she was not alone in her pain. He also hoped the tightness in his chest he felt after talking to her would soon pass, because the truth was, the tale he told her was only partly true. Yes, he had loved his early years with his family, and yes, he appreciated the opportunity to make them proud by entering seminary. But, as far as the lesson his parishioner had tried to teach him? No, he had not learned to walk free as he told Allison. Oh, that made a good story—like his early sermons that left the taste of metal in his mouth—and on some days it appeared true. But on just as many other days, Danny still felt bound to his terrifying memories of Seamus. He held his head in his hands, knowing he should look to the crucifix for relief, for hope. Instead, he watched the sun set behind the Front. Then he considered how he could help both Allison and Ron.

He thought back on his prenuptial sessions with Ron and Jolene, how Ron seemed to be on a solid path, what with his work at Fresh Air and his plans to marry. But when Jolene mentioned that Ron was going for drug counseling at the Center for Hope, he seemed vague when Danny asked how the therapy was working. Danny wondered now if Ron hadn't been forthcoming, that maybe—given what Allison just told him—Ron was in Vance Carmichael's Viewpoint Program for sex offenders and hadn't told Jolene. He stood, walked to his desk, and made a note to call Vance the next morning.

Vance tipped the person who delivered the order of chicken broccoli and Szechuan beef, opened the bag, and passed a plate and chopsticks across his desk to Danny. "The way Viewpoint works," he said, "is we get men who look like they're headed for trouble with a nonrefundable ticket." He dug into his meal then continued. "Some have done time. Some are about to if they don't shape up. Most have a history of alcohol or drugs or both. They've all got histories of crimes against women. We get them work and therapy, so they have a chance at living clean."

Viewpoint, he said, was as good as any program in the state.

"That's good. That's good." Danny set down his chopsticks and leaned forward. "Vance, I don't want to waste your time, so may I get to the reason I'm here?"

"Shoot."

"I'm trying to find out about a man in your program. Ron Jenkins."

Vance pushed his plate away on his desk. "You know better than that," he said. "Giving out information on program members— even to men of the cloth? That would be like you breaking the seal of the confessional."

Danny nodded and leaned back, giving Vance time to open up. If he was going to.

Vance wadded up his napkin, tossed it into a nearby trash can and spoke again. "Why you want to know?"

Danny shook his head. "I can't trust you if you can't trust me."

"Good point." Vance had never been fond of the priests at Saint Michael's. The parish had never supported the Center's programs. But Danny seemed open to changing that. It wouldn't hurt to start building trust between themselves. "Ron's been with us around two years now. Seems like the treatment's taking hold. He's got support from a close friend. A fiancée, too."

"Did he do time before he got into Viewpoint?"

Vance shook his head. "He probably should have. Once his denial cracked, he spilled a history that didn't allow for much hope until he came here." Vance rested his elbows on the arms of his chair, clasped his hands, and leaned forward. "What are you up to, Father Dan?"

Danny knew he wouldn't get more information from Vance without giving some himself. "A young woman I know believes Ron raped her a few years ago. She left town a while but now she's back. Ron fixed her furnace the other day."

"She's thinking of pressing charges?"

Danny shrugged. "She's scared, hurt."

Vance backed his chair away from his desk and stood. Their discussion was over.

CHAPTER TWENTY-SIX

Chet Mullen arrived at the Tyrone district attorney's office the morning after Allison met with Elizabeth Reedy. His silvery hair was, as usual, striking but tousled, his eyes a little droopy. He looked desperate for not only a decent night's sleep, but the oversized cup of takeout coffee he carried.

When Elizabeth gathered Allison's evidence and handed it to Chet, he accepted it but hesitated. He knew from experience that, when Elizabeth tilted her head just so, and allowed her usually flinty affect to soften, she needed a favor.

"You're looking at me like you always do when you want a rush on things."

"We've been working together too long." She cracked a smile. "Can you speed things up on this one? You know how fragile these young women can be while they're waiting."

"You're killing me," he said as he shook his head. "But, for you?" He smiled. "I'll do what I can. The official line'll still be that it'll take a month. Give or take."

"You're a good man." For Elizabeth, working with Chet was one of the few bright spots in her often-gloomy job. No need to wheedle and cajole, like she often had to with clients. No morphing into Cruella De Vil as she often did when dealing with defense attorneys.

He shrugged. "I'd rather get a big fat raise than a compliment."

"Wouldn't we all."

Elizabeth looked after Chet when he left the office. He wasn't a bad-looking guy. Decent, too. But why try? Neither of them had anywhere near enough time to commit to anything but their work.

⌒

When Chet called Elizabeth three weeks later, he confirmed that the DNA from the blood on the brush and semen on the quilt matched that of the blood on the paper towel Allison provided. "I'll pick the guy up tomorrow."

At six forty-five the next morning, warrant in hand, Chet drove to Fresh Air. He sat in the parking lot, waiting. He hated like hell to go after a guy who seemed to be making something of himself—a good worker, according to sources at Fresh Air—and someone who kept his commitments at Viewpoint. But with over two decades on the job, Chet knew that what he wanted to do and what his job required were often two very different things.

After Rusty showed up for work, Bud arrived fifteen minutes later. They were in the reception area, going over the day's assignments when Chet walked in.

"You're up early," Bud said, looking up from his desk. Bud knew Chet from their hunting lodge as well as in a professional capacity. "Your furnace on the fritz or you just paying a social call?" Bud laughed, though his eyes said, *Don't let this be true.*

"The furnace is working fine."

"So, what can we do for you?"

Chet turned toward Rusty. "Ronald Lee Jenkins?"

Rusty looked from Bud to Chet before he nodded.

"I have a warrant here that requests a DNA sample for an investigation involving you."

"An investigation?" Rusty knew his voice sounded as fearful as he felt.

"In connection with an attack on a woman named Allison Stephenson in July of 1988."

Allison Stephenson. Rusty repeated the name silently, remembering how, before the attack, her name sounded like water rippling over rocks in a creek. It just rolled on, nice and smooth. Then he remembered the furnace he fixed a few weeks back, on Silvermine. How the woman there seemed uneasy. And how he felt knocked off balance when he left her house. She didn't look like the girl from a few years back, and she didn't have the same name, but he'd had a feeling. He looked to Bud again, then back to Chet. "What do I need to do?" He tried to sound calm but could barely breathe.

"You need to come to the hospital and let the lab take a vial of your blood," Chet said. "To see if it matches DNA on the evidence we've collected."

"Whoa." Bud held up his hands. "He can talk to a lawyer first, can't he, Chet?" He knew from the time he hired Rusty, or any of the guys he had helped, things could turn sour in a heartbeat. But things were going so well for Ron.

Chet nodded.

"Wait here, Ron, while I make a call." Bud started toward his office, calling over his shoulder. "Don't say anything till I get back." Then he turned around. "On second thought, Ron, you come with me. And, Chet, you help yourself to coffee."

When Rusty followed him into his office, Bud closed the door. "Now let's just stay calm and act as cooperative as we can without doing anything to hurt you." Bud picked up the phone and nodded to the chair by his desk. "Have a seat."

Rusty sank into the chair. He sat with his eyes closed, head back, holding tight to the arms of his chair. He'd never been much on religion, but he knew enough from going to Saint Michael's with Jolene that he might as well call on God for help, because the pit opening under him was way too deep to get out of by himself.

"Sorry to get you so early, Duncan. Bud Johnson here. I got a fella in my office needs your help." When Bud described how Chet appeared at the office with a warrant, Duncan advised that

Ron go to the hospital, give the requested sample, but say nothing until Duncan got there.

"Let's go face the music," Bud said when he hung up and grabbed the keys to his Bronco. When they returned to the reception area, Bud told Chet he would drive Ron to the hospital.

"See you there in ten," Chet said, then left.

"The important thing is to keep your head and give the sample," Bud said once Chet left. "But don't say one word until Duncan gets to the hospital. Not hello, good-bye, nothing."

"I gotta call Quinn first," Rusty said. When Bud handed him the phone, Rusty rubbed his forehead while he counted five rings before Quinn answered. "The jig's up," he said. He told Quinn about Chet and the warrant, and how Bud was driving him to give a blood sample.

"You just hang on till I get to the hospital," Quinn said.

"I don't suppose there's anything you can do. Bud's got a lawyer friend comin'. I guess he's the one to call the shots now."

"Well, I don't give a good goddamn whether you think I can help or not. I'm comin' down anyway."

~

Not long after Bud and Rusty entered the lab reception area, a technician called Rusty into a small room. She motioned for him to have a seat, then tied a rubber tourniquet around his arm.

"Little stick," she said as she slipped the needle into his arm.

Little stick, my ass, Rusty thought as the blood spurted into the sample collection tube. *You could cut my arm off and catch a bucketful of blood and I wouldn't feel nothin'.* When the technician capped the tube with a purple stopper and wrote Rusty's name on it, he sprang from his seat then ran back to the reception area to wait for his lawyer.

Duncan Riordan arrived a few minutes later and led Rusty to a small conference room. The man was tall and thin, sharp-looking, Rusty thought, even after being called out of bed so early. Once they started talking, he made it seem like they were just two guys yapping over coffee, even though part of Rusty felt like he was watching a movie of his life, heading on fast forward to a bad ending.

"I done it," Rusty said, holding his hands up when Duncan asked for details about the assault. "I deserve what's comin' to me." He looked away. But when he turned back, Duncan wasn't acting like he'd said anything worse than "Today's Thursday."

Duncan leaned back in his chair. He had gone up against Elizabeth Reedy at least a dozen times on sexual violence cases and had been able to pull only three of his clients through without conviction. He wouldn't have thought much of that record, except that it was better than anyone else's in the county.

But Duncan had never had a client like Rusty. One who wasn't blaming the woman or the girl, or saying he was provoked, or that the woman consented. And he hadn't defended someone who had been in treatment for two years before being accused.

"What you've got coming," Duncan said, "is for the courts to decide." The important thing was for Rusty not to discuss the case with anyone and to keep going to counseling, to work, and to church. "You live clean as a whistle until we get this taken care of." Rusty nodded and Duncan packed up his briefcase. "Now let's both get back to work."

⌒

While Rusty talked with Duncan, Quinn arrived at the hospital and found his way to the lab where Bud was seated in the waiting area. "I appreciate your helpin' Rusty out," he said, after introducing himself and sitting down.

"He's done a heck of a job for me," Bud said, "and I'm not bailing on him now. We'll just take things day by day and get him through this as best we can." Bud checked his watch. "I gotta run," he said. "You can drive him back to the shop?"

"You bet."

Twenty minutes later, when he heard the conference room door open down the hall, Quinn looked up to see Rusty following

Duncan into the reception area. He hoped it was just the fluorescent lights that made Rusty look so green-ish and worn out. But when Rusty got up close, Quinn saw that the sparkle that had come back into his eyes was replaced by hollow despair.

"This here's the lawyer," Rusty said.

Quinn set aside the *Sports Illustrated* he'd been leafing through and stood up.

"Duncan Riordan."

When Duncan extended his hand, Quinn reached for it and asked the question he wasn't sure he wanted answered. "What're we lookin' at here?"

"Right now, we're not sure whether this will go to trial. A lot can happen before then." The most important thing, Duncan explained, was for Rusty to keep up with his program and listen to men in his support group who had gone to trial and could help him understand what to expect. Except for his one-on-one therapy, Rusty needed to keep quiet about details of the case. "The most vital things," Duncan said as he turned to Rusty, "are for you to keep clean and to not give up. Can you do that?"

Rusty nodded. "Yes, I can."

From the way Rusty avoided Duncan's eyes when he spoke, Quinn wasn't convinced.

In Quinn's Silverado, Rusty reached in his jacket pocket for a cigarette. It wasn't even nine o'clock, and he felt like he'd put in more than a full day's work. But instead of putting the Marlboro in his mouth, he slid it back into the pack. Nothing, he thought, *nothing* could make him feel better. No nicotine, no weed, no drink could fill the pit in his stomach. He pulled down the passenger's seat visor, looked in the mirror, then slapped it back against the roof. When Quinn started the engine and pulled out of his parking spot, Rusty ripped off his hat, slammed it against the dash. He told himself what he hadn't in a long time—that he was a no-good son of a gun and that no one ought to have to put up with him from the get-go.

Quinn glanced across the bench seat at Rusty, then turned his attention to the road. "If I was you," he said, trying to sound as casual as if he were saying how it looked like rain was coming in from the west, "I'd probably be feelin' plenty sorry for myself right about now. And I'd want to run."

Rusty worked his fists open and closed. He sank deeper into the seat.

"It's not gonna do one bit of good for you to act like an infant. You heard what the lawyer said. There's plenty of ins and outs we don't know about. It's up to him to give us the best advice he can."

Rusty scowled and said nothing.

"The only way outta this is through it, pal. Same as everything else. Now we got work to do."

Rusty wanted to grab Quinn by the throat and shake those useless words out of him. Easy for him to sit there and tell him to think positive, like he was suckin' it up to participate in some damn spelling bee. Didn't Quinn know what he was up against?

"First you got to call Jolene."

"I can't call Jolene."

"You don't want my opinion, it's okay." Quinn resisted the urge to pull the truck over, throw it into park, and throttle Rusty. "But I'm givin' you the best I got."

"How can I tell her about this? I still haven't told her nothin' about my past except sellin' weed."

Quinn stopped at the light on Cedar and Carbondale and looked at Rusty. *Tell me I didn't hear that.* "Just why is it you never told her?"

Rusty stared straight ahead, set his jaw, and went stone-cold silent.

"Look, I'm sorry I hollered. I just thought you told her months ago. About the program and all."

"Like I said before, her father done things to her." As he spoke, Rusty remembered how, at his first group meeting, he laughed at Mitchell for bawling when his girlfriend took off to California.

Mitchell's girl never came back. Now he realized Jolene might do the same thing. "What if she leaves me?"

"Whether you tell her or not, if there's a court case, she's gonna find out in some way. Papers. TV. But at least you'd know you did the right thing. If she leaves or stays, then you take care of her and your child like an honest man would."

Quinn pulled his truck into the Fresh Air parking lot and dropped Rusty at the door.

"Somehow sayin' thank you don't seem like the right thing," Rusty said as he opened the truck door. "But I'm glad you come and got me."

Quinn nodded. Rusty stepped from the truck and turned back before he closed the door.

"You still got that spare room set up?"

"Still waitin'."

On his way home, Rusty thought at first he should stop at the florist and buy Jolene flowers or grab a pizza for dinner. But he figured there was no flower pretty or sweet-smelling enough to cover up the truth, and even an extra-large, deep-dish pie, double cheese, wouldn't soften Jolene's reaction. Hell, he'd probably end up wearing it. So, he drove around awhile, away from town, thinking how hard he and Jolene worked to save up for the house they bought, how he installed a new heating and A/C system, and how she made it look good enough to be featured in one of those decorating magazines she was fond of. When he turned back to West MacMillan, he drove slowly so he could hold those memories close to his heart. By the time he got home, he figured he was as ready as he'd ever be to face the mother of his child. He went inside, hoping there was a God and that He was watching out for him.

"Where you been, hon?" Jolene walked toward Rusty and held his hand to her stomach when she kissed him. "I was gettin' worried."

"Had a little emergency is all." He held her close and looked around the kitchen thinking how homey Jolene made the place in the months they'd been there. He smelled his favorite chicken pot pie in the oven and saw the candles she put on the table, like she did once or twice a week. Then, with his hands on her arms, he stepped back from her. "I got somethin' to tell you. Hardest thing I've ever had to say. Let's sit down."

"What is it? You alright?" She wiped her hands on the towel hanging on the oven door handle and followed Rusty into the living room.

"Sit down," he said, motioning to the couch. "Please." When Jolene sat on the couch, Rusty paced from the television to the recliner and back. He could hardly breathe. She looked curious, then scared, then annoyed that he was taking so long to say what he had to say.

"Long time ago, I got into some trouble. You remember I told you about the drugs? How I sold weed to college kids?"

She sat forward. "You're not dealin' again, are you?"

He shook his head. "No, what I done, it's worse than dealin'." He paused, took as deep a breath as he could, then the words tumbled out. "I hurt a girl. A long while ago." For the first time since he walked in the house, he looked straight at her to see how she was taking his news.

"You mean rape?"

When he heard the high-pitched tone in her voice and saw the way her face seemed to struggle to find its natural shape, he swallowed hard. "That's what I mean."

Jolene fitted her hands around her full stomach. "Who'd you rape?"

"There was a couple I tried to mess with. One more serious than others. Here in town. Now she wants to take me to court."

"How long ago?" The question squeaked out of her.

"Three years."

"You mean you could go to jail?"

He nodded.

"For how long?"

"Five to ten."

She looked at him as if he were speaking a strange language, one she didn't understand and one she didn't want to. "Why?"

"Why'd I do it or why didn't I tell you?"

"Why didn't you tell me?" she screamed, her face red. "You knew about my father. Why didn't you tell me?" She grabbed a pillow from the sofa and held it to her belly. Something to hang onto. Anything.

"I was afraid you'd leave me. Now that you're pregnant, I'm even more afraid."

"Oh," she said, "poor you. If you'd told me before, I would've at least known I could trust you to tell the truth. Now I'm wonderin' what else you're hidin' from me."

"The only other thing is that I've been gettin' help for this problem. Over to the Center. For two years now."

She stood, still holding the pillow. "You mean everybody but me knows about this?"

"Not everybody. Just Quinn and the guys in my group."

"You're sayin' they're more important than me?" She slammed the pillow on the couch. He went to her, but she ran to the other side of the room. "Don't you dare come near me."

He clenched his fists, trying to anchor himself. "No one's more important than you, Jolene. No one. I was afraid, because of what your father did, you'd think I was the same as him and you'd hate me the way you hate him."

"Well," she said, "you got a point there." She reached to her neck and fumbled with the cross she wore on a delicate gold chain. "I covered up for him for all those years and guess what?"

"What?"

She marched to the kitchen, turned off the oven, grabbed a towel, wrapped it around the casserole, and carried it to the door. "I'm not coverin' up nothin' no more." She kicked open the screen door and pitched the pot pie over the porch railing. The dish hit the ground and rolled, spreading chicken and carrots and peas and gravy across the lawn. "Enjoy your dinner," she said. "And when you're done, don't even think about tryin' to get back in this house."

Rusty knew he deserved to be tossed out like yesterday's trash. He only wanted to take away the pain he was causing her. Right now, he figured, that wasn't possible. He went to their bedroom and stuffed a few things in his gym bag before he headed to Quinn's. When he came out, Jolene had locked herself in the spare bedroom they had painted yellow and called the nursery.

He went to the door and heard her rocking in the chair they set next to the crib. "I know this may be hard to believe right now." He spoke loudly enough so she could hear, his voice quavering, his body shaking. "But I'm not who I was when I did those things, mostly because you loved me into bein' a different man." When Jolene said nothing and all he could hear was the rocking chair on the creaking floorboards, he turned and left the house.

After she heard Rusty leave the house, Jolene went to the front door and locked it. She went to the bathroom, then turned on the shower and took off her clothes. Instead of stepping into the tub, she looked at herself in the mirror. She glanced down at her belly, fitting her hands along the sides of it. It was still a wonder that, inside her, a little person—part Rusty, part her—was growing eyes and teeth and hair and feet. "It's a boy, I bet you ten to one," Nancy Cummings said almost every time she saw her daughter, once Jolene's stomach started to fill out. "I carried your brother high like that. I only hope your baby is quicker to come out than J.J. was."

For the last two months, since her mother first voiced her prediction, Jolene sometimes imagined how Rusty looked when he was small. She had no pictures of him to go by except the one his Nana gave Rusty of him and his father. And that was taken in the first hours after Rusty was born, when he was squirming and squinty and red. At first, Jolene hoped Nancy's prediction was

correct and their son would look every inch his father, not just
so there would be two men in the world she adored, but also so
Rusty could, in some way, relive the childhood he missed because
of Lorraine's lack of attention.

But as Jolene rubbed her hands over her belly, she hoped the
baby looked as little like Rusty as possible and was a girl. At least
then there was a chance she could turn out to be worth something.
She loosened her long ponytail and noticed how full and heavy
her breasts hung and how the nipples had darkened and spread.
Even though she was mad enough to spit nails, she looked resolute.

Still, a dirty feeling had come over her when Rusty admitted
his past. She remembered what her father told her when he did
things to her—that if she wasn't so pretty, he wouldn't have done
what he did. She poured lavender bubble bath into the tub, then
stepped into the warm water to wash herself clean, ready to begin
a new life for herself and her child.

CHAPTER TWENTY-SEVEN

On the morning of Lehanna's departure from the village, Nathalie came to her room in the staff residence with a small package tied with raffia. "For you," she said, holding out the bundle.

"But I have nothing for you," Lehanna said. "If I had known—"

Nathalie shook her head and reached for Lehanna's hand. "You gave me a gift long ago when you stayed with me when my spirit wanted to leave."

That wasn't true, Lehanna wanted to say, but she recalled what Jacques said the day she arrived at the clinic: she had played a role in Nathalie's healing whether or not she chose to acknowledge that. She smiled, sat on the bed, unwrapped the little package, and took out the carving of a zebu, the sacred ox, on a leather cord.

"To bring you prosperity, peace, and happiness." Nathalie smiled. "And if you or someone you love is in danger, you can invoke the zebu's strength for her, too."

Lehanna stood and circled her arms around her friend.

They were still hugging, promising to write, when Allain, who had returned to the village to escort Lehanna back to Tana, came to the door. Clouds were rolling in from the west, he said, promising heavy rain. "We need to leave now."

The women embraced again, then Lehanna made a quick sweep through the clinic buildings to say good-bye to the other staff. Then, as she and Allain set out for Tana, she promised herself that she would return to this community where her contribution was valued and where doubt and self-deprecation were not tolerated.

⁓

I'd like to invite you to dinner tonight."

Lehanna looked up from her university office desk. She and Jacques had had dinner six or seven times since her return to Tana from the clinic. Each time, he'd simply asked if she was free or where she wanted to go.

She leaned back in her chair. "I feel an 'and' or a 'but' at the end of that sentence."

Jacques shrugged and smiled.

She had never before seen him divert his eyes. Was it possible he was capable of even the slightest self-doubt? She thought of how, a few years back, she heard him address the Global Health Organization's New York symposium. How he stood in front of a couple hundred potential patrons and said, no matter how deep they dug into their pockets to help Worldwide Health, it wouldn't be deep enough. He told them that American medical schools prepared graduates to manage their investment portfolios, but not to hold the hand of a man dying of AIDS or to console a woman whose child had died from treatable malaria. When a few stood to leave because of his pointed accusations, he called after them.

"You can walk out," he said. But hadn't they turned their backs on these same brothers and sisters too many times? Was it asking too much to trade the cost of one limousine ride for a child's well-being?

"I challenge you to look at this before you head to 21 or Le Cirque," he said, clicking through his presentation slides to one of children picking through a dumpster in an Antananarivo alley, searching for the makings of a meal.

Some still left, without looking back. But those who stayed that night contributed over five hundred thousand dollars to the clinic and to programs to help locals learn to farm their land without depleting it, so the next generation would have a chance to eat better, grow stronger, and raise healthier children.

Lehanna had seen Jacques stare down deadlier challengers, including AIDS and malaria, without a tremor. But now, asking her to dinner, hands clasped behind his back, eyes searching, he looked tentative.

She smiled. "Dinner would be lovely."

As soon as the words were out, the momentary uncertainty left Jacques's eyes. She looked back to the open notebook on the desk, scribbled a few words, and stowed it in her bag. "What time?"

"Seven."

"Okay, good." She stood, organized into piles the materials to send to Swenson. When she picked up her bag, smiled, and prepared to walk to her apartment on the other side of campus, she wondered why she was leaving this man, when she wanted to reach to him, put her head to his chest, allow herself to be held.

"And," he said, "wear your dancing shoes."

"My dancing shoes?"

He nodded.

"I guess that means we're not going to one of your favorite faculty haunts?"

"That's correct."

She adjusted the tote on her shoulder. "No hints?"

"I'd rather surprise you."

"You have a way of doing that." She wanted to look away but couldn't. "Surprising me, I mean."

He moved closer. He took the bag from her hand and set it on the floor. The distance between them—eighteen inches, a foot, six inches—began to close. He held his hand to her face. He stroked her hair.

She wondered if he could feel her heart racing. Could he hear her swallowing, her attempt to satisfy the thirst she just now noticed?

He said nothing.

She pulled away and tossed her hair over her shoulder. "I need to do my hair, of course." She smiled and reached for her bag on the floor. "And change my shoes." Then she headed for the door. "*Àu bientôt.*" She waved but didn't look back.

Outside the building, Lehanna stood in the gentle rain that had begun to fall. She looked at the sky, gray, wet, and full. Closing her eyes, she tilted her head back and felt the cool air on her face. Then she opened her mouth and caught raindrops on her tongue. She swallowed and felt less thirsty. Still, she wanted more to drink.

When Lehanna opened her apartment door that evening, she found Jacques standing with his hands clasped behind his back. "You did some shopping in Paris," Lehanna said, admiring his new suit.

"I did." He smiled, then handed her the box he held behind him, wrapped in blue paper, tied with a silver bow. "Also from Paris," he said. "I hope you like it."

She looked at the box, at Jacques, at the box again. "May I open it now?"

"I wish you would."

She pulled at the bow, then removed the paper more slowly than she wanted to. When she looked inside the box at the silvery shawl of appliquéd organza, she stroked her hand along it in its tissue nest.

"I hope you like it," he said again.

"I do," she said, although she still didn't take it out of the box. "It's so delicate. And elegant."

"It made me think of you."

"I'm touched." She removed the shawl from the box and wrapped it around her. It felt light as mist on her shoulders, her arms. "Thank you," she said. "So much."

"You'll wear it tonight?"

"Of course." She walked to the one mirror, over the bureau.

When she looked at herself, still enveloping the shawl over the long, rose-colored crepe-de-chine dress she bought that afternoon, she pulled her hair back and up and secured it with combs. Then she turned to him and presented herself.

"You look beautiful."

She smiled and took his arm. If she had spoken her thoughts, she would have said, *I feel beautiful, too.*

They sidestepped the puddles left by the afternoon's showers. He opened the car for her, tucked the hem of her skirt in so it wouldn't catch when he closed the door.

"And," she said, when he took his seat behind the wheel, "we're going where?"

He smiled. "Still a surprise." He drove to the *haute ville,* the section of Tana where many wealthy residents and government officials lived. "I used to live right there," he said, when they passed a red brick house on one of the tree-lined streets.

Lehanna warmed when he shared this detail of his early past. The first.

Two blocks farther, he pulled in front of an elegant, white-columned building, set back from the road, lit by torches, guarded by granite lions atop pillars at the base of the steps. When the valet came to take the car, Jacques escorted Lehanna into the restaurant. A discreet brass door plate identified it as *La Vague de la Mer.*

"My father's name is still influential enough to get a table here," he said, nodding to a group of guests in the lobby, all dressed in fashionable evening attire. As they walked into the dining room, Lehanna's steps slowed. If someone had shown her a photo of the place, she might have guessed it was in New York or Paris. But the terrace plantings were too lush and voluptuous for New York, and the waitstaff too welcoming for Paris. The *maître d'* escorted them to their table overlooking the gardens, handed them hand-written menus, then recited the evening's specials.

"No *achards* or *romazava*?" Her eyes sparkled as she whispered across the table.

Jacques smiled. "No *gris,* either."

While the waiter stood, hands clasped behind his back, gaze fixed on an imaginary point across the dining room, they settled on Coquilles-Saint Jacques, followed by Cornish hens. "And Dom Perignon to start." Jacques handed back both menus, though his eyes focused on Lehanna.

She tilted her head, wondering what warranted the champagne. "You've had a successful trip, yes?" he asked.

She smiled. "Very," she said. "Swenson's pleased. I am, too."

"And you look too lovely not to celebrate."

"It would be difficult to not at least feel lovely in this place."

"Maybe, maybe not. But *you* look lovely."

In the background a band started playing, and Lehanna felt she might have been transported to a Bogart movie set, and that her lines should have been scripted for Bacall. Or Hepburn. She reeled in her thoughts. "How did things go in Paris?"

He told how he negotiated additional clinic support from a group of Parisian businessmen and that things went as well as could be expected with his children. "It's going to take them time to trust me again." He reached for his napkin and spread it on his lap. "I neglected them. I admit that."

There was no point, Lehanna decided, in trying to assuage his regret. His work had supplanted his family. At least he could acknowledge the truth.

When he asked how she felt about going back to the States, she looked wistful. "It's ironic that I've come halfway around the world to feel like I belong. Maybe not in this place." She gestured around the dining room. "But in the clinic, the village."

"Maybe the reason you feel at home here is that this place needs so much healing. The country is raw and bleeding and there's not enough food. We ravaged her and abandoned her, and now we wonder why she won't pull herself together and sustain us."

They sat in silence for a moment, then Jacques spoke again, as if he had been waiting for the right moment to say what he wanted. "You remember the *famadihana*? The one Haja ordered for Nathalie?"

She leaned back in her chair. "Of course."

"You recall, then, the joy the village experienced at the exhumation? How happy everyone was to be in Nathalie's ancestor's presence?"

She nodded slowly. She wasn't certain she wanted to follow where Jacques was leading.

"And how, once the bones were turned, and put back in the tomb, the villagers believed results would follow. Then they got on with their lives?"

"I know where you're going with this—" When her voice took on a crisp tone, he retreated.

"Well, if you know where I'm going, there's no point in my continuing." He reached across the table for a slice of bread and buttered it.

"I'm sorry. It's just that—"

"Just what? That you refuse to move on because you're afraid of being hurt again? That you would rather hide behind helping other people than help yourself? That you feel you're different? That you don't need anyone else?" He hesitated. "You don't need to make the same mistake I did. Burying yourself in your work, then waking up one day and finding you've hurt—not just yourself, but others, too—not by what you accomplished, but by what you didn't do."

She turned to look at the middle-aged couple on the dance floor, leading and following as they probably had for twenty years or more. She hadn't danced in a long, long time. She thought of the lesson she tried to teach Allison. *It's wounds that make a healer.* Jacques was right. She had buried herself so deep in her wounds and her desire, her *need* to help others, that she left her own healing behind. But she thought, too, of what Haja told her the night they sat beneath the stars. *This is not your home.*

"The plants and the drugs are one part of the equation," Jacques continued, the pace of his words quickening. "Many of them work, not just because they set off chemical reactions that boost immune systems or gobble up parasites and render them impotent. They work because people believe they will work. Because they are administered with faith and hope and love. One human being to another. And if you continue to shut yourself off from the possibility of that love, or if you continue to let it all flow out and none of it flow back in? There you'll be, empty and parched, with only the fossils of memories to sustain you."

She looked at him, blinking, her lips parting slightly as if she wanted to make words but couldn't. On the one hand, she didn't appreciate his preaching. On the other, he was right. But if she admitted that truth, she felt it would swallow her.

"I don't know all the reasons you've gone inside yourself. But I know Jonathan loved you, and you loved him, and that is something that can never be replaced." His tone softened as he leaned toward her. "But there can be more love. In fact, there must be, or there is no reason to go on." She tried to take her hands from the table, but he took them in his. "Raise up Jonathan and anyone else who is holding you back. Lift them and your own heart out of the tomb where you've placed them. Celebrate him, and anyone else who is there, but reclaim your heart."

It's time now. She thought of her last visit to Taughannock Falls. How she burned Jonathan's letters there, thinking she had let go of him and moved on. "It's not that easy to forget—"

"No one's asking you to forget. Only that, while you're healing other people, you make sure you're nourished, too."

She took her hands from his and looked across the table at him, then lowered her eyes. It was one thing for her to know the truth about herself, but quite another for someone else to discover what she had tried, for almost twenty years, to keep contained, deep inside. She steadied herself, then looked directly at Jacques.

"I'm better at helping other people heal than I am at healing myself."

When the words came out, she felt small. She should have seen how removed she had become, how she had barricaded herself behind her healing arts, while not integrating what she knew into her own life. And why? Because she had lost people important to her, her father, Jonathan. It was so much easier to avoid attachment than to risk the possibility of loss or hurt. Isn't that what she had done, even with Allison? Avoided commitment, responsibility?

"That's just it," Jacques said. "We can't heal in isolation. I think my clinic patients have no idea how much they help me when they persevere. They would tell you it's me who helps them. And, of course, on the physical level, that's true. But when they choose to trust in me and my work, and to believe that healing is possible, I benefit as much as they do. Maybe more."

"But I—"

"No buts." His voice was softer, but still insistent. "I know I'm a fine one to talk, on the verge of divorce, needing to work double-time with my kids because I ignored them for too long. All I'm trying to say is that we each have an opportunity. To repair what we can—in ourselves and our relationships—then see what awaits us. The clinic is far enough along to run without me now, at least on a day-to-day basis. Once Charles finishes his studies, he'll be able to tend to it while I'm away. I'll never leave it, or Madagascar, not totally, but it's no longer my whole life."

Lehanna looked beyond the terrace, over Tana, toward the distant hills. She recalled that Fourth of July, when, as a child, she saw Jonathan's death. Hadn't she learned since then that she couldn't control his life or death, or her father's, or anyone else's? Still, she hung on to the feeling that she *should* be able to. And while assuming that responsibility kept her from hurt, it also prevented possibility. She looked back to Jacques, thinking how Haja had told her the Great Red Island was not her home. He hadn't said Jacques wasn't the right man to make a home with though. If not in the village or Tana, maybe in Paris, or the States.

Yet had *he* really moved on? He hadn't yet mentioned Celeste, except to say she had taken the children to Paris.

When Jacques reached across the table again, Lehanna looked at the hands that had first welcomed her to the Great Red Island twenty years earlier. She remembered the feeling she had on that first visit, that she was linked to him, in a way she didn't yet know. But now she knew that, regardless of what progress he had or hadn't made in his own life, he was right: she would never be able to shake off her fear or come out of isolation on her own.

The waiter arrived and set a champagne flute in front of each of them, then deftly turned the bottle until its cork released with a soft sigh. He poured a small amount into Jacques's glass. "Perfect," Jacques said.

They finished dinner, then their coffee and profiteroles. When the band played again, they danced out to the terrace and sat on the steps leading to the gardens below, brimming red and pink. They didn't speak. Their gestures—the way she touched his face, as if to make sure he was really there, the way he took her hand in his, and traced his finger along her palm—said what mattered, at least in that moment. Together, she promised herself, they would learn to live differently than they had before.

Around midnight, they left the club and drove to her university apartment. The next morning, they woke and started their day the way they finished the last.

⌒

Swenson landed at Ivato airport with two agendas. First, he would review the information Lehanna had catalogued to complete their drug patent applications. Second, he would try to recruit Lehanna and Jacques to join him when he changed jobs.

"He looks happy about something," Lehanna said when she and Jacques spotted George crossing the tarmac, waving and smiling.

They didn't need to wait long for him to spill his good news. Once they were driving out of the airport, he leaned forward from the back seat of Jacques's Renault. "What would you say," he asked Jacques, "to an offer for a year-long appointment to set up a program at MacMillan University?"

"You're talking so fast, even I can't keep up," Jacques said. "What kind of program? And why at MacMillan and not Cornell?"

George grinned. "Let me start over. I've been in the air for eighteen hours, not counting the six hours I spent sleeping on a plastic chair at Charles de Gaulle." He shook his head, as if to dislodge cobwebs that had settled in, then told them how, before he left for Madagascar, he received a call from MacMillan's dean of the College of Medicine. "Harvey Lerner. Remember him?" Jacques nodded and Swenson told how Lerner had finally convinced the school to pilot a program for health care students—not just doctors, but nurses, physician's assistants, dentists—who wanted to work in developing countries. He envisioned interdisciplinary courses on everything from how to set up a clinic to how to work with traditional healers to how to breach cultural differences, all in a new Department of Alternative Medicine.

Jacques looked across the seat at Lehanna, then in the rearview mirror where he could catch Swenson's eye. Had he heard correctly? He had been after schools in the States to at least acknowledge developing countries' unique health care needs for more than a decade. If an elite American university offered a specialized curriculum, that would be a fine start. If he developed and ran the program? Even better.

"You're serious," Jacques said.

Swenson adjusted his wire-rimmed glasses. "Very."

"Well, hallelujah." Jacques intentionally swerved the car, causing Lehanna and George to grip their seats, then laugh.

"Provided you haven't killed yourself, and us, before you get there," George said when he regained his balance. "You'd pretty much get *carte blanche* as far as curriculum and faculty go—though you'd have to deal with academia's usual rigamarole. Plus, a couple paid trips back to Madagascar to check on the clinic." He paused. "What do you say?"

Jacques reached across the seat and squeezed Lehanna's hand, sending Swenson the first signal that the two had become more than business associates. When Lehanna nodded, Jacques smiled into the rearview mirror. "I'm thrilled. But," he said, catching George's reflection again, "you're still grinning like a little kid who very badly wants to tell a secret."

"I never could pull anything over on you, Merthin." George reached forward and slapped Jacques on the back. "If I had a non-disclosure agreement in my pocket, I'd ask both of you to sign. I've got your word you won't get on the phone to your hundred or so nearest and dearest family and friends, or enemies, for that matter?"

When they both agreed, George revealed that Lerner had cleared the way for George to move to MacMillan, too, as head of a new ethnobotany research program. "And you," he said, tapping Lehanna on the shoulder, "will be my very first hire."

Lehanna turned to George, wishing she hadn't agreed to secrecy. She wanted to open her window and shout the news. The three of them would all be working to further the advancement of traditional healing practices, not just at the clinic but around the globe. As for Jacques and her? She smiled and sat back into the Renault's comfortably worn leather seat.

CHAPTER TWENTY-EIGHT

As Allison drove to Richard and Corinne's house, the overly confident radio weatherman promised only a dusting of snow. She knew better. A storm was headed MacMillan's way. Not just because the clouds overhead looked lead-bellied, but also because she was about to deliver unsettling news.

Driving onto Tranche Street, Allison remembered the last time it snowed on Thanksgiving. The year she turned twelve. Her mother helped her build a snowman in the shape of a pilgrim. "We'll name him Miles Standish," Lucy said, and they dressed him in a woolen top hat made from an old black coat. They built a mate for Miles, too, called Priscilla, and Lucy and Allison draped cranberry beads around her neck and an orange cape over her scrawny stick-arms.

When she pulled the car next to the barren weeping cherries, she turned off the ignition and sat staring at the house. She still half-expected Lucy to come to the door and welcome her. She could hear her mother. "Careful not to slip on the marble floor." When the door didn't open, Allison considered turning around and going back to her place. But Eamon and Danny had gone to Ireland to visit their mother over the holiday break, and the thought of spending the day alone seemed almost as threatening as the sky. Besides, she reminded herself, this wasn't a social call. She had work to do. She walked to the front steps and rang the bell.

Corinne answered the door with a larger than necessary smile, and a flourish of her arm that sent her gold bracelets tinkling. *Too many bracelets, too much perfume, and too many teeth,* Allison thought. When she walked inside, she reminded herself to be civil. That way her news would have greater impact.

"Happy Thanksgiving," she said, handing over the pumpkin pie she made for dessert.

"And Happy Thanksgiving to you." Corinne reached to take the pie. "It's a chilly one, isn't it?"

She wondered if Corinne was referring to the tone of Allison's greeting or the weather, but she didn't have long to decide. Richard came out of the kitchen into the hall, carrying two mugs of mulled cider.

"Hi, Ali." He kissed her cheek. "A little something to warm you up." He handed one cup to Ali then reached to take her coat.

"Thanks." She wrapped her hands around the mug. In spite of herself, she felt comforted breathing in the cider's cinnamon and clove scent. "Smells good." If there were basil in the fire, and a mince pie baking, and if Corinne hadn't overdone her perfume, Allison thought, the house would smell like it had every Thanksgiving that she and Lucy and Richard had lived there. She reminded herself not to get too cozy.

"Come sit by the fire." Corinne led Allison into the family room, where Stephanie was watching the Macy's parade on television while Devon polished her nails. "Allison's here, girls." Devon and Stephanie, both younger, blonder versions of Corinne, looked up. They smiled, said hello as if politely greeting a neighbor or family acquaintance, then went back to watching and polishing.

"The girls have been home since Tuesday," Corinne said, motioning to Allison to have a seat.

Home? Do they really consider my mother's house their home? Allison remained standing.

"I could use some help in the kitchen," Corinne said to the girls.

Though Stephanie got up and bounced after her mother, Devon dawdled. "They're not dry yet," she said, fluttering her nails through the air.

"Now!" Devon stood then dawdled after Stephanie when Corinne, like a stylishly dressed crossing guard, pointed to the kitchen.

Allison watched after them, wishing all three would keep on walking, out the back door, down the ravine, into the chilly creek, and float away. She sat on the couch.

"Almost time," Corinne called as she pulled the turkey from the oven. "Just make yourself at home."

Richard came into the family room as Allison rolled her eyes toward Corinne. *Make myself at home? It* is *my home. Or it was.*

"Everything okay?" he said.

"Peachy."

"Good." After putting on his reading glasses, Richard reached for the current issue of *The New York Review of Books* from the magazine rack.

"If I yelled 'fire,'" she muttered, "would you hear me?"

"What's that?"

"Nothing." She turned her attention to the television. "There he is," Poppie Grant said. "The Cat in the Hat. One hundred fifty feet tall. Guess how long it took to fill him with helium, Andrew?" Allison didn't try to answer the question. Instead, she imagined Corrine as a guest on Poppie's early morning show, the two of them yucking it up like two long-lost sorority sisters.

"Okay, everyone," Corinne called a few minutes later. "Dinner is served."

Devon was already seated when Allison and Richard entered the dining room. Stephanie was filling their water glasses from a crystal pitcher. Richard took his place at the head of the table and Allison sat across from the girls as Corinne brought in a platter piled with turkey and dressing, set it in front of Richard like a gift, then ran back to the kitchen for the Brussels sprouts and sweet potatoes. "Devon," she said over her shoulder. "I need another set of hands for this cranberry sauce and gravy."

Devon tested her nail polish again, deemed it dry, then slouched out to the kitchen.

"Smells delicious, love," Richard called.

Allison wondered how Richard had transitioned from her mother to Corinne so effortlessly. Were they so easily exchangeable, one for the other? Relationship Legos that snapped into place? Was it the sex? Allison shoveled turkey onto her plate while Devon and Stephanie—more Legos—snickered over Richard's term of endearment.

When Corinne returned to the dining room, she passed a bowl of Brussels sprouts to Stephanie. "We're so glad we can all finally be together," she said. "You're sure you don't want cranberry sauce, Allison?"

Before Allison could answer, Corinne looked around the table, smiling. "Now before Richard says grace, we want to share this year's special reason for feeling thankful."

Richard was about to say grace? Allison couldn't remember a time her father had uttered anything remotely spiritual. Except, when Lucy tried getting him to church, and he commented that religion was the Vicodin of the masses.

Corinne nodded to Richard. He drank from his wine glass, wiped his mouth with his napkin, then settled his hands on the arms of his chair. "Yes," he said with an uneasy little cough. "We do." He turned to Devon and Stephanie. "Your mother and I . . ." Then he turned to Allison. "Corinne and I, are going to be married."

Devon and Stephanie looked at each other, then at their mother. Richard smiled. Corinne beamed.

"When?" Devon asked.

"Valentine's Day." Corinne reached across the table for her daughter's hand. "We want each of you to be in the wedding."

Devon and Stephanie glanced at each other again, then giggled. "Bridesmaids?"

Allison looked from Richard to Corinne, then back to Richard. She reminded herself that she, too, had news to share, and that she suspected it would surprise Richard and Corinne even more than their announcement had unsettled her. She lifted her wine glass. "To the happy couple," she said.

⌒

"We're going to Lauren's, Mom," Dev and Steph—as their mother called them—announced after they put away the crystal and silver. They seemed as anxious to see their boarding school friend as Allison was for them to leave. While Corinne set the rules for their visit—Be home by nine. Thank Mrs. Carmody for inviting you—Allison rehearsed again what she had come to tell her father and future stepmother.

"Pour us a brandy, will you, honey?" When Corinne called to Richard in the family room, Allison heard the newspaper rustle. She imagined he would pout because his reading had been interrupted. Then she heard him rummaging in the sideboard for the decanter and snifters. When Corinne and Allison walked into the room, he held out a glass to each, then poured himself a bourbon.

"Sit." Corinne smiled and patted the sofa next to her.

Allison dismissed her first thought—that Corinne considered her on par with a trained cockapoo. *Arf!* She sat, placed her brandy on the table next to her, leaned forward, and clasped her crossed legs. "You two look very happy."

"We are." Corinne smiled at Richard, then encircled her hands around her glass. She looked at Allison. "I would imagine this is awkward for you. With all your memories of your mother and holidays here."

"Awkward? I guess awkward is as good a word as any."

Corinne set her drink on the coffee table and reached for Allison's hand. "I'm sure this isn't easy, and—"

Allison pulled away.

"Allison—" Richard ventured into the conversation, but Allison cut him off.

"You two aren't the only ones with news today." She smiled and sipped her brandy.

"Oh?" Corinne looked at Richard as if to say *I told you she and Eamon would get married.* She smiled.

Allison set down her glass. "I want to tell you about something that happened a long time ago." She spoke slowly, as if gathering preschoolers for story time. One with a lesson requiring their close attention. "And what I'm doing about it."

Corinne blanched. This wasn't what she hoped for. Richard sat, right leg crossed over left, the paper on his lap. He knew his daughter. Whatever Allison was going to say would attempt to shock. He took off his glasses, folded them, and set them on the table. "What is it, Ali?"

"The summer before I left for school," she said, still speaking slowly. "The summer Mother died." Her voice cracked. She took a deep breath. "I was raped."

Corinne's mouth opened in the shape of a small *O*, but no sound came out.

The muscles in Richard's jaw worked. He blinked twice but said nothing.

"Here," Allison went on. "In this house. In my room. Devon's room."

"Ali?" Richard sat forward. "When?" He had expected high drama, but she wouldn't fabricate this story, would she? But if it were true, why hadn't she said something before?

"I'd like to finish."

Richard sat back in his chair.

"It was a few weeks before Mother died. The man broke in. It was late." She continued telling how the man attacked her and threatened to hurt Lucy if she screamed for help or told anyone afterwards.

Corinne put her hand on the sofa next to Allison. "Honey, why didn't you tell us?"

Wondering how Corinne could ask a question with such an obvious answer, Allison snapped. "Because Mother was ill. I didn't want her to know what I had done. And I was afraid he would hurt her. Or hurt me again."

"But you didn't do anything."

Allison's voice softened. Even though the attempted reprieve came from Corinne, she welcomed it. "When it happened, I didn't want her to leave me thinking I was bad, a disappointment. That maybe I had done something to make him think——" She picked up her brandy and finished it. "Now," she said, finding her voice again, "I know who did it, and I'm taking him to court."

"Who was it, Ali?" Corinne put her hand on Allison's leg. "Have you known all along?"

She shook her head. "I never saw him that night. He attacked me from behind. But I met him a few weeks ago. I know who he is."

Richard leaned forward. He held up his hands as if unable to find meaning in an inscrutable text. "If you never saw him that night, how did you recognize him?"

Allison froze. In Richard's impatience, she read disbelief. *Why don't you believe me?* Then she remembered her mission: to punish Ron Jenkins so she would be free of fear. Not only of him. Of anyone. She raised her eyes to look directly at her father. "By the smell, mostly. And his voice."

Corinne reached to stroke Allison's hair. "How awful."

Allison breathed deeper when she felt Corinne's touch. Maybe she wasn't as manipulative as Allison thought. Maybe . . .

But no. Corinne wasn't to be trusted. Allison edged away from her.

"I felt awful when it happened. I was afraid all the time. That maybe he would find me. That one day he would break through a different window or come after me on a dark street. That's part of the reason I got involved with those men at school." She turned to Richard, who leaned forward in his chair, but remained mute. "I was afraid to be alone. And being hurt by them? I don't know. It felt like if they hurt me, he couldn't. I know that sounds mixed up. But now that I know who he is, I don't feel so terrible." She sat up straight again. "Now it's his turn to be scared." She explained how she had seen Elizabeth Reedy and that an investigation was underway. "Then there'll be a hearing. Maybe a trial. And then Mr. Jenkins will go to jail for five to ten years."

"Mr. Jenkins?"

"Yes. Ronny Lee Jenkins. He goes by Rusty. Or Ron. I know he's in your program, Corinne."

Corinne sat back into the couch. She had known Ron since he started in Viewpoint. He was doing everything right to turn his life around. "You're sure? That it was Ron, I mean."

"I'm sure."

Allison looked to Richard, still in his chair, his eyes narrowed and straining, as if he couldn't tell whether he was dreaming or awake.

"Can't you say something?" She yelled to Richard. "You're the one who translates obscure texts. You win awards for teaching students how to think and speak and write. But now, you just sit there?"

Richard's lips parted slightly. He shook his head, but whatever he might have said stuck in his throat.

"Allison," Corinne said, filling the void that Richard couldn't, "if you never saw the man, how can you prove it was Ron?"

"I have evidence," she said. "My quilt with his stinking semen on it. And—"

"In this house?"

Allison and Corinne both looked to Richard, who had finally spoken.

"It happened in this house?" Richard sounded like he wanted his daughter, please, to admit her story was a ploy for attention, for money, for something else. "It happened when I moved out? And you were alone with your mother? When she was sick?"

When Allison saw the way her father's face contorted, the way he seemed desperate to shape sense from her story, she pressed her lips together. She had hurt him. But now that she had gotten what she wanted—the certainty that her father could feel—she wasn't as satisfied as she hoped she would be.

Allison left alone, even though her father wanted her to spend the night, or at least let him drive her home. "You can come back for the car tomorrow," he said. "Or you can stay in the guest room. Upstairs." His shaky pleading pleased her. But she also wanted to run to him, to say she was sorry. What Elizabeth told her was true. This wasn't going to be easy. Still, she left alone.

When he closed the front door, after walking Allison to her car and watching her drive off, Richard went back to the family room. He tossed back the rest of his bourbon. Then he poured himself another. He said nothing to Corinne, who was gathering glasses and leftovers from the coffee table to take to the kitchen. While he stared into the fireplace, he hoped something—the fire, the alcohol, anything—would take a hammer to the guilt in his chest, break it up, and disperse it.

Corinne came back into the room. She stood for a moment watching Richard, his back still toward her. "I'm shocked," she said finally, hoping he would reply. When he didn't, she went to the sofa and sat down.

"It was wrong," he said finally, still looking into the fire. "It was wrong for us to take her home away from her. We booted her out like a scraggly stray we grew tired of tossing kitchen scraps to."

Corinne waited for him to continue, but he didn't. She leaned forward and spoke. "We did the best we could at the time. With the information we had. And Stanley's advice and all."

"To hell with Stanley's advice." He turned to her and slammed his bourbon on the side table. "And to hell with your advice, too. All along, whether you've known it or not, you've been pushing Allison away from me, cutting her off like a dead tree limb. You can't do that anymore."

"I only did what I thought was right. What I thought Lucy . . ." She looked down at her lap, spread her hands over her knees, unable to continue.

"Did Lucy know?"

"Know what?"

"About the rape?"

"Of course not. At least I don't think so. You heard Allison. She didn't tell anyone. "

"Not Paige?"

"Not that I know. Besides, Paige wouldn't have told me. That's privileged information."

"Not you?"

"I know you're upset, but you heard Allison. She told no one."

"I need to help her." He turned back to the fireplace.

"Of course, honey. She's going to need your support, especially if there's a trial." Then she paused. "I'm in a tricky spot here, Richard. Ron Jenkins is one of Viewpoint's success stories. I can't let him down, either."

He spun away from the fireplace and flung out his arm. "He raped my daughter, for God's sake."

She stiffened when he yelled. When a chill scurried down her spine, she felt the way she did when her former husband blamed her, diminished her. "I know that." She fought back tears. "Or at least I think that, based on what Allison said."

"You don't believe her?"

"All I'm saying is that all the facts aren't in yet, and I have a professional responsibility to Ron."

The phone rang and Richard grabbed it. It was Allison calling to say she had returned home safely. "Keep a light on," he told her before he hung up, knowing what a feeble and belated attempt he was making at trying to protect his daughter. He put the phone down, turned off the stereo, and walked out of the room. He took his coat from the hall closet without speaking to Corinne, then walked out the door.

The snow was beginning to spread an innocent white blanket on the town as he walked the mile and a half to campus. When he reached Wellington Hall, which was silent and dark except for the foyer and hall lights, he climbed three flights to his office, thankful he had a place to go to think about what he had done, what he hadn't done, and what he needed to do next. He settled into his familiar leather chair, pulled it up to his desk, and rested his face in his hands, trying to rub away the fatigue and confusion that had settled in like thick fog. After scarcely moving for an hour, he shuffled a few papers on his desk, stacking them into tidy, manageable piles. He took a copy of Dante's *Inferno* from his bookshelf. When dawn crept over the ridge to the east, he was still reading.

CHAPTER TWENTY-NINE

Rusty checked his watch after pulling into the rectory parking lot. Three forty-five. Fifteen minutes early. He decided to go in anyway. It wouldn't hurt to have a little time with Father Dan before Allison Stephenson arrived.

For the last three weeks, since he had been charged with rape, aggravated assault, and breaking and entering the Stephenson house on an evening in July 1988, Rusty had been checking in with Danny every few days. He still hadn't heard from Jolene, so without hope they could patch things up, he was leaning on Danny and Quinn, along with Vance and his Viewpoint group. Even with their help he still felt close to dead inside, like a hollowed-out pumpkin with a face carved out of it. As Danny suggested, he started every day with a prayer: if God was willing to give him another chance, he wouldn't let Him down. No matter how scared he got, no matter how much he wanted to run, all he asked was the strength to do the right thing.

So, a few days earlier when Danny proposed a meeting with Allison, Rusty consented. If she were willing to face him, he couldn't very well try to weasel out of it, even though the ghoul in his head was screeching *run, run, run*. Besides, Danny had taught him that prayer—Saint Patrick's Breastplate, he called it: *Christ within me, Christ behind me, Christ before me, Christ beside me*—and if Christ really was covering the bases, maybe the voice in his head would shut the hell up.

"Come in, come in, Ron." Rusty shook Father Danny's hand and followed him into his study. He paused when he entered the room. He had come to feel safe there, especially late afternoons, like now. The light shining in from behind the Front always settled on the crucifix this time of day, helping him focus. *Christ within me, Christ behind me . . .*

"Have a seat." Danny motioned to two chairs in front of his desk. "What are your thoughts before Allison arrives?"

Rusty suspected Danny wanted to hear that he had faith he—and Jolene and his child—would be protected and provided for, spiritually speaking, anyway. What he really wanted, though, was to curl up in a ball and say nothing. "Just that I want to do the right thing." He wiped the sweat from his upper lip.

Danny sat at his desk and nodded. "If I were in your chair right now," he said, "I might be tempted to say what I thought my spiritual advisor wanted to hear."

Rusty turned away, then looked back. "You're right. That's what I'm doin'. Truth is, I'm scared'er than I've ever been. If it was just me goin' up for what I did, that would be bad enough. But maybe losin' Jolene and my child? That's what's weighin' on me heaviest." He glanced to the crucifix. "I keep thinkin' that if I had as much faith as I say I got, I wouldn't feel this way."

Danny clasped his hands on his desk. "I'd be surprised if you weren't afraid. If we were all perfect in our faith," he said, pointing to the crucifix, "we might start thinking we don't need Him anymore."

Rusty felt his chest loosen up. Maybe there was still hope. But when the doorbell rang and Danny excused himself to let Allison in, his thoughts started spinning again. *What if this? What if that?* With his foot tapping as fierce as it was, all he could do was keep his eyes on the cross. If He knew what it felt like to hang down from there, His hands and feet nailed to it, He might just have some idea how he felt, sitting there waiting for Allison to come into the room.

As she walked in the office, Rusty stood. But when she shot him a quick, sharp look, he sat back down, braced his elbows on the armrests, and folded his hands in front of him.

"Tea?" Danny offered.

Allison reached for the empty chair in front of Danny's desk and edged it away from Rusty. She sat down and shook her head.

"No," Rusty said. "Thank you."

Danny poured himself a cup, mostly to stall. He wanted the conversation to start slowly. He swiveled his chair so he could look out the window. The late afternoon sun was setting behind the Allegheny Front. Whereas Rusty had agreed to this meeting without coaxing, Allison had balked, then only reluctantly decided to come. Her resolve to punish Rusty still seemed as unshakable as that escarpment must have seemed to Martin MacMillan before he tunneled his way through it over a hundred years earlier. But as streaks of amber and amethyst light reflected through the stained glass and across the floor and his desk, Danny invoked the words of the Gospel of Matthew. *If you have faith as small as a mustard seed, you can say to this mountain, "move from here to there," and it will move. Nothing will be impossible for you.*

"This can't feel very good for either of you now, can it?" He set his tea down and brought his chair closer to the desk. Rusty focused on the floor about a yard in front of his feet. Allison looked straight at Danny.

"This is no court of law," Danny continued. "Anything either of you say is going no further than this room unless you're the ones to speak of it." He looked first at Rusty, then Allison. "Do you understand that?" Rusty nodded. Allison kept looking at Danny, expressionless. "And do you trust me?" Rusty nodded again, but Allison remained motionless. "Allison, do you trust that I'm not going to tell anyone outside this room what we talk about today?"

Trust? Allison looked away from him. She trusted no one. Still, Danny had told her that story of his own rape. He knew in some way how she felt. Besides, Lucy often said Father Malone was the most compassionate priest ever to come to Saint Michael's. "Yes."

Danny reviewed the facts as he understood them. First, that Allison believed Rusty had broken into her mother's home and raped her. "Is that what you believe, Allison?"

She nodded, though she didn't just believe what Danny had said. She knew it.

"And you believe you have evidence that could be admissible in a court of law to prove that to be true?"

"Yes."

"And Rusty—without admitting to anything here, that's what the courts are for—you believe what Allison's saying could be true, since at the time you were behaving in ways you no longer do?"

"Yes, sir. I mean, yes, Father."

"Why then, Rusty, are you willing to meet with me and Allison today? You didn't have to, did you?"

"I didn't have to, if you mean is I wasn't legally required."

"Then why did you come, Rusty? Why, when you're risking going to jail over something Allison says you may have done?"

"Because back then I did things I'm not proud of. Mean things. I found out over at Viewpoint that what was leadin' me around then was fear and anger. I wanted to prove I wasn't dirt." He shook his head. "And what did I do? I hurt people. And I felt dirtier than I did to begin with. So, yeah, it's a fact that back then I would've done almost anything to try to feel better. It's no excuse. I'm just sayin' I didn't know the only way to feel better was to do the right thing, not the things I thought I wanted to do."

Allison tightened her grip on the arms of her chair. She looked only at Danny. She said nothing.

"And what happened, Rusty? To make you want to do something different with your life, I mean."

Rusty shrugged. "I got caught. Not by the law. By an old friend. He made me see how wrong what I was doin' was, and how, if I kept livin' that way, I'd never have the kind of life I really wanted. He gave me hope it wasn't too late to try."

"And what did you do?"

"I called over at the Center and got in Viewpoint."

Allison winced. The thought that Corinne's program helped men like Rusty evade responsibility and feel better, while victims like her continued to suffer? It was more than unfair. It was wrong.

"When was that?" Danny asked.

"Two years ago, this past May."

"I see." Danny motioned from Rusty to Allison. "Do you have anything to say to Allison?"

Rusty shifted in his chair. "Only that I wouldn't blame her if she couldn't find it in her heart to forgive me." His voice softened. He looked down at his hands. "That nothin' that was done to me was excuse enough for me to behave how I used to." He paused. "And that I'll take what I got comin'."

Allison turned to Rusty. She saw a lean, strong young man whose face seemed creased with experience and wisdom beyond his twenty-five or so years. Sure, that was regret etched in his forehead. Yet his eyes looked peaceful.

She looked up at the crucifix behind Danny's desk, the wounds piercing the pale figure's side, the droop of His head, the nails through His hands, His feet. She asked herself the same question she asked when she first visited Danny. How could His wounds relate to hers?

She thought of Danny's story about his early years as a priest. How his sermons about forgiveness skated from his mouth like blades on ice. She tasted the cold metal of what it was like to hang onto the past. But, no, she could not, she would not, let it go. She would do whatever she could to rob Ron of his peace. Then, she believed, she would have hers.

Without speaking, she rose from her chair and left the room, closing the door behind her.

CHAPTER THIRTY

Allison waved to Mr. Shaffer when he tipped his cap to her on his way out of Metaphors. "And you have a good day, too."

But when the bells on the shop's door announced another customer's arrival, Allison shifted her eyes to the woman who entered. The one dressed in a deep red cape and long black skirt. Allison's heart beat faster. The woman was tall and slender, and her long hair framed her face in soft waves. Like Lehanna's. But Lehanna was in Madagascar. At least Allison thought she was.

The woman spoke to the tall dark-haired man who walked beside her and brushed her cheek with a kiss. Then she turned to Allison, opened her arms, and rushed toward the counter. "I found you."

When Allison heard Lehanna's familiar voice, she stuffed the cash Mr. Shaffer had given her into the register, left the drawer open, and ran to meet her.

"I've been worried about you," Lehanna said, holding Allison to her heart, then at arm's length to admire her. "But look at you. You look wonderful!"

It didn't occur to Allison to ask the most obvious question: What are you doing here? She didn't care why Lehanna had come, only that she had come. When they let go of each other, Lehanna motioned to Jacques. "You remember Jacques?"

Allison nodded and extended her hand when he approached. "Of course," she said. "From the Worldwide Health fundraiser." But she wasn't interested in chatting with Jacques. She wanted Lehanna to herself so she could ask what had happened since they last saw each other. She wanted to tell her about Eamon, and the upcoming hearing.

"We have wonderful news," Lehanna said.

"You're getting married?"

"No." Lehanna laughed when Jacques pulled her toward him and kissed her hair. "But we're going to be in MacMillan, for a year. Maybe longer. After we make a quick trip back to Madagascar, Jacques's going to set up an alternative medicine program with George Swenson. Remember George?"

"Sure," Allison said.

"George is head of research now at MacU. He and Jacques are designing the curriculum over the next six months. Then he'll run the department and commute to Madagascar to check on the clinic when he needs to."

"And you?" Allison held her breath, hoping to hear what she wanted.

"After I go back to Madagascar to finish up there, I'll be in MacMillan, too, working with George, in his ethnobotany program. I know it's a lot to absorb. It all happened so fast I didn't make time to let you know."

Allison smiled but said nothing. This wasn't the time to tell her friend about her case against Rusty, or that she and Eamon decided to study in Ireland after the trial.

Lehanna took both Allison's hands. "We've got to get back to campus," she said. "When can you and I catch up?"

"Dinner tomorrow? At my place? Eamon's working late."

"Eamon?"

"I'll explain tomorrow." She ran back to the counter, scribbled her phone number and address on a card, and handed it to Lehanna. "How's six?"

"Perfect."

⌒

Allison was checking on the chicken roasting in the oven when Lehanna rang the bell. She washed her hands, went to the front door, and found her friend smiling and holding out a globe-shaped topiary.

"Rosemary," Lehanna said. "For remembrance."

Allison held the plant to her face and breathed in its savory aroma. "It's beautiful," she said, smiling, "but totally unnecessary. You're the only present I want." While that wasn't quite true—Allison hoped for a grander gift, release from fear when Rusty Jenkins ended up in jail—she said it anyway. Besides, if she remembered her Shakespeare well enough, Ophelia's reference to the herb presaged tragedy, not the hopeful resolution Allison anticipated for herself.

She set the plant on the hallway table. "It looks good here, I think. It'll get just enough filtered sunlight."

Allison hugged Lehanna, then asked her to close her eyes. "I've got something to show you out back."

"Don't I even get to see your place?"

"First things first." She led Lehanna through the living room and kitchen, then flicked on the backyard lights. She guided her out the back door and down the steps, then along the path to the garden. The Thanksgiving snow had come and gone, but a few icy spots lingered. "Careful," she said. "These flagstones are slippery." When they reached the bench Eamon built, facing the pond, Allison sat Lehanna down, then let go of her hand. "Now open your eyes."

Lehanna held her hands to her face. She spoke slowly. "I could smell the hardy sage as we were walking," she said. "And remnants of last season's lavender and rosemary. But I wasn't prepared for all this." She waved her arms toward the Celtic knot garden formation, the arborvitae that stood guard in a semi-circle behind it, and the pond farther back. "This is all yours?"

Allison nodded. "I wish you could have seen it when I moved in. It wasn't much more than a heap of sticks and overgrowth. But I worked on it every day, weather permitting. Eamon helped, too. Of course, nothing's in bloom now. When we go inside, I'll show you the sketches I made last summer so you can see how it looks at its best."

"All right," Lehanna said. "No more delay. Who is Eamon?"

Allison stood, pulled Lehanna to standing, and put her arm through her friend's as they walked toward the house.

"Remember how you told me, back when I was certain no one would ever be able to care for me—"

"You were so utterly convinced you were unlovable."

"But you said that, if I just kept doing what was put in front of me, someone, the right someone, would just drop out of the sky?"

"Yes, I remember."

"Well, Eamon didn't exactly fly down from the heavens. He rode in on his bike, walked into Metaphors, and since then those nasty habits and fears began to melt."

They reached the house, moved into the kitchen, and Allison motioned for Lehanna to have a seat at the table. She put a pot of water on for tea.

"So, tell me about him," Lehanna said.

"He's from Ireland and came to MacMillan to study comp lit, though I won't hold that against him."

"Sounds like there's still a little fence-mending to do with your father."

The tea kettle whistled. Allison lifted it from the stove. "Chamomile?"

"Please."

Allison served Lehanna a cup of tea, avoiding talk about her father. "You hungry?"

"Starved."

Allison checked the oven timer. "Only about ten minutes to go."

She sat at the table, sipped her tea, then began telling how she wrote to Lehanna after she left for Madagascar. "But after a while, when I didn't hear from you . . ." She shrugged. "I felt abandoned again.

"I went back to believing I had as much value as used Kleenex. So, I looked for it in all the wrong places—you know that old song—and I ended up with terrible men, mean men, one who did a pretty good number on me."

Lehanna reached to stroke her arm, but Allison withdrew it. "It's fine now, really.

"When I moved back to MacMillan and my father helped me buy this place, I started feeling at home again. It was the garden mostly. When it came to life, I did, too." She smiled. "And that day Eamon walked into Metaphors, I began thinking I might not want to be alone anymore. It was as simple as that."

Allison took Lehanna's hands in hers. "Now tell me about Jacques." She tried to sound excited, though she still had misgivings about the man.

Lehanna shrugged as if there wasn't much to tell, even though her smile said otherwise. "I knew even when I met him twenty years ago that he was determined to do good in the world. He was like Jonathan in that way, but with a strong enough will and personality to work on a greater scale. When I left Madagascar back in the sixties, I wrote to him once in a while. He kept me up to date on the clinic, but I didn't take it further than that because he was married and had two kids. But before I went back to the Island, I heard from Swenson that Jacques's marriage wasn't working out. And if I'm really honest, I suspected, from the time of the *famadihana* we both participated in back then that we would end up together." She took her hands from Allison's. "But I built a wall around me just like you did. Maybe it wasn't obvious, but I was using other people's wounds, their need to be healed, to block out the possibility of my being hurt again. I even did that with you. Do you understand that now?"

Allison nodded.

"Even when Jacques called me on it, I tried to keep him at bay. But he told me he had learned a couple lessons along the way—mostly from his rift with Celeste and his children—so, he persisted." She shrugged. "And I'm glad he did."

"He's divorced now?"

Lehanna shook her head. "It's not final, but it's in process."

Allison drank from her tea. She had the same feeling about Jacques now as she did when she met him at the Worldwide Health conference. Yes, he was a man who did good. And, yes, he seemed infatuated with Lehanna. Was he capable of committing to her, even though he hadn't stayed with his family? Even though he had grand plans for Worldwide Health? And why was the divorce taking so long? She tilted her head and searched for words to express her reservations. Before she could, Lehanna interrupted her thoughts.

"Now, you said you had something else to tell me."

Allison finished her tea. The time wasn't right to talk about Jacques. She leaned forward. "Going on two months ago," she said, "I ran into the man who raped me."

Lehanna put a hand to her cheek. "Where?"

"He came here to fix the furnace. I knew it was him, by the smell, his voice. After I did some research, I went to the district attorney to see if I could still prosecute—I have DNA evidence— and she told me I could. So, that's what I'm doing."

Allison looked to Lehanna, waiting. For approval, praise, a pat on the head. *Good job, Allison! You're standing up for yourself. You're getting justice! You're healing!* When she got none, her mouth turned down. "You're not saying anything."

Lehanna tilted her head. Her eyes narrowed. "I'm not sure what to say."

Why Lehanna looked somber, Allison didn't know. This was good news.

"Who is he?"

"His name's Ronny Lee Jenkins. He's from MacMillan, but

he sold drugs all over for a while. And he hurt other women."
Allison's pace slowed. "I don't know if he actually raped them.
But he did enough to qualify for a treatment program, the one
Corinne Kramer started." She waved her hand. "That's another
whole story. Anyway, his fiancée's pregnant—I'm not sure they're
still together—but I think he's going to hurt a lot more now than
when . . . Why are you looking at me like that?"

   "I just want to understand. You're saying he's come clean and
he's making something of his life?"

   Allison hesitated. "That's one way to look at it." She shifted
in her chair. "The other is that he hurt me, and he might hurt
other women. Recidivism is higher among sex offenders than for
any other criminals." Her impatience building, Allison continued.
"And when this is over with, he's going to know what it's like to
be afraid that someone, or something, is going to jump out of
nowhere and hurt *him*. Isn't that what happens in prison? Especially to sex offenders? It does on *Law and Order,* anyway." She
crossed her arms and smiled. "Best of all, he'll lose a part of his
life that he'll never get back. Like I did."

   Lehanna held her teacup and swirled the remaining tea around
and around, looking into it.

   Allison wasn't sure whether her friend was stalling or searching
for answers. Traveling to a different country? Falling in love with
a man Allison wasn't sure was as committed as Lehanna thought?
Did all that weaken her loyalty, her friendship? She wouldn't know
until Lehanna said more. Something, anything would be better
than her silence.

   "I guess no one knows for sure," Lehanna said finally.

   "Knows what?" Allison held onto the table's edge to steady
herself. She was starting to feel small and foul. "I just want justice,
and to put the whole thing to rest."

   "Of course you want to put it behind you. I'm just wondering.
Do you really believe that if you send this man—what's his name
again?"

   "Ron. Ron Jenkins."

"That if you send Ron to jail, you'll feel better? That you'll get the kind of justice that counts?" Though Allison glared, Lehanna continued. "And what about his family? His child?"

"He's not married yet," Allison snapped. "And Elizabeth—she's the assistant DA—says, if his girlfriend has nothing to do with him, it'll help our case. The judge, and the jury, if there's a trial, might think she doesn't feel safe with him."

Lehanna looked directly at Allison. She kept her voice calm. "But he's trying to make a new life."

When the kitchen timer sounded, Allison stood abruptly, her chair screeching along the tile floor. She went to the oven, took out the chicken, and set it on the stovetop. "So am I," she said, her back to Lehanna, her heart pounding. She slammed the oven door closed.

"I don't want to upset you," Lehanna said. "I just want to know if you really feel sending Ron to jail will help you."

Allison turned to face Lehanna. "What *I* need to know," she said deliberately, "is that he's going to pay for the years I've lost. And the terror he caused me."

Lehanna stood and walked to Allison, reaching for her. "I know how hard this has been on you. Awful. I just—" When Allison pulled away to turn off the oven, Lehanna asked how Eamon felt about the case.

"He says he'll support whatever I decide."

Lehanna knew she needed to tread lightly. She also knew she needed to say what she felt was true. "You've got what sounds like a wonderful future with Eamon. Support, the chance to visit and study in a different place. If you're going to start fresh in Ireland with him, and if Ron won't be a threat to you—or anyone else if he keeps following his program—how will putting him in jail help you?"

Allison spun around from the stove. "Whose side are you on?"

Lehanna shook her head. "That's just it, love, there are no sides here. Not if Ron's changing. And not if you really want to heal. You do believe in change, don't you? Look at the work you've done. With your job, your garden, with Eamon. I know it probably doesn't feel this way right now, but you have an opportunity here."

"Opportunity?" Allison crossed her arms and shook her head. "You're kidding, right?"

"I'm not." Lehanna hesitated. "Whatever you decide, you're going to take a step—a big one—on your journey. What you need to ask yourself is whether sending Ron to jail will help release the understandable grip he's had on you, or whether it will keep you tethered to him by unresolved anger and fear and hate."

Allison didn't look at her but allowed Lehanna to take her hands when she reached for them. Lehanna's beliefs about journeys and forgiveness and healing had all sounded soothing and possible back at Artemis, with its frothy curtains and fairyland decor. But now her mentor sounded naïve, misguided. As if she didn't understand that, in the real world, the rules were different.

"I don't want anything or anyone to hurt you," Lehanna said. "Not ever again. I'm just not sure that punishing someone else will end your own suffering."

Allison took her hands from Lehanna's. She looked away and pressed her lips together, unsure whether she was trying to hold back tears or more vitriol.

"I want what's best for you," Lehanna said. "And I'm not sure a public trial and damaging someone else's life *is* best. If he were a threat to you, or to other women, I would feel differently. But he's trying to do the right thing. Most men who do what Ron did to you? They're acting out of anger caused by hurt done to them.

"I'm not excusing their behavior. I just don't want you to think you want revenge, only to find out it's as corrosive as the hurt you wanted to be rid of."

Lehanna's placating tone began to disgust Allison. "And how would you know about wanting revenge and not getting it?"

Allison's reaction neither surprised nor angered Lehanna. She understood what it was like to want recompense for a debt that couldn't be repaid. "Remember the story I told you about the man named Quinn? How I tried to blame him for Jonathan's death, even though, when I was a child, I foresaw that Jonathan was going to die in the war?"

Allison reluctantly nodded.

"I needed to hold someone responsible. At least I thought I did. But when I met Quinn, when I saw his heart bleeding from his own guilt and regret, I was given the strength to try to help him." She paused. "Don't get the idea I didn't want to hurt or even hate him.

"I know my situation wasn't the same as yours. And it happened twenty years ago. I just wonder how *you'll* feel in twenty years. Can you, just for a minute, try to step out of the present and look back and imagine that?"

Allison crossed her arms. "I won't feel afraid. I know that much."

"Maybe. But what about the fact that you kept a father from his child for five years?"

Allison shook her head. She looked at Lehanna as if her friend had gone mad. "My father stayed away longer than that. He didn't go to jail. He just buried himself in his books and his students and his writing."

"And if you punish this man—Ron—will you get back those years you lost with your father?"

Allison looked away again. She shook. She began to cry. When Lehanna reached to her, she allowed herself to be held.

"May I make a suggestion," Lehanna asked.

Allison nodded.

"Will you consider going to your father and making some sort of peace with him, then deciding whether to go ahead with the case?"

"My father's got nothing to do with Ron. Besides, *he's* the parent! He's the one who left me!" Allison tore herself away. "Why are you so intent on easing other people's pain? Why can't you hear *me*?"

"Okay. It was only a suggestion." Lehanna turned to collect her purse and her coat. "Maybe it would be better if we got together another time."

"Don't go," Allison whimpered.

"I don't know what else to say. It's not that I want you to hurt more. Just the opposite. I want you to be free. I want you to see that forgiveness isn't only something you give others—it's also a gift to yourself. When you honestly forgive someone, you let go of the anger and fear and bitterness. It's the only way they lose their grip on you."

Now, Allison thought, Lehanna sounded like Danny. Two people in the healing business. Two people who had been hurt and learned to be free.

When Allison turned from her, Lehanna put on her coat, picked up her purse, and started for the door.

"What would I say?"

When Allison turned back to her, Lehanna stepped closer. "I'm sorry, I didn't hear you."

"What would I say to my father?"

"Whatever you feel. And if you don't know what you feel, tell him that. Just make some gesture to narrow the distance between you and see where it leads." Lehanna slid back into the chair at the table. "I'm not suggesting you become his best friend, or even that you immediately and wholeheartedly clean the slate of everything he's done. Just take one step toward him and see what happens."

Allison bit her lower lip. "One step?"

"Just one. And if you don't like what happens, you can go back to feeling the way you do now." Lehanna held Allison's hand. "What do you think?"

"I think we can still have dinner if you want to stay."

"Good." Lehanna let go of Allison. She slipped off her coat and draped it over her chair. "Because I'm starved."

While Allison carved the chicken, Lehanna reached under the neckline of her sweater and pulled out the cord on which she wore the carved zebu Nathalie had given her in Madagascar. She took off the necklace, held it briefly to remind herself of her young friend at the clinic, hoping Nathalie's promise of the zebu's protection was true.

When Allison served the meal and sat down, Lehanna handed her the necklace and explained how, on the Great Red Island, the zebu offered strength in time of need. "Nathalie would want you to have it." Allison smiled and thanked her friend, then she admired the charm. But instead of hanging it around her neck, she clutched it in her hand and didn't let go.

CHAPTER THIRTY-ONE

Allison took her time climbing the three flights of stairs to Wellington Hall's top floor. Walking into the Comp Lit office, she was relieved to see that the reception desk was unattended. Her conversation would be difficult enough. She didn't need Jacqueline listening in. The door to her father's office was closed, so she knocked.

"Who is it?"

"Allison."

Richard got up from his desk and hurried to the door. "Ali. Hi." With awkward, anxious gestures, he motioned her inside. "Can I take your coat?"

She shook her head. "I just came for a minute." She hadn't seen him since Thanksgiving. The gray circles under his eyes made him look tired and a little lost. His rumpled shirt and cords gave away the fact that he had taken to sleeping in his office.

She walked to the chair stamped with the Yale crest and pulled it up to Richard's desk. She looked around at the shelves jammed with books and empty coffee mugs and piles of old *New Yorkers, New York Review of Books,* and *New York Times* magazines that crowded the dark little place her father preferred, she thought, to any other in the world. In one corner, on a stack of papers, still sat the globe showing the constellations that Lucy gave him one Christmas. On a shelf to the left were postage stamp–sized photos of Allison as a baby.

He sat at his desk before he spoke. "You haven't been here in a long time."

She nodded, thinking back to the times when she and Lucy used to visit. "Remember the year we came on your birthday? We brought hats and horns and a cake that looked like the cover of *The Canterbury Tales.*"

"I was in a rush as usual, wasn't I?"

"I don't think we even got through the first line of *Happy Birthday* before you ran to a faculty meeting. Or somewhere."

He took off his glasses and rubbed his eyes, then propped his elbow on the chair and rested his chin on his hand. "If I could do things over, Ali, I would. Every day since you told me about the . . . I can't even say the word . . ."

"The rape," she said.

"Yes, the rape. Ever since then I've wished I'd been in that house that night. Maybe it never would have happened. Or maybe you wouldn't have left the way you did. Without telling anyone." He paused, then looked at her, his eyes searching for reprieve. "Do you think it would have made a difference?"

His voice was so small. "I don't know," she said, looking away, trying to retreat into the usual distance she kept from him. But she heard Lehanna. *Just one step.* "Yes," she said, looking back to him. "Maybe."

He sat forward, folding his hands on his desk. "Ali, I'm sorry. So sorry."

When she heard his voice crack, she wasn't sure what to do. She'd never seen him cry.

"Can you forgive me?" His voice was an old man's, thin and frail.

She bit her lower lip and thought for a moment. "Not yet," she spoke slowly, looking at him across the desk. "But I want to."

He stood and walked around his desk. He took the chair next to hers and pulled it close. When he held her hands, she didn't stiffen or freeze.

"Will you let me help you through this mess?" he asked. "The hearing? And the trial if there is one?"

She breathed in the citrusy smell of his aftershave, the same scent he'd worn as long as she could remember. Everything else about her father seemed new. Then a stubborn knot loosened in her chest, and she began to cry.

"Do you miss her?" she asked.

He nodded. "I miss your mother every day."

She turned and wiped at her tears with her hand. "I miss her, too, Daddy." She hugged him, then separated from him. "I need to get back to work."

At the door she stopped and turned back. "Yes, Daddy. I want you to help me."

⌒

Cornelia hung up her phone then looked to Allison. "You can see Attorney Reedy now." She motioned down the hall then adjusted an ornament on the small Christmas tree atop her desk. "You know the way?"

Allison nodded. Then she and Lehanna walked past other ADA's cubicles until they reached Elizabeth's. When Elizabeth looked up from her desk, Allison diverted her eyes.

"I brought a friend," Allison said. "This is Lehanna Stanislaus."

Elizabeth stood then hesitated before shaking Lehanna's hand. She motioned for her visitors to sit down, but not before taking a deep breath, wishing she hadn't given up smoking a couple months earlier. She'd been doing her job long enough to know that when a client scheduled an appointment for no apparent reason, and brought someone with her, she usually wanted to amend her previous statements or, worse, drop charges against her assailant.

Elizabeth picked up a pen and began tapping it on her desk. "What can I do for you?"

Allison looked to Lehanna, then to Elizabeth. "I've changed my mind."

Elizabeth's eyes went dark, her tone sharpened. "About?"

"About the case. I want to drop the charges."

Elizabeth set down her pen. She had been through this routine with dozens of sexual violence survivors over the years. More often with victims of acquaintance rape than in cases like Allison's. It wasn't unusual for women who were involved with their attackers to want to kiss and make up after time passed. *He didn't mean it. I misunderstood. We're getting married.* She'd heard it all. Those women usually regretted their decisions, and sometimes found themselves back on Elizabeth's doorstep months or years later, provided they lived to tell about the next attack.

She folded her hands on her desk, her foot tapping on her chair beneath. "You changed your mind?"

"I know I've taken a lot of your time." Allison's words raced out. Not only because she wanted to apologize, but because she wasn't yet completely convinced that Father Malone and Lehanna were correct. That forgiveness would heal. "It's just that, when I thought about it, it didn't make sense to ruin this guy's—Mr. Jenkins's—life. Not when I don't think he's going to hurt me again."

Elizabeth sat back. She quelled the desire to reach across the desk and shake Allison. Not only had she taken time from other women who had to wait in line until Elizabeth could work them into her schedule, but because sexual offenders, more than any other criminals, were likely to strike again. How many times had she tried to drive that point home to Allison? "This happens sometimes," she said. "That women change their minds. Most often with women who knew their attacker."

When Allison began to relax—maybe this wouldn't be so hard—Elizabeth slammed her palm on her desk. Allison started at the sound.

"Then," Elizabeth said, "they get back with their lover or their husband and he's sweet as pie until the charges are dropped."

Rattled, Allison looked to Lehanna, who nodded encouragement.

"I don't think I have to worry about him." She knew her voice sounded shaky. "I mean, he's in his program."

Elizabeth leaned forward. "*You* don't have to worry about him. That's my job. And that's why, once a complaint is filed against a man in a sexual violence case, I proceed. No matter what."

Allison sat taller in her chair. "Then I won't testify."

Elizabeth leaned forward, clasping her hands on her desk. Her eyes went cold. "That won't help my case. And I can't force you to take the stand. But I have to proceed with the hearing based on the information in your preliminary statement and the evidence you provided."

Allison looked again at Lehanna, who tried to position things another way. "It's just that, under the circumstances, Allison has come to believe that it would be wrong to threaten the new life of a man who's trying to correct his mistakes."

Elizabeth snickered and shook her head. "Maybe she's right. Maybe Ron Jenkins is one in a million. Maybe he'll straighten up and fly right and never again hurt even a flea." She picked up her pen and decisively stashed it in the pencil holder on her desk. "But I can't take that risk. I need to protect the public welfare."

"There wasn't a knife."

Elizabeth's eyes narrowed. "You're saying now that your previous statement was incorrect?"

"Not incorrect, exactly. I mean I felt something against my side that might have been a knife. But it might have been a belt buckle. Or something."

Elizabeth shook her head and crossed her arms as her chances for a sexual assault conviction dissipated. "Just to be clear, if you change your statement, your credibility will be shot and your case—for rape anyway—goes up in smoke."

Allison nodded. "I might have known him before, too."

"And now you're saying you might have consented to have intercourse with him?"

When Allison nodded, Elizabeth considered—as she had many times—retiring at age thirty-nine. She could buy a condo in Santa Fe and paint desert landscapes or make fake turquoise jewelry. But, no, not when so many women needed her help. It would be easy to drop the charges against Mr. Jenkins and check off another case on her roster. Still, she knew what sexual offenders were capable of, and she didn't want to feel responsible if a year or two from now another young woman walked into her office and said that a man named Ronny Lee Jenkins Jr. had attacked her, too. On the other hand, she had learned it was wrong for her to force her ethics and opinions on a survivor. Not as wrong as it was for a man to force a woman to have sex. But wrong anyway.

"You're sure about this?"

Allison nodded.

"Okay." Elizabeth turned to her filing cabinet and pulled out Allison's previous statement. "Let's take it from the top."

When Allison and Lehanna left her office, Elizabeth pushed away from her desk and turned her chair to the window overlooking Municipal Park. Clouds were rolling in from the west, over the Front. Maybe it would rain or snow, and their unusually warm December would end. She kicked off her shoes, propped her feet on a stack of briefs, files, and never-read copies of *The Times* and *The Journal,* and leaned back to weigh her options.

The easiest thing would be to grant Allison her wishes and drop the charges. Chet's preliminary investigation had verified Jenkins's statement that he was living clean, attending the Viewpoint program, doing a good job at Fresh Air, and that a young woman was carrying his child. Taken together with Allison's revised statement, Elizabeth figured her chances of a conviction, on a felony anyway, had melted like a snow cone at a Fourth of July picnic.

Also, as of his phone call last week, Duncan Riordan was hoping to work out a plea to a misdemeanor charge instead of a felony. That would mean the difference between a mandatory five-year jail sentence and a sentence of probation and community service. She hated like hell to give Duncan the satisfaction of seeing the charges superseded, especially since she had brushed him off when she still felt assured of conviction. But the case wasn't about her ego. In the end, damn it, the case wasn't about her at all. She flipped through her Rolodex and dialed Duncan's number.

"Duncan? Elizabeth Reedy here."

By the time she hung up, Elizabeth agreed to supersede the rape charge in return for Ronny Lee Jenkins's guilty plea to a charge of indecent assault, with a two-year maximum sentence, and to corruption of a minor with a five-year maximum. The recommended sentence would be five years' probation with three years' community service. In addition, Jenkins would be required to continue one-on-one counseling, to attend the Viewpoint program, and to refrain from contact with the complainant.

Before she left her office, she called the Probation and Parole Department and arranged for a preliminary report to facilitate sentencing at the Court of Common Pleas hearing. Why prolong the agony? It would be one more case down. And if Elizabeth Reedy knew anything at all, dozens were waiting to take its place.

Richard sampled the Merlot, then nodded his approval. The waiter filled Corinne's glass, then Richard's, and set the bottle in the center of the table.

"May I take your dinner orders?"

Richard looked at the young man, pen in hand, eager to do a good job in return for a solid tip. He wished that the task ahead of him was uncomplicated as the young man's job of rattling off the evening's specials.

"We need a little more time."

It was the week before Ron Jenkins's court appearance, and Richard had wanted to postpone this talk with Corinne until after the proceeding. But he knew what he had to say would never be easy. He drank from his wine glass and forced a tentative smile. "You look good, Corinne."

"So do you."

The weekend after Allison told Richard and Corinne about the rape, Richard rented an apartment near campus with a month-to-month lease. He needed time to think, he told Corinne, not unaware of how he had said those same words to Lucy four years earlier. By the first week in December, when Allison was preparing for the hearing, Richard knew he and Corinne had moved too fast. He hadn't given himself time to feel the loss of Lucy, or to explore where he wanted his life to go in her absence.

After he talked over the possibility with Allison, he called Nina Whyte and put his house on the market. He would negotiate as flexible a closing date as possible to give Corinne and the girls time to find another place to live. But no matter what he and Corinne decided, he needed to put that house—Lucy's house, the house where Allison was raped—in the past.

"This is awkward." He fidgeted with his wine glass.

"It is." Corinne smiled her cheery smile, even though, like everyone else in Richard's circle, she had seen him change since Thanksgiving. Allison's announcement seemed to snap him out of a perpetual summer afternoon's nap. He paid attention. He spoke as confidently and clearly outside the classroom as he did inside. She couldn't manipulate him anymore.

"Allison's moving to Ireland," he said. "With Eamon. I'm not sure it's permanent. They may come back after he finishes his degree." Even though Corinne had wedged herself between him and Allison, he knew she was vulnerable. He also knew she had been a good friend to Lucy, that Graham had given her a hard time with the divorce, and that she had two daughters to raise. He just wished she wasn't trying to look so cheerful.

"I've decided—rather, Allison and I have decided—that I'll move into her place while she's in Ireland. We'll put the house on Tranche Street on the market." When Richard saw Corinne's lower lip quiver, he decided he preferred that she try to look pleasant after all. He reached across the table to take her hand, but she held it back. "I'm not saying we, I mean you and I, can't move forward. Just not now."

Even if she hadn't read all those books—the ones about how, when men are divorced or widowed, they never end up marrying the first woman they get involved with—Corinne knew he was right. She looked down at the table, trying to dispel the illusion of a life with Richard she had been trying to hammer and chisel into reality.

"You're smart and lovely and you do an admirable job with Dev and Steph."

"Then what is it?" She knew the answer, but she blurted the question anyway.

"We went too fast. And for the wrong reasons."

She moved her hands to the table's edge, farther out of reach.

"Is there someone else?" she asked, almost too softly for Richard to hear. When he chuckled, she shot him a sharp look. "That's funny?"

"I'm not laughing at you, Corinne. It's just that my plate's heaped full enough as it is now that I can see my life with some kind of clarity." He reached across the table again. This time she let him take her hand. "Can you understand that? Even a little?"

She managed a thin smile. "This hasn't been easy for any of us."

"No, it hasn't." He breathed deeper. The worst of the evening was over.

She took her hand from his. "But let's not kid ourselves."

Richard tilted his head, as if asking Corinne to clarify.

"When we move forward, it won't be together. Not now, not ever." She stood. Bracelets tinkling, she removed her coat from the back of her chair. "Good-bye, Richard."

He knew he should feel hurt or sad. Instead, he felt relieved.

CHAPTER THIRTY-TWO

The Tuesday morning after the New Year, Allison dressed to attend Ronny Lee Jenkins Jr.'s appearance in the Court of Common Pleas. After she put on the blue suit she wore on her college interviews, she studied her reflection in the closet door mirror. In the weeks after discovering Ron was her assailant, she had stopped eating much of anything except carrots and tortilla chips. Her single-minded purpose, to retrieve her lost freedom and security, left her hungry for little but justice. But after Lehanna encouraged her to find freedom in letting go of revenge rather than clutching it close, she started eating again. A little chicken here, a small salad there, and, of course, the holiday gingerbread she made from Lucy's recipe. While the suit—and her decision to drop rape charges—still didn't fit perfectly, she had begun to fill out, both physically and with the possibility that she could move on.

When she reached for her mascara and leaned closer to the mirror, she struggled to focus. The fact that she had curled next to Eamon without sleeping the night before no doubt contributed to the fuzziness the day had taken on, even though the sun outside reflected brightly on the thin layer of snow that had fallen early that morning.

She had come to believe Lehanna's opinion, that guilty or not, putting Ron Jenkins in prison would probably not help him, his family, or her. So, why, as she tried to apply her makeup, did her hands still shake a little? Could she ever know she wouldn't be attacked—or worse—tomorrow? Next month? Years from now?

Even if Ron wouldn't or couldn't hurt her again, someone or something might. No platitudes, herbal remedies, or reassurances could guarantee perfect protection. The best anyone could offer was what Danny and Lehanna had said, each in their own way. If she wanted to walk free, she needed to trust and at least try to forgive.

She stood back again. This time as she looked at her reflection, she smiled, despite her doubts. Dressed in her suit and her sensible shoes, her hair restored to its natural brown, she could be mistaken for a banker or lawyer or businesswoman. In truth, she wasn't quite sure who or what she was. But if she believed Lehanna and Danny—and she was at least willing to try—her life could begin to take shape in new and unexpected ways, once this day was behind her.

~

When Allison walked into the courtroom, her footsteps echoed on the marble floor as she approached Elizabeth, seated at the table at the left facing the judge's bench. Elizabeth stood and nodded, then shook hands with her client's companions as Allison took the chair next to her. Once the others settled into the front row of seats behind Allison, Lehanna excused herself to go to the ladies' room.

Elizabeth reviewed her notes, then looked to her client. "You ready?" she asked, her affect and tone flat.

Allison nodded. "I'm ready." She felt Elizabeth's disappointment in her and now wished she could repay the woman for the time she spent on her case. But when the courtroom doors opened again, she turned to them. Ronny Lee Jenkins walked in, wearing a blazer and tie, his hair newly trimmed, his khakis neatly pressed. A tall, soap-opera-star-looking man carrying a Stetson walked with him. Ron no longer looked like a threat, but Allison's stomach grabbed anyway. Her eyes continued to focus on him as Duncan Riordan motioned Ron and his friend to the table on the right side of the room. Duncan then opened his briefcase. After removing a file and speaking with his client, he turned to Elizabeth and nodded.

It was nine forty-five, according to the clock on the back wall. Elizabeth rose from her chair. As she had already explained to Allison, before the official proceedings started, Elizabeth would meet with Duncan in the witness room off the hallway to finalize the plea agreement they had discussed.

As Elizabeth walked away, Lehanna returned to the courtroom, but stopped abruptly halfway down the center aisle. As if she had called his name, the man with the wavy brown hair, the one seated next to Ron, turned and saw her. He tilted his head—*What are you doing here?*—then nodded. Lehanna shrugged. It would take a long conversation to fully explain how she ended up in MacMillan. She smiled, then continued to the front row and took her seat next to Richard.

A few minutes later, when she heard the courtroom door open again, Allison turned to see Rusty's pregnant fiancée walk in—at least she used to be his fiancée—and sit by herself in the back row of chairs. Whether she came to support Ron, or to hope for justice, Allison couldn't know. But when the woman looked to her, expressionless, Allison faced forward again.

At five minutes to ten, Elizabeth and Duncan walked back to their seats. When she sat down, Elizabeth turned to Allison. "Mr. Jenkins has agreed to plead guilty to indecent assault and corruption of a minor," she said, her affect flat, her tone even. "When the judge comes in, we'll present the plea, and he'll make the final determination."

"That's good, isn't it?" Allison asked, wishing Elizabeth would, for even a moment, reassure her, even forgive her.

Elizabeth focused on the papers in Allison's file. "It's what we hoped for. Whether or not it's good, time will tell."

Allison sat back, chiding herself for trying to win Elizabeth's approval. She forced herself to remember why she had changed her mind about prosecuting Ron for the rape. She gripped the arms of her chair, hoping she had made the right choice, not just to please Lehanna, or Danny, but to secure her freedom.

At ten o'clock, Judge Arthur Greenbaum, black robes dwarfing his slight frame, entered the courtroom. He settled into his chair behind the bench, peered down over his half-glasses to those gathered, and motioned to the clerk on his left. The first item on the morning's docket, the clerk announced, was the case of the Commonwealth versus Jenkins.

"Permission to approach, your honor." When Elizabeth made her request, she and Duncan walked to the pit in front of the bench. She reported that she and Attorney Riordan had reached a plea agreement that they believed would satisfy the court. "Permission to submit for the court's consideration, a pre-sentence probation officer's report, prepared by Mr. Jenkins's prospective probation officer."

When the judge nodded Elizabeth said the report indicated that Ronny Lee Jenkins Jr. had participated in a sexual offenders' rehabilitation program for two years and that he had held a job for the same duration. "During that period," she admitted, "he demonstrated no inclination to his previous behavior."

When the judge held out his hand, Elizabeth proffered the report. He reviewed it, then looked down to Rusty. "Mr. Jenkins?"

Duncan motioned for Rusty to stand.

Heart pounding, hands clasped in front of him, Rusty stood. *Christ within me,* he repeated to himself. *Christ behind me . . .*

Did he understand, Judge Greenbaum asked, that if convicted of the rape charge with which he had formerly been accused, he could serve a jail sentence of up to ten years?

"Yes, your honor."

In his discussions with his attorney, had he been promised anything when he agreed to plead guilty to a lesser charge?

"Only that I might receive a sentence of probation and community service, your honor."

Nothing else?

"Nothing, sir . . . I mean, your honor."

Did he plead guilty to the charge voluntarily?

"Yes, your honor."

Then the judge asked Rusty to describe what he remembered of the events of the 1988 July evening in question. Rusty told, in a clear but quiet voice, how he followed Allison home from the Three Bears. How he broke into the Stephensons' home. How he attacked Allison. As Duncan advised, he kept his eyes on the judge's. "It was a terrible thing I done."

Arthur Greenbaum leaned back in his chair. Like Elizabeth, he'd seen dozens of men, dressed in their Sunday best, in his court-room, vowing they'd never again hurt a woman. Most often he figured their rehabilitation was temporary, and he was known to overturn a plea's sentencing recommendation in favor of a stiffer ruling. But as much as he wanted to safeguard his tough reputation, he heard no false note in Rusty's admission. He saw no duplicity in the young man's eyes.

He looked to the two attorneys and said he was satisfied there was a basis for the plea, that Rusty understood the charges against him, and that he showed remorse for his actions. The judge leaned forward. "In a situation like this," he said, "I usually assign a sentence after a week or so." He removed his glasses and tapped them on the bench. "But since the pre-sentence probation report has already been filed, there's no point in delay."

Ronny Lee Jenkins Jr. was sentenced to five years' probation, with three years' community service, arrangements for which would be made by the probation officer assigned to his case. He was required to continue one-on-one counseling, to participate in the Viewpoint program, and was prohibited from contact with Allison.

"The proceedings," the judge said, "are complete." He banged his gavel. When he rose to leave the courtroom, Allison, like the others, stood.

"It's over," Elizabeth said, when she returned to Allison's side.

"Over?" Allison knew her question sounded dubious.

Elizabeth hesitated. There was no point in saying that, in her experience, the effects of sexual assault were never really over. They lingered, no matter what a healer, like Lehanna, or a spiritual adviser, like Father Malone, might promise. There was also no point in saying—again—that there was a greater than fifty percent chance that sexual assault wasn't over for Mr. Jenkins either, no matter how committed he was to his new life and to Viewpoint. "Give it time," she said.

Time? Allison kept her eyes on Elizabeth's as she shook her hand. But her confidence in the freedom Lehanna and Danny had promised began to wobble. She looked from Elizabeth to Lehanna, then decided she couldn't afford to debate which woman would prove correct. She had made her decision.

As Elizabeth left the room, Allison turned to Eamon, Lehanna, and Richard. She reached to her father, who held her to his chest and stroked her hair. "It's going to be okay, Ali." She knew his words were meant to comfort her but also to try to assuage the guilt he still felt for not preventing the assault. She felt the warmth of his arms around her and wanted to believe he could provide the protection she now understood was impossible for him—or anyone—to guarantee. It still unsettled her that she had begun to grow, to mature, while her father continued to flounder with his ability to, or lack of ability to, know what she needed and wanted from him. *He's the parent.* But she also knew that faulting him would only prevent her from receiving whatever affection and constancy he could provide. She hugged him close then broke away and prepared to leave the room.

When she stepped into the center aisle, Ron turned to face her. Her heart sped. She reached to Eamon and squeezed his hand. Then she reminded herself of what Lehanna had counseled before Allison began to reconcile with her father—just take one step and see where it leads. She released Eamon's hand and walked toward Ron, one slow, measured step at a time. Within three feet of him, she stopped.

Ron took a step to close the distance between them, but when Allison raised her hand to signal for him to come no closer, he stopped. For a moment she looked beyond him, out the courthouse window, where the Allegheny Front stood, regal, silent. Like every other schoolkid in MacMillan, Allison had learned how that seemingly impenetrable landmass had formed millions of years ago, through violent continental collisions that bumped east against west, separating them, seemingly permanently. Not unlike her life had been broken into two parts: before the rape, and after. But Martin MacMillan, through hard work, imagination, and belief in himself had dug a tunnel through the escarpment, allowing east and west to begin to reconcile their division. She, too, had the choice to mend or not. When she heard Ron speaking, she turned to him.

"I know there's no way I can make up to you for what I did," he said. "I only hope you can know, even a little, how sorry I am."

The air is so still, Allison thought. *So thick and warm and still.* She kept her eyes on his, so blue, with no hint of malice. She repeated to herself—*I forgive you. I forgive you*—the words she hoped—or at least Lehanna and Danny hoped—would set her free. But they struck her as premature, not quite ready to deliver.

She debated what might happen if she said them anyway, even if she didn't yet believe them. She and Ron would no doubt go their separate ways and live their own lives. But she would have sacrificed a part of herself, she would have surrendered truth for the sake of harmony. She remembered Lehanna's counsel from their time in Ithaca. How each person had to do her own work, on her own path. *No*, Allison decided. *This is no time to do or say what someone, even Lehanna, wants, not if my words and actions aren't true.* Besides, even Martin MacMillan's tunnel uniting east and west took years to construct. She would take her time, *her time*, in working through the barriers between her and Ron. When she forgave him, and she hoped one day she could, she would speak from her own heart, in her own words, with the satisfaction of knowing she had been truthful.

Her eyes still on his, she nodded slowly, then took one more step toward him. All dressed up, all cleaned up, no remnant of the swamp smell that had clung to him before remained.

"Yes," she said. "I can see that." When Ron's shoulders relaxed and he closed his eyes, as if in prayer, she breathed deeply. She had taken the step *she* believed was meant to be taken at this time, in this place. Then she turned to Eamon who opened his arms and leaned close to whisper to her as they walked from the room.

Richard followed, but Lehanna held back. "You're coming?" he asked when he turned to her.

"In a minute. Meet you out front?"

"Sure."

As Richard left, Lehanna turned to Quinn across the room. He smiled and motioned that he would be right over. "Head out to the car and I'll catch up with you," he told Rusty. He walked to Lehanna. They stood face to face, silent at first. "I'm not gonna even ask why it is you're here," Quinn eventually said.

"It's a long story," Lehanna said as she felt herself drifting back to their time together years earlier. There were those green eyes, that wavy hair, that delicious body, lean and strong. A dull longing for him pressed on her chest. "I met Allison when she was at college. In Ithaca," she said. "Not long after . . ." She stopped. "I'm here with a friend. He's teaching at the university."

He thought she might be more forthcoming if the man meant much to her, but it wasn't his place to ask. No matter how much he wanted to. "I see." He turned his hat end over end. "I knew Rusty's mother, back when he was a kid. Then I run into him a couple years ago, before he came clean."

"Before you helped him come clean?" She figured from the way Rusty looked at him for encouragement during the proceedings that Quinn was more than a casual acquaintance.

"I guess you could say that, yeah." He shifted his weight, left to right, right to left, uncomfortable with credit.

"You did a wonderful thing by helping him." She hesitated. "You look well."

"You look better than well. The guy's good to you?"

She nodded, though her eyes remained on his.

"I'm glad."

They stood silent for a moment. Then, reluctant to say more, they turned to go their separate ways.

As Quinn watched Lehanna catching up with Allison, Richard, and Eamon, he saw Rusty at the back of the courtroom with Jolene. He didn't want to interrupt, even though it looked as if they weren't speaking much. Rusty's face, moments earlier relieved when the judge pronounced his sentence, now looked as drawn as it had when he entered the courtroom. Jolene held her hand around her belly, her face betraying nothing of her feelings. Then she turned from Rusty and left the room.

When Quinn reached Rusty, he put his hand on his friend's shoulder and squeezed it, wishing he had a magic wand to wave over him, or at least a pint of Beam to ease his pain. "She showed up," Quinn said. "There's somethin' to be said for that. Now—and this is the hard part—you gotta give her time."

CHAPTER THIRTY-THREE

The day after Rusty's sentencing, Allison went to her grand-father's house and knocked on the door. Marie was apparently out, so Allison walked in. "Grandpa?" She heard his faint, raspy breath, but he didn't invite her to enter his room. She went in anyway.

Lying in his bed, he looked like a memory of his stormy self. His hair, which had always been trimmed precisely, splayed from his head in ragged tufts. His skin, like gray crêpe, slipped over his face and sank into the hollows of his cheeks. When she neared the bed, his eyes opened, and he waved her away.

"I know you don't want me here, Grandpa," she said. "I won't stay long." She stood at the foot of the bed, holding the footboard. "I want you to know I'm sorry if I hurt you, and I don't want you to leave without knowing that."

Charles licked his dry lips. He raised his right hand off the quilt, then let it drop. When he didn't try to confront or resist her, Allison walked around the side of the bed. She took off her gloves and reached for his hand. "Marie called me last night," she said. "About the last stroke." He looked away.

"I know you miss them, Grandpa," she said, nodding to the picture of Lucy and Emily on the bedside table. "Mother and Grandma, I mean. And I'm sure they don't want you to suffer more than you already have." She paused between each sentence to allow Charles time to absorb her words. "I don't want you to either."

"Tired," was all he said. At least that's what Allison thought he said. "So tired."

"I know." She stroked the hair from his face, waiting until he looked at her. His eyes were heavy, but clear. She thought they asked unvoiced questions. *How much longer do I have to carry on with this insult? This cold, hard-hearted imitation of life?*

"You don't have to go on longer than you want, Grandpa." He didn't move, but Allison saw a flicker of light in his eyes. "I'm not going to hurt you, but I know how to help you when you want to go."

His breath slowed. He looked up at her, a hint of a smile on his face. He didn't try to ask how she would help or whether there would be pain. Any temporary discomfort would be more tolerable than the merciless drop-by-drop pace at which he was passing. He didn't fear death. It was indignity, degradation, and shame that he found unbearable.

"I'll let you think about it," she said. "And I'll come back tomorrow?"

He nodded.

"I can answer any questions you have or make any arrangements you want. Okay?"

He squeezed her hand. Then she turned to leave. When she reached the door and looked back, Charles lifted his hand off the bed a few inches and wriggled his fingers to wave good-bye.

Allison spent that afternoon reviewing Lehanna's folios. She determined the amounts of nightshade and black mushroom extract that would induce lethally high blood flow yet pass out of the body so Charles's death certificate would read *natural causes*. She prepared a vial of extracts from the supply Lehanna had given her. Then she filled another vial with angelica essence.

The formulas would take twelve hours to work. After she mixed them, she gathered everything she needed to make her grandfather's last day as comfortable as she could. She took a few books she thought he might like her to read from, and the Bible. She packed a photo album, showing pictures of Emily and Charles at their wedding, all the way through Allison's high school years. Out of her trunk she took the book of poems she had written, and Lucy's sketches from their field trips to the Pennsylvania Highlands. Then she drove to Charles's house, stopping to buy a bottle of his favorite port. She would suspend the essences in it so they would feel warm and friendly going down.

When Allison arrived, Marie met her at the door. "I don't want you upsetting him now," she said.

Allison knew she had mistreated the woman in the past. "I promise I won't," she said. "I came to stay with him so you can have the night off."

Marie looked her up and down, gauging Allison's sincerity. "I appreciate that," Marie said. "It's been hard."

"I'm sure it has."

Marie showed Allison the dinner she had made for Charles, then explained his new medication schedule.

When Marie left the house, Allison went to Charles's room. He was sleeping, so she arranged the books and the vials and the port on the table next to his bed. She brought a crystal goblet in from the dining room china cabinet, then opened the vials of nightshade and mushroom extracts and poured them into the glass. She added in a little port and gently swirled it. While she waited for Charles to waken, she leafed through the Lucy's portfolio, with its photos and sketches and poems.

Allison ran her hands down the pages, as if touching each sketch or photo or poem would better ingrain her memories of each trip. She regretted she hadn't let Lucy continue them after she turned thirteen. But she knew it was impossible to undo the past. And memories, good or bad, could go just so far to shape the present and the future. Only in letting go of the past would she move forward and embrace new opportunities. She closed the book, took her grandfather's hand, and held it until he wakened half an hour later.

"I'm here, Grandpa."

His eyes adjusted to the light in the room, then focused on Allison. "I'm glad," he said. "I-I-I'm rrready."

She kissed Charles's cheek, then reached for the glass of port on the bedside table. She lifted his head off the pillow and raised the goblet to his lips. He looked sideways at her as he sipped from the glass, as if he wanted to keep the image of her with him as long as he could. When he finished drinking, he let his head rest back into Allison's hand. She set the empty goblet on the bedside table and nestled him into the pillow. Then she twisted the stopper from a vial of clear liquid. "Angelica is the angel of the garden." She dabbed a drop on his forehead, another on his lips. "To help ensure a safe crossing." She capped the vial, set it down, and stroked his face. "Is there anything else I can do for you, Grandpa?"

"Hooold myyy haaand."

Allison took her grandfather's hand between both of hers. "I'm glad we had this time together." His eyes were closed, but his mouth turned up in a little smile. "Will you tell Mother I miss her very much?" He nodded. "And Grandma, too?" He nodded again. "And that I'm doing better with my father?" Charles didn't respond to Allison's last question. He had already fallen into deep, safe sleep.

Allison and Eamon were scheduled to leave for Ireland the last week in January. But with news of Charles's death, they postponed their departure until the first week in February. In the days before the funeral, they moved their belongings into the attic so Richard could move in while they were away.

Lehanna and Jacques packed, too, for a short trip to Madagascar before Jacques got MacU's alternative medicine program up and running. They all gathered at Fiore's for a farewell dinner with Richard the night before leaving to catch their flights to Kennedy then their overseas flights.

The next day they shared a taxi to MacMillan's airport. After arriving in New York and clearing security at the International Terminal, Lehanna and Allison held each other. Then Allison stepped away, holding Lehanna's arms, her eyes on her mentor's.

"What is it?" Lehanna asked.

"You remember the things you told me that Haja taught you?"

"You mean that I had a mandate to work in ethnobotany? And to heal?"

Allison shook her head. "I know he said you would work wonders in others' lives. But I knew that years ago. Look what you've done for me!" She laughed and took Lehanna's hands. "He also said you still needed to learn to wait, and listen, and to help yourself as well as others." She paused. "And that Madagascar's not your home. Not now anyway."

Lehanna released Allison's hands. She adjusted the tote she carried on her shoulder. "Yes, of course. Our trip back is a quick one. And, when I return to MacMillan, I'll work on the *Sutherlandia* project."

Lehanna's smile looked a little forced, almost girlish. Along with the fact that she'd said nothing about taking care of herself, it did nothing to conceal her denial of Allison's observation. That her teacher, her friend seemed to be sacrificing too much of herself in order to please and help others.

Allison considered for a moment that her comments might have affronted Lehanna for one selfish reason: she hoped that, not long from now, they would again see each other, maybe work and learn together.

But in the last weeks as she watched Lehanna and Jacques, her heart had spoken to her. As when she spoke to Rusty at his hearing, the lessons Lehanna had taught her at Artemis came to her, especially how each woman needed to follow her own path, do her own work, but with the guidance of others. Back then Lehanna's words had often seemed jarring and unwelcome. As unsettling as those she had just spoken. But, as Allison's were now, they had been spoken in love, in the hope that her friend might grow into them. No, Allison decided, she didn't regret what she said.

"You've learned your lessons too well," Lehanna said.

"I've learned them, yes," Allison said, "but not too well, I don't think. I want you to know that whatever path you choose, you will always have a home in my heart."

Lehanna placed her hand on her own heart. "And you in mine."

They reached to each other again.

"This time we'll stay in touch?" Allison said.

"We will."

When they separated, Allison slipped her camera off her shoulder. She handed it to Eamon for one more picture of her with Lehanna. Then the two women wiped away tears, and the men shook hands. They picked up their bags, and Allison and Eamon walked toward the gate at the terminal's eastern end, where they were to catch their plane to Shannon. Lehanna and Jacques went the opposite way, toward the gate for their flights to Paris, then Antananarivo.

After they parted, Lehanna turned around once to wave again, but her friends were already halfway down the hall. Eamon had wrapped his arm around Allison's waist. She was leaning her head on him as he held her, telling her one more time how new stars were forming, at that very moment, in the sword of Orion, the warrior, the protector of the winter sky.

ABOUT THE AUTHOR

Marleen Pasch's novel, *At the End of the Storm,* received the gold medal in contemporary fiction in the 2021 Global Book Awards. Her short fiction, creative nonfiction and articles on health, healing and spirituality appear in select journals and anthologies, including *Intima—A Journal of Narrative Medicine* and *Dozen—The Best of Breath and Shadow.* She earned her bachelor's degree in English Literature at Cornell University and has done graduate work in psychology and women in religion. As a lecturer, workshop facilitator, and writing coach, she helps emerging and established writers find their power on the page. Previous to moving to South Florida, she served on the Connecticut Festival of Words planning committee.

www.marleenpasch.com

PUBLISHER'S NOTE

Thank you for the opportunity to serve you. If you would like to help share this book, here are some popular ways:

- **Reviews:** Write an online review; in social media posts, tag #starsintheirinfancy and #marleenpasch

- **Giving:** Gift this book to friends, family, and colleagues

- **Book Clubs:** Request the Reading Group Guide and an author appearance

- **Speaking:** Invite Marleen Pasch as a speaker

- **Bulk Orders:** Email Sales@CitrinePublishing.com

- **Contact Information:** +1-828-585-7030

We appreciate your book reviews, letters, and shares.

Made in the USA
Middletown, DE
22 July 2022